Praise for Michael Genelin's
Commander Jana Matinova Series

"A terrific novel by a man who knows crime, knows Europe, and knows how to write…. [A] genuine pleasure."
—Thomas Perry, author of *Strip*

"[T]he resourceful and prodigiously insightful Jana seems to have no flaws. It isn't her feats of superheroism that give the story its chilly sense of reality; it's her casual acceptance of the almost universal corruption of everyone who lives in her world." —*The New York Times Book Review*

"Readers hungry for a fresh crime setting will be enormously satisfied with Michael Genelin's Jana Matinova novels, based in Bratislava, Slovakia…. Here, tough-as-nails Matinova goes head-to-head with a beloved childhood friend whose budding political career is in crash mode because of an affair…. The portrayal of life in post-Communist Slovakia is riveting."
—*USA Today*

"A truly fine novel. It's filled with exactitude of place and people, taking us into a world that seethes with dangerous secrets. On the treacherous journey, Michael Genelin makes unfamiliar worlds seem knowable, and does so with great style." —Pete Hamill, author of *North River*

"Genelin weaves a compelling plot with a unique central feature…. Plan on getting the first Matinova novel, *Siren of the Waters*, too. You're not going to want to miss an episode."
—*Globe and Mail* (Toronto)

"Jana Matinova is an attractive character.... Genelin has allowed his readers to understand an area of the world hidden from Western eyes for a long time."   —*Oregonian*

"Plenty of misdirection and suspense.... In the end, we must acknowledge that we have been held spellbound by a master storyteller."   —*Library Journal* (Starred Review)

"[Genelin] writes with a sharp, clear style that lights up his characters.... It's hard not to see *Dark Dreams* at or near the top of many best-books-of-the-year lists."
     —Dick Adler, *Barnes & Noble Review*

"As an international mystery, *Siren* provides more for the reader than depositing bloody and charred bodies in exotic settings. International noir provides all the thrills and mental exercise of the mystery genre while also offering a glimpse into another culture. The change in mental scenery is refreshing."   —*Sacramento News & Review*

Dark Dreams

Dark Dreams

Michael Genelin

Published by
Soho Press, Inc.
853 Broadway
New York, NY 10003

Library of Congress Cataloging-in-Publication Data
Genelin, Michael.
Dark dreams / Michael Genelin.
     p. cm.
ISBN 978-1-56947-557-7
1. Women police chiefs—Fiction.   2. Police—Slovakia—
Fiction.   3. Slovakia—Fiction.   I. Title.
PS3607.E53D37 2009
813'.6—dc22
2008038730

Paperback ISBN 978-1-56947-649-9

10 9 8 7 6 5 4 3 2 1

For the ladies in my life,
SUSY AND NORA,
who keep me involved and
focused on what's truly important,
and NOAH,
who always shows me the need for
loving humor in the world.

Acknowledgments

Once again, my special thanks for their friendship, help, and inspiration go to Miro, Adriana, Emilia, Dano, and Professor Mathern, and to all the police, judges, procurators, legislators, NGOs, interested citizens, and all the other people I toiled with in Slovakia. They are all still committed and hard at work making their wonderful country even better. My gratitude to Cecilia Brainard, Lauren Brainard, and John Allen for their continuing friendship and their aid in strengthening my resolve, and my work as a novelist. I would also like to credit Penelope Masson and Abigail Altman for their assistance. My appreciation to Terrance Gelenter. And, although I dedicated this book to her, I also want it to be very clear that Susan Genelin's first read of the manuscript, and her instinctive good taste and judgment contributed mightily to the quality of this book. Finally, as I've said before, a very special acknowledgment to my editor, Laura Hruska, particularly on this book. Blame me for the bad parts; thank her for the good ones.

Chapter 1

Solti had taken a chance. He was not ordinarily a risk-taker: he did not believe in tempting the fates. You could not rely on luck. Controlling events, even small ones, was the only sane way. And if nothing else, Solti was eminently sane. Which did not explain why he had joined the hash run today.

He satisfied himself for the seventh or eighth time that no one was paying particular attention to him, that his position in the hiking group was just crowded with walkers not willing to expend energy by being frontrunners in ninety-five-degree heat. Their sweat—and all of them were sweating profusely—reinforced a collective decision to go slowly. That resolve was bolstered even further by the high humidity, which added its ration of discomfort to the late afternoon air.

The Hash House Harriers, in Nepal as elsewhere, consisted primarily of people from outside their home countries taking a Saturday group run—or, in Soti's sub-group, perambulation. The line of men and women stretched toward the top of the hill as they went chugging through the irregular rice paddies and fields of excrement-scented vegetables basking in the heat. Solti's group at the rear was made up primarily of non-athletes along for the camaraderie of other expatriates who could talk or listen to English with some comprehension.

Their Saturday topics in Nepal were almost always the same: they exchanged local gossip, shared complaints about the bouts of diarrhea they had experienced, and griped about problems with corruption and the government bureaucrats who always had their hands out. To a man they all jabbered fervently of their eagerness for the monsoon, hoping it would come soon enough to dispel the heat that was making life miserable for everyone. There was also an anticipated pleasure they shared: the drinking that everybody did after the hash was over: sloe gin fizz, beer and more beer, Campari and soda. In fact, anything that was chilled and alcoholic.

Solti again wondered why he had joined the hash.

Wouldn't he have been better off at the hotel? Yes and no, he answered himself. Safer. More comfortable. But what about his *mental* state?

The weeks of waiting in a hotel room with only the occasional foray into the lobby were like being in prison, an experience he'd had not so long ago: agonizing in its constriction of movement and boring beyond the limits of tolerance. So Solti, surprising himself, pried his body out of its safe shelter and, at the suggestion of a desk clerk, decided to take part in an event that would provide the safety of numbers, a group of people who didn't care who Solti was as long as he showed them a modicum of courtesy in the course of the temporary bonding that the human race seems to require. He was like them, Solti thought. Monkey, ape, human—social animals all, keeping their sanity and safety through togetherness.

They crossed the mud bridge between two paddies, careful not to slip down into the water, the sweeper at the rear urging the last of the stragglers to chance the crossing. Solti was beginning to feel invigorated, even excited that he had taken the risk of participation. He would be able to tolerate the hotel room for another few days after this. Maybe he'd even come again next Saturday if the contact had not yet been made.

He looked to the top of the small hill they were climbing. At its apex there was a large elephant, its back loaded with what appeared to be palm fronds, being urged on by a mahout. The elephant intersected their path, suddenly coming to a stop, blocking the way of the runners, forcing the whole hash line to constrict as the gaps closed between the hashers, all of them impatiently waiting for the mahout to get his elephant out of their way.

Solti began to feel a vague discomfort creep through his body. The scene did not quite ring true. Why wasn't the mahout able to prod the beast on again? Why had it stopped directly in the path of the hash? Almost without intention, Solti found himself falling back toward the very back of the group, letting the stragglers pass him by as his eyes darted over the surrounding areas.

There were a few Nepalese women tending the paddy to the right side of the mud path. To his left and across the paddy was a mud wall high enough so he could not look over it. No apparent danger from the front or sides . . . yet. Solti looked back. A minute or two ago, the hash had crossed a small dirt road. Now, clunking their way up the road was a pair of tuk-tuks, the ubiquitous three-wheeled jitneys with Chinese two-cylinder engines that often served as transportation for the city Nepalese. The eight-seat vehicles were struggling up the slight incline, their motors, barely larger than sewing machines, emitting an inordinate amount of noise and exhaust fumes.

Solti felt a chill radiating from his stomach. This could not be a regular run for a tuk-tuk. Maybe he would have believed one tuk-tuk, motoring out by chance into the countryside as they were completing the hash run, but not two. It was wrong. Frantically, he looked around for a safe place. The way up the hill was blocked. The tuk-tuks barred the rear. The only possible safety was through the paddies. Solti scrambled down the bank to his left, finally reaching the bottom, not even bothering to take off his shoes when he slipped into the water. As he began to slosh across the paddy, the hash sweeper yelled at him to come back. The man's voice only added to Solti's fear. He had to get away from the group, away from the tuk-tuks, away from the elephant. He was sure of it: they were looking for him.

Stumbling through the muddy water, Solti glanced back at the tuk-tuks. Both jitneys had pulled to a stop with a ragtag group of Nepalese piling out, the men carrying an assortment of weapons from shotguns to AK-47's. One of the men even brandished a sword, another a long-handled ax. They began trotting up the hill.

Solti swiveled around to face uphill. The elephant and his mahout had been joined by more Nepalis, all armed like the group below. They began coming down the path.

Ambush! Solti tried to believe the armed groups were here to kill other members of the hash. Then he considered another possibility: Maybe they were just robbers? Maybe they were diehard Maoists down from the surrounding mountains, bringing their brand of organized terror to the people in the valleys below? Solti shook off these notions as fantasies. He was here, they were here, and every instinct he had screamed at him that he was their target.

His breath came in gasps as he tried to go faster, hoping against hope that the men wouldn't see that he had broken away from the line of hashers. If he could get across the paddy and hide behind the dirt bulk of its enclosing side, he might make it.

Solti reached the wall of the paddy, frantically scrambling up on his hands and knees, finally reaching the top lip.

Three Nepalese were waiting for him. The man carrying the kukri didn't hesitate for a second. He thrust the long, curved knife through Solti's belly. Solti looked down as the man pulled the knife out, his life spilling out, following the knife. It didn't hurt. Solti was numb with the thought that he was going to be dead very soon.

One of the other Nepalese men carried an old pump-action shotgun. He pumped the slide once and then fired across the few feet separating them. Solti's body was catapulted back into the paddy below. The gunman took his time, surveying Solti, now half-submerged in the muddy water, then descended, put the shotgun muzzle close to Solti's head, and fired a last shell, blowing Solti's head apart.

The man looked down at the body, now satisfied, then made his leisurely way up the embankment to join the other two. The third member of the trio was a woman, her hair covered in the Moslem style, wearing sunglasses. The name she used was Rana, a common enough name in Nepal. Rana pulled a red bandanna from a recess of her sari and waved it in the air, yelling something in Nepalese at both armed groups on the hill. She waited to make sure the bands of men had seen her signal, nodding as the men piled into the tuk-tuks, driving away. The uphill group disappeared the way they had come, the elephant the last of the party to lumber over the crest of the hill and vanish.

A second later, the killers trotted away, disappearing behind an abandoned farmhouse.

The survivors of the hash told the authorities various distorted stories of what they had seen or heard. The Nepalese police, not very efficient in any case, put it down as an unsolved crime, gathered Solti's belongings from his hotel room, and had the hotel staff wrap and ship them back to the home address Solti had left at the registration desk. When the belongings arrived at the European destination listed on the package, nobody living there had ever heard of Solti. Rather than take the trouble of returning it to the post office, the residents stored the package in a corner of their small basement. They did not open it to look inside. It might appear dishonest. After all, someone might come to claim the package, and they had their reputations to uphold in the neighborhood.

In a week, they forgot about it. In Nepal, the monsoon rains began.

Chapter 2

Sofia, Jana Matinova's old chum, called Jana from Transparency in Government, the anti-corruption organization. Sofia had helped set up a chapter in Slovakia three years earlier. They had not talked for some time, not because of any animosity but because each of them had set off in the world in a different direction that required very separate activities, both professionally and socially.

Sofia had assumed she would find the right path for herself, but it had taken her a little longer than Jana, who was now a commander in the Slovak Police. Sofia had first gone with a bank, then a statistical information firm doing corporate analysis, followed by a freelance interpreter's job for the expatriate business community, loathing each job in turn. But her latest work had opened a door to vast opportunities.

After a few weeks of studying the issues, Sofia had started out with a bang, calling a news conference to deride the government's award of a building contract to a firm whose head was not only related to a cabinet minister, but a heavy contributor to the present government. Even worse, one of the school buildings that the man had constructed was already beginning to crumble, due to the inferior concrete used in the construction. The story was broadcast on all the television networks and headlined in the newspapers. Even the United States took notice, and Sofia was called in by the

American ambassador to Slovakia and publicly commended for her action in revealing the corrupt practice.

That was only Sofia's first step. Sofia called for reform, not only in government procurement, but in government accounting procedures, for filing property and financial statements by all civil servants and the passage of freedom-of-information laws. She sponsored citizen hotlines to encourage the reporting of corrupt activities and criticized licensing practices that resulted in enormous payoffs being required to obtain business permits. Then she went after the government as a whole. Sofia's demands called for a massive overhaul of the electoral process and a total review and reform of the way government departments did business.

In the process, with an energy that astonished everyone who knew her, Sofia traveled all over the country, meeting with groups of people, manufacturers and regional representatives of government, attending international conferences and becoming a major figure in Eastern Europe in the anti-corruption fight. Everyone was aware of her; everyone in Slovakia admired her.

Through it all, Sofia and Jana had maintained their friendship. They saw each other less, they telephoned less frequently, but they retained the feeling they'd had for each other since they had been children. To each of them, the other was the same person who had seen a friend through the powerless years of childhood, through the hard teen years, and finally into adulthood.

Today began another chapter.

Sofia's voice on the telephone was excited, urging Jana to meet her for lunch at a vegetarian restaurant they both liked on Laurinska, halfway between them, almost in the exact center of Bratislava. Sofia assured Jana she had something of great importance to discuss and needed Jana's input.

Jana tried to put her off until the evening, but Sofia was so enthusiastic, so insistent that Jana agreed to meet her at noon.

Jana generally did not eat lunch, instead snacking on one thing or another that she brought from home. Today, when she finally queued up in the line outside, she was ravenous and glad she had come. The restaurant served a limited numbers of items, cafeteria style. The servers, on the other side of the counter, plopped large portions of the food on customers' plates when they went by, portions that would satisfy much larger people than Jana. It was not gourmet food, but pleasant enough, and cheap by any standard, so for a police officer it was a good place to eat.

As usual, Sofia was late when she joined Jana in line. A number of people who recognized her from her coverage by the media murmured encouragement to Sofia; one woman even insisted on shaking her hand. Sofia was patient, finally breaking free of her admirers to hug Jana and, still breathless from racing to the restaurant from a meeting that had run on and on, apologized, as she always did, for being late.

"I'm sorry; more than sorry."

"I accept your expression of remorse," Jana said, a smile on her face. "True friends are required to accept apologies."

"Even police officer friends?"

"Particularly police officer friends."

They hugged again; then Sofia got right to the point. "I'm so happy, Jana. I think I may be starting on an incredible adventure that will bring me the job of my dreams. A new profession."

Jana was shocked that Sofia was even thinking of leaving work she was so good at and which she obviously enjoyed. "I thought you already had the job of your dreams. You told me on the phone only this morning how wonderful it was, how satisfied you were when you went home. It's what you're good at."

"I am, I am, Jana. But, if you look at it right, this new job is really an extension of what I'm doing now. I've already talked to other people at work. I even spoke to the people at international headquarters in Berlin, and they all gave me the go-ahead. In fact, they urged me to do it. Of course, I won't be able to keep working at Transparency. It would be a conflict of interest. But if I want to come back, the job will probably be waiting for me."

"Okay." Jana tried to keep an open mind. "Here I am, your old friend Jana, the arbiter of all things good for Sofia, waiting with hope in my heart and open arms for your glad tidings. So, what's the new job, Sofia?"

"Jana, I've been asked to campaign in the general election for the reform coalition. They've promised me a position on the slate. If we get enough votes I'll become a member of parliament." She stared at Jana, waiting for approval, her face lit up with excitement. "It's a tremendous leap up, an opportunity to be involved in something even more important, a job that will allow me to make changes directly in the way the government does business. I can be a real advocate for the people."

Jana thought it over. It was not all that hard for her to follow Sofia's logic and to understand Sofia's enthusiasm. The present government was far from wonderful. It was crooked, led by a man who was a dangerous demagogue. His secret police used strongarm tactics and were becoming even more extreme. A change would be a good thing. Even so, Jana's main concern was her friend and her friend's future: would Sofia's move into politics benefit Sofia?

"You've never talked to me before about wanting to be a politician."

"Jana, what I've been doing over the last years is political."

"Wrong," said Jana. "Now you're your own master.

You don't have to answer to the voters. You don't have to kowtow to a political party. You don't have to consider expediency and make compromises."

"Jana, I've examined all the arguments for and against."

"That's the right start."

"I'll tell you something I've never told even you. This has always been my secret dream. I pushed it back into a corner of my mind. I never thought that I could get there. Inside, I always see a powerless person in my mirror. How could a powerless woman become a member of the National Council of the Slovak Republic? How could I become a person who people look up to? That Sofia in my mirror could never be a member of parliament. Then, like a gift from the gods, it's offered to me on a silver platter."

"If the party wins."

"Why shouldn't the party win? This regime of criminals is ready to crumble. The people are turning against it. I can help the slate. They want the people to know that there are reformers in the party. I've been working for Transparency; I'm well known as a speaker for truth, so I'm perfect for them. It is a great fit."

Jana sighed. "The opposition, the newspapers, all the media, will look for everything and anything that they can use against you, not only during the election but all the while you hold office. You'll have no privacy. The people who voted for you will demand your attention; everyone will be ready to criticize, and to criticize unfairly." Jana was trying to lay it on as thick as possible so Sofia would realize what she was getting into. "There'll be blame heaped on you for both what you do wrong and what you didn't manage to get done and, in reality, couldn't be expected to do. You'll only have brief moments of love from the voters, and lots of moments of anger and rejection." Jana finally ran down. "Can you face that?"

Sofia did not even bother to reflect.

"I am ready for anything and everything." She threw back her head, raising her fists in the air in triumph. "It can all come, and I'll survive it; I'll eat it all up and lick my lips afterward." Her arms came down. "Will you help your friend Sofia, Jana?"

Jana responded to the plea as any good friend would have. "If you're sure, then I'll help."

Sofia began clapping her hands and jumping up and down in glee. "I knew you would approve; I knew you'd support me!!"

The line moved forward. The two of them went into the café, picked up their trays, and moved to the serving line. There was a moment of silence as they ordered and the food was passed across the counter onto their trays. Sofia's voice, when she spoke again, was more subdued, scarcely above a whisper.

"The party has plans for a number of us to make a bicycle trip around the country, from city to city, village to village, talking directly to the people. They've asked me to participate, and I've agreed. I'll be one of their major spokespersons. And we'll change Slovakia for the better."

Jana winced at the thought of all the speeches, all the hand-shaking, and all the holding of babies as their mothers thrust them forward. "Not something I would want. But maybe it's right for you. You were always daring."

Sofia giggled. "I can be both daring and good at the same time."

"Just remember the 'good' part," Jana whispered back.

After they paid, Sofia glanced around the room looking for a place to sit and eat. Her eyes stopped at a table where there was only one person. Even seated you could see that he was tall and dressed in a suit more expensive than the ordinary Slovak could afford, with a dark blue tie and a very white starched shirt.

"Jana!" She nudged her friend with an elbow. "I know that man. He's already a member of parliament."

Jana recognized him from television. "I've seen him." She remembered the man as a good speaker with tremendous poise. Even sitting, eating and reading a newspaper, he projected a strong presence. There were not that many people who looked good while putting food in their mouths. "He's handsome."

"He's even better when you get closer."

Sofia started moving toward his table, Jana following close behind.

"We'll be interrupting him," Jana warned.

"All politicians want people to admire them, which is what we're now going to work at doing."

Jana thought about the Sofia she had seen today. "Sofia, maybe you're right for this job after all."

"Ah, suddenly I'm right for the job?"

"Maybe it's not so sudden. You were almost always willing to do whatever was necessary to get to where you wanted to go, and damn the consequences."

"You may take out the 'almost.'"

The man looked up just as they reached his table.

"Do you mind if we join you?" Sofia asked. "Most of the other seats are taken."

He waved a welcoming hand at the chairs, watching them as they sat, his eyes resting longer on Sofia. Jana could see that Sofia was right about one thing: he looked even better up close, a sprinkling of gray in his carefully combed hair, a straight boned nose, and rather large ears which seemed, for some reason, to add a soft touch to what otherwise might have been too stern a face.

"We know each other," he said to Sofia. "I'm trying to remember from where."

"It's not good for a politician to forget names and events."

He snapped his fingers in a flash of pleased recognition. "Yes, the lady from Transparency who is always trying to reform the political process. I remember now. We met briefly at that strategy session on the Freedom for Expression bill. You spoke."

"Right."

"Now that I've remembered, does that put me back in your graces?"

"You were never out of my good graces."

He reached over and shook Sofia's hand, then held his hand out to Jana. "My name is Ivan Boryda."

"The member of parliament?"

He nodded, pleased that she recognized him.

"My name is Jana Matinova. This is Sofia Senec."

"I remembered Sofia. I promise that I'll remember you too."

"I hope we're not taking you away from anything important." Sofia indicated the newspaper.

He shrugged, folding the paper up, setting it down next to his empty dish. "They conducted a poll. According to the poll, the present prime minister is going to win the next election. His party took the poll. Since I know how much money they steal, and how much they skew their figures, I would deduct at least twenty percent from their totals, which means we're ahead."

"I agree," said Sofia, staring openly at Boryda. Jana kicked her under the table, trying to bring her back to reality. There was a wedding ring on the man's finger. As usual, where men were concerned, Sofia paid little attention to Jana.

"I am going into the political arena myself," Sofia informed him.

He looked at her with new interest. "How so?"

"I'll be campaigning for our party."

"Our party?"

"I'm going on the bicycle junket. I think we will be on the same program."

He stared at her for a long moment. "Then we're already close associates."

"I hope so." Sofia started to reach out, almost as if to take his hand, and then pulled it back. "We're on a mission together."

"Here's to the mission." He raised his water glass in a toast, the two women joining him, clinking their glasses against his, sipping the water. He set his glass down. "I have to go." Boryda got up. "Jana, Sofia, I know we'll all see each other again very soon. Sofia, you and I will have fun together on the campaign trail." He inclined his head, then walked away.

Sofia's eyes followed him all of the way out the door, then, through the window, as he walked down the street.

"Sofia, he's married," Jana warned.

"Just lusting in my mind."

"Sofia, you're going to be a politician. Scandals aren't good for officeholders."

"I'm aware of what I can do and what I can't do." Her voice showed her irritation. "You're not my mother, Jana."

"Yes, I am." Jana changed her tone. "Eat your food, darling Sofia," ordered Jana, in her best maternal command voice. "The greens will be good for you."

Sofia grimaced, then smiled. "Maybe you *are* my mother."

They began eating. Sofia got a few words out between bites. "I'll remember your advice. Don't worry, Jana."

"I promise I won't worry," Jana replied, knowing she already was.

Over the next weeks, Sofia resigned her position at

Transparency. Several months later, at a press conference given by the coalition parties, Sofia walked to the dais to endorse the fight against the government. Seated next to her was Ivan Boryda, the man they had met in the restaurant.

Chapter 3

During the early part of the campaign, Jana did no work for the coalition slate trying to win the elections. She'd not been asked. Then the election took a different turn. The strategists of the party had decided that those who had participated in the bicycle tour of the countryside would come to Bratislava and, with all their other supporters, saturate the capital with appearances. Hundreds of worker bees were to spread their message, meeting every potential voter they could possibly contact, trying to squeeze out the last potential ballot they could for their candidate.

When the call came from Sofia, Jana was glad her friend thought she could help. Until then, Jana had been happy to be left out of the campaign. Nevertheless, since Sofia had called, Jana responded. As a precaution, before she saw Sofia, Jana went to her supervisors to discuss what she could and couldn't do because she was a police officer. They told her emphatically that she was precluded from getting involved in politics.

After that meeting, Jana was relieved. Her participation in the election was going to have to be limited, perhaps to her presence in the audience or better still to something as simple as stuffing envelopes with flyers. Of course she would have to be out of uniform.

She called her friend, who sounded harried and had little time to talk on the phone. Sofia asked Jana to meet with her and others that night. There would be a mixed group of volunteers at a small meeting room the party had rented in the Stara Radnica, the old town hall.

Crossing the square in her "civilian" clothes, Jana saw the town hall's yellow tower and red tiles. She'd always liked the building, but now she felt a certain sense of dread as she neared it. She was hoping that the meeting would be called off. Her wish was not granted.

At least fifty people were crowded into the room, seated on folding chairs, more of which had to be brought for latecomers. That left a good twenty people still standing. Everyone was talking at once, their conversations reluctantly trailing off when the meeting began.

Sofia sat at a table in the front of the room next to Lesna, the small, energetic and very bright man who ran the coalition of opposition parties and who would be prime minister if they won. On his other side was Ivan Boryda, the legislator she and Sofia had met. Jana had seen Boryda and Sofia together on television several times; each time Sofia had a big smile on her face and they had looked very comfortable together.

Sofia beckoned to Jana. She introduced her to Lesna, proclaiming her the best police officer in Slovakia. Lesna made nice noises, saying he'd heard of her and her work, and thanked her for giving up her free time to assist their efforts. When he turned away to say a few words to another campaign worker, Sofia began to reintroduce Jana to Boryda, who interrupted Sofia.

"Jana Matinova, from the restaurant. I told you I wouldn't forget your name."

Sofia reached up to affectionately pat Boryda's shoulder. "He remembers everyone's name. I think he knows all five million people in Slovakia by name." She brushed lint off his arm in a familiar way, running her fingers down to his hand. "Ivan is brilliant."

"I've read that in the papers. I generally distrust the news-papers, but since *you* say it, I know it must be true," Jana replied.

They all laughed, Boryda looking appropriately abashed.

Jana watched their interaction, the way they leaned against each other, the way Sofia constantly touched Boryda, the way she looked at him, the way she said his name. Sofia was in love. There was no doubt in Jana's mind that the two had begun an affair. "I wish you a huge sweep of the election and a change for the good in the government."

Boryda thanked her, but he was already trolling the room with his eyes to find the next person to charm.

As others came up to talk to Sofia and Boryda, Jana began backing away. "You'll do the country proud," she murmured, hoping against hope that they would. She was also aware of the possibility of a scandal that might destroy both their careers. Slovakia was still a very proper country when it came to politicians' personal lives. And Boryda was a mar-ried man.

Jana sat in the back of the room, watching the proceed-ings. The mayor introduced the three dignitaries, and then called on Lesna to speak. There was loud applause when he stood up, which became a rhythmic clap of appreciation, until he finally held up his hand to quiet his audience.

When he spoke, Jana was riveted. Not that he used grand gestures or a stentorian voice to command attention. He seemed sincere, all-inclusive in his gentle, direct approach, and captivated everyone in the room. It was a huge change from the man who was currently in power, a change for the better. Jana was glad that Sofia was in his camp. He was the right man for the job.

Lesna apologized for having to leave the meeting early, departing as soon as he was through. Sofia and Boryda remained to get the needed commitments from the people in the room, not only to vote for them but to campaign in their neighborhoods, to get their friends and neighbors to campaign, and, perhaps, to give small contributions to help win the victory they were all working so hard to achieve.

Sofia gave a persuasive talk, emphasizing the need to curtail the illegal activities of the people in power, their nepotism and cronyism. She reminded her audience over and over of her past work with Transparency in trying to open government to public scrutiny. She did exactly what she had been brought into the campaign for, lending needed authenticity to the party's calls for honest government. Her prior reputation added almost a religious note of conviction. The response to her speech was good, though it lacked the aura of veneration that Lesna had received just a few minutes earlier.

Boryda was the last to speak. He started slowly, his voice gradually building in volume, his gestures becoming broader as his speech progressed. His words, starting off mildly, reached a roar of reproach for the current regime. His eyes flashed, his posture was assertive. He carried the audience with him, held them in his hands and lifted them up with him in a final burst of exhortation. There was a split second of silence when he ended. Then the audience jumped to their feet, screaming approval, applauding, the applause becoming a chant. They bathed Boryda in adoration.

Boryda glowed, beaming when the people began pushing forward, crowding around him, patting him on the back, complimenting him. Finally, as a pair of bodyguards appeared out of nowhere, Boryda edged away from his admirers and was escorted to the door, a retinue like a comet's tail trailing after him. Sofia, who had stayed behind to talk to the few supporters who remained, walked over to Jana.

"Did you like Lesna?" she inquired, although Boryda was the man she really wanted to talk about. "So logical, so clear in his perception of what should be done for this country. A good man."

"I think he's a wonderful man, particularly for a politician."

"Jana, I'm now a politician."

"I'll ignore that fact," Jana teased. "And continue to think of you as my friend instead."

Sofia kissed her on the cheek. "I know. I always think of you as Jana, my old pal, and not as a threatening police officer."

"I've never threatened you, Sofia."

"It's just how you look in a uniform."

"That's one of the reasons I left the uniform home. Let's talk about the new man in your life."

"A new man? Me?" Sofia asked in mock innocence.

"We both know, Sofia."

"He was wonderful, wasn't he, Jana?" Her face flushed with emotion, the words gushed out of her mouth. "He's a genius, the greatest public speaker I've ever seen. He seizes audiences and carries them with him."

"To heaven or hell?" Jana asked.

"No, not to hell. He will take us to where *we* want to go."

"No, Sofia," Jana corrected. "He will take us to where *he* wants us to go."

"Why do you say that, Jana? I know Ivan Boryda; you don't."

"I listened to his speech. Demagoguery. He loves power. He supports Lesna and the coalition now. He is the kind of man who, when he is ready, will try to get rid of them. He wants center stage. He *wants!* He sees himself as the prime minister. He'll always need more, Sofia." Jana considered, then decided to plunge ahead. "And he'll want another woman after you, Sofia."

"Jana, please." Sofia looked around to see if anyone was listening. She took Jana's arm, leading her to the door. "Let's talk about the elections instead. We both want our side to win. That's why I'm doing this."

"That's why you started doing this. Are you sure you're not out for power yourself?"

"Jana, enough. I want power, but just to get the program we need adopted by this country. The election is paramount."

Jana sighed. "Okay, I'll focus on the election."

Sofia relaxed, finally reaching the subject of Jana's role in the campaign. "We'd like you to make door-to-door presentations for us; perhaps even neighborhood presentations. You're a police officer. If you wear your uniform when you talk to people, they will know who to vote for."

"Wear my uniform? I can't do that, Sofia."

Sofia stopped walking. "You said you'd support our efforts." She frowned. "Is this because you don't approve of Ivan? A moral judgment?"

"It has nothing to do with you or Ivan Boryda. I asked my supervisors if I could campaign. Public employees, particularly police officers, are not supposed to work actively for political causes. And you want me to do my preaching to the people of Bratislava in uniform, making it clear that I'm a police officer. Sofia, I wouldn't be on the police force for long if I did that. I'd be dismissed for abusing my office."

"When we win, we'll have you reinstated."

Jana didn't like what she was hearing. "You're telling me that you'd put me at risk? Make me suffer that kind of anguish? You'd let them dismiss me to get what you want?" Jana looked at her friend. This was not the Sofia she knew, the Sofia who had worked for Transparency and opposed corruption. This wasn't Sofia, her friend. "Being a police officer is the work I always wanted to do. You want to be a politician. Would you sacrifice me for your ambition?"

"I said we would have you reinstated."

"I'm not looking for reinstatement, Sofia." When had this insensitivity, this disregard for other people's needs and happiness, appeared? "I'd be dismissed, my friends on the police force would shun me, all just to gain you a few votes?" They had reached the door. "Sofia, I'll sit in the audience as a civilian. I'll applaud everything you or Lesna say. But I won't do it on your terms. Understood?"

Sofia looked at her without expression, then turned to another supporter who'd come up to her.

Angry, Jana walked out of the room.

Chapter 4

The reform slate was elected. Lesna was now the prime minister, Sofia a member of parliament. Today the streets of Bratislava were covered by sleet that was still pouring down, the wet pellets immediately turning to slush, forming a cold, soggy carpet. The slush turned dark gray as it mixed with street oil, city dirt, and discarded papers that had been laid down in a glutinous mixture for weeks by the passing cars. Galoshes-clad people slogged through the muck.

Jana trudged through the wet sludge, her police greatcoat edged with beads of moisture, her police cap visor dripping water down her neck. She pulled the collar closer, wondering at the speed at which the beautiful white snow of early morning had turned to mire. A truck passed, sloshing dirty water onto the sidewalk. Jana skipped quickly out of the way, almost falling when she slipped on a patch of black ice. She turned to yell at the truck driver, but immediately caught herself, feeling guilty. It was not appropriate for a police commander to shout at passing vehicles. Looking around, she saw the structure she was aiming for, quickly crossed the street, and passed through the shop-lined tunnel that led to the next block, where the Gremium Café was located.

Jana tried to peer through its fogged-up windows. She saw only vague shapes inside. Jana sidled under the half-open awning that was spilling liquid onto passing customers, went through the front door and was immediately struck by the smell of wet clothing mixed with the aroma of burned coffee. She checked out the people inside, a police habit. The customers eyed her in return, resenting her presence. Now they'd have to be on guard as to what they said, did, or smoked.

Jana stared down the people who were peering at her. Most broke eye contact. Then she saw Sofia. Her friend was graced with her usual stylish hairdo and makeup which, of course, because it was Sofia, and Sofia always looked her best, had not been spoiled by the weather. Now her friend's clothes were in the latest Western style. She smiled as Jana came to greet her. They exchanged hugs and quick pecks on the cheek; Sofia helped Jana off with her greatcoat, Jana tossed it over the back of a spare chair. They sat, and Sofia slid a glass of steaming apple tea over to Jana.

Jana took a grateful sip, than warmed her hands around the cup, nodding in appreciation

"You're always on time, so I could order and know it would still be hot for you."

"You remembered I love apples."

"Slovakia doesn't have much, but it has lots of apples," Sofia laughed. "And, being good Slovaks, we were always munching them as girls, the two of us sitting on the porch chewing away."

"I remember."

"Cops, and people who run for public office, we always remember."

"We were friends first."

"Thank you for that." Sofia paused. "I thought you might not come." She smiled ruefully. "You might damage your reputation by associating with me."

"Friends come when they're called."

"I thought you would. But who knows?" Sofia winced. "Things are bad."

Jana smiled wryly. "In this small country one would have to be deaf, dumb, and blind not to be aware of a scandal." She took a sip of her tea, trying to find the right words. "I've been worried. I was glad you called. All the innuendos have to be hurtful, even for a politician."

Sofia tried to shrug it off. "A politico gets used to it."

"They're keeping up the drumbeat. Every day it's on the front pages."

"Sex. They love sex. Readers underline the good parts. So they keep it up." Sofia patted her hair reflexively. "People are people. If it weren't about me, I'd probably lap up every word."

Jana studied her friend. She seemed even smaller, her shoulders slightly bowed. Jana had always admired her eyes since they'd been young girls, but now, despite Sofia's makeup, they were darker and more shadowed than usual. The lines around her mouth and on her forehead had not been there before.

Jana tried to be encouraging. "Sofia, I know you. You'll get through this."

Sofia grimaced, her lips thinning, then tried to sound light-hearted. "I like your optimism. In the dark of the night, when I can't sleep, I'll hold on to it. It'll be my comfort blanket, protecting me against the dark." She sighed. "At least I'll *try* to hold on to it." She took a sip of her own tea, reflecting. "I won't hide it from you. I'm in a pit and I don't see my way out."

"I'm sorry, Sofia."

Sofia reached over and touched Jana's wrist in appreciation, then took a deep breath. "They're after us like hounds closing in on their prey."

"How is he taking it?"

"Not well. We can't see each other. No phone calls. He thinks, from the information they've put out, that they've bribed some secretary, or the telephone company, or the land-lord to record our conversations. The dogs want every chunk of us, every small bite, until they kill us." She paused, reflect-ing on her life, trying not to sound too angry. Still, bitterness colored her words. "We pass in the halls and try not to look at each other. For us, life has shut down."

"And his wife?"

Sofia's lips tightened. "I think she was the one who first told the reporters. He says no, that she seemed shocked to learn of our 'love nest,' as they call it. She pretends it is not happening. She is brave, he says. I say nothing, but think *horseshit*. She knew. And she is the kind of woman who won't admit it."

"I've heard wives are always supposed to know when a husband is unfaithful."

Sofia nodded, then fixed her eyes on Jana, studying her.

"Did you know when your husband cheated on you?"

"I don't know if he was unfaithful, so I can't answer the question." Jana hesitated, trying to force herself to utter the words. "When he . . . when he died, I didn't sense that any other woman had been involved in our lives."

Sofia made a rude noise. "All men cheat."

They sat in silence, each alone with her thoughts. Jana considered her life with Daniel. It had been hard, but not because of women. He had been a revolutionary, had robbed banks for his cause. A handsome man, charismatic, opinionated, willful. But, Jana thought, he had not chased other women. And, finally, when his world imploded, he'd committed suicide. The literal truth was that he *had* been unfaithful, but not in the way Sofia meant. There are many ways to be disloyal, to leave a mate, to renege on your word, to destroy trust. Her husband had promised, even though it was an implicit promise, that he would, at the least, do his best to stay alive for her. It is that one ultimate, unbreakable promise that every married couple makes. And Jana's husband's suicide had left its mark. He'd promised, then lied, and deserted her for eternity. The pain was still there.

Jana turned her attention back to Sofia. "Sofia, you had to know when you began this affair that it was dangerous for an elected official to have a romance with another politician, particularly one who was married. He's a deputy prime minister, Sofia. You're a member of the Slovak parliament. Eventually, someone had to find out. It would be irresistible to the media."

Tears began flowing down Sofia's cheeks. After a few seconds she began to rub them away, to pretend they were not there, as she struggled to remain in control of her emotions. "You don't have to rebuke me, Jana. I know. I wake up in the morning, barely hold my tears concealed inside me all day, then go to sleep sobbing on my pillow at night."

Jana had not come to criticize her friend. Sofia was having a hard enough time. "The words just came out. I apologize." She reached over and took Sofia's hand, squeezing it reassuringly. "I'm a fool. I was insensitive."

"No. I'm the insensitive one. I always have been." Sofia squeezed Jana's hand back. She was silent for a moment, then, as if explaining her actions to herself, said, "I couldn't stay away from him. One step led to another, then another, then it was irrevocable, and I was locked in. And so, here we are." She pulled a compact out of her handbag, using one of the napkins on the table to try to wipe off her smeared makeup. She was only somewhat successful. "Better to talk about pleasant times when we were innocent, when we were young. We dreamed, you and I."

"Everyone has hopes. Young, old, we all have them."

"Some are fantasies." Sofia winced, then managed a slight smile. "Your father was a wise man. You remember him telling us to be careful what we wished for?"

Jana remembered. "Be careful what you wish for. Castles in the sky can turn out to be dark dungeons."

"I'm living in one, Jana."

"We'll get through it, Sofia."

Sofia's cell phone rang. She reached into her purse and pulled it out, barking an impatient "Yes." While Sofia talked on the phone, Jana glanced around the café, once more surveying the customers. A number were looking at Jana's table, peering at Sofia. Their expressions, particularly the women's, were not kind. Sofia was right: her fantasy had turned into a nightmare.

Sofia finally terminated her phone call.

"Politics," she explained. "They never let you rest. A meeting has just been called. I must go." She started to rise.

Jana touched her arm, stopping her. "Sofia, you phoned and asked me to meet you here. There was urgency in your voice. You wanted something. What is it you need? Help of some kind?"

Sofia stared at Jana as if about to speak, an anxious look on her face. Then she stifled the impulse, quickly standing to don her coat and scarf. She paused long enough to lean over and give Jana a quick peck on the cheek.

"I just wanted to see you and talk."

Jana stood, gave her friend a hug, then held her at arm's length, looking directly at her. "We have known each other forever. You know you can confide in me, right?"

"Of course I know that." Sofia pulled away. "We will always be friends." She smiled, gave Jana another quick kiss on the cheek, and hurried out of the café.

Jana looked after her. The smile and the kiss had been a politician's smile and kiss, not a friend's. Sofia had always confided in Jana when things were bad. If she didn't feel comfortable enough to open up, then Sofia was in the worst kind of trouble. And Jana had no idea how to help her.

Jana's friend was truly living in a dark place.

Perhaps even worse than the one she'd been in when they were young.

Chapter 5

The Bratislava of that long-past day had not been unkind to the young, just indifferent. Certainly the Slovaks had taken care of their children under communism, then under the new government after the communists fell. Things were harder, but parents managed to feed their children and keep them clothed, if not stylishly dressed; and if the clothes were second-hand, they were at least carefully patched. But there were no places for children to play among the gray soot-stained buildings of the Austro-Hungarian Empire; or to run free between the drab edifices built during the not-so-glorious reign of the Bolsheviks, structures which were decaying even faster than the older ones around them. So, like kids everywhere, they made do, carving playgrounds out of garbage-littered lots, dashing after a soccer ball through moldering back streets, making do amid the stoops of dreary, half-empty structures. Or they whiled away the afternoons when school was over by talking with a best friend.

Jana and Sofia had been best friends since they had met at school and found out that they both disliked their teacher, a man named Adolphus. It had been easy to dislike him. He found ways, in every class, almost on an hourly basis, to praise the current government for its commitment to warm relations with Russia and to disdain the West. Unfortunately for him, since everyone knew he was of German, not Slovak, descent, he was axiomatically, uniformly distrusted.

Today Jana's mother was visiting Jana's sick grandmother, and Sofia's mother was working in her small hat shop, so the two youngsters had been free to walk through the streets holding hands and to settle down on the front steps of a closed cinema that still displayed posters of the last film it had shown over a year ago. Sofia was holding forth on the subject of boys, which still didn't interest Jana much, but which was irresistible to Sofia.

"I like them looking at me," proclaimed Sofia, smoothing a stray lock of hair. "Then I like to ignore them, or sneer at them. Then they get mad."

"Why do you want to make them mad?"

"'Cause I noticed that they come back and stare even harder." She snickered. "Then they bring you a present or something. Just to interest you. Most of the time I ignore that too."

"Why do you care?" snapped Jana, a little irritated. "They're not supposed to give you presents. And you're not supposed to take them."

Sofia shrugged off Jana's criticism, turning her nose up, assuming a haughty attitude. "They're not worth much, so I throw them back." They had both seen that done in a movie they'd gone to. The heroine of the film was a good girl, and everyone believed she had done the right thing, so Jana nodded her approval.

They chatted away for another few moments until Sofia noticed a black government-licensed Zil limousine pass by. She smiled at the man who looked out from behind the partially open curtain of the back-seat window. The car slowed.

Jana slapped at Sofia's knee in disapproval, her voice taking on an edge. "Stop smiling. The man is ugly, and his thoughts are uglier."

Sofia's smile lost a bit of sparkle. "He's respectable. He has a big car. And it's a Zil. He must be a high official if he has a Zil instead of one of those ugly, noisy Tatras."

"Government officials are never respectable, particularly the older ones. Everyone knows that."

The curtain in the back seat dropped as the car picked up speed.

Sofia watched the limousine move away, making a small moue of regret. She hadn't had her chance to really flirt and to enjoy the results, which was the whole point of flirting.

"Who says they're not respectable?" she asked.

"My father, sometimes, and he's a judge so he should know. He says they steal, and other things."

"What other things?" a suddenly pugnacious Sofia demanded, her jaw jutting, a little angry at being reproached for exercising her newly found skill.

"You know." Jana's voice took on more assurance. "They don't want me to hear so they drop their voices. Or my mother tells my father to be quiet."

"She's brave to do that."

"Why?"

"He's a judge."

"They're married," explained Jana. "She's louder than he is."

The two of them nodded, both understanding that louder was better.

"Marrieds always argue."

"No, they don't."

Jana tried to think of one pair of married neighbors who seemed happy. There were two, both sisters married to a pair of brothers.

"The Slavins."

"They're not Slovak."

"Yes, they are."

"They are also brothers who married two neighbor sisters. That's different."

"I fight with my brother."

"They're also Jews. Jews keep it quiet."

"How can you keep an argument quiet?"

"That's what Jews do. My uncle says they have secrets they only tell other Jews."

"What does that have to do with them arguing?"

"That's the reason you don't hear them arguing."

The Zil drove slowly down the block again, crawling as it neared the two girls. Sofia smiled, giving the occupant of the car a little wave. When Jana grabbed Sofia's hand, Sofia pulled away.

The sedan stopped at the curb directly in front of them.

Jana was uneasy, embarrassed and upset. She edged away from Sofia, trying to ignore the car, pretending it was not there. But after a few seconds Jana couldn't help herself and she sneaked a glance at the car. The back-seat window curtain was pulled back completely this time, and a man's face was pressed against the glass. His lips were slightly parted, the yellow-green color of his teeth showing; his teeth seemed to fit badly in his mouth. His eyes caught the light through the window. Their color was like wet ashes, devoid of even a tinge of human warmth.

The man beckoned to Sofia, and Sofia, seemingly oblivious to what Jana observed, walked over to the door as it opened. A hand came from within, holding out a map to Sofia as if he were going to ask directions. Sofia focused on the map.

Instinct told Jana it was all wrong. Why would the passenger of a limousine ask directions, rather than the driver? And what government driver didn't know every part of Bratislava by heart? Warning signals flashed in Jana's mind. Sofia was in danger!

Jana broke into a run, lunging forward, screaming at her friend to come back.

Too late.

The man grabbed Sofia, pulling her into the car. The door closed behind her with a thud just as Jana reached it. The man glanced at Jana through the window as the curtain dropped. The Zil drove off, Jana running after it, trying to keep up, screaming for help, screaming at the car, screaming at the sky in frustration as the vehicle picked up speed. Frantic now, Jana tried to find a weapon, anything to use against the fortress of a car that seemed impregnable to her.

Jana finally scooped up a stone from the side of the road, stopped for a fraction of a second to get set, and threw the rock with force. The stone bounced off the rear window of the car, leaving a small star-shaped crack in the glass.

The car accelerated, reached the intersection and turned, out of Jana's sight. Jana ran harder, desperate to save Sofia. When she got to the intersection, the car was no longer in view.

Panting from exertion and shock, Jana looked from road to alley and back, trying to decide which way to go. She scanned the street frantically, looking for someone to assist her, some pedestrian to ask for direction or advice. A store owner was rearranging a display of fruit in front of his shop, sprinkling the older fruit and vegetables with water to make them shiny and fresh-looking. Jana ran over to him.

"A black car; a black Zil," Jana panted. "It passed by here. Which street did it take?" The man shrugged, indifferent, returning to his work without a moment's thought. A woman came out of another store. Jana darted over to her. "Did you see it? The black government car. It was just here."

"What?" The woman's eyes shifted from side to side as if she were being accused of something. "I saw nothing. Nothing!" She scurried away, afraid to be associated with an event, no matter how trivial, which might involve her with the government. No one in Slovakia wanted to be involved in anything that might attract the attention of the bureaucracy.

Jana screamed with grief and frustration. The fruit dealer quickly walked inside his shop, closing the door behind him with finality. The woman scuttled down the street, her shoes rapidly click-clacking on the cement of the sidewalk as she put distance between herself and the young girl who was going to get them all in trouble. Jana forced herself to become calmer. She needed to think, to use her eyes more effectively. Her eyes swept the street and the alleys intently. At the head of one stood a puddle of water. Immediately behind the puddle were tire tracks, fresh tracks, still damp. It had to be the Zil.

Jana ran down the alley, and kept on running over to the next street. Then arbitrarily, because she had no other leads, she ran through the nameless maze of corridors that made up that section of Bratislava, scouring the alleys trying to search. One street radiated into another. She forced herself to keep on until she was exhausted, and still she kept going.

She did not find the car.

An hour and a half later, she found Sofia.

She was at another street corner, sitting on a curb, feet in the gutter, her clothes disheveled, her hair hanging down, looking like just another Gypsy child to the people who passed by without really looking at her, without realizing that she was in distress. Maybe they didn't want to notice. Jana hesitated, wondering what to do, how to act. She finally settled down on the curb next to Sofia, murmuring "hello." Sofia continued to stare vacantly at the ground without acknowledging Jana.

After five minutes of silence, Jana moved closer, just close enough to angle her body so she could look out of the corners of her eyes at Sofia. There was a small scratch on Sofia's nose, running almost parallel to the tracks tears were leaving on her cheeks. Her blouse was torn on the side closest to Jana; the blouse itself was buttoned askew. When Jana faced Sofia, she saw that one of her friend's shoes was missing, that blood stained Sofia's once-white sock. A very thin trail of blood ran up the length of Sofia's calf, up to a smudge of blood half revealed on her thigh, the rest concealed by her skirt.

Jana thought it over.

Even a twelve-year-old girl in Bratislava knew enough about men and women to be aware of what these signs indicated. The mothers of Slovakia, where so many girls become pregnant before they marry young, told their daughters the facts of life early and frequently in the hope that they would be able to avoid the worst. Sofia had listened, but not heard. Jana had been more receptive.

They sat quietly for another half hour. Eventually, Jana put her arm around her friend. Sofia, still silent, leaned on Jana's shoulder. Then, judging the time was right, Jana attempted to straighten her friend's blouse.

"I want to clean up," Sofia whispered.

"I know," Jana whispered back.

"I can't go home this way."

"We can go to my house," Jana assured her, kissing her on the ear. "My parents aren't home."

Sofia nodded.

"Now, let's go." Jana urged Sofia to her feet, supporting her to make sure she did not fall, then smoothed her friend's hair into a semblance of order.

"Thank you," whispered Sofia. "I'm a mess. Everything is a mess, just a big mess."

"I'm your friend. As long as we're friends it will be okay. We're friends for life, right, Sofia?"

Sofia nodded.

"That's a good thing for both of us to remember."

Sofia nodded again. She held up what looked like the handle from the inside of a door. "I grabbed it trying to get out. It broke off in my hand. I hit him with it."

"You did the right thing." Jana's heart went out to her friend. She managed to hold her tears back. "I'm proud of you, Sofia."

They began to walk. Sofia was stiff, moaning softly from pain as she moved. Jana put her arm around her friend's waist, trying to ease her distress.

"Friends for life," Sofia got out.

"Yes," said Jana. "Forever."

They reached Jana's house twenty-five minutes later. Immediately, Jana drew a hot bath for Sofia, helped her into the water and watched her friend try to recover from her ordeal. Sofia sat in the bath until the water was cold. Then Jana helped a dispirited Sofia dry herself, at the same time supporting her to make sure she didn't fall. She walked Sofia into her own bedroom and found a fresh pair of panties and a clean blouse to take the place of Sofia's torn ones. After a few minutes, Jana managed to comb Sofia's hair, then made arrangements with Sofia's parents for her to stay with Jana overnight without telling either of their mothers what had happened.

The next day Jana confided in her father. Her father was the only one she trusted enough to ask for advice. He listened carefully until she was finished.

"You acted bravely," he told her. "She was foolish."

"What should I do, Father?"

"Sofia hasn't told anybody?"

"She doesn't want people to know. It would be horrible for her."

The judge thought about it. "The man in the Zil had to be a high government official." He sat quietly for another long moment. "You must do what you think you should. But I believe she's right to want this to be kept silent." He leaned closer to Jana trying to convey his thoughts without imposing his will on his daughter and, by influencing Jana, imposing his will on Sofia. "If, in the future, this man were identified, I don't think it would make any difference. Not under these circumstances. They'd do nothing. The police, the government, would remain deaf. Or worse. And Sofia? Well, I think Sofia wouldn't fare very well. They'd call her names. They'd make her out to be something terrible, a person of no morals, even a prostitute who deserved what she got. They would heap scorn on her, and on her family. I've seen it done before when one of *them* is involved. It's always the person's fault, not the official's."

Jana considered what her father had tried to convey. Even at the age of twelve, she could comprehend the possible future that her father had outlined. She projected the results of bringing the government into Sofia's life. Sofia would suffer more. It was a terrible truth, but still the truth.

Jana conceded. "The neighbors, her family, they would all blame her."

"All of them," her father agreed.

"But this isn't justice," Jana finally got out.

"Sometimes justice has to wait." Her father pursed his lips. "Sometimes there is no justice."

"I don't like that." Jana was furious at the thought of Sofia's brutalizer walking around free after what he had done. "And I don't accept it. Perhaps justice will have to wait, but just for a few days."

Her father kissed her on the cheek. "Maybe more than a few days," he offered. He saw the anger and disappointment on his daughter's face. He tried to reassure her. "Things eventually work out," he said. "He'll be punished."

"Of course, Father. But by whom?"

He shrugged, not knowing what to say.

"There must be someone," Jana suggested.

She listened to her own words: there had to be someone. That same day Jana began to search, first for the Zil.

The window will need repair, she thought, which meant it would be brought to the government auto repair area, the large facility where all of the ministries' autos are brought for servicing. No one stopped Jana as she walked quickly and surely onto the lot, looking as if she had business there. Almost immediately she found the car; the workmen were just finishing the replacement of the rear window.

"A lovely car," Jana admiringly told one of them. "I want to be a high government person when I grow up so I can have one of these. Who does it belong to?" Jana smiled sweetly.

"Kamin, the minister of the interior," the man told her.

He's in charge of the police, thought Jana. Her father had been right. Sofia would not have gotten justice. She smiled again at the workers, left the lot, and the next day, immediately after breakfast, went to the building housing the Ministry of the Interior. By this time, the car had to have been repaired and returned to the minister. A few minutes later, she saw the limousine drive up and the man get out of the car. There was no mistaking the same ugly mouth, the eyes. It was him! Kamin. And he had a bandage over his left eyebrow.

Sofia had hit him with the broken door handle, and hit him hard enough to require medical treatment. Yes, said Jana to herself, she was proud of Sofia.

Jana didn't tell Sofia what she'd learned, or seen. Sofia had to recover. They both had to grow up, to be able to protect themselves. But there would come a time. Jana promised herself: they would be ready.

Three weeks later Sofia threw Jana a surprise un-birthday party, as she called it. It was not even Jana's name day. How Sofia did it, rounding up all the kids that they both knew, and getting Jana's mother to host it without telling Jana, was a feat that Jana never quite got over.

Birthdays, not to speak of un-birthdays, are not celebrated with much fanfare in Slovakia. But the kids who came even brought small presents. Sofia baked a cake, not the best cake in the world, but splendid-looking, and Sofia was Miss Personality at the party, organizing everything, making sure that all the things she had planned went well.

After the party, when most of the guests had gone home, Sofia kissed Jana on the cheek. It was her way of saying thank you for what Jana had done for her on that terrible day.

They remained the closest of friends. But, as with all friendships, the bonds fracture or strengthen, depending upon fate. Jana did not tell Sofia about her discovery of the identity of the rapist until a couple of years later, when they were in their teens. And it took a stressful event to make her divulge that information.

Jana and Sofia had gone to Bratislava's main square, Hlavne Namestie, to visit the Christmas Fair. They had money to spend because they had been working, selling live carp for Christmas dinners from a temporary stand on Frantiskanska, near the main post office. Although the job hadn't paid much, it had already provided Jana with a pair of shoes at a discount, and Sofia with a dress which she could not possibly have afforded otherwise. Each still had a few crowns left in her pocket. Sofia was dying to spend hers, and she had dragged Jana along to keep her company, all the while encouraging Jana to "live a little less like a timid old aunt," to be audacious for once.

They wandered through the Christmas stands and, at Sofia's insistence, each had a glass of spiced wine when a man had offered it to them. After they finished the wine, the man kept asking them what else he could buy them and, despite their efforts to shoo him away, kept following them, demanding more. Jana was embarrassed at what Sofia finally did to rid them of the fellow.

Talking in a loud voice so that everyone in the crowd around them could hear, she pleaded with the fairgoers to help them because a depraved man was following them. He had bought them wine and was trying to get "terrible" things from two innocent girls. It didn't take long for the crowd to begin closing in on the man, throwing things at him, screaming imprecations, even calling for the police.

He fled.

Afterwards, using their own money, they'd settled at a small table inside Meyer's, ordered hot, thick chocolate to drink and two large pastries to go with the chocolate. Sofia did most of the eating.

It was hard for Jana to muster an appetite. Her stomach was still churning. Through her impetuous conduct, Sofia had involved Jana in a situation that neither of them should have been in. The first time it had happened, two years earlier, it resulted in the horrible assault on Sofia. Now, as a result of Sofia's conduct, Jana had been forced to participate in an embarrassing incident.

Jana continued to be upset, reviewing her own behavior. After a few sips of the hot chocolate, she decided, between sips, that it was time to vent her simmering anger.

"If you weren't my one true friend, I would kick you, and kick you hard, for what you put us through."

Sofia wasn't fazed.

"What sin did I commit? The man offered to buy us spiced wine. I like spiced wine; you like spiced wine. What was wrong with letting him buy us the wine? Nothing. We got the wine and he got the pleasure of buying two pretty girls glasses of wine. We even gave him pleasant conversation and our attention while we drank the wine."

"Sofia, he expected more."

"I didn't tell him he could have more. He had no right to expect more."

"Both of us knew that he would expect more."

"Jana, if you felt that way, you didn't have to drink the wine." There was triumph in Sofia's eyes. She had Jana, and she knew it. "As your one true friend, I'd like to point out that I acted in the best possible way for both of us. He was a pest, and becoming a worse pest. Even you'll admit, he was uncomfortable to be around."

"We didn't have to get to that point, Sofia."

"We did, after he wouldn't leave us alone."

"Sofia, we're friends, but I won't be put in that position again. It should never have happened."

Sofia regarded Jana with a faintly disdainful look.

"You were never *put* in any position. I took responsibility for the man following us; I took the responsibility, and the action needed to get rid of him. Now, all I'm interested in is my pastry and chocolate."

"I'm not going to be fobbed off that easily."

"I'm not fobbing you off."

"You have to listen to me."

Sofia took another forkful of pastry, savoring the taste.

"My mother tells me I won't be able to eat like this when I get older, so I'm enjoying it now, while I can. You should enjoy yours."

Jana pushed the remains of her dessert away. "I don't want any more."

"Don't be this way."

"I'm the one who began this talk by asking you not to act in a certain way. You refuse to listen."

Sofia pushed her now-empty plate to the center of the table, where it touched Jana's. "See, even our plates are friends."

Jana persisted, wanting to make what she thought was an important point, so she raised the subject neither had talked about since the event that had occurred two years ago.

"Kamin, that's the name of the man who did what he did to you in the car."

Sofia's widening eyes and mouth revealed the shock she felt.

"You know who he is?"

"I found out."

"How did you find out?"

"I found his car. Then I found him."

"When?"

"A day or so after."

"You didn't tell me? You should have told me." Sofia's mouth snapped shut. "You should have told me!"

"I *am* telling you."

"*Then!* You should have told me then."

"What would you have done if I told you then? Who would you have gone to? Your parents? You didn't want them to know. You didn't want your neighbors to know. You didn't want any of our friends to know. Have you changed your mind? Do you want everyone in Bratislava to know? Are you going to tell them?"

Sofia's body seemed to shrink into the seat. She looked down at the plates, wiping her hands with a napkin as if she were trying to scrub off deeply embedded dirt. When she put the napkin down, Jana thought she might be ready to listen.

"You let the man buy us the spiced wine; you walked up to that car. You're right: the man who had bought us the wine had no right to expect anything more than to have us drink the wine, and maybe talk with him for a little while. It was just like the man in the car. He had no right to think that because you walked up to the car he was entitled to drag you inside and do those things to you. But some people do crazy things. They'll abuse you if they can. So you can't put yourself in a position where they can."

Sofia straightened her shoulders, an angry, determined look on her face.

"I know people want things. *I* want things. *You* want things. We take chances to get them."

Jana phrased her answer carefully.

"My father says that risks are a part of life. But the risks have to be thought out. You can't just play with danger. If you do, the danger gets you. You have to weigh a negative outcome against a positive one, to decide if you want to chance it. You don't take a risk just for the thrill of it."

The two of them sat quietly for a long time. Jana was beginning to despair, fearing that she had gotten nowhere with Sofia until, at last, her friend nodded.

"Your father is right. I'll try to consider the risk in the future, I promise you."

Jana felt relieved and happy. It had been worth the effort. Now she had to give Sofia a little nurturing and confess her own inadequacy.

"I should also have considered the risk this time. I didn't. So I'm sorry."

Sofia gave Jana an impish smile. "There's one thing I know, Jana."

"What?"

"I'm still hungry, and there is still pastry left on your plate."

Jana pushed her plate over to Sofia.

Sofia quickly finished the remainder of the confection. When she finally laid her fork down, she voiced one more thought.

"I'll try to think about people, Jana. And men! I'll be careful. But when I find the one I want, I'll make him love me, not just *want* something from me. And I'll love him back with everything I have."

They finished their chocolate, paid the check, and left.

Chapter 6

Jana was at the police academy, and Sofia was a teaching assistant at the university, when they next encountered Kamin. There had been a change in government, and the Velvet Revolution was imminent. It had taken Sofia and Jana a long time to become ready, emotionally, to confront Kamin.

Jana had a day off from the academy. She called Sofia, who was able to break away from her duties at the university. The two of them agreed to meet in Bratislava's central square and to take a walk through the Old Town.

The Slovak government had decided to begin the resurrection of Bratislava after years of neglect first under the communists, and then under the Czech-dominated government in Prague. They had been even worse off, in a way, under the Czechs, who regarded their Slovak cousins as poor relations, as a drain on the country as a whole, as inferiors who deserved second-best when it came to the expenditure of tax revenues, and, of course, as undeserving of any say in the affairs of the country. So, with some regrets, particularly for the loss of Prague as their capital, the Slovaks had taken themselves out of their union with the Czechs. They now had their own country. Their own capital, Bratislava, had to be spruced up. Building reconstruction was going on everywhere.

Both women had been involved in brief affairs. Jana's beau had not been serious enough; Sofia's had been too serious.

As they walked, the two young women were confessing to the awkwardness of breaking up with men. Eventually, they strolled into the area around the Primate's Palace. A number of missing tiles were being reset on the mosaic of the tympanum on the roof, and, as they were looking up at the daring young men working on it, Kamin emerged and strode to a waiting car, passing as close to them as one could without touching.

Jana heard Sofia draw a breath, gasping. She followed Sofia's eyes, and quickly broke out in a cold sweat. He was so close that through his cologne they could smell the body odor he was trying to conceal. The scar on his left eyebrow where Sofia had hit him with the window handle was still there. She had left her signature.

They watched Kamin's chauffeur open the passenger door for him. Sofia came out of her shock with a start and began to walk toward the car, her fingers curved into talons. Jana grabbed Sofia's arm, pulling her back, using a police hold on her arm, forcing her toward the opposite end of the square. Kamin was driven away without ever realizing that Sofia had been close.

Not that he would have known who she was. Sofia, a mature woman, was much different from the child who he had raped. But they both still knew him.

Jana ultimately felt it was safe to let Sofia go. Sofia pulled away, panting from exertion. She stared at the corner around which Kamin's vehicle had disappeared, then swung around to face Jana, teeth bared, ready to fight her.

"You would have been beaten by the chauffeur if you had tried to attack Kamin," Jana countered. "Or shot. These men have chauffeurs who double as armed bodyguards."

Sofia's fists began to uncurl. She took several deep breaths and her body began to relax. "I want to kill him. It's the only way."

"If you want to suffer afterwards, yes, that's the way. However, that would be foolish and wasteful. I've seen the inside of prisons, Sofia. They're not nice places to live in. You would surely go to prison if you killed him, no matter what he'd done to you in the past."

"It wouldn't matter."

"It matters to both of us, Sofia. Neither of us wants our lives destroyed because of him." She put her arm around Sofia's shoulder, and they began to walk. It would only be a matter of time, Jana thought. Time and planning.

Unfortunately, their planning was put on hold. The next day, Kamin left the country. Rumors swirled through the media, some of them confirmed: he was a leader of organized crime; his wife had recently been killed in a vehicle collision and Kamin was suspected of murdering her; a large amount of money had been embezzled from the government and Kamin was believed to be the mastermind behind it; Kamin had fled because the tax police were after him. Investigations were commenced, none of which ever resulted in charges being filed.

Chapter 7

Mehta made use of his shoulders and elbows to get through the ocean of people. He would never get used to this smother of humanity. Mumbai was always like this: masses spilling into the streets, its inhabitants darting among, around, and through the huge, boiling, swirling crowd. They sweated, screamed, talked to themselves or to anyone else, as they pushed and squeezed their way through countless bodies, walking, running, and dashing through the stream of cars and carts and bullocks that wandered freely, or stood uncaring as they blocked traffic.

Mehta felt himself start to become angry as an older woman screamed at him for blocking her way. Another man was screaming at her, telling her to shut up. The two of them were still arguing as they moved away from each other, forgetting in that split second what had started the altercation.

Mehta put his own emotions behind him. It wasn't good to be angry at work, and today he had business to conduct. It had been hard to live in this Indian city, now the size of Australia's total population. Bollywood, the film capital of Asia, computers, diamond-cutting, cars that poured off assembly lines, international engineering firms, and all the offices and housing for their employees piled on top of buildings, higher and higher. It stifled one's soul.

It had taken Salman Mehta, as he called himself, a month to acclimate to Mumbai sufficiently to feel that he could conduct his business at an acceptable level of safety. His job required patience, not the too-quick hands and jerky movements that impatience generates. He was holding a paper-wrapped package; it was not heavy, but awkward to carry through the crowded streets. Mehta did not want the contents of the package jostled. He checked his watch, looking in the direction the vehicle would come from, unsuccessfully trying to see through the gaps in the crowd. He felt water on his face. A solid mass of dark clouds loomed; the daily monsoon deluge was about to begin. He tugged a plastic envelope out of his inner jacket pocket and unfolded a rain cape, slipping it over his head and shoulders. The gray plastic covered him to his mid-thighs.

He was just in time. The sky opened, the rain pelting down hard enough to hurt. Mehta pulled the plastic hood over his head, then took another look down the street. He saw the small canvas-covered truck slowly plowing down the middle of the road a few minutes early.

He didn't wait. He let the truck pass, then quickly hoisted himself up and into the open rear of the vehicle and knocked on the back of the driver's cab to let him know that he was there, as the truck inched over the curb.

Pedestrians hurried out of the way, angry at being forced out of their path, banging their fists in disapproval on the fenders and sides of the truck. The driver gave them one long blast of the horn to let them know that he was angry at them, too. As previously instructed, he stayed in the driver's seat. He heard the tailgate of the truck come down, the sound of a motorcycle revving up, and the truck shuddering as the motorcycle leaped out of the back of the truck, roared down the street through the rain-slowed traffic, and was quickly lost to sight in the moving flood of water, vehicles and pedestrians. The driver heaved a sigh of relief, glad he had not seen the man who was now on the motorcycle. He'd heard enough stories to know the necessity of avoiding such a meeting.

The motorcycle zigzagged through the streets. The crowds in the Dharavi slums were even denser. Mehta took to the sidewalk, weaving through the people clustered near the storefronts in their effort to avoid being hit or soaked by the additional water the wheels of the motorcycle kicked up. A path on the sidewalk opened up. There was no real reason to worry about being stopped by the police. These were relatively minor transgressions. And although the Mumbai police are considered among the best in India, they rarely entered the slums, and if they did, it was over something much more serious than traffic violations.

Mehta swung into an alley, behind tenements that spewed forth a stink of sewage and offal, and rolled about ten meters to an open lot, a rare area large enough to hold a large tent. Clutching umbrellas, newspapers held over their heads, jackets pulled off their backs and offered to the sky as a defense against the pouring rain, a line of men, women, and children were filing into the tent. Everyone was being welcomed by young women clutching parasols that offered scant protection against the slashing downpour. The young women wore light blue clothes that darkened as they became soaked. They escorted the people into the tent to be seated, females to one side, males on the other.

Mehta braked along the outside of the tent, bringing the cycle to a stop near a side-gap entrance. He dismounted, took his parcel from the rear storage box of the cycle, then walked past a blue-uniformed usherette and into the tent. Mehta knew what he would see. He had been through this twice before on previous weekends, identifying exactly which seat he wanted to occupy: one near his entry point and ten

steps away from the raised throne that occupied a place in
the exact center of the front of the tent. All Mehta had to do
now was to wait. The Church of the Universal Master would
do the rest.

Mehta slipped his raincoat off so his movements would
not be restricted, then crushed it into a ball, casually placing
it on the seat next to him. The rows of seats were rapidly filling up, with every class and caste. Mehta had to admire the
church founder, simply called the Master. The church practiced no segregation by birth or economic wealth, openly
welcoming untouchables. The church acknowledged only
one God, but preached universal benevolence and connection. All were equals, although everyone acknowledged that
the current Master was slightly more equal. He was exalted
above everyone else due to his ability to interpret the word
of God.

Gradually the parade of incoming parishioners trickled to
a halt; the usherettes took seats near the doors, and a trio of
musicians in one of the corners of the room began to play.
The second number was a psalm that everyone, almost as a
single person, stood and sang. This was followed by another
hymn. They remained standing as the Master made his
entrance. He walked through the same gap in the tent that
Mehta had used and was helped up in a graceful swirl by several of the blue-clad usherettes to his place on the throne.

The Master, now comfortably seated, had a smile on his
face, nodding to his followers, all of them shouting, murmuring, singing, mumbling greetings until the Master held up
his hand and the room immediately fell silent. The Master,
a pleasant-faced man with a dark beard, his head framed by
a white turban, gave everyone a huge smile that seemed to
light the whole tent. He surveyed his flock, nodding, his
head bowing slightly, then coming erect as his smile faded.

He waited an additional moment, creating the dramatic tension he wanted, then began to address his flock.

His voice became a drone to Mehta. He was not interested; he was rehearsing in his mind's eye, exactly what he had to do. Mehta checked his watch: the sermon would take fifteen minutes, his walk to the throne perhaps thirty seconds; going outside to his cycle, forty-five seconds; starting the cycle and then leaving the immediate vicinity, two minutes. Satisfied, Mehta reached down for the bundle he had carried into the tent and placed under his seat, pulled some of the wrapping aside, and punched a pre-set button. A very low buzz came from the package. Satisfied, he sat back, again focusing on the Master.

As Mehta anticipated, the sermon was over in exactly fifteen minutes. The Master was quite predictable in his habits. Several of his followers came forward to put gift offerings in an area set aside for them next to the throne, then bent to kiss the Master's feet. Mehta stood, walked to the throne, and waited to let the people already lined up kiss the Master's feet, then edged close to the Master, looking up at him. Very impressive, Mehta thought; then without any hesitation, Mehta reached under his jacket to his hidden shoulder holster, drew his semi-automatic, snapped off the safety, and pumped half of the gun's magazine into the man above him.

Chaos reigned. People screamed, ran down the aisles, cowered in their seats, some not understanding what had happened, only that something dreadful had befallen them, others climbing over each other trying to get out of the tent. And above, on his high seat, the Master leaned back against his throne as if he was asleep, unchanged except for the bloody tears on his once all-white garments.

One of the blue-suited usherettes tried to stop Mehta as he walked toward the flap in the tent. Without hesitating, Mehta fired once, the bullet propelling her back into the general seating area, knocking over a file of chairs as she hit the floor. Unhurried, Mehta continued out of the tent, holstered his pistol, climbed onto his motorcycle and rode down the alley, away from the tent. Thirty seconds later, the bomb that he had left under his chair went off and blew the tent apart.

Later police accounts reckoned that there were eighteen dead and sixty-three injured in what they attributed to a probable suicide-bomber attack by a rival church group. Whoever had done this was a fanatic. They questioned the survivors, but no one could identify the man who had killed the Master and left the bomb, so the Mumbai police were stymied.

There were a large number of mourners at the Master's funeral. Most of those who attended came from other Churches of the Universal Master, located in New York, Amsterdam, Bremen, San Francisco, Kathmandu, and New Delhi. Not many parishioners from the local church could attend, since they were either dead or in the hospital.

The worshipers could not assemble for a month after the killing. Then, with amazingly little disagreement, they selected one of the old Master's acolytes as the new Master and held a church service in their new tent.

The service went well.

Chapter 8

The gray Soviet-style central police building had been transformed into a very stale-looking gingerbread house by the storm. The windowsills were layered with snow that looked yellow in the light from inside the building. Unfortunately, the yellow snow did not change the structure's appearance for the better: its concrete walls continued to look brutally ugly and cruelly unappetizing. It would always say "police."

Jana trudged up the stairs to the building's entrance, kicking her boots on the top step to knock the slush away, and returned the salute of the guard at the entrance. His name was Jarov, a decent cop who was now doing sentry penance outside in the freezing sleet, instead of inside the vestibule, because of a minor infraction. He'd been monitoring a right-wing demonstration and one of the demonstrators had spit on him. Jarov had returned the favor, with interest: a smack alongside the head of the miscreant. The media had caught it on camera, which was Jarov's sin, so now he was stamping around trying to keep his toes from frostbite.

"Commander," he grimaced at her. "I am freezing my balls off." And, as she was going past, "I could use a piss break, Commander. They seem to have forgotten that I'm out here."

"Maybe you should have brought a wool scarf for your balls?" She nodded. "Hold on to them a while longer. I'll send someone out." She walked inside.

It was only slightly less frigid inside. The cold rose from the barren cement floor in icy waves, bleeding even more heat from the air, the chill only beginning to abate when Jana took the elevator up to her floor. To supplement the inadequate central heating, a number of space heaters lined the corridor. They whined at full blast, their warmth almost tempting her to remain in the hall. After toasting her hands for a moment at the last heater before her office, Jana walked in, only to find her warrant officer, Seges, going through her desk.

Seges was so involved in his search that he didn't see her at first. When he did, he snapped upright, his face contorting with the effort of controlling his shock at being observed going through his supervisor's desk. He took one step back, then one step to the side, as if trying to distance himself from the scene of his crime.

"Find anything incriminating?" Jana asked

She took off her greatcoat, slinging it onto the antlers of her clothes tree, which teetered slightly from the force and weight of the coat, its legs jittering on the floor before it decided not to fall over. Jana checked out the top of the desk before she sat. Seges used the opportunity to sidle to the front of the desk, growing more nervous as he watched her go through its drawers.

Jana was surprised. At least Seges had left them neat, perhaps even neater than they'd been. She would have expected a mess, like the one he made of his case reports, which meant that he had placed importance on conducting his search with care, more care than was required if he'd just been afraid she'd find out what he had done. Her guess was that he had been put up to it by someone. Except, what sensational find was there to be made in her desk?

She stared at Seges, wondering what was going through his mind.

Since Seges had been posted as her aide against her will, he had proved incompetent: reports were not written, he neglected to interview witnesses, he avoided making decisions, and whatever he did was done badly. She'd tried to get rid of him a number of times, but it was always a matter of regulations and much red tape before a liability like Seges could be transferred. No one wanted him. They'd fight tooth and nail to keep him away. It would be even harder to get the man dismissed. He was like a fungus that you tried to scrape away or kill with a spray; no matter, it kept coming back. That was a good way to think of him, she thought: a fungus, and this fungus was standing in front of her.

"Tell me," she ordered.

"Tell you what, Commander?"

Her voice got louder. "The desk!" She slapped its top, taking some small satisfaction from seeing him jump. "Why were you searching through the drawers?"

He hesitated, his face betraying his struggle to come up with an answer.

"You were searching my desk." She managed to control her volume. "I want to know why."

"The colonel wanted me to find you," he finally blurted out.

"So?"

"I called. Your cell phone was off . . . I think."

Jana hesitated, then pulled her cell phone out of her bag, checking its setting. "It's on, ready to receive calls."

"I thought you might have a . . . new . . . number," he stammered. "So I was looking for it."

"Let's see if it has been changed." She picked up her desk phone and dialed her cell number. Almost immediately the cell phone rang. Jana put it to one ear, the desk phone to the other. "Have you heard that Seges is a liar?" she asked, speaking into the desk phone. "Yes, I heard. There is no question about it." She replied, "Thank you for your information." She hung up both phones.

"Did you hear that?" she asked Seges. "My goodness! Both said you were a liar."

"No, Commander," he got out.

"All you had to do was call Communications to find if I had been assigned a new number." She put her cell phone away. "If I catch you going through my papers again, I will make sure you never forget it." She tried to relax, finally noticing the dampness of the clothes clinging to her body. Even her galoshes had not kept water from seeping into her socks. And she was now tired.

"What did you learn at the scene of the crime?" Seges asked, trying to make small talk, hoping she would forget his transgression. She had been investigating a death while he had been ransacking her desk.

"A suicide. Not for us. I left it for the patrol officers to report and the coroner to make his own finding."

"Good," said Seges. "That means our caseload stays the same."

"Too much work, Seges?"

"We all work hard, Commander."

"I have a little more work for the hard-working man that you are," she said, keeping a straight face. "Relieve Jarov at the building entrance. You have a two-hour shift. Dress warmly."

"Me?" He looked aghast.

"You," she agreed. "Now!"

Seges scrambled out of the office.

Jana smiled to herself, shaking her head at Seges's idiocy. If he had not been so incompetent, he might have been dangerous. She checked her appearance in the small wall mirror, then walked to the colonel's office.

The door was ajar, inviting visitors, so she tapped on the metal frame before entering.

Trokan was going through a stack of papers. He looked up briefly, then wagged a finger at her to close the door, following with another waggle that invited her to sit. He took a last look at his papers, then moved them to the corner of his desk. He was wearing a Chinese police officer's cap, whose bill jutted out aggressively. It was part of his collection of police headwear from all parts of the world. Most of the caps sat on shelves around the office.

"Why are you wearing that cap?" she asked. "Thinking of transferring to China?"

"It cuts down the fluorescent light glare, so I don't go blind."

"Do you like Chinese food?"

"Who doesn't like Chinese food?" He took the cap off and laid it on his desk. "Where were you?"

"With someone."

"With 'someone,' as in sex?" He gave her a fake leer topped with an eyebrow twitch. "No, you don't look satisfied enough. You were with your friend, the member of parliament. What's her name?"

Jana studied Trokan. He knew about her meeting with Sofia. How? The meeting was not a secret, but the arrangement had been last-minute. If he'd been aware that she was going to meet with Sofia, and wanted more information, he would simply have asked, knowing she would answer him truthfully. No, he hadn't been notified about the meeting before she'd gone to the café. Trokan was her superior, but also a friend and a longtime supporter. Someone had to have been concerned enough about the two of them having tea together to tell Trokan.

"Don't bother telling me the name of your friend. I know it. She's the one who's the current illicit sex interest of the nation." He twitched his eyebrows again. "Okay, so I'm making bad jokes."

"How did you know I was with her?"

"I'm a colonel in the Criminal Police, remember? I have informants everywhere. They tell me everything." He thought about that for a moment. "Okay, so I don't get told everything." His scratched his head, studying her. "You look upset, too upset for it to be about me knowing you were meeting the M.P."

"I walked in on my adjutant, Seges, going through my desk."

"Naturally. He's spying on you."

Jana shifted, uneasy in her seat. "Why would he do that?"

"Our anti-corruption crew opened an investigation of your politician friend. They had a watcher across the street when you two sipped your tea together. They called me to warn me about your conduct."

"Conduct of mine?"

"That you were meeting with her, naturally."

"Wonderful. Now I'm a co-suspect."

"I think not. Just a friendly warning to me. So I told Seges to find you. When he couldn't, I told him to call you. I did it knowing he would use the opportunity to try to find anything that was suspicious in your office."

"Why?"

"Because I knew he would find nothing, and he'd tell them that, which is what I wanted. It'll make them feel better and less aggressive toward you."

"How long has he been working for them?"

"He wants to get out of here just as much as you want him

out. Except the shitface wants to land in a cushy job. He picked the anti-corruption unit, and they called me when he got in touch with them, and. . . ." He waved his hands in the air to show it had progressed from there. "It was okay with me. I know their spy. They know I know. That way all of us are covered."

"This is getting to be too devious a business."

"It always was." He looked her over. "You look like a drowned rat."

"I feel like one."

Trokan checked his watch. "It's late enough for the men not to feel too put-upon if you go home a little early. Go home, take a bath, and change into something warm, but nicer than a police uniform."

Jana got up and went to the door.

Trokan called after her. "What did you do with 'Seges the Spy' after you found him searching your desk?"

"He's doing relief guard duty outside the building in the snow."

"Good." Trokan smiled. "At least it'll stop him from going through your desk drawers." Trokan tapped his forehead. "I just remembered the other reason I wanted you. The Guzak brothers have left Ukraine. They're supposed to be either en route back to Bratislava, or already here."

"More trouble."

"A bad pair. We'll look for them at the borders. Except they know how to get in and out under the radar. The older one is psychotic, a genuine madman. You remember the case with Giles?"

"I remember the case. I was going to see Giles anyway. I'll warn him," Jana said.

The colonel nodded, returning to the papers he had been studying as Jana walked out the door. Trokan hummed tonelessly. After a moment he stopped going through the papers, picked up the Chinese police officer's cap, buffed the bill with his sleeve, then put it back on his head.

A satisfied look on his face, he bent over his papers again.

Chapter 9

Jana returned to her small house in the Rusovce District after buying a few cherries from a street vendor nearby. She waved at a neighbor, Mrs. Miklanova, who ducked her head, pretending that she had not seen Jana.

Jana had stopped Mrs. Miklanova's husband from beating her up some years back. The husband had to spend a few days in the hospital, which she had never forgiven Jana for. Jana opened her door, wondering if the woman had ever considered what would have happened to her if she hadn't stopped him. Mrs. Miklanova had already been bleeding from a broken nose and a scalp wound when Jana intervened. And, to Jana's knowledge, he had never beaten his wife again. After all, the police officer who'd put him in the hospital was still living across the street; he only enjoyed beating his wife when there was no one to stop him. Jana had thought briefly of moving, but she was not going to be forced out by a cowardly wife-beater, or by the anger of his victim.

She walked through her unlocked front door.

At first she didn't know what was hanging from a red ribbon tacked to a ceiling beam in the middle of the room. It swung slowly back and forth in the air current. Jana slowly closed the door behind her, stepping closer to the object. A simple necklace of gold links was dangling from the ribbon. Hanging from this chain was a diamond. The diamond was the size of a small candy egg. Jana turned a lamp on, moving closer to the necklace to examine it.

The facets glittered sharp and bright, demanding to be looked at, with a piercing luminosity that seemed to grow sharper and brighter as she focused on the gem. The stone looked even larger from up close. It seemed to consume the light in the space around it. It had its own life, demanding to be looked at.

Jana managed to pull back, forcing herself to look away. Someone had been in the house, and perhaps was still there. She snapped her holster open, ready to use her gun if she had to, cautiously but quickly going through the house to make sure she was alone. Then she walked back to the gem.

The diamond was still there.

It was hypnotic. It said, "You want me. You need me. We are meant to be together."

Jana was amazed at the effect the diamond had on her. First, greed and lust. Then came a feeling of unease at her reaction. It was followed by dread that she might so easily be corrupted by such a thing. It was crazy, and wrong.

Why had someone hung the diamond in her home?

Jana pulled the stone and its gold chain off the ribbon. It felt cold in her hand. She now wanted to cast it off, to throw it away. Anything to get rid of it. Her fear increased. She was a police officer. Whoever had put it in her home had placed her in jeopardy.

How could such an inanimate object be so threatening? Not only the diamond, but what it represented. Danger. Personal danger. It had been hung in her house for a reason. The stone was too expensive to be a gift. It meant . . . something else!

Hide it! She started toward her couch, thinking to conceal it under a cushion, then halted. The ludicrousness of hiding the diamond under a cushion jolted her. What was she thinking? She forced herself to stop. Yes, her own department might be kicking down her door at any moment, ready to arrest her for corruption, or theft, whatever crime the diamond would implicate her in. But this was no way to deal with the issue. Jana calmed herself.

She would get out of her wet clothes, take a bath, let the hot water soothe her. She had to think. The cherries were still in her other hand, half crushed. She took them with her into the bathroom, laying them next to the tub, then ran a hot bath. Knocking sounds began emanating from the hot-water heater as if someone imprisoned inside the tank was demanding to be let out. It had been repaired twice before by Brod, the handyman, the man who did repairs for everyone. Unfortunately, he also jury-rigged failing parts so he didn't have to buy expensive new ones, and sooner, rather than later, the item he serviced would break down again. She listened to the sounds, focusing on them, trying to take her mind off the diamond.

Jana had purchased a small bottle of bath oil in a little town just over the Austrian border. She poured the remaining contents of the bottle into the tub, regretting for a brief moment that she had none left for her future baths, her regrets vanishing as she slipped into the water. She tried to luxuriate in the heat, lying mostly submerged, eating an occasional cherry, safe from the snow-turned-to-sleet outside. The bath oil would smooth her skin, which Peter would like . . . and she wanted Peter to like it.

Jana tried to forget, to think only of the evening ahead, seeing Peter of the dark, dark eyes and the contrasting pale skin waiting for her outside the opera just a short two hours from now. Peter, the only man she had been this attracted to since her husband's death.

Jana had met Peter by chance when she had been asked

to address a small committee of legislators at the parliament building. The minister of the interior had told Trokan he wanted her to speak in favor of a bill to prevent human trafficking that the government had ordered its members of parliament to pass. Some of them had misgivings because the penalties attached to the bill went beyond the limits imposed by EU treaty and UN conventions. She was to convince the swing votes that dealers in human flesh would keep their trade out of Slovakia, or at least limit it, when they became aware of how much more severely Slovakia would punish them than the surrounding, less-punitive states. Also, it was a good bill to pass just before an election, and played well in the more conservative parts of the country.

Unfortunately, the day she met Peter was also the day she saw Kamin again.

Jana had been sent over to parliament at the last moment. She met Sila Covic, known to all as the Red Devil, at the front entrance to the great lobby of the parliament building. The woman handled public relations and logistics for parliament. Covic was very short and dressed in conservative clothing, and would have seemed undistinguished had it not been for her deep, raspy, penetrating voice that forced everybody in the immediate vicinity to look at her.

Sila had gotten her nickname because she had once been a communist activist, and still often mouthed communist dogma even though she was now an avowed democrat. There was another reason as well: when she got angry, her face was suffused with a startlingly red flush. And Sila Covic got angry very often. So everyone tried to steer clear of her, except when business forced them to deal with her.

The Red Devil did not bother with amenities when she met Jana, hustling her toward the staircase leading to the parliament's meeting rooms.

"I wish you had come earlier," Sila rasped, her irritation apparent. "You could have had individual meetings. Now, you will face the four members who control the committee. One is with the SDL party, so he's probably lost anyway, no matter what you say. The other three are vacillating; they're the ones you have to focus on. They sent over a man from the attorney general's office, their chief trial lawyer. He can talk about legality if they raise any questions."

"Did this prosecutor write the bill?"

"He had input. You have a brief moment to discuss it with him. Brief!" she warned, her voice becoming even more penetrating. "They've made changes."

"I haven't seen them."

"He'll inform you. That's his area anyway."

They walked through the halls toward the meeting room, turned a corner, and Jana almost immediately bumped into Peter Saris, who was sipping a mug of coffee. The collision slopped coffee on both of them. Each immediately offered apologies; each tried to wipe the coffee droplets off the other and became embarrassed upon realizing they were touching a person they hadn't even met, a person who was terribly attractive.

"This is Procurator Peter Saris of the attorney general's office." The Red Devil indicated Peter. "And this is Commander Jana Matinova." Sila surveyed the two of them, goggling at each other. She snickered, and then, after a second of silence, said, "I think the spilled-coffee routine worked." Her voice took on an acerbic edge. "You can repair to the nearest hotel room later. Talk about the statute now." She laughed, her voice like the braying of a mule. "In here." She pointed to the meeting room. "Two minutes." She entered the room, leaving them standing in the hallway.

As soon as the Red Devil left them, Jana and Peter realized they were still staring. Both tried to bring themselves back to business. Jana's heartbeat was so loud, she thought that he must hear it. She felt the urgent need to reach out and touch his face and repressed the impulse with difficulty.

"I—," he began, then stopped.

"I think," Jana began, and also stopped.

They started to laugh.

"We should talk . . . about the law," he mumbled.

"Yes, we should," she responded. She thought about it for a moment. "What law?"

"Cupid's," he suggested.

"I didn't know he made laws," she murmured.

"Oh, yes," he got out. "And they can't be broken."

"Well," she finally responded, "we're both in law enforcement, and it would look bad if we broke any laws."

"Absolutely!"

"How about the other law?" she wondered. "You know, the one we came to discuss?"

"Hard to care about it right now."

Jana felt the same way.

The door to the meeting room opened; the Red Devil peered out.

"Time to talk to the committee members."

Peter and Jana nodded and walked past Sila Covac into the conference room.

"And keep your minds on the meeting," she snarled as they went in. "Or you'll deal with me later!" She hitched herself up to her full height and followed them in.

The meeting went well, despite Jana and Peter having to try hard to keep their hands to themselves and focus on the bill. After it was over, they walked down the stairs together and left the building, going to the lot where Jana had parked her car. She offered Peter a lift. To her disappointment, he declined, explaining that he had business at the office. Dry-mouthed,

Jana left wondering what she had done to drive him away. Was he married and doing the honorable thing before they became so besotted they'd both regret what would unquestionably have happened?

As Peter left, Jana saw a limousine drive off. She recognized the passenger, which brought a chill to her. Almost in a daze, she got in her car and followed him. The limousine drove to a large house in the suburbs. Jana parked nearby, turned off her cell phone, and watched the house gradually fill with people arriving for a dinner party.

Kamin, the man who had ravaged Sofia inside the limousine, had returned to Slovakia and was in that house. Three hours later the guests began leaving, couple by couple, and the lights were turned off. When the house was dark and Kamin hadn't left with the guests, Jana knew she had found his home. Now she could leave. He'd be there when she came back.

Kamin had evaded justice before. Jana wouldn't let him get away again.

Chapter 10

Jana sat in the tub thinking about Kamin's return until the water became frigid, her skin wrinkled from its long immersion in the water. She put Kamin out of her mind. The diamond was the issue she had to deal with now.

Slowly toweling herself off, Jana mulled over the few facts she knew. The diamond could have been placed where it was by anyone. Jana usually left her doors unlocked. If she'd locked them, anyone wanting to get inside would force the lock. It would only take an instant. Or they would go to the rear and punch out a glass window and be inside just as quickly. Besides, everyone in the neighborhood knew that Jana was a police commander. Thieves were stupid, but not so stupid that they'd break into a police officer's house.

No, not a thief. What kind of thief would leave this kind of present behind him? Whoever had left the diamond knew that Jana lived there. And they'd hung the diamond up for her to see for a reason.

Jana picked up the diamond, then walked into her bedroom, deciding to wear one of her uniforms. The evening's social activities would have to be put on hold. She had to be a police officer for a while longer. Jana finished dressing and called Trokan's cell phone.

Trokan complained he had been sent out to a market

by his wife, to pick up groceries. A demeaning job for a colonel! And who in the world needed green peppers after a hard day's work, he grumbled. Trokan eventually suggested that they meet in the bus kiosk at the front of the market.

Jana reached the kiosk first, just in time to watch Trokan trudge through the slush toward her. With a groan, setting his packages on the bench, he sat next to Jana.

"Why are you still in uniform?"

"I have a police problem, I think."

"Good police, or bad police?"

"Bad police."

"So bad it could not wait until tomorrow."

"Yes."

He heaved a sigh. "This is probably going to be worse than the green peppers. Okay, tell me."

"I went home, and the problem was inside my living room."

He stared at her. "What did you find?"

"This." She pulled the diamond from her pocket, swinging it by its chain like a pendulum. After they both stared at it for a moment she handed it to him. "It was hanging by a ribbon from a beam in the room. Needless to say, I had never seen it before."

Trokan examined the diamond for a full minute, finally breaking away from its fascination. "A real diamond like this captures one's attention, doesn't it?"

"That's why everyone wants them."

"Did you want it?"

"For a very brief instant."

"Now you want to get rid of it?"

"It was never mine to keep."

"Well, don't expect *me* to take it. What am I supposed to

do, take it home to my wife? She would want it, too. Then what do I do? So you keep it for now."

"It doesn't feel right for me to hold on to such a stone. It's dangerous for a police officer to have it."

He thought about this.

"In the morning I'll write a report about your finding the diamond, seal it in an envelope, and give it to one of the secretaries to tuck away. That way, if anyone asks what you are doing with the diamond, we can show them the memorandum to prove I set up an investigation. You, on the other hand are a police investigator. So, investigate and find out how it got into your living room."

He tossed the diamond pendant back to her.

"I give you one week, then we tell the corruption investigation team about it. You understand the need for that? It is called covering your colonel's ass."

"Agreed."

"Your first move in the investigation?"

Jana thought about it. "I'll call Grosse at Europol. See if he can check on the diamond's provenance."

"He's a good man. Tell him you ran it by me. Have him link up with Interpol. Make a large sweep. One more step in covering our backsides. Okay?"

"Okay."

Jana put the diamond back in her pocket. Trokan shook his finger at her. "Be careful with the stone. You don't want to lose it. It's your job if you do."

"Sure you don't want to keep it for me?"

"I didn't have the misfortune to find it in my home."

They both got up.

"You think this thing has anything to do with the internal affairs investigation? With Seges going through my desk?"

"Maybe. Then again, maybe not." He patted her on the shoulder. "At the risk of sounding sarcastic, have a good evening."

He picked up his groceries and trudged away through the parking area.

Jana called Europol on her cell phone, then walked back to her car. She already knew what her next move was going to be.

Chapter 11

Giles lived and worked at his furniture store on Obchodná Ulica near Postová. They sold legitimate furniture at the store, but his real business was dealing in high-priced stolen antiques and anything else not nailed down by its original owner, from jewelry to high-end cameras to stolen luxury cars, particularly Mercedes.

Jana had been involved in the only investigation that had ever taken Giles off the street and put him in prison for a time. A body had been found in the back seat of one of Giles's stolen cars being shipped to Albania. Giles would send the cars there for corrective surgery: specialists would remove the vehicle's real motor and chassis numbers, stamp false numbers on the car, and provide false registration, all to allow Giles to resell the car for a large markup in the Czech Republic, Austria, or Italy.

In order to obtain a lighter sentence, at Jana's urging, Giles had given the police evidence that proved who had committed the murder. The killer was the elder of the two Guzak brothers, both ordinarily smugglers with a penchant for violence that had resulted in the dead man in the Mercedes. Both brothers had run to Ukraine to escape prosecution. Both had vowed to kill Giles in retaliation, a threat not to be taken lightly when it came from one of the Guzaks, neither of whom was above practicing any form of brutality that had ever been thought of.

Of course, the brothers were not the only ones who wanted to eviscerate Giles. Long-term criminals make lots of long-term enemies. And Giles had made so many of them that he lived in his headquarters above his furniture store, and left the premises only in the direst of emergencies.

When Giles was released from prison, he had come back to his old haunts and begun his activities again. He and Jana had stayed on relatively friendly terms. Giles had refrained from violence, at least in Slovakia, and his other games were not played in Jana's jurisdiction, so she had no urgent need to take him down. Besides, he was a good source of information. But every so often Jana was required to help him in return for his knowledge of the criminal world. As the saying goes, "One hand washes the other."

Jana drove to his block, saw the large sign over the store reading "Antiques of the Golden Ages," parked the police car, crossed the street to the store, wiping her feet at the entrance, then walked through its baroque, carved-wood-framed doors into the shop. Jana's eyes adjusted to the dim lighting as she threaded her way through its inventory of fake Louis Treize tables, Thonet chairs, Restoration chairs, Rococo framed mirrors, heavy Biedermeyer armoires, Empire busts, Art Nouveau lamps, mixed pieces from Limoges and a hundred other porcelain works, along with a thousand other exemplars of the faux antique business.

The furniture occupied the floor space except for two narrow parallel paths that led through the objets d'art facsimiles to the rear of the store. Giles did not sell his genuine antique pieces with their questionable chains of title through the front door. They were reserved for people who had real money and were willing to spend it without asking questions to get the piece they wanted. That form of business was consummated upstairs, where Giles had his office and living quarters.

Jana paused to admire a pair of pretty crystal chandeliers hanging from the ceiling, wondering, for a brief second, if they were truly antiques, then laughed at herself for not knowing better.

One of the two salespersons on the floor came over; then, recognizing Jana's uniform, quickly pretended she did not exist and beat a retreat. As expected, Giles was not on the main floor. Jana walked to the back, avoiding the furniture encroaching on the aisle. A stairway led up to the loft area, the way barred by a gate that was ornate enough to have previously belonged at the entrance of a bordello. There was also a German-made steel-and-titanium U-bolt sealing the gate, which would have taken very heavy equipment to open if you did not have the lock combination.

Spis, Giles's bodyguard, a man of medium height with an incredibly thick-trunked body, stepped out of the shadows behind the stairs. He carried an old heavy-caliber Webley pistol in one hand; the other held a cell phone dwarfed by his large fingers. The cell was raised to a cauliflowered ear, the most apparent effect of one too many street fights. Spis grunted into the phone, then pocketed it, standing his ground, even more solid and formidable than the gateway he was protecting.

"He told you to open the gate, didn't he, Spis?"

The tree trunk pretending to be a man continued to stare at her without moving. Jana opened her greatcoat to display her holstered Makarov.

"I have a gun too, Spis." Jana kept her voice low. "My gun is better. It comes with a license that allows me to kill people, particularly when they have a weapon. If I have to shoot you to get in, I will tell my supervisors that you were threatening to kill me, and they will thank me. But if *you* shoot *me*, you will go to jail forever—if one of my fellow officers doesn't kill you first. Which I think would happen. 'Spis Commits Suicide' will be the headline. Now, open the gate, Spis." She waited a second, then unsnapped her holster.

Spis opened the gate.

"Thank you, Spis."

Jana mounted the stairs, the gate closing behind her. At the top, she looked down. Spis was gazing up through the bars at her, wishing he had killed her. She made a pistol of her thumb and forefinger, pointing down at him. "Bang," she said. "Spis is dead."

She strolled to the back of the loft where Giles's office was located.

He sat on an overstuffed red couch, a small table with a demitasse of coffee in front of him. He was a little man, his hands always moving, his appearance immaculate, even dandyish. He stared at Jana, stroking his carefully brushed-back hair, his too-big mouth simulating a smile, his slightly pop eyes peering a little uneasily at her through jeweled women's glasses. The eyeglasses were a prop Giles had affected throughout the years Jana had known him. Giles was not gay. He made regular use of a steady stream of middle-aged prostitutes whom Spis would bring up to his office. When he had gone out in public, he had worn the bejeweled frames as an eccentricity to attract attention. It made up for his small stature and lack of a commanding presence.

Giles carefully poured Jana a cup of coffee from a carafe, holding the cup out to her when she sat in one of the chairs across from him.

"I assume you are bringing trouble? You always bring trouble, you know. It's the essence of being a police officer, which is the reason most people don't like them."

Jana nodded.

Giles took a quick taste of his own coffee. "It's always a

milestone in my life, an event of importance . . . no, *major* importance, when you appear at the top of my stairs."

Jana nodded again, looking at his glasses. "Still wearing the spectacles. Add any new gems?"

Giles got excited. "Yes, a new sapphire." He took the glasses off, pointing to the sparkling blue stone mounted just above one of the lenses. "I got it from an old piece of jewelry that nobody seemed to know the value of, so it was a steal."

"You're sure you didn't just steal it?"

He slipped the glasses back on, a little irked. "Of course not. Prison cured me of those bad habits. I do everything legitimately. I'm very careful about what I buy now."

They sat in silence, each sipping coffee. Giles liked to settle in with his visitors. When he put his cup back on the tray, it was a signal that he was ready to talk business.

"How can I help you?"

"First, a complaint: your man downstairs didn't want to let me in. I told him I would kill him if he didn't."

Giles shifted uneasily. "Forgive him. Police make him angry. He still thinks he's a criminal gang member."

"He still is."

"But, he's *my* gang member," Giles half apologized. "I'll talk to him about it." He fiddled with his glasses. "You want information?"

"Yes."

"I take it you are prepared to make it worth my while?"

"As always."

"What's the payment to be?"

"You go into my 'future favors' book. When you are in trouble, and you will be, I'll be there for you. Or you get a small piece of information in return now, and forget the future favor."

He thought about it. "I'm not into long-term investments. So, payment now."

"I want information from you first."

"You have no trust! A typical policeman. But go ahead. I'm magnanimous. I shall forgive you for not believing in me. Ask your questions."

Jana took the diamond out of her pocket, dangling it in front of the little man. The gem pulled Giles in as it had Jana. Giles's eyes seemed to get even bigger, and he began gnawing on the knuckle of one of his hands. "May I . . . hold it?"

Jana nodded, bringing it closer to Giles. He took it, pulled a loupe from his jacket pocket, blew it free of lint, then inserted it in his eye socket, inspecting the diamond. "Lovely. A lovely thing," he murmured to himself.

He took the loupe out of his eye and held the diamond out above him, watching the jewel twist on its chain. "Look! It lights up the space. It's as if the full moon has come into this room." He let out a long sigh. "Are we at all interested in selling this piece of the heavens?" He hesitated. "By any chance, is it stolen merchandise? Less money, but for this one I am willing to make an exception. How much?" He took his eyes off the diamond, glancing at Jana, wincing when he saw the expression on her face. She was not going to sell him the diamond.

"For this stone, I had to try," he mumbled by way of an apology. "I will give you the particulars. It's blue-white, clear, class G, no faults. Approximately five and a half carats, beautifully cut, about a hundred and seventy-five thousand plus in U.S. dollars."

Jana nodded, stunned by the price.

"A very nice bauble." Giles kept turning the gem over and over in his hands, an avid look on his face. Reluctantly, he handed the diamond back to Jana. "Another few minutes and I would probably be willing to murder you for it. A gem that cut and size, that color, with no faults . . . is rare."

"I would think so."

"Very high-quality goods," he murmured. "So, why did you bring it here?"

"Tell me about the gem market in this area of the world."

"Not much to tell. Diamonds like these are hard to come by locally. With some exceptions, they're too expensive for Middle or Eastern Europe." His face took on a wan look. "Surely too expensive for most Slovaks. Maybe one of the fine jewelry outlets in Austria? Vienna would be the place to ask."

"You think it came from Vienna?"

He turned the question over in his mind, taking his glasses off to wave them in her direction. "Since you made my day by bringing me the diamond, you can now have an additional contribution from me for an entry in your 'future favors' book. It is my belief the chain is probably Indian. The weave is not European. The gold is too soft, probably 22 or 24 carat. Most Europeans would not want to use such soft gold for such a big stone. They would be afraid it might work its way loose. There is also a small flower mark on the clasp. I have seen it on goods that came from the East. It could have been cut and set in Europe, but I don't think so."

"I thought diamonds came from South Africa."

He laughed. "Most good diamonds still do, but they have to be cut and polished. The Indians are taking over from the Dutch Jews. It's no longer the old India of the Raj. Indians have computerized and brought diamond cutting to a high art, and a cheap art. Everybody else is being eliminated."

"Can someone track this diamond back to its source?"

"Maybe. But I would think, at the moment, no."

"Why not?"

He ran his fingers through his hair, then wiped them on his jacket. "Because you came here, which means you are looking for a lead. I assume your Customs or Europol or Interpol would have told you the diamond was not declared in the normal course of business. So my guess is it was brought in under the table."

"Who is handling under-the-table business besides you, these days?"

He frowned at her. "I told you I'm no longer in the business."

"That will be the day the Slovak police celebrate."

He decided to ignore her jibe. "Are you asking about volume pieces?"

"At the moment, just quality merchandise, like this."

She held the diamond so that it swayed on its chain, both of them watching it glitter. "Odd how a piece of aged, compressed carbon can make people yearn so much."

Giles continued to stare at it. When he managed to break away, he was out of breath from the effort. He held up a finger. "No more from Giles." He wiped his forehead with the back of his hand. "Time you furnish the information you have for me."

Jana nodded. It was time to pay the little man. "The Guzak brothers. Rumor has it that they have come back from Ukraine and are on their way to Bratislava."

Giles sat back on the couch. His face took on a gray cast; his shoulders slumped. Then a visible shudder passed over his body.

"They are coming after me?"

"Whatever business they have here, some part of it will always include coming after you. I'm sorry, Giles. Perhaps we can get them first."

Giles looked up. "Besides you, who else on the police force in Slovakia can take care of the Guzak brothers? Nobody. And I should know: I'm on the other side."

Jana put the diamond in her pocket.

"We have some good officers, Giles."

"Not likely." He took a deep breath, finally managing a wan smile. "How about giving old Giles something to pick up his spirits? Euros, not dollars: 150,000 Euros for the diamond."

"You know I am not going to sell it to you, Giles."

"Just a thought. It's my nature," he shrugged. "An animal cannot change what he is."

Jana nodded at him, turned, and walked to the stairs, descending without looking back.

Chapter 12

Jana phoned the office the next morning. They told her Peter had called the night before. Since he was a procurator, they had given him her number. Jana's elation overcame her anger at seeing Kamin back in Slovakia. She called Peter at the number he had left, but his phone was turned off.

She dressed, hoping he would try again while she was home, and just as she was slipping on her shoes, her phone rang. Jana jumped to answer it. Her heart racing, she forced herself to swallow, and wet her dry lips, calming herself before picking up the phone. To her disappointment, it was one of the legislators, wanting to ask a few more questions about issues raised by members who had not been at the committee meeting the previous day. Fighting back the urge to hang up to leave the phone free for Peter, she managed to remain polite and patient enough to answer his questions, then sat staring at the phone after she had finished the conversation, wondering how long she could hold out before she tried Peter again.

Jana finished getting ready, walked to the door and this time locked it behind her. She had not taken two steps when the phone rang again. Fumbling with the key, Jana opened the door and darted to the phone.

"Hello, I'm here," she blurted out. "Jana Matinova," she mumbled, compelled to keep talking. "How can I help you?"

"Hello, Commander." He addressed her formally. Even

so, and even through the distortion of a telephone, Peter's voice had an instantaneous effect on her. "I don't know if you remember me?" he asked. "I'm the procurator you met at the parliament building yesterday."

Jana took a deep breath. Then she had a moment of disquiet. He had used her title so easily. Was he trying to tell her that this was the level at which he wanted to keep their relationship?

"Of course I remember you." She tried to think of something encouraging. "You spoke very articulately yesterday before the members of the committee."

"I wondered if you might like to . . . ?" He hesitated. "I gather you like music."

"How did you find out I liked music?" she asked, surprised.

"I . . . well . . . I asked the . . . head of the Traffic Police. I thought he might know you. He asked around, and called me."

Oh, God, she thought. Everybody in the police department, the inspectors, the street police, all of them would now know that a man was interested in her, and not just as a police officer. She was about to reprove him, then managed to stop herself. He had cared enough to go through the trouble of finding out something personal about her. He was romantically interested.

"Yes, I like opera," she got out. "There is a good one at the National Theatre tonight. Puccini's *La Bohème*. They even have an Italian tenor singing Rodolfo." Jana wondered if she was being too eager. "Or perhaps you would rather not?" Hesitate, she told herself. Show him that you're not too eager. "There might be trouble getting tickets at this late date." She regretted saying this as soon as she uttered the words.

"I have them."

He had the tickets already. Why was she playing coy? She was no longer a girl who had to put on a performance. "You bought the tickets. Lovely of you to do that."

"I could only get balcony seats. The tourists had already snapped up the rest."

"The balcony is perfect," she gushed, angry at the flutter in her voice. "You can see everything from there."

"Dinner before or after?"

She almost ground her teeth in frustration at having to turn him down. "I won't be able to have dinner. I will need time to change after work."

"Drinks, and a snack after the opera?"

"I would love that."

They decided to meet at the opera.

Jana didn't want the conversation to end. She had no choice. He had to go . . . and there was the matter of Kamin to attend to.

Jana had to assume her objective, tough police mentality, so she used a method that was radical but always worked. She had learned it from another policewoman who used it when personal events interfered with her job. It was not hard: She thought back to the time she had first learned how to swim. At the beginning, at one time or another, she would go underwater and almost drown. She couldn't breathe, suffocating, going down and down, trying to fight her way back up. She finally made it to the surface, gasping for air, but forgetting everything except the here-and-now of survival. Live it again, now, she told herself. Choke on the water, frantic with the need to take in air, feel the fear, then come up and out of it, taking deep breaths.

The exercise worked. Peter was, for the moment, pushed to the back of her mind. She was free to focus on Kamin.

Jana drove to her office and began making phone calls,

personally speaking to ranking officers in each of the directories of the police, issuing queries about Kamin. The state had never filed charges against him for any crime. Not enough proof, no one would testify, books missing, investigations coming up empty when it came to vital evidence. Kamin had always covered himself, an eel slipping through the fishing nets. Now, Jana heard the same thing again. The only difference was that Jana wanted current information; she wasn't interested in past investigative problems. Kamin was back in the country. What had he been doing all this time?

It was time to talk to Sofia, to share last night's events with her. Jana headed toward Sofia's house, realizing she should have called first. She hadn't because she was too concerned about Sofia's reaction if Jana told her on the phone that she had seen Kamin. Jana had to be there to stop Sofia, as she'd done before, when they had first run into Kamin years after the assault on Sofia. Sofia had been prepared to kill the man, and damn the consequences.

Jana drove to Čunovo, where Sofia was now living. Her parents had added a second story, creating an apartment for their daughter, a common practice in the country when the young could not afford to buy a house on their own. There was even a small office in the apartment where Sofia did much of her parliamentary business. A separate entrance allowed the people she worked with to come and go without interfering with her now-widowed mother downstairs.

Jana climbed the stairs. There was a sign on the door that said COME IN in big block letters; then, in deep blue lettering, *Nech So Paci*, AT YOUR SERVICE, and Sofia's name and parliamentary title. The door was kept open, day and night, to show Sofia's constituency that she was always there for them. Jana rapped lightly at the door, then entered.

Sofia was sitting on a small couch in the room. Next to the couch, in an armchair, sat Kamin.

Shock slowed the moment into a tableau. Then it began to accelerate into separate timeframes; then there was an abrupt explosion into action as Jana started to draw her gun. Sofia bolted up, rushing toward her friend.

"No, Jana!" Sofia interposed her body as a shield between Jana and Kamin. "It's all right. Mr. Kamin and I are talking about the country's interests. Government needs." She turned to Kamin. "*Prepacte*. If you would excuse us for a moment?" She nudged Jana back through the door, then down to the bottom of the steps.

"Sofia, that is Kamin, the man who assaulted you."

"I know who he is, Jana. And I can hardly stand to be in the same room with him." She paused, choosing her words. "I was asked to meet with him by our party leader in parliament."

"The party leader? To meet with that monster? What kind of a Slovak National Council catastrophe is pending that would require this of you? Unless Kamin is preparing to be the savior of Slovakia, and I know he isn't, he should be locked up and the key thrown away."

Sofia rubbed her forehead, as if trying to marshal her thoughts. "He's apologized for what he did to me. Truly, contritely apologized for all the misery he caused me. He's begged me to accept his apology, and I've done so."

"How can an apology make up for his horrific attack on you? You were a young girl. How can you invite him into your office and sit down next to him without vomiting?"

"It's over! I've done what I could. I'm the victim, not you, Jana. It's my decision, not yours, to make. I believe he's a changed individual."

"There is no way he's changed."

"You can't know that." Sofia took several steps, then

slowly returned to Jana. "There is a problem between the political parties in the coalition. They have asked me to work out an agreement so that the government will survive an upcoming vote. I intend to do that. And this man, if I can call him that, is vital to any agreement. He can influence a number of votes."

"Do they know what this man is?"

"I've let them know. Not in detail, but enough so they understand how hard this is for me."

"Why not a hundred other people instead of you? Why should you be put through this?"

"I have to go back upstairs, Jana, and talk to him. Please go."

Jana focused on Sofia's face, then carefully took in her whole appearance. She was wearing a crisp business suit, her face was carefully made up, not a hair was out of place. Only her eyes betrayed that she was under strain, and it was doubtful that anyone but Jana could have seen that. Sofia was very much in control of herself, and not afraid.

"You're sure you want me to go?"

Sofia nodded. "I need to get back to work."

"Yes. I guess you do. What's the expression? Ah, yes, I remember: 'Politics makes strange bedfellows.'"

"That's not appropriate, or kind, Jana."

"Go upstairs, Sofia."

Sofia very calmly walked up the steps and into her office.

Chapter 13

Jana met Peter in front of the National Theatre steps. She had pushed her meeting with Sofia to the back of her mind and returned home in time to put her evening clothes on, a black pantsuit with a velvet collar and cuffs. The trousers were flared enough so she could carry a small pistol in an ankle holster. Not that she would need it, but in case she was called out of the performance to handle a police emergency, she would be armed.

Her first sight of Peter made her weak in the knees. He was gorgeous, his eyes as beautiful as she remembered from yesterday, and his black suit and matching tie making him look even more masculine. They joked about their being dressed to match, twins of the mind and spirit.

Their seats were in the center balcony. The opera house, a remnant of the old empire, still looked every inch a part of its old Austro-Hungarian Hapsburg past, with all its gilt and ornamentation echoed by the operagoers dressed in their finest. The orchestra members entered the pit, tuned up, and, as the lights dimmed, the overture began . . . and Peter leaned over and kissed her on the cheek, taking her hand and holding it for the rest of the opera.

Jana did not remember much of the opera after Peter kissed her; she registered very little when they drove back to her house together after the performance. Her senses only returned full-blast when they walked into the house. Peter turned her to face him and kissed her. He kissed her again, and again, and somehow their clothes disappeared as they went from kiss to kiss into the bedroom, and made love. Then made love again.

When they lay there afterward, spent, she realized that this was the man she wanted to spend the rest of her life with. She hoped he felt the same way.

Kamin could wait until tomorrow, or the tomorrow after that, or maybe next year.

But of course, as things turned out, he wouldn't wait.

Chapter 14

Vienna is the city of many people's dreams. Their dreams are varied. Some of them want the monarchy back, with its capes and carriages, when men still fought duels and women made a spectacle of public mourning if their lover was killed. For others, it is still the Vienna of Haydn and Mozart and Beethoven, when the grand gesture in music and the great musical soloists of the *Konzert Kulture* thrilled the world. For a few, it is Freud and the ferment of the fin de siècle when great intellectual leaps forward made it the capital of the intellectual world. For Jana, none of this was the case. She admired its palace architecture and liked its pretzels. Otherwise, she found Vienna an uneasy city to be in. It was the Austrian temperament, so law-abiding that it suppressed everything spontaneous or unusual. Jana was always cautious, even down to very carefully obeying the traffic lights, when she visited the Austrian capital.

Today she was with Trokan and a Slovak customs official named Halco, walking up Neustiftgasse toward the Ringstrasse, the circle of streets that surrounded the inner city, the old town that was the center of Vienna. They had been sent to Vienna to attend an international customs meeting.

Trokan never went to Austria if he could help it; he would send Jana or some volunteer who wanted to spend time in the Austrian capital and could afford its exorbitant prices. Halco was a Slovak bureaucrat, an expert on policy issues. The three of them were told to listen and, after the Austrians got through, to do a little complaining of their own. The Austrians were being difficult about Slovaks crossing the border into Austria and taking Austrian jobs away from Austrians. In their turn, the Slovaks, through Trokan, were to complain about the illegal laundering of Slovak gray money with the complicity of Austrian banks.

Trokan had been a last-minute replacement, and because Jana had recently investigated a murder that had involved Slovak money deposited in Austrian banks, he had ordered her to accompany him to explain the practical aspects of the problems. Of the three, only Halco was enjoying himself. He had married an Austrian woman and was looking forward to meeting her and his Austrian in-laws for dinner at the posh Sacher Hotel, since his father-in-law would pick up the check. He went on and on about it, as both Trokan and Jana tried to ignore him.

Trokan and Jana were in civilian clothes. Jana was snacking on a huge salted pretzel she had just bought from a kiosk that advertised thirteen types of pretzels, trying not to pay attention to the other pedestrians who gave her critical stares for munching as she walked their pristine streets. The three had just crossed the Ringstrasse when Jana saw Kamin. He was striding along next to a woman who easily kept pace with him, a woman who had that mixture of Asian and European features that made passing men take second and third looks at her.

Jana touched Trokan on the arm, indicating Kamin. Trokan took a few seconds to recognize him. Then his face reflected his anger.

"There goes the man who has been responsible for half of the major criminal acts in Slovakia. No," he corrected himself. "Judas Iscariot is dead, so more than half."

"He was never caught."

"'Never' might not include today." Trokan quickly decided that he could dispense with Jana's presence at the meeting. "Follow him. See where he's going."

Jana broke away from Trokan and Halco, crossed the street, and increased her pace to catch up with Kamin and his companion, then slowed her stride to match theirs. Kamin and the woman appeared not in the least interested in conversing with each other, nor concerned with the stores, buildings, or people they passed. They entered a cozy-looking café that blended in with the other storefronts lining the *Strasse*.

Jana waited to let them get settled and involved in selection from the menu, then casually walked in, peering around for a table. The café was small enough that any table she took would give her a good view of her quarry. Jana quickly chose one at the rear. The waitress came over, setting a small plastic holder with the specials of the day in front of Jana, who picked it up to study, while looking over the top at Kamin and the woman. Then she ordered a *Kaffee mit Schlag*.

They had been joined by a bullet-headed, pig-featured man with a scruffy blond goatee that was more a flag of challenge than an asset. They were arguing with him. Kamin was gesturing angrily. His voice did not carry, but she saw him snarl. The newcomer leaned forward, threateningly, and knocked Kamin's hand off the table, then shoved Kamin back in his chair and stood, towering over him.

Kamin did not appear fazed. He stared up at the man intently. The bullet-headed man, as a last defiant gesture, took his own chair and tossed it across the floor. The few customers in the restaurant got to their feet at this disturbance of the fabled Viennese *Gemütlichkeit*. The manager scurried over to pick up the chair, but was afraid to bring it back to the table.

The bullet-headed man mouthed a curse and stalked out of the restaurant. Almost immediately, the woman rose to her feet and followed him. Kamin remaining seated. Jana's instinct urged her to follow the woman. She had a quick sip of the coffee the waitress had set in front of her, then dropped a bill on the table in payment. As casually as possible, she got to her feet and went after the woman.

Outside, she saw the woman catch up to the bullet-headed man. He heard her coming and swiveled around to face her. As soon as he turned, another man came up behind him and smashed him across the back of his neck with what looked like a pipe, hit him again, this time on the head, and continued to beat him as he lay on the sidewalk.

As soon as the fight started, the pedestrians began to flee, interfering with Jana's view. She ran forward, only to stop short when she saw the woman turn to face her and point a gun directly at her. She gestured with it for Jana to retreat; Jana backed up without taking her eyes off the woman and her partner. He went to the driver's seat of a car that had been parked at the curb. The woman casually approached the passenger side of the vehicle. They drove off.

Jana went to the man on the sidewalk. His skull had been fractured and he had been beaten to death. Nothing could be done for him, so Jana raced back to the café. The waitress told Jana that Kamin had left through the rear door.

Jana ran out the back door. As she had expected, Kamin was gone.

It is hard for a police officer to witness a murder and not be able to do anything about it. It's even worse to have an opportunity to apprehend the man responsible, and miss that opportunity as well. The Austrian police said they could take no action against Kamin. How could they prove he had sent the man and woman to do the killing? Kamin was not a resident of Austria as far as they knew. As for the man and woman, who were they?

No arrests.

No charges.

Jana liked Vienna even less after that.

She had to go to Vienna on police business on a regular basis. Austria and a number of other countries shared a border, so a regional liaison group had been established to deal with the prevention and suppression of cross-border crime. There were other meetings, higher-level meetings than the one Jana was now going to attend, that dealt with matters of policy, working agreements, treaties on mutual cross-border needs in criminal prosecutions, and the like. Jana only participated in those events as a briefer, an expert behind the scenes. The meeting today involved a fairly convivial group, professionals in law enforcement who generally believed in what they did. Jana had been struck by how their national characteristics were reflected in the way the individuals interacted. The Swiss seldom talked; the Hungarians always seemed to be talking; the French punctuated most of their communicating with facial expressions and extravagant gestures. The Germans were always suspicious of police representatives from the other countries; they might themselves be involved in criminal activity. The others knew how the Germans felt, but, for the sake of appearances, tolerated them. Despite all their differences, they managed a substantial degree of cooperation and assisted each other when the need arose.

Today the group discussed communications, methodology of selected crimes, and trends in cross-border crime.

Of course, like cops everywhere, they always discussed the cases they were personally involved in after the agenda was covered. After the official business was over, the troop converged on a local beer hall to swap stories, drink a glass of pilsner, briefly mention their families, and then return to their own home country. That meant catching the last train to Bratislava, which was only sixty-four kilometers from Vienna, for the Slovaks. Today, the group had selected Grosslik's, an old beer hall and eatery whose menu boasted that Hitler used to enjoy its wonderful breakfasts. By unspoken agreement, they studiously avoided commenting on this fact to the Germans. They settled in with their mugs of beer, enjoying the others' old war stories and telling a few of their own.

They were well into their second beer as Andras, the Hungarian, held forth on his personal brilliance in breaking up a criminal ring.

"Two groups were involved, both Hungarian, and they met a third group's representative, a Slovak. It was set up by another Slovak, a man they called Midi." Andras inclined his head to Jana in acknowledgment of her countrymen's participation. "They met in an up-market chocolate shop. When we finally broke in, they didn't understand how we could have overheard them. They must have felt like idiots when they found out we were listening in on their conversations via a mike concealed in an elephant made of bittersweet chocolate." He laughed. "I took a photograph of the elephant and showed it to my children."

They laughed at his story. After that, there was a moment of silence. Most of them used this opportunity to finish the last of their beer and stood, ready to call it a day. Jana gestured at Andras to stay as the others said their good-byes. She ordered another round of beer for the two of them. Something Andras had said earlier had engaged her interest.

"You mentioned the man who set the scheme up, a man called Midi. That doesn't sound Hungarian or Slovak. Italian, perhaps?"

"We never found out."

The waiter set two beers down; Andras sipped his. "A very clever man, Midi. He put up the money for the venture, planned it, but stayed away from meetings, using the Slovak we caught at the chocolate place as his representative. The Slovak gave us Midi's name."

"What else did he say about this Midi?

"Not much. Our Slovak was afraid of him. We had to drag the facts out of him, which means you always miss something. He said this Midi helped him get out of prison early but didn't know why he was selected. Perhaps it was because he had been sent to prison for smuggling and Midi wanted a professional in that line."

"How did Midi arrange to get the smuggler get out of prison early?"

Andras held his hand up and rubbed his thumb against his first two fingers. "Remarkable what people can do with dollars, euros, pounds, Swiss francs, or whatever. Greed is universal."

Jana smiled. "Did they speak English together? Hungarian? Maybe even Slovak? What language were they comfortable in?"

"Midi spoke good Slovak. But the smuggler said that Midi also knew English, a little Hungarian, and, on at least one occasion, spoke German."

Jana mulled it over: four languages, but one thing seemed important. "English and German are in common use all over Europe. The smuggler said Midi spoke a little Hungarian, but he spoke Slovak well. There are only five or six million Slovaks. And Slovak is not spoken by the rest of Europe. Which means to me that Midi was probably Slovak."

"So?" Andras asked.

"It puts this man called Midi in my jurisdiction, someone for me to watch out for." She continued, "You said your bad guys made a number of trips into Slovakia?"

"And into Austria, and back to Hungary, and the Balkans, even to France. They delivered goods to others in France and Italy, which they thought were destined for Canada and the U.S. They said one shipment went to Mexico on a Spanish ship. They were delivering packages all over the fucking place."

"Not so hard to understand. It's easy when there are no border controls. But what were they shipping out of the Euro area?"

"When the group was first set up, one condition was laid down: the goods were prepackaged, waiting at a pickup point. The instructions were explicit: nobody was to open a package. If a package was opened on the job, no matter who tampered with it, they would be held responsible."

"Being thieves, I'm surprised they didn't look anyway."

"One of the teams may have. Our Slovak smuggler told us that two of the original group were found floating in Lake Como early in the game."

"Italy?"

"Yes. Everyone believed that Midi had arranged their deaths because the team had fiddled with the contents of one of the packages."

"What was in the packages?"

"Nobody knew. After the killings, they never asked. They were paid very well, and they left it at that."

"Were the packages all the same size?"

"No. Some were very small, some not so small. The wrappings were not alike, so there was no clue there. And the addresses for the pickup and delivery were varied."

"So what did you arrest them for, if you didn't even know what they were carrying?"

"You said it yourself: thieves will be thieves. They couldn't just transport the goods they were scheduled to carry. They got into the transportation of narcotics to make a little extra money. There are too many informants in the narcotics trade. That's what led us to them."

"And Midi's description?"

"Your Slovak was all over the place in his description of the man. The most trustworthy part of the picture that he painted was that there was nothing really outstanding about the man, except for his eyes. He said the man had cold eyes, eyes the color of wet ashes."

The description jolted Jana. "Wet ashes." She probed her memory, remembering. "I once knew a man like that: a Slovak." A picture popped into Jana's mind. "Did he have a scar through one of his eyebrows?"

Andras looked surprised. "You know him?"

Jana sat back in her seat, mulling over the information. It had to be him. Kamin! Sofia's rapist. He was close.

She finished her beer.

"Ever hear of Midi again?"

"Not Midi. Three days later, the Slovak smuggler was murdered in jail. Throat cut."

"You had no leads?"

"Nothing." He dropped his voice, leaning closer. "He was in a locked cell. We never figured out how the murderer got in or out." He shifted nervously in his seat. "Maybe a jailhouse guard was bribed?" He laughed. This time there was an edge of nervousness to the sound.

They finished off the remainder of their beer; Jana paid for the last round. She left quickly, glad to be going home.

Chapter 15

J ana and Peter decided to spend a few nights out of town together. It was one of those intervals when each had a lull in official responsibilities. They jumped at the chance to get away.

A relative of Peter's was the manager of a hotel in Piešt'any, a spa town that claimed miraculous cures for its hot mineral baths. It catered to not only the Slovaks but also to tourists from a dozen other countries, particularly Germans, Czechs, and Russians, who had a long tradition of patronizing the waters. Their vivid testimonials about the curative value of the spa's thermal pools and sulfurous mud were advertised in international magazines, bringing in a constant flow of new pilgrims intent on experiencing miraculous cures.

Despite a certain cynicism about what the curative waters of the spa did for people, Peter's cousin Vilem took pride in the way his hotel treated its customers. He claimed that the staff, which he had trained, was attentive; besides, he bragged, although the hotel was one of the oldest of the numerous hotels in the city, it sat next to a small, bucolic stream, and, despite its age and Spartan decor, it was charming. To further induce Peter to come, his cousin offered them free immersion in the steaming hot springs, glorious mud baths, and all the free massages they wanted, from morning until just before midnight.

It was an easy eighty-kilometer drive from Bratislava.

Before Jana and Peter arrived, they had decided that since it would not be seemly for the two of them to room together, they would get rooms on different floors, each paying for his own. However, they also made sure that one of the rooms came with a king-size bed.

They each insisted on taking up their own bag to their own room, where they quickly put belongings away and freshened up, then met in Peter's suite. He had ordered a bottle of Russian champagne. They were too much involved with teasing and kissing and slowly undressing each other to be critical of their surroundings, making glorious, undisturbed love for the next two hours.

They lazed around for another hour, drank the rest of the champagne, and decided to try the mud baths. Changing into their bathing suits, they went down to the baths and had themselves coated with the soft, brown sulfurous goo. The experience ended with showers, topped off with a luxurious massage. After that, they were both so agreeably tired that they went back up to Peter's room and fell asleep, not waking up until dinnertime, both now ravenously hungry.

Since Cousin Vilem and Peter had not seen each other for a while, they decided to all go out to a Hungarian restaurant to have dinner. It was a small place but comfortable. Cousin Vilem provided the entertainment. He was a very pleasant man, almost chivalrous in his courtesy to Jana, complaining about the terrible girls that Peter had dated when they were both young, and complimenting Peter for finally bagging a lady who was not only good-looking and bright, but who had a gun that she could use to protect him. He laughed uproariously at his own joke.

The small talk continued through dinner. They began affectionately calling Peter's cousin "Groucho" because his moustache and wry humor reminded them of one of the

Marx Brothers. Groucho's jokes began tapering off just after dessert, when Peter's cousin, a perceptive man, claimed that he had to get back to his duties at the hotel.

The two of them sipped their after-dinner drinks, glad to be alone together. With some trepidation, Jana decided that it was also time for them to talk more about themselves and their pasts, particularly hers.

"We have to recognize who each of us is, and where we have come from. No," she stopped herself, "it's more important that you know about me. If nobody's told you or if they have said something, I want you to know my truth. How it actually was with me before, and how it is now."

"What's there to know? I love being with you. We fit together. We talk and have fun, and you let me tell stupid jokes and stories and laugh at them, and I think you love me, which is even more important. So what else is there to say?"

"I was married."

"You told me you'd been married. You said he was dead."

"Did you know he was a criminal?"

Peter's eyes opened wide in surprise.

"Ah, you didn't know." Jana thought about how she should phrase this, then plunged ahead. "He was not a criminal when I married him. He was the love of my life, I thought. And he was, for a while. Then he went off somewhere. It was not because of me; it was because of how he saw himself, the government, the whole world. He decided he wanted to be a man who robbed the rich and gave to the poor. I loved him, but I couldn't help him. No one really could. It was heartbreaking. Along the way, the man he was disappeared. And, when there was nothing left of him, he died. By his own hand."

Peter took her hand, pressing it to his mouth to reassure her.

"You think his being a criminal would hurt me, or have

some effect on me? The answer is no. And, since you're still a commander in the police, I imagine the government agrees." He held his hands up, as if to surrender. "The past has to be let go of . . . by both of us."

Jana thought about the next problem. It was harder to talk about than the first one, and more serious.

"Another truth to tell: we had a child, a daughter."

Peter did not let go of her hand. "Then he left you with a wonderful present. I hope you've told her about me. What did she say?"

"My daughter married an American. They were both killed in an auto accident."

Peter felt her anguish. "Hard. So hard! I am sorry, Jana."

"She had something wrong with her . . . approach to life. Maybe she was too much like her father." Jana grieved for her daughter's life, and her death. There was a void, a deep hole inside herself, because of that death. "She also had a daughter." Jana forced a laugh. "You didn't know you were making love to a grandmother, did you?"

"Is that all?"

Jana managed to get out a weak "Yes," waiting for his response.

He kissed her hand again. "The youngest, prettiest, and sexiest grandmother I have ever seen."

"You're sure?"

"I think that I'm surer than you are."

Jana had to continue, the words tumbling out. "I may be a good police officer, but I couldn't help my family." She grimaced. "Peter, please believe me, I truly loved them both. It didn't help. They died anyway."

"Anyone who knew you would know that you loved them. Where is your granddaughter?"

"She lives with her father's parents in the United States. Right now, they're in Switzerland for a time."

"Have you seen her lately?"

"We talk at least once a month." She laughed, a little shaky and embarrassed. "She doesn't speak Slovak except for a few words; but she wants to come visit me. My daughter's in-laws have refused. I think I'm ready to visit her in Switzerland without going into hysterics when I have to leave. I believe her other grandparents will let me see her there."

"I am glad it is all right between you and your grandchild."

"It may not be all right if she learns more about her mother and me."

"It was . . . bad with your daughter?"

"Very bad, because of my relationship with her father at the end of my marriage. She was angry and blamed me."

"You and your granddaughter haven't talked about her?"

"I've told my granddaughter how much I loved her mother, and that she was a good girl and a bright girl and a pretty girl, with little anecdotes sprinkled in. As far as she knows, her mother was wonderful. That's all."

"I don't think it would have benefited you or her if you had told her anything else."

"You think I did the right thing?"

"I know so!"

Jana felt a wave of relief. "You're a lovely man."

"I'm just a man who feels both love and admiration for the woman sitting next to him. Thanks for confiding in me."

"I had to tell you sometime."

Peter smiled. "That sometime is now officially over. One last question: Do I get to meet her when she eventually comes to Slovakia?"

Jana stared at Peter, a weight lifting from her shoulders. He had accepted her past without rejecting her. She leaned over and planted a firm, lingering kiss on his mouth before settling back in her seat.

"I liked the kiss," he said.

"I liked the kiss too; I like you," Jana whispered.

"You're supposed to," Peter insisted.

"I'm going to see her soon in Switzerland."

"When?" asked Peter.

"In six weeks. She has a break from classes then."

"I think she'll look like you."

Jana found herself blushing. "It doesn't matter what she looks like, as long as I can see her."

"So," said Peter, "shall we go back to the hotel?"

"Your room or my room?" Jana teased.

"My bed is made up with two pillows, and it's larger."

They walked out of the restaurant with their arms around each other's waists.

Chapter 16

Jana was at home in bed when the body of the Guzak brothers' mother was discovered near Nový Most bus station. Her younger son, Milan, was found lying in the garden of Saint Martin's Cathedral, around the corner from the front entrance.

A priest had telephoned after hearing shots just before a midnight mass. The officers who were dispatched to the location found the son first, lying face up, his arms outstretched, legs together, the blood on the body making it look as if he were a modern Christ, crucified on the ground. The mother was found during the police sweep of the area, her small frame crumpled like a sack of garbage in the bus underpass at Nový Most.

As soon as the officers at the location reported the murders, Jana dispatched a forensics crew to the scene, and made sure the homicide investigators who were on night duty were experienced. When she realized that the name of the dead man was Guzak, she went to the scene herself.

Portable lights had been strung up at both sites. The police vehicle's headlights also had been left on to provide further illumination. Jana stopped first at the bus underpass, figuring that she would spend a short time there, then would quickly go to the church where the woman's son had been killed. She expected to spend more time at the second location.

The son had probably been the target. The man was too deeply involved in criminal activity not to be the primary objective.

The bus underpass was eerie in the artificial light, support pillars casting huge, impenetrable shadows around the few illuminated areas. The officers had already marked off the murder site and were making a spiral search of the ground, commencing with the perimeter around the body. They could not do a wider search until daylight gave them confidence that they wouldn't miss anything.

Jana walked over to the woman's body. The photographer had finished. She put on the regulation plastic gloves and, using her flashlight to give her added light, checked the corpse. Her clothes were sedate: she could not possibly have been mistaken for a streetwalker trying to pick up customers in the bus depot area. The woman had been in her early fifties, with nothing to distinguish her except the apparent cause of death: her throat had been cut, the slash so deep that the woman's head was hanging by a thread. Jana looked closer at the wound.

The cut was wide and clean, so the knife that inflicted it had been large and very sharp, with no obstructions on the blade such as scaling notches that might have torn the edges of the wound. Whoever had done the killing must have been very strong to create this kind of deep slash without any sawing, just a single blow.

Jana checked the woman's hair. There was a small patch missing from the top and just to the right side of her head, with a very small amount of blood on the scalp itself. The murderer had obtained leverage by grabbing a handful of hair, then pulled her head back to expose her throat. From the direction of the cut and the position of the missing hair and bloody scalp, the murderer had used his right hand to bring her head back, wielding the knife with his left. It was a small thing but might be an item in the chain of evidence.

Jana scanned the woman's clothing. It was not particularly disheveled, nothing was torn, the dress was fully buttoned, her shoes still on her feet. She pulled the woman's dress up: panties intact and not pulled down, so there had been no sexual assault. Jana checked the wrists and fingers: no watch, but a wedding ring still there. There was no necklace. Jana checked the immediate vicinity to determine if it might have been jerked or cut off. A few feet away she found a small gold chain in a crack on the sidewalk. A very small pavé diamond pendant was still on the chain, the clasp intact. One of the links had been broken. Again, Jana thought, the murderer was very strong. She looked around for the woman's purse. It was not there. This did not appear to have been a robbery, so the handbag should have been in the immediate area.

"Do any of you have the woman's purse?" she yelled at the working officers.

One of the patrol officers held his hand up. "I do."

"I want it."

The man quickly trotted over to his vehicle, took out the woman's handbag, and bought it over to Jana.

"Was this by the body?"

"Yes, Commander."

"You picked it up and put it in your car before the photographer got his shots of its position in relation to the body?"

The officer thought. "I wanted to safeguard the contents."

"Commendable. Unfortunately, it interfered with the investigation. The next time, leave evidence where it is until the police assigned to investigate the homicide arrive at the scene."

"Yes, Commander."

She went through the contents of the purse, which were relatively orderly. It was probable that the purse had not been searched by the murderer. The money was still there. She gave the purse back to the patrol officer. "Put this in the same spot where you found it. Have the photographer take a few pictures. Then have a detective make a note of what you have done, so it is clear in the written reports, and tell him I want the purse and its contents on my desk in the morning."

The man scurried off.

Within a few minutes, Jana was at the scene of the second murder. This examination had progressed about as far as the other.

Milan, the dead Guzak brother, was in his twenties. He had been shot several times. She rolled the body on its side, checking the wounds: once in the back, twice in the chest, and once through the head. The shot in the back had left no visible powder burns, so it was probably fired from more than three feet away. Jana tilted the body. There was one exit wound on his back; the bullet from the other shot was probably still in the body. She checked the ground under the body. A large slug, mashed beyond ballistics comparison, had gone through the body and smacked into the stones underneath. As the slug was on the ground under the body, the bullets in the chest probably had been fired straight down while Guzak was on the ground and helpless. Jana carefully replaced the body. She wanted to make sure that the bullet was recovered and not overlooked, so she told the crime-scene detectives that there was a slug under the torso of the corpse.

Jana examined the head of the dead man. There was a contact wound in a tight ring of scorched powder, and, from what she could tell, burning inside the wound. Two bullets in the chest and the one in the back had not been enough for the killer. He wanted to make absolutely sure that his victim went to hell. It was an execution.

Jana stood, perusing the surroundings. A priest was standing to one side being interviewed by an officer. The shots had occurred just before the midnight mass. The killings of both mother and son had to be related, so Jana could hazard a few reasonable guesses: The mother and son had intended to attend the midnight mass. It was a time that her son, a man wanted for questioning in connection with several crimes, would have felt it would be safe enough to leave whatever hole he had been hiding in. So, Jana conjectured, Mother Guzak had wanted to go to mass, and not having seen mama for awhile, and wanting to do the Slovak thing of protecting one's mother when she went out at night, or perhaps even listening to her entreaties to save his soul, he had accompanied her.

Unfortunately for them both, someone knew they were coming. Perhaps knowing that the sons were in Slovakia, someone had been watching the mother's house and had seen her and one of her sons take the bus to the area under the overpass and get off to walk to the cathedral.

The first contact with the murderer had been at the bus stop. The mother was quickly eliminated, probably so there would be no witness. It also meant it was possible that the mother had known the killer. The son had run, perhaps thinking his mother would not be harmed. He'd headed to the one area he thought might be safe: the cathedral where the mass was to be celebrated. He'd almost made it, but was cut down before he reached a place of refuge. Perhaps he had staggered a few feet, twisting, falling on his back, and the killer had come up to him, firing straight down into his chest. Then the killer had made damned sure that Milan Guzak would never get up and run away again by putting the gun to his head and firing the last shot.

Jana thought about the huge old Webley that Giles's bodyguard had displayed when she'd visited. Ballistics from the two slugs still in the body, the one in the chest and the one in the head, would give them an indication of the type of gun that had fired the slug. If they found the gun, they might get a match.

In the scenario Jana had constructed, there were at least two killers. While one was killing the mother, the other had to have chased the son and caught up to him before he got to the safety of the cathedral.

Could one of the men have been Giles? Jana thought about it for a second. Possibly. He could be violent. And he certainly was afraid of the Guzak brothers, and wanted them out of his life. But to kill, Giles would have had to be under enormous and immediate threat. If Giles's bodyguard had been part of the murder team, and not Giles, the bodyguard could have worked with someone else, someone who would also be able to commit cold blooded murder. There were certainly enough criminals in the world to choose from.

Jana sighed. She'd wait for the autopsy report and the ballistics reports. As well, she'd look through the mother's purse in the morning to see if there was anything of interest inside.

Then she went home to bed.

Chapter 17

The man who had called himself Salman Mehta in India was now going by Soros, a suitably Hungarian name while in Hungary. He had passed the time while waiting for his associate to arrive by visiting the Benedictine monastery on the outskirts of Györ; then he had walked around the slow-moving city center near the river before driving to the house that they had designated just outside the small community of Vac, north of Budapest and some ways east of Györ. His associate was to meet him there.

It was irritating to wait, and the trip from Austria, to the northwest, had not been easy. Most of the roads were good, but icy, and after spending months in India, driving on the left, driving on the right now created additional stress.

Soros found the house a few minutes before he was scheduled to arrive. He parked two hundred away and scanned the street. The few houses were widely scattered, so there were only a few people to worry about. There were no danger signs, not too much pedestrian traffic, nor indications of surveillance other than his own.

He focused on the front of the house: a small porch, two windows with the drapes drawn. Good. He could not see within, but once inside no one would be able to see him. He checked the back of the house. Unlike the neighbors, it had no garden, just trees and large bushes which blocked any real view of the rear. Just like a petty criminal, Soros thought:

the occupant had wanted a way to get out of the house safely without being observed if anything threatened him. No doubt he had a car in a lot or on the street somewhere nearby, which he would use to get away once he got out beyond the trees. They would have to take that into account.

Soros saw another car approaching from the other end of the street. The vehicle parked. Almost immediately, his cell phone began ringing. Soros answered, knowing who would be on the other end of the line.

"I saw you park. Wait about three minutes to allow me to get to the back, then walk to the front door and knock. Okay?" Soros hung up, took out a cigarette and lit it, then left his car, casually pretending to be a man out for a stroll, just a local smoking his cigarette without a care in the world.

When he felt he was close enough, he cut through an empty lot, angling toward the house. He took off at a sprint when he heard the back door close. Their quarry had not run far when Soros caught him and dragged him back inside. The woman who had been called Rana in Nepal, and who now called herself Eva, was already waiting for him within. She had changed from her sari and head scarf into an inconspicuous ski jacket and heavy slacks. She now looked very Western, her hair carefully blonde-streaked.

Eva eyed the man on the kitchen floor. "He knew we were coming," she remarked.

"He's a thief. They develop a sixth sense for danger." Without warning, Soros kicked the man on the floor, who let out a muffled grunt, skittering back to get as far from Soros as the small kitchen would allow.

"How was prison, Vlad?" Soros asked.

"Who are you?" Vlad got out.

"Friends of Solti," Eva answered.

"Then where is Solti?" Vlad asked. He answered his own

question, worrying his lip with his teeth. "Not a good question. I know what happened. He expected you; I expected you. You've already met with him."

"Congratulations on your assessment of the situation." Eva's pretended admiration mocked him.

"I can see the pieces," Vlad scowled at her. "How many of us are left?"

"Why do you want to know, Vlad?"

Eva moved to the small stove, which had a coffeepot on it. She touched it to feel if it was warm, then sniffed at the top of the pot, making a face. "Old. Undrinkable. If you're to receive guests properly, the least you could do is to make a fresh cup." She put the pot in the sink, running water over it, letting the water continue to run. "Cleanliness is next to godliness, right?" Vlad didn't respond. "Would you rather speak to me, Vlad? Or would you prefer that my colleague speak to you?"

Vlad shot a quick glance at Soros, then nodded at her. "You!" The word seemed to be forced out.

"Wonderful, Vlad. I appreciate the confidence you have in me." She unzipped her ski jacket, pulling out a small automatic from a clip-on belt holster, snapping off the safety, levering a shell into the chamber.

"I'll take a look around the house," Soros announced, walking out of the kitchen.

Eva waved her gun at the man on the floor. "You can see how much confidence my partner has in me by the fact that he's left me here alone with you."

"You have a gun."

"It helps," she acknowledged. "Tell me, how was prison, Vlad?"

"Like all prisons."

"I've never been. Actually, I'm just making small talk so you feel more comfortable."

"How could your being here possibly make me more comfortable?"

"I'll be going in a little while."

"Will I still be alive to enjoy your departure?"

They heard the sound of breaking furniture coming from the front of the house.

"My associate is very clumsy. It is always best to get out of his way." There were more crashes. "As he ages, he just gets worse."

"Can I have a cigarette?"

"I don't like the smoke."

"*He* smokes."

"I have to tolerate his habits but not yours. Perhaps a drink?"

"In the cabinet." He pointed.

Keeping her eyes on him, Eva opened the cabinet, pulling out a half-empty bottle of red wine. She stepped back several feet, then placed it on the floor between them. "Pick it up slowly and uncork it. Drink from the bottle."

He uncorked the bottle, taking a long drink, then wiping his lips.

"Can we talk?" he asked.

"We *are* talking."

"I've already told everyone, your people, my people, that I don't have what you're after."

"I'm inclined to believe you. We're just making sure."

The sound of additional breakage came from the other rooms.

"If you don't think I have it, why not let me live?"

"You know why not."

"How can I help you so you'll let me live?"

"You're absolutely sure you don't have it?"

He took another swig of wine from the bottle. "If I had the package, would I be staying here?"

"Probably not."

"Good." He thought for a moment. "I could help you with the others. I know some of them."

"We know them all."

"I'll go anywhere you wish. Do anything you wish." He took another swig out of the bottle. "What more can a man offer?"

"If I can't think of anything and you can't think of anything, then there's nothing."

The man who had called himself Mehta and who now called himself Soros came back into the room. Staring down at Vlad, he talked to his partner. "Not here. It could be under the house, or buried next to a tree in the back, or at the bottom of some pond in a godforsaken part of Budapest, but it's not here."

"He doesn't have it; he doesn't know where it is."

"You're sure?"

"He's the type who would have given it to me under the circumstances. He's not sure who has it." She talked directly to the man on the floor. "Do you have the vaguest idea who has it, Vlad?"

"I could guess." He took another swig, almost finishing the wine.

"Save a little of the wine, Vlad."

Vlad brought the bottle down between his legs.

"Do you have any reason to suspect any one of them over the others?"

Vlad thought about it. Finally he said, "No."

"I think it's time to finish this." She looked over to Soros. "You agree?"

"Yes."

"Good." She took a small cameo-topped pillbox out of her pocket. "I bought this box in a little shop in Budapest before I got here. He said it was early nineteenth century, but I think he lied. All those small shopkeepers lie." She tossed the pillbox to Vlad. "Take the pills inside. The wine will help."

He examined the box, then opened it, staring at the pills inside.

"They will kill me."

"Yes."

"I would rather be shot."

"If you wish. But you should know that we're going to cut you up after you die."

"Cut me up?" His face twisted in fright. "Why do you need to do this to me?"

"As an example. We have to set an example."

"I don't want you to cut me up."

"Then take the pills."

He thought about it. "Will you leave my face untouched if I take the pills?"

She and Soros exchanged looks. "Okay. We'll leave your face alone."

"And my balls."

"And your balls also," Soros agreed.

Vlad poured the pills into his hand, hesitated, and then popped them all into his mouth, slugging them down with the wine.

"You're a brave man, Vlad," Eva said. "I'll tell people that."

"No, you won't." Vlad's eyes looked sad. "I know your kind."

"Yes, you know my kind."

They watched silently for the next five minutes while Vlad drifted away. He made a last effort to lift his head.

"Don't forget what you promised."

"I won't."

He seemed to hear her, then his head slumped. His breathing stopped.

The two watched the body for a moment. Soros prodded the body with the toe of his shoe; the corpse toppled over.

"Surprised he took the poison."

"You shouldn't have been. Being shot, taking the poison, no matter. He knew he was going to die." She put her gun away. "Look at it this way: he saved his testicles from being cut off. Very important to a man."

"He wasn't going to be able to use them again."

"True."

"And his face?"

"The first thing you look at in the mirror every morning. It says you're who you think you are. Maybe he wanted to make sure they knew who he was when they found him?"

"Maybe." He turned the running water off. "Let's save some for cleaning up later." Soros started rummaging through the kitchen drawers.

"I hope he has some sharp knives in here."

Chapter 18

J ana entered her office and, as she had requested, found the Guzak woman's pocketbook on her desk, along with its contents and an inventory of the contents in a plastic envelope. The son's wallet was also there in another envelope, along with a few papers, a pen, some bills, and a dirty handkerchief that had drops of blood on it. Jana took out the son's wallet first.

There was not much to examine: a Ukrainian driver's license with the dead man's photograph but a different name on it, a membership card for a strip club in Bratislava that advertised "totally nude" artistic dancing, and one crumpled piece of paper with an address in Kremenchuk and a telephone number scribbled on it. Kremenchuk was a city in Ukraine. In the billfold section of the wallet Jana found a folded, well-fingered piece of paper. Another telephone number was scribbled on this piece of paper with the word "Vienna" under it, to her mild surprise. Why would a man like the younger Guzak have a Vienna number? It was not a place that anyone like Guzak would think of visiting to have a good time.

Jana turned the paper over, looking for further notes. There were none. She then looked collectively at the group of objects taken from Guzak, feeling that there was something missing. After a few seconds, it came to her: there were no keys. Virtually everyone carried keys. She put the items back into their plastic bag.

Jana poured the contents of the mother's evidence envelope onto the desk: coins, a small purse with a few bills, an identity card in a plastic folder, and keys, which she assumed were for her house or apartment. Jana pocketed the keys, along with the woman's identity card for its photo in case she had occasion to show it to anyone, as well as a small vial of perfume, which Jana sniffed, making a face over the sweetness of the scent.

Jana picked up the large handbag, opened it, and looked inside. It was empty. She then turned it upside down and shook it. Nothing came out. Jana carefully felt around the inside lining of the purse. Nothing. She weighed the pocketbook in her hand. It was heavy leather and, judging by the maker's label, an expensive item.

Jana thought back. The mother had been a small woman, older, and not strong. Why would she have carried such a large and fairly empty purse? Older women don't like to carry heavy handbags unless it's really necessary. She pictured the woman's clothes: clean, but cheap and dowdy. The clothes did not match the bag, nor did the money that it would have cost jibe with the woman's cheap clothes. Maybe the bag had been a present? Not likely, not from anyone in the circle of friends she would have had. A gift from an admirer? No, the woman was too old. Perhaps one of the sons, a husband, or some other relative. Jana made a mental note to determine, when she checked the woman's other possessions, if she owned anything else that was expensive or that might have been purchased for her by anyone else.

Jana put the bag aside and had just put the mother's things back in their evidence envelope when Seges came in. He was carrying a number of 20-by-30 centimeter glossy photographs.

"I brought you the blowups of the bodies and the immediate area around the bodies, Commander." He sounded very pleased with himself. "I knew you would want these." He laid them in front of her.

"Trying to make up for searching my desk yesterday, Seges?" Without waiting for an answer, she began going through the photographs, looking closely at them as she spoke. "You figure kissing my fanny a little bit will make it all right? Not so, Seges."

He shifted his feet uneasily. "Just doing my job, Commander."

"I want to tell you that it will take an awful lot more than kissing my behind to make up for your fingers tripping through my desk, Seges."

"It was . . . a mistake, Commander."

"It was suicidal, Seges. You have a death wish."

"Not so, Commander."

She stopped at one of the photographs, looking at it closer, then took a felt-tip pen from a cup of pens on her desk and circled the area she had focused on.

"Tell me what you see, Seges."

She passed the photo over to Seges. He looked carefully at the photo while she finished examining the others.

"What is interesting in the photograph, Seges?"

"Aside from the fact that it shows a man who was murdered, Commander?"

"Aside from that, Seges."

She got up from her desk and put on her greatcoat and cap, picking up her purse, slinging it over her shoulder.

"So, Seges?"

"I don't know, Commander."

"His pants pocket is torn open. It might have been ripped when he fell, but it's too large for that kind of tear. There were no objects that could have torn the pocket where he fell. It was deliberately torn open in a hasty search of the body." Jana gestured at Guzak's evidence envelope. "His money is there, but someone wanted to find out what that pocket contained. Do you have keys, Seges?"

"Do you want one of my keys, Commander?"

She took a deep, irritated breath. "No. I want the dead man's keys. There were none in his belongings. Why not? I think he had them in that pocket. The person who killed him took them. And that key, or keys, may open up the secret box that contains the reason the decedent was killed."

"Wonderful thinking, Commander."

"More ass-kissing, Seges?" She went to the door. "Get your coat. We have a long drive to Devín Castle. The dead woman lived just north of there." She walked out, then leaned back in. "Leave the photo on the desk."

She walked out. Seges dropped the photo on the desk and hurried after her.

It took nearly an hour to reach their destination, a small village outside the immediate area but within sight of the ruined ramparts of the old castle blasted apart by Napoleon. They drove down the village's main street, which was lined with elderly but fairly well kept houses, in back of which were plots of vegetables and vineyards on the hillside above them. The frame house of Mrs. Guzakova was one of the smallest on the street. It jutted out at a slight angle to the rest of them. It was also more run down. Slovaks are proud of taking care of their aging parents. The dead man, or whoever else was taking care of her and giving her expensive pocketbooks, had not been doing it as well as he should.

They parked the police car in front of the house. The neighbors immediately came out of their homes and warily stared at them. Their kids went to look in the police car, even as their mothers and fathers hurried to pull them away from it. Typically Slovak: it was still not thought wise to mix with the police.

Jana and Seges walked up to the front door. Jana took out the keys she had removed from the mother's evidence envelope, checked the lock, and inserted what she thought was probably the right key.

"A perfect fit."

Jana knocked on the door, waited a half second, and then unlocked it. She slowly eased her way inside, turning on a light.

The place was a shambles: a jumble of furniture, broken tables, smashed vases, and overturned chairs with their stuffing leaking out. It looked like a huge food blender had been inserted in the house and turned on high. It was not a place anyone would have expected to come home to, and it would have reduced any unsuspecting homeowner to tears.

"I think we now know why the dead man's keys were taken from him. The murderer wanted to make sure he could get in to look for what he wanted."

They made their way through the carnage to the other rooms. One bedroom was in the same state as the living room, as was the kitchen. Virtually all of its crockery had been smashed on the floor.

Jana pointed toward the front door and the street outside. "Talk to the neighbors. See if any of them saw or heard anything here last night. They'll probably all be close-mouthed. See no evil, hear no evil, and speak no evil. But try anyway, Seges."

He left. Jana continued to sift through the debris, going back through the rooms. There was a rear entrance leading to the back yard. Jana stepped into the yard and walked over to a small shed near the side of the house. A clatter came from the shed.

Jana eased her gun from the holster, walked to the shed door and, without exposing herself, pulled it open. Then, slowly, she eased around the doorjamb, her gun at the ready.

There was a sad-looking little mutt inside, shaking with fear, looking up at her with large, sorrowful eyes.

"It's all right, little doggie. I promise not to hurt you." She verified that there was no one inside, holstered her weapon, then picked the mutt up, cradling it in her arms, petting it, as she studied the interior of the shed. Whoever had savaged the inside of the house had done the same to the shed. A small cot had been turned on its end; the linen that had covered the bed had been dumped on the floor. A small lamp had been shattered, a chair broken, and, in the far corner, a suitcase had been torn apart and clothing strewn around it.

Jana kneeled by the suitcase, holding the dog in one arm while she picked through the clothing. Men's clothes: a jacket with its lining ripped out, underwear, a shirt, worn socks. Nothing remained in the suitcase except the inner lining, which had been slashed. Whatever the slasher had been looking for then must have been small enough to have been hidden inside the lining.

A person had been living in the shed, most probably the dead man. So the younger of the Guzak brothers had come to stay with his mother. From the fierce nature of the search, the destruction in the house and the shed, the searchers, whoever they were, had been more than merely thorough in their search: they had been angry. To Jana, that meant that whatever they were looking for had not been found. And, since the two Guzak brothers had been traveling together, the searchers, who were probably the killers of the younger one, would now be hunting for the other Guzak brother.

Unless Jana found the other brother first, he was going to be very dead, very soon.

Chapter 19

Tracking the surviving Guzak brother began with the neighbors. She went into the street, now leading the dog by a piece of twine she had found to use as a leash, and walked over to several of the locals who were standing in a cluster across the street. Seges was two houses down the block, interviewing a homeowner, which Jana thought was all for the best, as she approached the small cluster of women. Several small children clutched at their skirts, staring at Jana in awe and fear.

Jana introduced herself, only to be met with sullen stares. She said, "I have this little dog I found out in back of Mrs. Guzakova's house. He's frightened, and probably has not been fed or had anything to drink since yesterday evening. Do you think one of you could get a small bowl of water for the poor little thing?"

A mother yelled over to an older girl who was still prowling around Jana's police vehicle, ordering her to go inside her house to get a bowl of water and some leftovers from the night before. They watched the little mutt lap up the water first, then begin eating the meat. Jana thanked the girl, who sat next on the ground next to the puppy, petting him; then Jana turned back to the mother.

"I'll have to find somebody to take the dog. Do you think you might want him?"

The woman shook her head. "I have three children. They give me enough trouble without worrying about a dog."

"Thank you anyway." Jana looked at the other women. "Any of you?"

The rest of the women stared back, except for a younger one holding a baby. She stared at the ground, avoiding eye contact.

Jana was glad to see her. The rule is to always focus on the shy ones. When they finally talk, they usually have a lot to say. Jana put warmth into her voice. "Will you tell me your name?"

The woman finally looking up. "Lenka Lalikova."

"Lenka. A good name. My mother's name," Jana lied. Little lies were occasionally needed, and this one did no one any harm. "I loved my mother, even when I was taking care of her in her old age."

One of the other women chimed in, "That's what children are for, to love you as you get older."

There was a general murmur of assent.

"I'm glad you agree. All of you know that Mrs. Guzakova was killed last night?"

All of them, even the shy one, nodded now.

"And her son also," she added. "A terrible thing."

"Terrible," they all agreed.

"I think her son died protecting her," Jana offered. "Although we're not altogether sure."

"I'm surprised," the shy one got out.

"Yes?" Jana probed.

"He and his brother weren't around so much."

"You mean they were *never* around!" one of the other women asserted.

There was a general murmur of assent.

"And the older one has been a miserable human being from the beginning of his life," an older one tacked on.

"The younger one followed the older one's example. Both awful," another woman chimed in.

Jana watched them, convinced that they were now ready to answer her serious questions.

"Has anyone seen the surviving brother?" They made noises indicating they had not. "Or the father?" There was a general round of shrugs.

"We never saw a father. She never talked about a husband," an older woman said.

"Except once," Lenka chipped in, to their surprise. "She said he was in Hungary. Then, one day, she told me he had died there."

"Thank you, Lenka." Jana smiled her appreciation. "So the mother used to talk to you, eh?"

"Only sometimes. I took cookies to her once in a while because she was alone. We would exchange a few words."

"Did she ever say what her sons did for a living, or talk about where they were?"

"She never talked about them," one of the others responded. "I'm surprised she spoke to Lenka. She never talked to anyone else."

"I can keep my mouth shut," said Lenka proudly. "She knew I would never repeat anything to anyone."

"You became her friend," Jana suggested.

"Not exactly her friend, but I think she liked me."

"She didn't like anyone," said the older woman.

There was another murmur of assent.

"She even told me once that she had a brother."

"Did she tell you his name, or where he lived?" Jana waited expectantly.

Lenka took a while to think about it. "She never told me his name, but she said he bought her house for her."

"A nice brother," said Jana. She thought about the expensive purse, which she had left back in her office. "He must have been very well off to be able to afford to buy his sister a house."

"I guess so," Lenka agreed.

"Do you remember his name?"

"No," Lenka admitted, a little sad that she could not provide the information.

"Does anyone here know what Mrs. Guzakova's maiden name was?"

The women shook their heads. Then the woman who had sent her daughter to fetch the water finally volunteered. "I think it was like the politician, Dalingo, or Durinka, something like that."

"Good," Jana encouraged. "Does anyone remember when Mrs. Guzakova and her sons moved in?"

The same woman answered. "I was here when she came. Ten, no . . . twelve years back."

"Did her sons move her in?" Jana pushed her. "Or perhaps she used a furniture-moving business? Can you remember?"

"Who remembers that far back?"

"Was she a churchgoer?"

There was a chorus of "no's" and "never's."

"Did any of you see them leave last night?"

There was another chorus of negatives.

"Thank you, ladies, for your assistance." Jana wound up the conversation, then picked up the dog. "Oh," she added, "are you sure that none of you can keep the dog?" For a second, Jana thought that Lenka would take the little thing. Jana could see her hesitate, then decide against it. "I may be back to talk to you all again. Good-bye."

Jana began walking toward her car. Seges was slowly ambling toward the vehicle as if he had not a care in the world. Jana was willing to bet he had found out nothing. She stopped, looking back, then beckoned Lenka to come over. Jana took her arm, leaning close to her, and the two of them went to the car.

"Lenka, could I ask you something?"

"Yes," said Lenka, timidly.

"It is important that no one enter the house. I'm going to have a forensic team come out here, but they are busy and won't arrive until late today. It's important that *nobody* go inside the house, and, knowing the natural curiosity people have about this type of case, someone might be tempted to peek in, perhaps go inside and take a souvenir or two. That would contaminate the scene, making it very difficult for our people to perform the necessary tests. So, could I ask you to make sure that people don't go inside the house? You know, shoo them away. I would give you whatever authority you feel you need to do that."

"I won't be able to stop them if they try to force their way in," Lenka mumbled.

"I'd never expect you to do that. But the other neighbors will listen if they know that I'll ask you to report and that I'd deal with them."

Lenka finally agreed.

"And one more thing, the little dog. Do you think you could keep him until the forensic men come? If you don't want to keep him then, they'll take him from you."

Without waiting for an answer, Jana handed the dog's leash to Lenka, patted her on the arm, and got into the car. Seges was already in the driver's seat.

"Anything?" he asked.

"Bits and pieces."

"You want to tell me?" He put the car in gear. "I might be able to help."

Seges's description of himself as a potential helper was contrary to anything she knew about him.

"Did *you* discover anything?" she asked.

"No."

"Then let's leave it that way. Drive!"

Seges shrugged, then started back to Bratislava. Jana relaxed and tried to clear her mind. Unbidden, the thought of Andras, the Hungarian police officer she had talked to in Vienna, popped into her head. She hadn't bothered to ask him a very important question when he'd told her about the smuggling operation he'd broken in Hungary. She mentally kicked herself for being too stupid or lazy to ask for so simple and basic a piece of information.

She prodded Seges to go faster, promising to let him off the hook for going through her desk, at least for the moment, if he cut thirty minutes off their time from the village. He almost made it.

Once in her office, Jana immediately dialed Andras's number, waiting impatiently until he answered.

When he did, she made sure to be friendly. "Andras, how have you been since our meeting in Vienna?"

"Budapest is always better for me," he replied, then went right to business. "Why has the smartest lady in the whole Slovak police department called a simple detective from Hungary?"

"I need to test your memory, Andras."

"That's all? I was hoping for more."

"Just a quick item, my friend. The case you described when we were last in Vienna. The smuggling case. You mentioned that one of the defendants was a Slovak. He was killed in his jail cell. Did you confirm his name? Were you satisfied it was not a false name, an alias?"

"I'm not a dolt, Jana. Of course I confirmed it. He had

arrests going back for years. His fingerprints and photo matched."

"Please tell me his last name."

Jana could almost hear the cells in Andras's brain click as he dredged up the name of the man she wanted.

"His name was Durajka."

"Thank you, Andras. Can you send me his file?"

"What else are police friends good for? I'll get it out to you immediately."

"Wonderful."

She hung up.

It would have to be confirmed when the file arrived, but Jana had no real doubts that Durajka had been Guzakova's maiden name. Guzakova's brother had paid for her house. And there was the pocketbook. There are no coincidences. The woman's brother had been the Slovak man involved in the smuggling operation, the one who had been murdered in his cell. Brother killed, sister killed, one nephew killed; they had to be connected. And if Jana didn't get lucky, Guzakova's older son was either going to have his throat slit or a bullet in his head before she could talk to him. Whoever was after the brothers was quite efficient.

Jana got on the phone again, asking Trokan for permission to authorize overtime for her men, then assigned them to the now-extended search for the remaining Guzak brother. They would do a door-to-door inquiry, showing the older brother's mug shots to anyone and everyone on the streets, in businesses or dwellings. They'd also display the photo taken from the younger brother's Ukrainian driver's license and see if that registered with anyone. Trolling of the side-street apartments near the murder scene for witnesses to the two murders would also be extended. As an afterthought, Jana told her men to hand out fliers with the photos to people on the *Ulicas* riding the trams, and have the cab drivers alerted to see if the elder Guzak had taken one of their cabs. Bulletins were already out to all the police stations in Slovakia, and Jana made sure that one went to the neighboring countries just in case the brother had fled across the border.

Perhaps it would pay off; perhaps not.

Jana called the Ukraine *militsia* in Kiev and tried to contact Mikhail Grushov, an old friend of hers from that police force. Jana felt a stab of irritation when she learned that Grushov had retired and left Ukraine. The answering officer referring her to a police captain she didn't know. The captain was none too pleased to get a call from Slovakia, which would mean extra work for him; but when Jana promised him a bottle of *Borovicka*, the white-lightning alcohol that Slovakia specialized in, he quickly changed his tone, asked her to call him Alexi, began calling her by her first name, and invited her to a quiet dinner for two.

Jana chatted for a minute, then came to the point of the call, asking him to check on the Kremenchuk address found in the wallet of the younger Guzak brother, as well as the Kiev address on the fake Ukraine driver's license the dead man was carrying. She got his fax number so she could send a copy of the license to him, then agreed to come visit him when she had the time, both of them knowing that was just phone flirtation protocol.

They both hung up, Jana delighted by his agreement to help. The Ukraine police were not esteemed for their sense of duty, and even less for their cooperation with other police departments. She hoped this would be an exception.

Jana pondered her next step. The only items she had left were the card for the strip club that the dead man had in his possession, and the telephone number in Vienna. She sighed: Austria would have to wait. As for the club, she had been there before on police business. Like all these clubs, it had a history of prostitution that no one ever did anything about. Prostitution was not a crime in Slovakia, as long as the man did the propositioning. She checked the club's card. It didn't open until late evening, so she had to wait before she paid it a visit.

She needed a backup officer. Seges would love this type of club, but he would probably spend his time ogling the girls rather than paying attention to the reason for the visit. But she reluctantly decided that it had to be him: all of her other men were out combing the city. Besides, she thought, she needed to put Seges's invasion of her desk's privacy behind her. It would do no good to condemn him. Even if he was not an investigator in any sense of the word, she needed a body to watch her back while she did the investigating. She couldn't go to a place like this club without another officer to provide extra eyes and hands. As little as Seges might help, he would at least make the visit official, and safe.

Jana turned next to the dead woman.

She ran a national identity request on Guzakova. The result came back almost immediately. It had the usual place of birth, date of birth, and current address, as well as other useless bits of information. The date of birth was hard to believe when she compared it to the face and appearance of the woman she had seen last night. The woman must have had a hard life. Belonging to a family of thieves couldn't have helped. Jana mulled over what she knew of the woman and her family. Since the rest of them were thieves, maybe the little old lady, as Jana thought of her now, was a thief as well?

And the husband? He was supposed to be dead. Maybe yes; maybe no. Jana had to find out about him as well. And she would have to do it herself.

It was time to visit the club advertised on the card taken from the dead Guzak brother. They drove to Gorkého, parking near the Gremium, the café where Sofia and Jana had met to discuss the sex scandal that Sofia had found herself in. Since the Gremium was a favorite hangout of Sofia's, as well as of a number of other politicians, Jana stepped inside to see if she might be there.

A Klezmer band was playing Yiddish tunes, a small audience clapping in time to the music. Jana scanned the customers. They were having fun. She wanted to stay there, to hear the music, to laugh, to simply feel good. But it was impossible tonight. Jana went outside. Seges, in a first for himself as far as ambition went, was already four doors down the block, in front of the sex club.

The club was dark. A new steel gate barred the entrance. The wind had pushed bits and pieces of paper and other debris through the grating in front of the entrance. It had not been swept in some time. The place was definitely closed down. Even the posters on the walls advertising "Theatre Erotique," "Sex Between Women," and "Lap Dancing" were starting to peel.

Seges was pleased. Perhaps he could go home early.

"Locked tight!" He pulled on the bars to show how closed the club was.

Jana stepped close to the gate and discovered a small slip

of paper tacked to the door inside the bars. She read it with the aid of her flashlight, turning back to Seges when she was through.

"Back to the Gremium. They left a referral to Medzil, the manager of the café."

Seges followed Jana, reluctantly bringing up the rear as they trudged back to the Gremium. The band was even louder now, the clarinet leading the group. Jana and Seges went to the counter where the cashier-manager was counting the money in the till. The customers quickly surveyed the two police officers; then, satisfied that nothing traumatic was about to happen, turned back to the band. The manager reluctantly looked up from stuffing money into the register.

"I hope you're having a profitable evening," Jana ventured.

"They"—he indicated the band—"have a following, so they bring in a decent crowd for a weekday."

"Good. You're Medzil?" Jana inquired.

"Yes." He pushed a menu toward her. "An evening coffee?" he suggested. "We have good strudel. There's a new baker who was trained in the old school. Very fine."

"No food, thank you. Just a few questions. The strip club down the street has closed. It has a card on the door referring people here to you for mail delivery."

The manager nodded; then he reached under a counter to pull out a bag, which he emptied on the countertop. "I never gave them permission to use this place as a mail drop. Nobody has come to pick up their crap. You can have it all if you want."

Jana picked up the mail without bothering to answer, thumbing through the envelopes. "Lots of bills." She opened a number of the envelopes to make sure that they were, in fact, bills. They club owners had not paid their debts for months back. There were no envelopes with contents of a personal nature. Not unexpected. Who sends personal letters to a strip club?

"I think the owner is a Gypsy," offered the manager. Anyone who didn't pay his bills in Slovakia was immediately labeled a Gypsy. "What do you expect from people who go into the business of selling sex?"

"Did they sell sex?"

"Clubs like that always sell sex. A couple of the young ones were all right, but the others had already gone saggy."

"You were inside the club?"

"Once. They ran out of food and asked for a delivery of pastry. I charged extra. All they had to do was walk the few steps to pick up what they wanted, and they asked for a delivery. Stupid."

A young couple came up to the counter to pay their bill. Jana turned her back, watching the audience while Medzil dealt with the couple. Two waitresses were working, one older, the other a very pretty young woman of perhaps seventeen or eighteen. Both of them were very industrious, bustling between the tables, the young one only pausing to clap with the audience when the Klezmer band finished a number. On a hunch, when the young woman came over to the pastry case and picked out a slice of Linzer torte for a customer, Jana approached her.

"I'm Commander Jana Matinova. Please put the cake back. I'd like to talk to you for a moment."

The waitress's body went rigid; her eyes took on the look of a frightened deer. Jana took the pastry out of her hand and put it back into the case, sliding its door shut.

"There is nothing to be afraid of. I am not enforcing immigration laws. We're investigating a larger crime." Jana looked to the back of the café, then over at the manager. His demeanor had changed, Medzil seeming almost as nervous as the waitress.

"I need a place to talk to this young lady. Is there an office in the back?"

He nodded.

Jana told Seges to wait by the front door, took the young waitress's arm, then walked her to the back, through a curtain and past the kitchen into a small, cramped office. There was a tiny desk, a tiny filing cabinet, and one chair in the middle of the room.

"Please sit down," Jana told the waitress. "You'll be more comfortable."

Instead, the waitress put her back against the wall and slowly slid to a squatting position.

"I'm not going to arrest you, if that's what you are afraid of," Jana reassured her. There was no response. Sixteen, Jana thought, seventeen at most. Jana sat down on the floor close to the girl, keeping her voice soft and non-threatening.

"Please don't be afraid. I'm sure you have a reason to be fearful, particularly of a police officer. To my own amazement, I found out early in my career that people were afraid of police, even when the people needed their help. That's not good for us, and not good for you. So, please don't be apprehensive. I have a few questions for you. I hope you'll feel comfortable enough to answer them. Please tell me your name."

"Karina," the young woman eventually murmured.

"Karina. A nice name."

"Thank you." The young girl looked up at Jana, studying her face. "You're not here to enforce the immigration laws?"

"No."

Karina let out a sigh and started to relax. "It's a hard floor." Karina gave Jana the barest semblance of a smile.

Jana shifted to make herself more comfortable. "You are right. It's hard."

Karina's smile became wider.

"I watched you outside," Jana told her. "You were having people point to the menu to tell you what they wanted. I can also hear a foreign accent when you speak Slovak. If you have a hard time understanding what I say, please tell me and I'll try to find another way to communicate. Okay?"

"Okay."

"Judging by your accent, you're from Ukraine. Right?"

Karina hesitated.

"There's no harm in telling me."

"Yes."

"Kiev?" Jana suggested.

Karina shook her head.

"Where, then?"

"Kremenchuk."

A connection.

"When did you come here?"

"Four months ago."

"Of course you're here illegally?"

After a long hesitation, Karina nodded.

"Am I right in believing that this isn't the first place that you've worked in Bratislava?"

Karina nodded again.

"Please tell me where else you've worked."

Karina shook her head very determinedly.

"Then I'll tell you where I think you worked. You were a 'hostess' in the strip club down the street."

Karina shuddered, clutching her knees to her chest, putting her face on her knees.

"It was very hard for you." Jana stroked the girl's hair. "Selling your body is a hard way to make a living."

Karina began to cry, tears rolling down her face.

"I'm sorry I made you think about it."

"That's all right," Karina got out, wiping her tears away. "No, it's not all right. I hated it."

"Yes. But you're here illegally. And they threatened you?"

"They hit me; they hit me over and over again. I had no place to go. They said they'd kill me and bury my body, and no one would ever know about it because there was no record of my being here."

"Yes, that's how they do it most of the time. They keep their girls scared." Jana took the waitress's hand in hers, squeezing it to give her reassurance. "Tell me about Kremenchuk. You were taken from there, across the border, by certain people. I'd like to know if you've ever heard the name Guzak."

Karina stiffened.

"The two brothers, right?" Jana said.

" . . . Yes."

"The younger one is dead. Did you know that?"

Karina nodded. "It was on television."

"Do you have any idea where in Bratislava the older one has come to roost?"

"No." Karina's voice was barely audible. "He was the worse of the two." She thought for a moment. "They were both bad."

"So, it's not a terrible thing that the young one is dead. You understand, that doesn't mean that he should have been murdered. What matters now is that I have to find out who killed him. That's my job. Do you have any idea who killed him?"

"Everyone at the club hated both brothers."

"But it wasn't 'everyone' who killed them." She paused, patting the girl on the hand. "I'll tell you how it was with you in Ukraine: You wanted to get out of a bad life in Kremenchuk. Some people offered to help. Maybe you even paid them. The brothers were the ones who ran you across the border?"

She nodded.

"When you were traveling to the border, things got even worse."

She nodded again. "The first night, the older one climbed on me. Then the other brother."

"Yes, very bad," murmured Jana. "No one should go through that."

"No one," murmured the girl.

"Then you were brought to the club and put to work?"

"Yes."

"The manager of the club, do you know where he is?"

Karina hesitated.

"I won't tell anyone that you told me. I swear it."

Again, hesitation. "I don't know where he lives. He did have a woman. The girls had a small party at her apartment once."

Jana pulled out her notebook, wrote down the address that Karina gave her, then got to her feet, helping Karina to hers.

"The manager here, Medzil, is he good to you?"

"Please don't make trouble for him," Karina pleaded. "He gave me shelter; he gave me a job. He's nice to me."

"He lets you keep the money you earn?"

"Always. And I don't have to share my tips, like the other waitress."

"Does he force you to have sex with him?"

"No."

"But you're having sex with him?"

Karina nodded. "He's kind of like my boyfriend."

Jana doubted that. For the manager, it was probably sex in exchange for a place to stay and for work. Should she turn the manager in? If she did, she would have to reveal what she had learned from the girl in her report, and she'd promised not to. If Jana revealed the young woman's identity, she would be in worse shape than she was now. They'd force her to go back to Ukraine, and lord knows what problems lurked for her there.

People made accommodations in their lives, and who was Jana to say what was right or wrong? Medzil, at least, was not pimping her. Jana decided to do nothing about the situation. She wrote her own home telephone number on her business card and gave it to Karina with instructions to call if she needed any kind of assistance, escorted the girl out of the room, and walked her back to her station.

"You can go back to work."

The girl mouthed a "Thank you" at Jana. Jana walked over to the manager, who was still nervous about what she might have found out, and even more nervous about what she might do about what she had discovered.

Jana leaned close to him. "If you are mean to that girl in any way, I'll find out, and then I'll come back here and make you pay and then pay some more. Do you understand me?"

"I haven't done anything," he insisted.

She grasped his shirt, pulling him forward.

"I asked if you 'understood.'"

" . . . Yes," he gulped.

"Good." She let him go and walked out of the cafe, Seges trailing after her.

"I don't like the customers at that café," said Seges.

"That's because you lack perception, Seges," said Jana.

Chapter 21

Jana and Seges left the café and drove directly to the
address that Karina had supplied. The word would get
back quickly to the girlfriend of the erotic club's manager
that they were looking for her. Of course, Seges felt that
their haste was unnecessary.

He did not complain about the need to talk to the woman,
because he knew Jana would be all over him. Instead, he
complained about the danger of the icy streets, the lack
of sufficient streetlights, the fear of getting into accidents,
his aches and pains, his wife's moans about his late nights,
all grievances geared to get Jana to change her mind about
where they were going, until she finally told him to shut up.
Her tone of voice brooked no argument. Seges kept quiet
until they got to the address, an old apartment building on
Cintorinska in the northeast section of Bratislava, an area of
small gray stores and even grayer buildings.

They parked directly in front, Jana leading the way into
the foyer. After they entered, Seges's first words were to
curse bitterly because the elevator was not working, not an
uncommon event in buildings this old. They climbed the
stairs to the fifth floor. Jana tuned his complaints out, thinking instead of what she needed to accomplish when they
arrived at the apartment. It would not be easy to get the
girlfriend to talk about her lover. Jana would probably need
some type of lever to pry the information out of her.

The fifth floor of the building was like the neighborhood, stained and colorless. An uneasy Seges drew his gun as the two of them walked down the torn and dirty hall carpet. Jana quietly told him to put it away. Seges began objecting. Jana was forced to raise a finger for silence as she paused to listen at the door of the woman's apartment. Music played inside.

"There are illegals inside. There is an off chance that there may be problems when one of them comes to the door. If the music is turned off before she gets here, then take your gun out and stand to the side." She pointed at the doorjamb. "If she leaves it on, there'll be no immediate trouble. She thinks she's safe."

The music stayed on. A woman's voice came through the door, querulous, asking who they were.

"Jana Matinova. Karina at the Gremium told me to look you up. She said we might be able to work together."

The slide-lock on the door rattled, the door opening, the woman's eyes getting big as she saw their uniforms. She tried to close the door but was not fast enough. Jana's foot was already in the way, her shoulder forcing the door aside.

"Hello," said Jana amiably, walking past the woman and into the apartment. Seges took the woman's arm, escorting her into the apartment with them. Three other woman were inside, in varying degrees of undress, frightened at seeing police officers. They wanted to run, but there was no place to go.

"I am not from immigration, ladies. No arrests for that tonight. So, please, all of you sit down." None of them complied. Jana raised her voice. "I said sit down!" They sat, and Jana's voice returned to normal. "Thank you, ladies."

She prowled through the other rooms, making sure no one was hiding. There were two very messy bedrooms, each with clothes strewn around. A small kitchen with a minuscule stove was cornered next to a bathroom, which had clothes-lines strung across it with wet underthings laid over the lines to dry.

When Jana walked back into the living room, Seges was eyeing the women, particularly one of them who had no top on. Jana told him to wait outside in the hallway. Reluctantly, grumbling under his breath, Seges left. Jana nodded to each of the women as Seges closed the door behind him.

"Let's relax, ladies." There were no other chairs, so Jana pulled over an end table, removed the cigarette-butt-filled ashtray set on top of it, and placed the ashtray on the arm of a tattered couch. She then sat on the table.

"We're now just friends together." She looked over to the woman who had opened the door. "You're Andreea?"

There was a reluctant nod.

The music was still on; glasses and several half-full liquor bottles were scattered around.

"A pleasure meeting you, Andreea." She widened the focus of her attention to include the other women. "I hope your little party was fun." She looked at the woman who was still topless. "If you want, you can get a blouse for yourself. Just come back here after you've put it on." The woman darted into one of the bedrooms. Jana waited for her. The woman quickly came out, having grabbed a sweater. Before the woman could sit, Jana pointed to the radio. "It's hard to talk when there's music playing. Please, turn it off." The woman turned the radio off, then stood there, unsure where to go. Jana motioned her back to her chair.

"If I were off duty," Jana talked, trying to relax the women, "I might even share a drink with you. However, I'm on duty. That means just business today. Did you all work at the Theatre Erotique before it closed down?" Jana eyed each one in turn. "I don't want to be impatient, but I've had a long couple of days and I'm tired, so if I have to pull the answers out of each of you I will probably lose my temper. Do we all understand that? I want to see some nods if you do."

There were slow nods of agreement from all of the women.

"Very good! You see, I told you we'd be friends." She looked back at Andreea. "You all share this apartment, but only one of you rented it. That person would assuredly be a Slovak. That means it was you, Andreea. Correct?"

" . . . Yes."

"How long have you had it?"

"Four months."

"Where were you born?"

"Poprad."

"And the other girls, where'd they come from?"

There was silence.

Jana heaved a sigh of exasperation. She focused even more pointedly on Andreea.

"If I speak to the others in this room and I find that they have accents that are not Slovak, I'll have to assume that, in fact, they're not Slovak, and that they're here illegally. In that case, I'll probably be forced to arrest them as aliens who are in this country without permission. All of them will unquestionably be deported if I take them into custody. So, it's up to you, Andreea, to speak for the group. Their lives depend upon your speaking truthfully. Do we all understand that?" She looked to each of the women. They understood the stakes, and eyed Andreea to make sure she knew, too.

"Andreea, I asked you a question. Please answer it. All of the girls are illegals, part of the group brought in for the club to use, true?"

Andreea finally nodded.

"And it was your job to 'take care' of them? To make

sure, in their time off, that they didn't play the game for themselves, work the streets, cut into the club's percentage; or perhaps to help them avoid 'difficulties' that might bring unwanted attention to the club. Right?"

" . . . Yes."

"The manager of the club was your boyfriend?"

Andreea remained silent. Jana's eyes swept around to the other women in warning.

"I don't think your friends are going to like you any more if you force them to speak."

Andreea quickly shot a glance at the other women. "Tell her!" one hissed, looking daggers at Andreea.

Andreea looked down at her bare feet; Jana waited her out. Andreea finally mumbled, "Yes, my boyfriend."

"What's his name?"

" . . . Veza."

"And where is Veza?"

She looked up, a small look of triumph on her face.

"He went to Kiev. Yesterday. So he's gone." Andreea saw the skeptical look on Jana's face. "Ask them." She motioned at the others. "They know he left."

"It's true!" the woman in the sweater said. "He is a son-of-a-bitch. I hope he dies there."

Jana looked back at Andreea.

"Your friend hopes your boyfriend dies. Do you?"

Andreea shrugged. "Whatever happens, happens."

"It sounds like he needed to leave Slovakia very quickly. Why?"

"He left. I didn't ask why."

"Did it have anything to do with the Guzak killings? Perhaps with the brother that's still alive? The older one?"

The breathing of all the women seemed to momentarily stop. Jana looked at them one by one, knowing, even before she looked, that the Guzak name had frightened them. Jana went back to questioning Andreea.

"Did your boyfriend kill the younger brother and his mother?"

" . . . I don't think so." She looked directly at Jana. "He's a coward. He's the kind of a man who only beats a woman if he's sure she won't hit him back."

There was a murmur of agreement from the other women.

"So he fled because was afraid."

" . . . Yes."

"Of who?"

"Others."

"What others?" Jana pressed her. "Give me their names."

"I don't know."

The woman in the sweater spoke up again.

"All of us talked about it. She doesn't know. None of us know."

Jana got up, then walked to a coffee table where there were a few scattered papers. She picked up a piece without any writing on it, then handed it, along with her pen, to Adreea.

"Write the address and telephone number in Kiev where your boyfriend is heading."

Andreea scribbled an address and phone number down on the paper, then handed the pen and paper back to Jana.

Jana looked at it, then passed it over to the woman in the sweater.

"Tell me if it's the correct address. Be very careful. If it's the wrong telephone number, if even one letter or number on the address is incorrect, I'm sorry to say our immigration people will come back here and you all will be in deep trouble. It'll mean jail, then you go back to your countries quicker than quick."

The rest of the women quickly gathered around the sweatered woman, chattering in several languages, none of them Slovak. The woman in the sweater took Jana's pen and made several corrections on the paper, then handed the items back to Jana.

"Now it's okay."

"Thank you." She looked at Andreea, who was again busy studying her bare feet. She had tried to mislead Jana. "Bad, bad girl," Jana chided. "He isn't worth it." Jana looked at the other women. "I'm glad that I'm not suspicious and that I didn't need to ask for your identity papers." Jana looked at the woman in the sweater. "As for you, you are obviously a Slovak."

As Jana walked into the hall, Seges immediately began his litany of complaints. Most of all, he whined about being deliberately sent away from the interview.

"They wouldn't have talked to me while you checked out their breasts."

"I would've made them talk quicker."

"You would have made them sullen and angry, not talkative."

He continued to complain, wearing Jana down. She decided to end the discussion.

"In the morning," Jana told him. "I'm very tired, and if you irritate me too much I'll unquestionably use my sidearm to shoot your tongue off."

The rest of the evening was blissfully quiet.

Chapter 22

In the morning, Jana telephoned Budapest and contacted Andras to update him on her investigation. After she finished, she asked if he had any information on other Hungarian criminals involved with the Slovaks, and whether they were still alive and out of prison. Unfortunately, Andras did not give her an answer she wanted to hear.

A body had been found in a small city in northwest Hungary. The victim had been dismembered, body parts neatly stacked up on the floor, the head in the kitchen stove. Whoever had dismembered the body had baked the head. The man's genitals had been stuck in his mouth like an apple propped between a roasted pig's lips.

"One of the Hungarians?"

"No question. We're trying to find the others. I don't think we'll find them alive."

"Any idea who might have done it?"

"Who knows? Except that whoever did him in apparently didn't like the man. Who cuts a man's balls off and sticks them in his mouth?"

"A person you don't want to meet on a dark night."

"The two cases, yours and mine, are probably connected."

"My conclusion also, Andras."

Andras had a man on his staff who spoke Slovak, so Jana promised to send him her files on the double murders in Bratislava.

"These seem to be killers operating on an international level," suggested Andras.

"There's some action in Ukraine as well," Jana told him. "A regional alert is in order."

"I'll put both our names on it as contacts when I get your file."

"Agreed. Was the victim shot? Stabbed?"

"Preliminary results indicate he was probably dead before they cut him up. No struggle. There was some bleed-out, but not much blood spatter, so the heart had already stopped. No slugs or cartridges found; no apparent bullet wounds. No blunt force. Strangulation ruled out. The coroner is examining the organs. He thinks the man may have been given some type of drug which was the cause of death. Although why they'd choose to give him a drug beforehand, when they were so willing to cut him up, is beyond me."

"Easier for them."

"I suppose."

"The question is, why did they cut him up in the first place?" She thought of their use of the plural for the murderers. Both she and Andras had come to the same conclusion.

"These are obviously not just psychopaths who love to kill, or love to dismember people." She thought a minute. "You said the body parts were neatly piled up, so whoever did the killing was not interrupted, and proceeded to do exactly what was intended."

"And the sexual organs in the mouth of the baked head?" Andras wanted to know.

"They wanted to show disdain for the man, to mock him, perhaps to show that they'd shut him up in the nastiest way they could. Revenge, maybe? More likely, I think, as an example to others who might be tempted to do whatever the victim did that made them angry enough to do this. The man's murder was deliberately brutal, absolutely ruthless, and the people who did it want everyone else to know it."

"You think a relative or ex-girlfriend or wife was involved?"

"I don't think so."

"Perhaps you might want to come to Hungary and help us solve this," Andras suggested, only half-joking.

They both laughed.

"That is your body, Andras. You're very competent. I have my own problems here. Besides, I think I have to go to Ukraine first."

"Budapest is lovely. Come here. Ukraine is a pit. Why go there?"

"Information. Any information I get, I'll share with you."

"That's why it's always such a pleasure doing business with you, Jana."

"One more thing: was the place ransacked?"

"Yes. Drawers pulled out, things on the floor, broken furniture. But other stuff not touched. Other places that I might have searched were left secure. So, not an all-out search. If they were looking, I don't think they looked very hard."

"They probably knew that whatever they were searching for was not there. My guess is that they'll pop up somewhere else. They made a mistake on this one."

"I don't see it. Tell me."

"They made the error of indicating that there is another person who they're looking for, the person who has whatever it is they want. So, we know they're still hunting."

"While we hunt them." Andras sighed. "Round and round it goes."

"Proceed with caution, Andras."

"I am, by nature, a cautious man."

"That's how we survive."

She wished him luck, then hung up, punching in the number for Alexi, the Ukrainian police officer she had talked to about the Guzaks. Alexi immediately asked her where the promised bottle of Borovicka was.

"I thought I might bring it myself," she responded.

"You're coming to Ukraine?"

"I'll even throw in a bottle of Slivovitza. Homemade. Of course, you may not be man enough to drink it."

A howl came over the phone line. Then, when Alexi calmed down, he said, "When are you coming to Ukraine, Slovak?"

"When you find a fugitive for me?"

There was a sigh from the other end.

"You're trying to get me to do more work for you."

"These are expensive refreshments I've promised to bring you."

"No more work without payment, Slovak."

"You're trying to hold me up."

"Liquor first," he insisted.

"You're forcing me to go up your chain of command to complain about the lack of cooperation I'm getting."

"Good. I have relatives up there, so nothing will happen to me." He laughed uproariously at how funny that was. "Listen, Slovak, you don't want them to assign someone else to do whatever it is you want. They're not very competent. So you need to stick with me."

"All I want you to do is to see if a man is living at an address. If he is, then I'll fly to Kiev with the two bottles in my luggage."

"If I arrest him, it will cost you another bottle."

"I don't want you to arrest him until I'm there."

"Okay, then, here's the agreement: you give me the information, I find out if this *blini* you want to question is there, then you bring me the presents, we have a glass or two, then we go out together and you talk to him."

"Close enough."

"Okay, Slovak. I agree." Another enormous belly laugh sounded. "I like you, Slovak."

Jana gave him the information she had obtained from Andreea and her friends about Veza, the pimp who had managed the Theatre Exotique. Alexi promised to call her as soon as he had answers for her.

Jana had to be ready if he called, so she walked down the corridor to Trokan's office. He glanced up at her as she came in.

"The two murders, the mother and son. Any progress?"

"I came in to talk to you about that."

One of his eyebrows shot up. She generally shied away from everyone when she was on a difficult case.

"You need a special favor from me?"

"Authorization to go to Kiev."

"I thought you were going to Switzerland to see your grandchild."

"I am. But I need to go to Kiev on this case. I could go to Switzerland to see my granddaughter; then, instead of coming back here, I would fly directly to Kiev from Geneva."

"No one who lives in Bratislava and can go to Vienna or Prague, which are just around the corner, would want to go to Kiev except on very pressing business that absolutely requires attention. Hence, knowing you, I am inclined to approve your request. Go!"

Trokan's quick approval surprised her.

"You're not your usual self." He usually stubbornly resisted requests like this. "Why are you simply agreeing? There must be questions. There always are."

"You told me that the trip is needed for the case you're working on, right? What else do I need to help me make the decision?"

"A detailed explanation about what I expect to find."

"Write up the request. Put everything in you think I should know, and I'll sign it."

"That was easy." She thought about his quick acquiescence. "Too easy." When it came to spending money for plane tickets or hotels, there was always a problem with the government. "You usually repeat how you have to watch expenses."

"As I get older, I get softer."

There was no question in Jana's mind that something else was motivating him. He wanted her out of town.

"It's something else. What?"

Trokan didn't deny what she had suggested, simply staring at her. The stare told her what she needed to know: he wanted to tell her, but he could not. And, knowing him, he was trying to communicate what he could not directly tell her.

Jana had to make her own assumptions. The only thing she could think of was the warning he had gotten about her from the corruption people. Jana decided to probe a little.

"Your friends from the corruption section have given you information. They're planning an operation and you want me out of town because of it?"

"Draw whatever conclusions you wish." He stared at her, trying to find something in her face. He nodded in satisfaction. "Good! There's no fear in your expression. That means you think you have nothing to make you fearful. It justifies my faith in you." He paused, finding the words he wanted to use. "As an old friend, I want you to listen to what I say and be guided by it without any questions."

Jana nodded.

"It's important for you to be out of Bratislava, particularly at the beginning of next week. Just go. Okay?"

"Okay."

"One more thing: that trinket that you showed me. Take it away with you." He looked at her knowingly. "The reason, if you are ever asked, is that I give you this advice to make sure that it is not stolen, or otherwise misplaced, while you are in the field to complete your investigation."

Trokan was building in an excuse for himself, and for her, if the issue was ever raised.

"Thank you, Colonel."

She saluted him, even though she rarely saluted him any more. He had just done her another favor to add to the long list of those in the past.

Jana did an about-face and went to her office. As soon as she walked in the door, her phone rang. Alexi was calling. An informant had confirmed that Veza was at the address Jana had given him. Jana told him that she would be flying to Kiev on Monday and would meet him at the main police station.

She put the phone down on its cradle. The Kiev call was a life-saver. Trokan had told her, indirectly, that her house was going to be searched in the upcoming days by the anti-corruption people. He wanted her, and the diamond, away at that time. It would save a lot of awkward questions and, possibly, help Jana keep her job.

It also meant that in all probability they were going to search Sofia's place as well. Unfortunately, there was no way that Jana could, or would, warn Sofia. Jana was still very much a part of the police department, and there was an ongoing investigation. Jana had to let them do their jobs.

It would all work out, she told herself.

She hoped so, for both their sakes.

Jana had one more errand to run before she got ready for her flight to Switzerland.

Chapter 23

In the morning, Jana stopped by to see Peter before she left for Geneva.

She parked, then walked from the lot to the front of the building that housed the appellate courts, the national court administration, and the attorney general and his staff. She angled up the steps, her path intersecting that of a pair of judges who Jana knew, and greeted them with a nod. She was hurrying, hoping to catch Peter before he got to his office. She stopped to wait for him just inside the front door. She was early enough to watch the attorney general himself arrive in his BMW sedan. Eventually, she decided that Peter must be an even earlier bird than she had supposed. After checking her ID, the guards allowed her to use their interoffice telephone to call Peter's office.

He insisted on coming to meet her, and within a few minutes she saw him bolting down the stairs. He approached her with a huge smile on his face, kissed her on both cheeks, then accompanied her to a wall bench, sitting as close to her as decorum allowed.

"You will notice that I conduct myself as a proper procurator while we are in a public building. Besides, how would it look if a police commander was embraced and passionately kissed? Which is what I want to do, with the whole judiciary and the attorney general himself as witnesses."

The attorney general was talking to a court of appeals

judge near the metal detectors. After finishing his conversation, he beckoned to Peter.

"No peace for the weary," Peter grumbled. "I'll only be a minute. Wait for me." He strode over to his boss. The two of them immediately fell into what appeared to be a lively conversation. The attorney general was apparently ordering a reluctant Peter to do something. It was clear that he was giving Peter an ultimatum. Peter made a gesture of compliance, and the attorney general, seemingly still miffed, walked toward his office. Peter watched him go, a resigned expression on his face; then he returned to Jana and sat next to her.

"Problems?" she asked.

"Some. A case I'm involved with. He wants me to do certain things and not do others. So I agreed, but I'm going to do what I have to do anyway." He looked grim. "If it backfires, I will have rain, squalls, typhoons, earthquakes, tsunamis, and hurricanes in my professional life."

"Charging directly into the storm," she teased. "That's my Peter."

He looked at her closely, a crooked smile on his face.

"I liked what you just said." He moved closer. "'*My* Peter,' you said. Did you mean that?"

She turned so they were face to face, almost touching noses, and looked directly into his eyes.

"Yes, I meant it."

"*My* Peter," he repeated. "Since I have no objection to your owning me, you now have all the responsibilities of ownership. I hope it means that you love your new possession, and will take care of it so that it's happy."

"People are watching us."

"You're avoiding the answer." He put his hand on her arm. "I'm keeping you prisoner until you reply."

"I love all my possessions."

His face dropped. "You mean there is nothing special about this one possession?"

She pretended to be thinking deeply. "I think this one may be unique," she eventually agreed.

"Not as much from you as I wanted. But, for today, it will have to do."

They moved farther apart. The two door guards had been watching them. One of them grinned, giving them a thumbs-up of approval. Peter returned the gesture.

"I told you they were watching us," Jana hissed, looking away in embarrassment.

"I see them every day. Today, they're both wishing they were me."

"They'll know we're lovers."

"The truth will out," he joked, a little embarrassed himself.

Jana returned to business, straightening up, moving even farther away from Peter so no one could question that she was there on business.

"I told you about my granddaughter. My son-in-law's parents and I have been talking back and forth. It's been tense. They've suggested that I visit her in Geneva. I can argue all I want; they won't agree to let her come to Bratislava. So I've agreed to go to Switzerland for the weekend to see her. If it goes well, they'll agree to another trip in a month or so, then another. I hope, when I've earned their trust, they'll let her visit me for a week, maybe two, in Bratislava."

"I'm sorry you can't bring her here now. I wanted to meet your granddaughter."

"It can't be helped."

"You plan to go this weekend?"

"Yes."

"I'll miss you."

Jana smiled. "That's good."

"You're hard-hearted."

"Never."

Peter shifted uneasily. "When I talked to the attorney general, he said a few words about you."

Jana came to full alert. "What did he say?"

"He ordered me to stay away from you until the case I'm working on is completed and has made its way through the courts."

"Why would he do that?" She felt herself getting angry. "He doesn't like his attorneys seeing police officers, is that it? That's idiotic. He can't mean it."

"Jana, it's because of the matter I'm working on. He's formed a special investigation unit. I'm in charge of the first case. We're targeting some people. That's all I can say. So, no more questions, please. I've already told you I'm not going to obey him. It simply means we have to be careful when and where we meet until this is over."

Jana calmed down. "Why would he single me out?"

"Jana, please. No questions!" He got up from the bench, taking her hand as she stood. "Call me from Geneva. And kiss your granddaughter for me."

He gave her a last smile as he headed for the stairs. Jana watched him go, then walked out of the building and went toward her car, almost turning back when she realized she had been so taken up with talking to him about seeing her granddaughter that she'd neglected to tell him she was going to Kiev when she finished her Geneva visit. She promised herself that she'd call him when she got to Geneva.

When she got into her car, something else came to mind. Colonel Trokan had told her that there was a special anti-corruption group that might be investigating her friend Sofia. They'd informed Trokan that they had seen Jana with

Sofia. Peter had been ordered to stay away from Jana. Was that the case Peter was working on? Because of her meeting with Sofia, was Peter also investigating her?

Thinking about it would not help. Jana was powerless. Besides, Peter was still going to see her. Since she couldn't interfere, it was best for her to forget it. She didn't want to carry any anxiety over into her meeting with her granddaughter. She was determined that the meeting in Switzerland was going to be a happy event.

In two hours, Jana was on her way to Geneva. The two bottles she had promised to take to Alexi in Kiev were in her luggage.

The diamond was wrapped in a small piece of velvet and safely tucked in her brassiere.

Chapter 24

Jana slept through the flight to Geneva. Still disoriented by the bustle of the large international airport, Jana was pleasantly surprised when she was met at the exit near the baggage area by a driver holding up a sign with "Matinova" written on it. Her in-laws had sent him to pick her up. The driver piloted the minivan through the traffic and they quickly reached her hotel, a few short blocks from the World Trade Organization headquarters on Rue de Lausanne. The man carried Jana's bag into the small, very functional-looking hotel, leaving her at the desk, where there was a terse message waiting for her. Her in-laws, the Conrads, would let Jana refresh herself, then would call on her in three hours.

Jana unpacked, took a quick shower, put on her best skirt and blouse, a pair of shoes with heels rather than the flats she had traveled in, and a new light leather coat. She decided to go out for some air rather than wait, nervously, in her room.

Jana checked the Geneva street map that the desk supplied. As a tourist, the least she could do was to see Lake Léman. She caught a taxi, ordering the driver to take her to the best viewpoint on the Geneva side of the lake. The cabbie dropped her near the lakefront on the Quai du Rhône. Just offshore, a huge fountain of water, perhaps two hundred meters high, shot up from the lake.

Jana paid the cab driver, then walked through the Jardin Anglais to the water's edge, all the while keeping her eye on the jet of water pulsing up into the sky. The wind suddenly shifted, blowing a light rain of liquid mist over the tourists watching. Everyone scattered to avoid the water, laughing. Jana was strangely jubilant, feeling once more like a child being hosed down in her front yard by her father on a pleasant Sunday. All of her built-up tension seemed to have been washed away by the lake water.

Then she saw a man observing her from across the street. She was the one he was interested in. To most people, the slight half turn the man made to face away from her would mean nothing; Jana recognized it as a piece of tradecraft. She angled over to a vendor selling chestnuts and bought a bag. As she extracted money from her purse she glanced at the man, confirming her perception. He was keeping pace with her. Jana turned back toward the town cathedral and began cracking the chestnuts open, munching on them as she walked, all the while considering the man behind her. He seemed to be a professional. That might indicate that he had a partner nearby, with whom he'd alternate to make sure that they didn't lose her. But, try as she might, she could not spot the other person tailing her until she reached St. Pierre Cathedral. Then a woman just down the street acknowledged him with a slight nod of her head. A mistake.

No matter how good tails are, if you're looking, you can generally find them. These two were good. Because of the distance between them, they had to be communicating with each other through a personal audio hookup. If one lost her, the other would pick her up. Jana approved. It was a good procedure. The primary question now was, why were they following her? Jana wanted a closer look at the both the man and the woman. She hailed a cab and, quickly consulting her map, directed the driver from street to street, taking a circular route through the area, forcing her followers to take cabs themselves to keep up.

It was all in the timing. Jana was not trying to lose them, just to force them to play catchup, perhaps to become careless enough to give her that brief moment she needed to see their faces up close. The circular route through the streets quickly brought them back to the cathedral area and Grand Rue. Jana threw more than enough money at the driver, pointing out where she wanted him to wait for her, then jumped out of the cab before it stopped, ducking behind a service truck, hurrying to a good position from which to see the two trailing her.

Grand Rue, despite its name, is a fairly narrow picturesque street, lined with small bookstores, art galleries, and antique shops. Within thirty seconds, the first of two cabs arrived, slowing as it passed her parked taxi. A woman got out, her face very clear to Jana. It only took Jana a moment to recognize her. Then she decided it was time to go after the man. She soon spotted him, sitting in a cab, talking into a lapel mike. They were trying to locate her.

Jana could see his face through the open passenger window of the cab. She walked up to the taxi, half leaning into the window.

"Good afternoon, Ludovit," she said.

The man's body jolted, his face going white.

"You and Sabina Postova are doing a fine job following me. I wanted to compliment you. When I get back to Bratislava, I'll be sure to tell your supervisor that you're both very diligent."

His face slowly reddened. He'd been made to seem less than professional, and his pride could not tolerate it. Ludovit turned to face the other side of the street, ignoring her.

"You're not an ostrich, Ludovit. There's no sand here to put your head in. Besides, who wants to put his head in sand?" She spoke in Slovak.

"I'm afraid you are mistaken," said Ludovit in very bad French, refusing to face Jana. "I am not this Ludovit person."

The absurdity of the situation kept Jana from becoming angry. "Strange, how you understand Slovak then. You realize, of course, that we are currently in the middle of Geneva in the country of Switzerland?"

In his badly accented French, still keeping his face averted, Ludovit ordered his taxi driver to drive on. The cab proceeded down the street, stopping momentarily to pick up Sabina, his partner. They would not be a happy couple.

Jana returned to her taxi, confused. Why was her own police department following her? Why were they so concerned about her activities that they would bear the expense of following her in another country? What reason could they have? Her trip was not a secret, but she hadn't told many people she was going to Switzerland. How had the people who authorized the surveillance learned of it? She had told Colonel Trokan. Could he have told the anti-corruption section? There was one other, very ugly possibility: could Peter have told them? But *why* were they following her?

Perhaps they thought she was visiting her money? "Jana the Corrupt," coming to visit her safety deposit box or Swiss bank account? I could buy a new water heater if I could only find this phantom account, she thought.

Jana ordered the driver of her cab to take her back to her hotel. She went up to her room, still mulling over what she now termed the Swiss Watch. Unfortunately, this watch had a bad movement. She smiled at her own joke.

The desk called to inform her that Mrs. Conrad was waiting for her in the dining room. Jana went downstairs.

As soon as Jana entered the restaurant, she saw Daniela. Her granddaughter was the very image of her own daughter, Katka, at that age, but with the deep-set eyes of her father and a touch of Jana in the nose and mouth. Jana had seen recent photographs of her, but her posture, the tilt of her head, her expression generated the personality that a photograph lacked, or that a voice on the telephone could not convey.

Jana was both elated and a little anxious as to how her granddaughter would react to her. She took smaller steps, trying to prepare for the moment when they would face each other, as she slowly walked to the table.

Daniela was engaged in animated conversation with a white-haired, expensively dressed, rather plain-looking woman. When Daniela finally looked toward Jana, she stopped eating and stood. Mrs. Conrad also rose, although reluctantly.

Jana was not sure whether to hold out her hand, or to embrace her. Daniela took the initiative, hugging Jana.

"Hello, Grandma."

"Hello, Daniela."

Jana broke away from Daniela to extend her hand to Mrs. Conrad, who took it, asking Jana to call her Mimi, trying to be welcoming. They sat stiffly until Daniela broke the silence.

"I finally get to see both my grandmothers. You look sooooo different." The elongated "so" made both women smile. "I'm glad you don't look like each other. It will be easy to tell you apart." She continued to stare at Jana. "I think you look a little like me."

"It would be better to say that you look like Grandmother Jana," Mimi corrected. "She came first."

"I guess so."

"Actually, I think you look a lot like your father," Jana said.

"Was he beautiful?"

"Very beautiful."

"I agree." Mimi's voice had an accent that was softer than most American speech. Jana had seen people in movies who were supposed to be from their South. Mimi's speech sounded like theirs.

"Granddaughters are supposed to look like their grand-mothers. It says so in all the books," Mimi joked. "And if they don't, which very seldom happens because the grand-mother's handbook refuses to let it happen, grandmothers will never admit it."

"She looks like both of us," Jana offered as a compromise.

"Are you very hungry?" Mimi asked.

"I'm too excited to eat much."

"I ordered a fondue for the three of us, so you can eat as much or as little as you want. It's supposed to be good here."

"The waiter said so," Daniela chimed in.

"And here he comes," Mimi added, as several waiters approached, one carrying a large fondue pot full of cheese. He set it over a portable burner, which he ignited. The two others carried plates filled with chunks of bread. With a touch of panache, the waiter distributing the fondue forks ceremoniously presented one to Daniela after spearing a piece of bread with its prongs.

"Dip," he suggested.

She took the fork and very tentatively dipped it into the fondue mix.

Daniela blew on the forkful, then gingerly bit a piece of it off, chewing. "It's good. I like it."

Between bites, they talked about simple things, pleasant events, fashion, movies, keeping the conversation light until the fondue serving dish was wiped clean. Mimi finally asked Daniela if she wanted a dessert.

"I saved space." Her words were emphatic. "I would like a dessert."

Mimi pointed to the other side of the room where a dessert cart stood.

"Go over there. Look the desserts over very carefully, then choose one that you are sure we'll all like. When you get back, you can order for all of us."

Daniela folded her napkin and put it on the table, then very carefully threaded her way through the other diners to the dessert table. The women exchanged glances. They could now talk freely about issues between them that had to be settled before Daniela came back.

"My husband sends his apologies for not being here. He had to attend a session of the World Trade Organization. William wanted to meet you in person, but he chairs the working group on Trade, Debt and Finance. There was no way to break loose.

"William and I agree, if you feel up to it and you want to try to get closer to Daniela, you can have her all day tomorrow."

Jana felt euphoric. "I would like that very much."

"We can let you have the car and driver for the day. I can even make a suggestion about where to go, a place that Daniela is dying to visit." Mimi sighed with regret. "We just haven't had a free day to take her."

"I don't know Switzerland, so all suggestions will be gratefully received." Jana reached over and took Mimi's hand in hers. "Thank you, Mimi."

"Nothing to thank me for. A little girl is better off with two grandmothers. Think of all the presents she'll get."

"We can both spoil her."

"We already have," admitted Mimi. "You should see the things William gets her."

"I'll have to work doubly hard, then," Jana joked, all the while wondering if she would be able to measure up to the Conrads.

Daniela came back to the table, looking satisfied. "I've made my selection."

"You considered all of them?" Jana asked, very seriously.

"All of them."

"Then what's it to be?" Mimi acted excited. "I can't wait."

"It was close, but I chose fudge cake."

"Wonderful," said Mimi.

"You did it!" exclaimed Jana. "I love fudge cake."

Mimi signaled to the waiter.

"Fudge cake for everyone," said Daniela.

Daniela leaned over to Jana, talking in a confidential voice.

"I knew Mimi liked fudge cake, so I ordered it. I really wanted the apricot tart."

Mimi heard her, staring for a moment, not quite approving. "I would have liked the apricot tart as well, Daniela."

"You were trying to please Grandmother Conrad." Jana smiled. "You did a nice thing."

"Yes."

"Then you've succeeded in pleasing both of us."

"Thank you, Daniela," said Mimi, following Jana's lead.

The waiter came back with the three pieces of fudge cake. Daniela was the first to take a bite.

"It's very good. So I would like to thank me, too."

Chapter 25

The sun was brilliant in the sky; with its ferocious reflection on the water it made the blue sheet that was Lake Léman hard to look at. Daniela was already in the car when the driver picked Jana up. Their first stop, as Mimi Conrad had suggested the night before, was to be Vevey, a small town halfway around the lake. It was the place that Daniela wanted to see, not because of its charm, although it had charm like most of the other small towns on the lake, but because it had a statue of Charlie Chaplin. Daniela loved Charlie Chaplin.

There was a movie channel on television "at home" that showed silent comedy films. The Little Tramp had been discovered. Daniela liked Chaplin so much that last Halloween she had dressed like him, moustache, outsized shoes, cane, and all, to go trick-or-treating. Chaplin had once lived on the lake, which was enough to make Daniela happy all the way across the Atlantic: She was going to see Charlie's home. And today was the day! It was what she had been waiting for.

There was a small picnic basket in the car. Within a few kilometers, Daniela was diving into the cookies, insisting on Jana trying each of the three types that had been packed. They agreed that a large vanilla wafer with coffee-flavored filling was their favorite.

"If my mother was your daughter, you must have taken care of her. So, what was my mother like?" Daniela asked with a mouth full of cookie.

The question generated a jolt in the pit of Jana's stomach. She expected questions from Daniela, and dreaded not quite knowing how to answer some of them honestly. Jana might be held responsible for not keeping Daniela's mother safe. Their relationship was very fragile; it could break at the slightest touch.

Finally, she said, "She left home when she was young, too young. I sent Katka to America, to go to school there. There were problems in Slovakia, so she had to be taught there."

"Then what?"

"She grew up."

"Then what?"

"She married your father."

Daniela doggedly kept pursuing her objective. "I know; then I was born. My father got a job in France, Mimi told me. Then he went away. Did my mother go with him?"

"She did."

"Where'd she go?"

"What has Grandma Mimi told you?"

"Grandma Mimi says my mother and father had business to take care of and they had to leave me with Grandma Mimi."

"I guess that's right. Grandmas can't be wrong. We can think of it as a trip."

Daniela realized that Jana had finished her cookie, reached inside the basket, and gave her another one.

"This one is orange."

"I like orange, too."

"Good."

They finally reached Vevey, on the northeast shore of the lake, stopping to watch the swans swim in the little cove on the lakefront before they drove into the town proper. It was, in many respects, a typical French village, with off-white and white one- and two-story buildings, though in a Swiss canton. Vevy also had a major corporate presence, the giant Nestlé's food company headquarters deliberately concealed so not to spoil the look of the town.

With the lake on one side, sitting at the foot of Mount Pelerin, the setting was picture-perfect. There was even a small market in progress in the center of the town. The driver parked the car in a lot placed close enough to make it easy for tourists to get to the city center and slumped down in the front seat to wait for them, while Jana and Daniela walked into the town to do their sightseeing.

They started with the market stalls, looked at the breads and pastries for sale, then the locally made cheeses, at meats in the cases that looked so red, and then they inspected the shops in the village proper. Jana was looking for a present to get Daniela: a pretty gift from her grandmother.

They eventually looked in a shop window that displayed local, hand-made clothing. Daniela's eyes lit up as she saw a small, colorfully beaded purse. Jana immediately noted the pleasure in her granddaughter's eyes and took her into the shop. When they left the store, Daniela was carrying the purse carefully by its little gold chain as they walked hand in hand through the rest of the town until they found the statue of Charlie Chaplin, standing with cane, derby hat, frock coat, and moustache, in front of a culinary museum. Jana assumed that the museum had put up the money for the statue as a tourist attraction. Perhaps that was the only way they could get the people who were passing through town to view their collection.

Suddenly, Jana saw Sabina, Ludovit's partner, not two stores down from them, leaning against the shop window, licking a gelato cone, not at all concerned about being seen. Any action Jana might otherwise have taken was out of the question with her granddaughter at her side. She repressed her anger, forcing herself to focus on Daniela. A few seconds later, they walked past Sabina.

Daniela was not bashful. As soon as she noticed the gelato cone Sabina was eating, she asked if the ice cream was good. Sabina nodded, never taking her eyes off Jana. Daniela insisted that she and Jana find the gelato stand.

Little girls are supposed to be spoiled by their grandparents, Jana told herself. Cookies, desserts, gelato, the goodies were all intended to make her granddaughter happy. And she truly appreciated the look of pleasure on Daniela's face when the little girl took her first taste. Jana's joy was only momentary.

The two of them had just purchased their cones when Jana saw Ludovit a few feet away, peering through an open stall at Jana. He was glaring daggers. If looks could kill, Jana would have been dead.

There was nothing she could do.

She and Daniela walked on.

On reflection, Jana blamed herself. She should have identified Ludovit but not ridiculed him. He would not forget. He would now think of Jana as a threat. It would be a black mark on his record if Jana told his supervisors what a *fine* job of trailing her he had been doing. And if his supervisors told others in the department about it, which they probably would, his associates would laugh at Ludovit. No, what she had done was not smart. As she and Daniela eased past the man, Jana was sure she could feel the heat of his rage.

Jana and her granddaughter were just approaching the parking lot when they heard a man shout from behind them; then several shots were fired, the light pop-pop of a small-caliber gun. Jana grabbed Daniela, bringing the little girl close to her own body to protect her, then carried her quickly to cover behind a large nearby tree.

"Stand here, behind the tree," she ordered Daniela. "I'll

come right back," she assured her. Jana peered around the tree. Thirty meters away, Jana could see someone lying in the street.

Wishing she had smuggled her gun into Switzerland despite the Swiss regulations, Jana began to approach the body, first checking to see if anyone was hiding, waiting to take a shot at her. There was no one, so she picked up her pace, jogging to present a fast-moving target if the shooter was still around. She reached the victim just as other pedestrians came running up.

He lay face down. Jana rolled the man over to look at his face. Ludovit no longer needed to worry about being embarrassed by her. Ludovit was dead.

Jana chose the largest male she could find in the crowd that gathered, telling him to make sure no one else touched the body; then she walked back to Daniela, picked her up, and told her they would have to wait here a little longer. A man had been hurt. The police would want to ask Jana a few questions about how it had happened.

Jana looked back. Sabina stood over Ludovit, staring at Jana. Jana wondered if Sabina thought she had killed him.

It would make things very difficult.

Chapter 26

The Swiss like to keep their cities clean. Their police do not like litter, particularly when foreigners are involved in the littering. They like it even less when the litter consists of murder victims. It was not that the Swiss police weren't nice to Jana; it was just that there was a faint aura of distaste about the event. The examination and recording of the crime scene was absolutely correct and precise, but performed with an air of fastidiousness that made Jana doubt that the Swiss police would do any of the dirty work that goes into solving most homicides.

They dealt with both Jana and Sabina in the same manner: cool, exact, and to the point. Eventually, both Jana and Sabina found themselves in a waiting room. Daniela had been taken away by a frightened and angry Mimi, who had made matters even worse by yelling at Jana.

"You should never have taken Daniela, and I should never have let you," she had shouted. "William warned me. He said you shouldn't be trusted with a child." She was very upset and needed to blame someone.

At least Mimi had allowed Jana to hug Daniela before she was driven away. It was hard for Jana to let her granddaughter go, even worse when she saw the car depart and realized that Daniela had left behind the little beaded purse.

The inspector in charge of the case had already summoned Jana twice. As Jana had anticipated, he had been intrigued by the fact that all of the principals—the dead man, Jana, and Sabina—were Slovak police officers. Then he became irate. The inspector was not angry at Jana, but at the Slovaks for sending police into Switzerland without alerting their Swiss colleagues and getting permission. He become even angrier when Jana told him that she had no information as to why the two were following her. After a few minutes, the inspector sent for Sabina. Jana was asked to wait outside. When Sabina emerged forty-five minutes later, the smug expression on her face when she glanced at Jana told her that Sabina had made it look as bad for her as she could. Jana was now the prime suspect, with no one else in sight.

The inspector called her back into his office for what had become an interrogation.

"You're a commander in the Slovak police?"

"I told you that."

"You didn't tell me that you were a major suspect in an investigation going on in Slovakia, and that the dead man was one of those who was a part of the investigation team assigned to gather evidence."

"I'm not aware of any charges, and I don't know about any investigation of my conduct. The only thing I was made aware of occurred yesterday, when I saw that two Slovak officers were following me."

The inspector tried sarcasm. "You knew they were police. Come on! Any fool with a minimum of common sense, particularly a commander with long experience, would know that they were there because you were suspected of a criminal act."

Jana studied the man, deciding she had to get as much information as she could from him. She needed to unravel the whole picture, not only here but in Slovakia.

"I think that after you talked to Sabina, you called Slovakia and confirmed what she told you. They must have informed you as to the scope of their investigation. I assure you that I'll tell you everything I know about any charges that may be pending. But I need to know what those charges are."

The inspector stared at her for a long time. "I had to assure the people in Slovakia that I would not reveal anything about their suspicions."

"You talked to my granddaughter before she left. She's a very bright little girl."

"Quite bright."

"Then she told you that I was with *her* when we heard the sounds of gunfire. You didn't find any gun in the area. I didn't have a gun, and I never left the scene of the murder." She threw the inspector's words back at him. "This has to mean, for any 'fool with common sense,' that I didn't kill anyone."

The inspector grimaced. "The dead man's partner, the other police officer, says you had a confederate lying in wait for the victim."

"Why would I want to kill that poor fool Ludovit? I knew they were both following me. I confronted them yesterday. So what? That wasn't motive for me to murder a man. Even more to the point, why would I kill a man knowing that he had a partner in the area? I saw her just before the killing. She must have told you that as well. I knew she was there. And, if I had set up a murder for a confederate to commit, I wouldn't have set it up where my granddaughter could witness it, or worse, might be in danger. You were the one who brought up the 'common sense' issue, Inspector."

Jana pressed on. "You informed whoever you talked to in Slovakia that you would keep the facts of their investigation secret. That doesn't mean that you'd keep the name of the person you talked to secret. That's not a *fact* of their investigation. So, who was it?"

The inspector thought about it for a moment, wondering whether he should divulge the person's name. "I prefer not to tell you. They said you were a very fine homicide detective." He paused, trying to decide if it was within his dignity to ask for her opinion, then decided to continue. "Tell me what you think happened, and perhaps—just perhaps, mind you—I may be able to give you some information."

Jana had been thinking about the events surrounding the killing anyway. Although she had not particularly enjoyed being followed by Ludovit, she wanted his killer caught.

"Remember, you interviewed the witnesses; I didn't. So I may be short on needed information." She ran the events of the killing through her mind. "However, I can try. What do you want from me?"

"Who were the man's enemies?"

"All police officers make enemies. His partner, Sabina, is in a better position to answer that."

"I asked her. She said there wasn't anyone she could point to."

"No witnesses saw the shooter run from the scene?"

"Too many people; too crowded. They saw no one."

"They all looked at the victim on the sidewalk, not at the person leaving the scene. Which means the shooter probably walked away without calling attention to himself."

"How do you kill someone in a sunlit market without being identified?"

"It's done all the time."

"Not here, in Switzerland."

"It happens."

"I suppose."

He still sounded reluctant to believe the killing had occurred, that a man had been murdered in his canton.

"Was he shot in the front or the back?" Jana asked.

"Body shots, both at a slight angle, from the right side."

"Close shots?"

"No powder burns, so not very close."

"Was there a wide spread to the entry wounds?"

"Yes, quite a wide spread."

"A face in the crowd then, standing at a distance from him." She thought about the position of the body and the shots. "He saw someone."

"The victim saw the murderer?"

"Yes. I also think it was a person he knew."

The inspector considered her statement.

"The victim shouted just before the shots," she reminded him. "Perhaps he was trying to yell at the murderer? Maybe trying to get someone's attention? It sounded like a command or an order. Or a warning."

"Perhaps a request for help?" the inspector suggested. "Other people heard the shout. So?"

"None of them understood his words, correct?"

"Correct."

"The tone of voice was very strong. No fear in it. So it was not a cry for help. The shout might have been garbled. But Ludovit shouted before he was hit. He spoke bad French, which might account for it seeming to be garbled. However, under the circumstances, the surprise, the speed of the events, I think he was probably shouting in Slovak. There were four Slovaks there: Sabina, me, Ludovit himself, and, I think, the murderer. Ludovit wasn't trying to call to Sabina. He was facing me. So he was either calling to me, or to the murderer. I think he was calling to the killer. I think he knew him. And I think the murderer already had his gun out, and Ludovit saw it."

The inspector looked impressed. "Okay, he was calling to you or to the murderer. How do you know the murderer already had the gun out?"

"The shout immediately preceded the gunshots. Unless the murderer was a quick draw, like in American Westerns, the murderer had already drawn his gun."

"Preparing to shoot the victim?"

"Maybe."

"Why 'maybe'?"

"Maybe the killer was going to shoot *me*."

The inspector's eyes widened. He had not considered that possibility.

"Do you know who it might be?"

"Not even a wild conjecture. I have no facts, Inspector."

The inspector considered the issues, finally nodding. "You've analyzed the facts very well."

"I gave you what I could. Now, it's your turn to give me a fact or two."

The inspector nodded, choosing his words carefully. "I made a promise to the person I talked to in Slovakia that I would not compromise the case being worked on. However, there was one thing, I believe, that had nothing to do with that case. The person spoke freely to me about you and Sabina and Ludovit. He explained why the two officers were here. He tried to explain that, due to the nature of the case and the importance of confidentiality, your police had not contacted us about operating in Switzerland." He hesitated.

"You promised a return for my help in the case, Inspector," Jana reminded him, trying to gain as much information as possible.

"I'm trying to think how to phrase this." He pursed his lips, rubbing his face, getting up steam. "The person I talked to was unhappy to hear about what had happened to his colleague, Ludovit. This person was not very concerned about Sabina, the other officer. However, this person was very concerned about you in a very, how shall I put it, in a very *caring* way. There was worry for your personal safety."

The last fact surprised Jana. It was not what she expected.

The inspector stood, somewhat reluctantly shook hands, and told her she was free to go after her statement was typed up and signed. He wished her a safe trip, then added one more thought. "When you see them, please tell your colleagues in Slovakia to keep Slovak concerns and criminal acts out of Switzerland. They only make my life harder." He went back to his work.

Jana walked into the waiting room and seated herself near Sabina. Sabina looked uncomfortable. She hadn't expected Jana to emerge from the inspector's office without handcuffs.

"Sabina," Jana began, trying to warm her up. "I am sorry about Ludovit. If you ask the inspector, I think he will tell you that he doesn't believe I had a hand in Ludovit's death."

"That's his opinion, not mine."

Jana stopped herself. There was no use trying to reason with the woman. She had to try a different approach.

Jana needed to find out who was in charge of the investigation, the person who had sent two Slovak police officers to follow Jana to Switzerland. Only two people, to Jana's knowledge, knew about her trip: Trokan and Peter. She had a suspicion, but it was hard for her to believe it was either one of them. No matter. She plunged ahead.

"When I was in his office, the inspector called the procurator assigned to your special investigation team. He told us *you* had to be considered a suspect in Ludovit's murder."

Sabina reacted with shock. "How could *I* be a suspect?"

"He said there was bad blood between you and Ludovit, and because of it he had considered not sending the two of you out of the country together."

"There was no bad blood between us! None at all!"

"Then why would Peter say there was?"

"He is absolutely mistaken."

"You will have to talk to Peter when you get back, to correct his impression."

"I can't understand why he would believe this."

"Probably a word or two from another police officer? Perhaps a co-worker who was jealous that you got to go out of the country?"

"I'll bet I know who it is." Sabine's voice had venom in it. "I'll take care of her when I get back."

"Good idea," Jana agreed, trying to relax, but finding it absolutely impossible. She now knew that Peter, her lover, the man she had begun to think of as her mate, was trying to put her in prison.

Her granddaughter had been taken away from her. Her lover was false. She was all alone again.

Jana went back to her hotel. Before she left Geneva she tried to telephone Mimi and her husband. There was no answer. She left messages. There was no response.

She almost called Peter. Almost.

The next day Jana flew to Ukraine.

Chapter 27

The flight to Kiev was uncomfortable. Turbulence tossed the passengers back and forth. Their discomfort was exacerbated by the attitudes of the Aeroflot crew's two stewardesses. They were more interested in conversing with each other through their clouds of cigarette smoke than in paying attention to the passengers. And the pilots apparently thought they were participating in an aerial circus. Coffee was dumped on passengers, children ran up and down the aisles while their mothers screamed at them, a fight broke out between two men, and the general level of conversation kept rising so the speakers could be heard above the din, which only added more noise. When they reached Boryspil Airport, instead of using a glide path, the cowboys in the cockpit, as Jana now thought of them, peeled off and powered in. Jana was happy to have survived, only recovering fully when she found that Alexi had sent a police officer to accelerate her passage through customs.

They deposited her baggage at the hotel and left immediately with the "package" she'd brought for the captain. The driver, siren wailing, drove like a madman. By the time they reached headquarters, Jana was convinced once more that all Ukrainians were insane.

The man escorted her to the captain's office and knocked. A yell in Ukrainian commanded Jana to enter. Alexi, a heavy-set man with a large paunch and the rosy complexion of a drinker, came bounding out of his chair with remarkable quickness and energy for a man of his size, enfolding her in a bear hug while quickly relieving her of the package she carried.

"I am so pleased to see you. You have come at just the right moment," he rattled on, this time in Russian so Jana could understand him better. "I have more information."

He ripped open the package Jana had carried from Slovakia, first pulling out the bottle of Borovicka, then the Slivovitza, heaving a sigh of pleasure as he set them on his desk. "You've kept your end of the bargain, so I will fulfill mine, with a small bonus. But first, a drink." He waved her to a chair. "Sit, sit; that was a long journey, and we have to make sure you're comfortable enough to enjoy our Ukrainian hospitality."

As if on cue, the officer who had met her brought in a tray with glasses. He was followed by another, carrying a coffee cup. He was Cziuba, his warrant officer, Alexi explained, who would be going with Jana to question Veza, the Club Exotique manager. Bilyk, the man who had picked Jana up, poured Borovicka into three glasses. As soon as he put the bottle down, Cziuba picked it up and filled his coffee cup.

Alexi scoffed at the glass in his hand. "The doctor says I have to drink less, so I must use these small things." He muttered a toast, all of them, except Cziuba, downing the Borovicka in one gulp. Cziuba sipped at the contents of his cup, not in any hurry to finish.

Alexi smacked his lips, looking longingly at the bottles, then told Bilyk to put them away. As Bylik left, Alexi settled in his chair with a groan of satisfaction, still savoring the drink. "I'm like the man dying of dehydration in the desert limited to two small sips of liquid per day. Not enough. It still leaves you with a horrible thirst."

Cziuba continued to sip, Alexi glaring at him.

"He does that deliberately, to torment me."

"Kremenchuk," Cziuba reminded him, peering over the cup rim.

"Yes, Kremenchuk." Alexi settled deeper into his seat, focusing on Jana.

"I had a good man check the place in Kremenchuk. He knew about it already. A bar that doubles as a place to buy women."

"Veza ran one in Slovakia." Jana leaned forward, getting even more interested. "It seems we are dealing with a society of pimps. Except I don't think that's what this is about."

Cziuba made a sound of agreement before tilting his cup to take another mouthful of Borovicka.

Alexi shot him an angry look, licking his lips again, swallowing hard, murmuring something at Cziuba that was not polite; then he refocused on Jana.

"My man in Kremenchuk asked about the Guzak brothers. No one had ever heard of them. My man says they were lying. They were terrified when he mentioned their names. I trust his judgment." He sneaked another envious look at Cziuba. "So, one or both of the Guzaks were there at one time or another. My guy thinks it was recently. He will continue to poke around, but he believes there is a problem. The criminal community isn't acting normally. Lots of turmoil. An argument between gangs, maybe? Even the worst thugs are afraid. So we can't depend upon obtaining information on the Guzaks in the next few days. If our man finds out why everyone is frightened, we'll let you know."

"They're very bad people down there." Cziuba took a last sip from the cup, holding it upside down so everyone could see it was empty, eliciting a grunt from Alexi. "They're all ruthless bastards. Whoever or whatever is scaring them has to be one son-of-a-bitch.

"Now, a nice piece of additional information for you." Alexi went into his top drawer and pulled out a folder, handing it to Jana. "Look at them."

Jana checked the two sheets of paper in the folder. "Telephone numbers?"

Alexi nodded, gesturing at Cziuba to explain.

"We got lucky. May I?" He took the folder from Jana. "The informant we used to locate Veza is involved in another investigation. The investigation has a telephone tap on the line where Veza is. We captured all the ingoing and outgoing calls. Not many. It was a dead line for conversation with nothing on it until Veza began using it again." He pointed out sections of the two pages to Jana. "The calls out are to Kremenchuk, Bratislava, and Vienna. There were four incoming calls. One came from a small town in Hungary, two from Bratislava. The other one was, from all places, Kathmandu in Nepal. Everything else was outgoing. We tracked the location of the Kremenchuk calls. They go to the bar our man checked out."

"That means Veza is tied in, one way or the other, with the Guzaks," Jana said. "Whether friend or enemy, still has to be answered. Have you matched the numbers with addresses?"

"Just the Kremenchuk ones; not yet as to the other numbers. It's hard to get information from the Austrians. They're always arguing invasion of privacy. We're working on it. The Bratislava numbers we figured you would help us with. There are only two of them. The Nepal call was from a hotel in Kathmandu. We haven't got to it yet. It's really too far away for me to worry about."

"I assume you recorded all the conversations?"

Cziuba handed the folder with the numbers back to Jana. "Yes. On the outgoing Veza calls, he identifies himself. Then the other party, no matter where the calls are made to, hangs up. Veza curses, screams at the dead phone, calls again begging whoever it is to not hang up, but they hang up as soon as they hear his voice."

Alexi laughed. "Whoever they are, his people have written him off. Veza stays in his apartment all day, only going out to shop. Once he went walking toward a movie. He strolled for a few blocks, then apparently thought better of it and ran back to his apartment in a panic. What set him off, we don't know. There was nothing there. I think he spooked himself."

"You said three incoming calls. That means you have recordings of what was said by the party calling in."

Cziuba pointed to the last page. All the calls had been picked up by an answering machine.

"One, Kathmandu. A man. He said, 'This is Solti. Tell me why I'm not seeing anyone.' Two was from a small Hungarian town. Whoever it was didn't leave a message. Three, two calls from Bratislava. One from a woman. She told him she loved him, then hung up. She said her name was Andreea."

Jana checked the numbers in Bratislava. One of them she immediately identified; the other one was familiar but just out of reach of her memory.

"I think I know who made one of these calls: I've met his girlfriend in Bratislava." She checked the date of the first phone call, thinking the woman might have warned him, but it had been made a week before Jana had confronted her in her apartment. Too early for her to tell the boyfriend that the Slovak police were looking for him. "I know the other number, but the file in my head isn't opening yet. I'll follow up on it when I'm back in Bratislava." She checked on the number of the call to Hungary. She recognized the town it had been made from. It was where the Hungarian smuggler had been cut to pieces.

More and more connections. The outlines of events were becoming faintly visible.

"Are we ready to go now?" Alexi asked Cziuba.

"Any time," Cziuba responded.

Alexi looked at Jana. "Ready to go talk to Veza?"

"That's why I came."

"We'll get you a vest in case there are any stray bullets to deal with. Anything else?"

"I couldn't bring my sidearm."

Alexi pulled an automatic in a waist-clip holster from the bottom drawer of his desk, sliding it over to her.

"Just so you don't feel naked. Don't fire it unless you absolutely have to. I don't want to answer questions as to why I gave you a gun. And don't shoot yourself in the foot."

"I promise not to shoot myself in the foot."

Jana had one last query. "What was the investigation about that made your people put a tap on the phone?"

"A botched bank robbery."

Cziuba shook his head in incredulity. "These people never learn. One criminal thug leads us to the other. The man who let Veza use his couch is Veza's cousin. His name is Omelchenko. We've held off arresting him because there were some other locals involved. We thought Omelchenko might lead us to them. He hasn't. But he led us to Veza. Now that his cousin Veza has come to visit, we can arrest them both."

"Omelchenko is a murderer," Alexi added. "Two people were killed in the bank robbery. Which is the reason I gave you the gun." His voice took on a mock-serious note. "You don't mind going along while we also do some Ukrainian business?"

"It's all part of the same business."

Both men nodded.

All of them understood: They were professionals.

Chapter 28

They drove to Svyatoshyn, the area where Veza had taken refuge, parking around the corner from the block of buildings where he was hiding. Seconds after their arrival two truckloads of Special Response Group police, bulked up with battle gear, squealed to a stop. The SRG team piled out and trotted to predesignated positions. The main group headed directly to the target's address. Jana noted with satisfaction that they appeared to be well trained, single-mindedly going about their tasks.

Jana and the two Ukrainian officers she'd come with dog-trotted behind the main body of SRG cops, watching them again break up into small teams as they reached the building. The flat they wanted was on the top floor of the six-story apartment house and, within minutes, elements of the assault unit were on the sixth floor of the building, signaling from a window that their people were in place.

Cziuba led the way into the structure, Jana and Bilyk following. Cziuba nodded at the two police officers who had secured the entry hall, and went to the elevator. Another police officer was inside it, at the control panel; he held the door for them, then punched the button for six. The car slowly ascended.

"This is your last opportunity to wait for us downstairs," Cziuba remarked.

"The elevator is already going up," Jana pointed out.

"Would you have taken my suggestion if I'd asked you before the doors closed?"

"No."

"So, what's the difference? The difference is this: if you now get killed, I can write in my report that I gave you the choice, you chose to go into danger, and I will have satisfied everyone who reviews the record. They'll know I tried to keep you safe."

"Brilliant foresight. I'm pleased that you did your best to keep me safe."

The door to the elevator door opened. They drew their guns as they got out. The SRG team had taken up positions in the corridor, having already knocked on most of the doors, removing the occupants from their apartments and taking them down the stairs. They were clearing the line of fire, protecting the residents from stray bullets.

"It might have been easier and safer to just kick in the door," Jana pointed out. "The sounds of people moving around will have alerted them."

"There was no choice. At least one of them inside is a shooter." He pointed to the metal door of an apartment they passed. "Their door is metal, too. Lots of people have metal doors now in Kiev; harder for thieves to break in."

"Thieves who are afraid of other thieves. I like that thought."

They reached the apartment door. A sapper was taping explosives around the frame, getting ready to blow it.

"Very efficient."

"It comes with experience."

"Are we sure that the two men we want are inside?"

"Surveillance confirms that they haven't come out."

"Are you just going to blow it without talking to them?"

"We blow the door, the entry team throws a pair of stun and flash grenades inside, and then we rush them."

"Since they probably know we're here, and there's no element of surprise, it won't hurt to talk to them first."

"They're armed. My guess is that they won't want to surrender."

"You used the word 'guess.' Let's take that out of the equation and reason with them."

Cziuba looked over to Bilyk, who nodded his approval, then handed Jana his cell phone. Jana had Veza's number from the telephone tap and punched it in. It was answered immediately.

The voice on the phone was so excited and disturbed that what he gabbled into the phone was unintelligible.

"Veza. *Volam sa* Jana Matinova." It calmed people down when you formally introduced yourself. Jana waited for a response. There was none. "Talk to me. Speak to me in Slovak, Veza."

Veza spoke again, quickly but articulately. "I am not afraid. Killing me won't be easy. We have weapons. Stay out!"

"Veza, we're the police. Why would we want to kill you? Listen, I've come all the way from Slovakia to talk. So let's talk."

"Don't fool with me. I know who you're from."

"Who am I from, Veza?" There was silence on the phone. "I'm not from the ones trying to murder you. I'm trying to find them; you're trying to get away from them. That's a perfect reason for us to cooperate. If we cooperate, we can each get what we need: we'll protect you; then you'll tell us about them, and we'll make sure they we get them before they get you. What do you think of this offer?"

There was another long silence.

"Veza, if you want, I'll come into the apartment alone so we can meet and talk things out. You have a gun. I'll leave my gun outside. How's that?"

The phone in the apartment was mute, except for the muffled voices Jana could hear arguing, an argument that went on for minutes before Veza finally came back on the phone.

"You can't come in."

"Your cousin doesn't want me inside, right?"

" . . . Yes."

"Tell him to get on the phone."

His hand came back over the phone, with another muffled argument taking place. Veza came back on. "He doesn't want to talk to you."

"Tell him that you're both dead men if he does not get on the phone."

The muffled argument that ensued was much louder and sharper. The cousin finally took the phone.

"Fuck you," were the first two words out of his mouth. "Fuck your mother," were the next three, all of them screamed into the phone. Jana waited, hoping the man would calm down. After a long silence, she began again, introducing herself, then asked his name.

"None of your business. Get off the phone and go to hell."

"I presume I am now talking to Mr. Omelchenko. Just listen to me, dear cousin of Veza. I think Cousin Veza is now my friend. If you listen to me like Cousin Veza did, you too may become my friend. Even better, you may still be alive at the end of the day."

Jana could hear Omelchenko's heavy breathing. At least he had stayed on the line.

"Here is what's going to happen if you don't do as I suggest. There are a dozen police officers on this floor. There are a dozen more in various places in the building. If you refuse to let them in, they've set explosive charges on the door and they will blow it open. It's possible that the charges are so large that they may blow you out into the street below. That would kill both of you." Jana waited, listening again. Omelchenko's breathing was louder. "When they blow the door, they won't wait for you to shoot at them. They'll toss in grenades. These aren't generally lethal grenades, although you could be killed by some of the small shrapnel particles.

"Our special operations group may choose to come in at that time. Needless to say, if you shoot at them they'll fire back at you with their assault weapons, probably killing both you and Veza immediately. If you're only wounded, they may take you into custody and you might survive if you get the correct medical treatment."

Jana waited for a moment to let all the implications of what she had said to sink in.

"A few more things to consider while you're deciding what you should do." The heavy breathing on the phone was now erratic. "If you're alive to shoot it out with the police, the police may simply roll a real grenade inside the room after they gain access. That will only leave pieces of you. Police don't arrest pieces of a person, so you'll save yourself from being arrested. If you shoot it out, and the police shoot their way in, which they eventually will, and if any of their comrades have been wounded in the fight, they'll assuredly take no prisoners. Either they will simply kill you on the spot, or maybe they'll just shoot you in the belly and watch you die slowly, in agony. But, either way, you die."

Omelchenko finally got a few words out. "Who are you?"

"I gave you my name."

"Can you speak for the police?"

"Who do you think I'm speaking for?"

"You guarantee my safety?" He was panting with fear. "I need your word."

"Cousin Omelchenko, I'll even guarantee your cousin's safety."

"I want to talk to Veza about this."

"Fine. Now I'll hang up."

"Why are you hanging up?" There was genuine fright in the man's voice. "I may want to talk more."

"No more conversation. In the next two minutes you knock loudly on the inside of the door to let us know you're coming out. You wait thirty seconds, then open the door and come out with your hands on your head. You walk to the opposite wall of the corridor and stand facing the wall. We'll then handcuff you and take you safely to jail. Of course, if we see you with a gun or any other weapon, we'll shoot you dead." She paused, letting the tension build. "Oh, I forgot something. There are snipers in the building across the street. I hope they don't shoot you before you come out."

Jana hung up.

Within two minutes they heard banging from inside the door. Thirty seconds later the two men were in custody. Cziuba and Bilyk were only slightly disappointed that they had not been required to shoot their way into the apartment.

When they got back to the police building, Alexi had already been informed. When he saw Jana, he kissed her on both cheeks.

The only one who seemed annoyed was Veza. He now had second thoughts about talking to Jana. He didn't want to talk to Cziuba or Bilyk, adamant that he didn't want to talk to any police. He wanted to be put in a cell and left alone.

Alexi had Cziuba take Veza to an interrogation room despite his protests. As Cziuba left, he winked at Jana before closing the door behind them.

Jana sat across from Veza at the small table in the middle of the interrogation area, simply looking at the man. He wouldn't meet her eyes. Andreea, Veza's girlfriend, was right: Veza was a coward. So was his cousin. Maybe it ran in the family.

Within five minutes, Veza was chattering, telling her everything he knew. It was not much information, but it was vital.

The next morning Jana flew back to Slovakia.

The trip had been worth it.

She couldn't wait to get back to Bratislava. She didn't even mind the aerobatics the pilots put the plane through.

Chapter 29

When the plane landed in Bratislava, Trokan was waiting. He would not have come to pick her up if it had not been important to see her immediately. His grim face told Jana he had bad news. She had her own car in the parking lot, but one of her aides would pick it up later. It was obviously imperative that she go with Trokan now. Aside from saying hello, Trokan and Jana did not exchange a word until they'd left the pickup zone.

"A fruitful trip?"

"I have more evidence to work with now."

"I'm happy we didn't waste the country's money." He braked to avoid a car that darted in front of them from an intersection. "An old person. Driving that way because he's night-blind."

"Just careless."

"I was wondering if you've been careless. Perhaps 'thoughtless' is a better word."

"Rotten traits in a police officer."

"Unhealthy qualities." He put the brakes on again; the car that had pulled ahead of them had slowed, then swerved off onto a side road. "That man is careless and thoughtless enough to get other people hurt."

"I drive carefully." Jana decided to stop being oblique. It was getting on her nerves. "Let's get to it: am I in trouble?"

"Your house is a mess. They searched it. I checked before I came by for you. You'll have a hell of job cleaning it up."

Jana's heart sank. She'd forgotten Trokan's warning. Jana felt the small lump the diamond made in her brassiere to reassure herself that it was still there.

"They also searched your office, and your adjutant's."

"I thought Seges was working with them."

"He is. They wanted to make it look good for him. He played his part afterward, loudly stating that he could not understand what had raised their suspicions about you, and therefore, him."

"I would appreciate your letting me ship him somewhere."

"Nobody wants him." He groaned. "I talked to Captain Bohumil. He wouldn't tell me what they found, or what they were looking for. Under the circumstances, I couldn't press for the information. I'm reasonably certain they took nothing from your office. You'll have to determine if they took anything from your home."

"There was nothing to take."

"Bohumil wanted to pick you up at the airport. I dissuaded him by agreeing to bring you to him as soon as you landed."

"We're going to headquarters? I just got back from a long flight."

"He's interrogating other people. He doesn't want you to talk to them before he talks to you."

"Not so stupid."

"He's a decent investigator."

They rolled into the city proper and were approaching the main police building. Trokan pulled the car to the side of the road next to a small park.

"I have a sudden need to relieve my bladder. If you feel the need to relieve yourself at this time of whatever it is you have to relieve yourself of, I suggest you do so as well. I'll be gone for a very brief time."

He got out of the car and walked into the park. There was no doubt what Trokan wanted Jana to do: hide the diamond so it was not on her when she was questioned. Jana pulled it out of her bra and felt around under the seat, then found an opening at the edge of the cloth above the springs and tucked the diamond inside. She could retrieve it later. Within a few seconds Trokan emerged from the park and got into the car, sighing in satisfaction.

"Now I feel better. I trust you do too."

He drove her to the police building. Very politely he wished her a good night, and left.

The policeman at the entrance saluted her when she came in but didn't exchange any of the usual pleasantries, keeping his eyes fixed straight ahead. The word that she was the subject of an investigation had gotten out. She would have to expect the same treatment from the other officers, perhaps worse. She would be a pariah.

Jana needed the exercise, so she walked up to the fifth floor, passing from what was a mostly deserted building into a beehive of activity. There were uniformed police, investigators, clerks, civilians, a number of politicians she had seen on television, as well as people she had never seen before, sitting hunched on benches. There were surprises as she recognized some of them. Sila Covic, the Red Devil, was there glaring at everyone. Jana recognized a man from the finance ministry she knew slightly, and another minor official from the ministry of justice. On one end of the crowded benches sat Ivan Boryda, and on the other end sat Sofia, each of them looking unhappy, both of them trying hard not to look at the other. She was walking toward Sofia when she was intercepted by Sabina Postova, the police officer who had followed her to Switzerland.

The woman was stiff, still angry, and pleased with herself for being in a position of command now. "Jana Matinova, you're to come with me."

Jana ignored the slight implied by the omission of her rank. She needed to remain calm and clearheaded, ready to dispel any notions they had developed about her in relationship to whatever it was they were investigating. Sabina walked her down the corridor and into the inner offices, finally selecting one in which another policewoman was waiting. Trokan was right to have Jana get rid of the diamond: she had to undergo a strip search.

Sabina enjoyed every second of what she perceived as Jana's humiliation, dragging it out as long as possible before permitting Jana to put her clothes back on. Sabina even gave Jana a slight push as she left the office.

"Sabina, one more push and you will regret *both* of them."

"Go ahead, tell me that you're innocent! I can't wait to hear that coming from your mouth."

The other officer tugged at Sabina's arm, muttering a caution, trying to calm her down.

"She was responsible for Ludovit's death," Sabina hissed. "You know that, and I know that, and she should be made to admit it."

The other woman kept talking to her, pulling her back into the room. She was forced to step in front of Postova to stop her from going after Jana as they walked to the captain's office.

Jana knew Captain Bohumil. It was impossible for Jana not to know everyone who was in the police hierarchy in Bratislava. But she did not know Bohumil well enough to predict his moods. They were not social friends, but each was aware of the other's reputation. Bohumil was solid, perhaps too solid; not inventive, but honest. And, of all the things Jana had going for her, she was still a commander in the police, and Bohumil was a captain. He could not forget that.

When Jana walked in, Bohumil had a recording unit on his desk and made a great show of activating it, perhaps to make her nervous enough to blurt out something incriminating. He waved an unhappy Sabina out of the office, asking Jana to sit down, motioning the other officer who had brought Jana into the room to sit in a chair that had been strategically placed to one side, in back of Jana.

"I'm Captain Bohumil." He recited the date and place of the interview for the benefit of the recording machine. "Please state your name for the record," he requested. Jana gave her name and police rank. Bohumil then related the rest of the required prelude to the questioning to set the stage for the interrogation. "We're here today to discuss an investigation of official corruption, violation of customs laws and regulations, bribery, money-laundering, and official misconduct." He droned on, citing at least a dozen felonies. At last Jana had some idea of what the investigation was about.

"Do you admit or deny any of these allegations?"

"I deny all of those charges, and any other charges. For the record, I protest the indignities I've already been forced to go through, and I'll report them to both the general and the minister."

"Your denial and protest are on the record."

He made a notation in a notebook he had on his desk, then closed the book with a snap. "I'll be frank. For the past six to eight weeks, we've been working on a case involving the smuggling of contraband both into the country and out of the country. Agencies from the other European states have been cooperating. The United States, Canada, and countries in Latin America are interested as well. Before we started the actual gathering of evidence, we heard rumors of an international criminal ring being involved in this. We began slowly gathering evidence, but it was not until six weeks ago that a credible source informed us that you were involved."

Jana wondered who this *credible* source was.

"Captain, I have been involved in the investigation and prosecution of crimes for years. There are lots of people out there who would swear that I've committed criminal acts just to get back at me. They'd do that without a qualm, despite the lack of truth to their charges."

"I said 'credible,' not 'criminal.'"

"Obviously it's someone who has a grievance against me."

"I'm sure this person doesn't."

"Who is the person?"

"That's confidential."

"Then tell me what the person said."

"That you have consistently given this criminal group inside information so they could avoid prosecution."

Jana straightened up, pressing herself against the back of her chair, fuming at the suggestion that she would compromise any case she investigated.

"Specifically, what cases have I investigated that I set out to destroy?"

"Not your cases, Commander. *My* cases."

Jana was shaken.

"Impossible. I don't know anything about your cases. How could I? Who would tell me?"

"Then how do you explain these reports that we found in your house after we searched it yesterday?" He took a folder from his desk and waved it in the air. "Not one case report, but three. How do you explain them?"

Jana gawked at the folder, making a huge effort to pull herself together, shaking her head in disbelief.

"Impossible. I didn't take them from this building. I didn't have them in my house." She started to rise and felt the hand of the officer behind her on her shoulder. She sat back down, telling herself to remain calm.

"I want to see these reports," she said.

"They're confidential."

"If I'd had them, I would've read them already, so the information they contain would no longer be secret. Consequently, there's no reason not to show me the reports."

Bohumil shook his head, refusing to let her examine the reports.

"Did you run the reports you recovered for fingerprints?"

Bohumil's eyes glazed over, then snapped back into focus. "That's none of your business."

"Don't be stupid. Of *course* it's my business. If I had brought those reports home and examined them closely enough to give someone information about their contents, I would have left my fingerprints on them." Jana couldn't stop the anger from bubbling up inside her. "You dolt, if my fingerprints were on the reports, that would be conclusive evidence that I'd handled them, hence of my guilt." Again, she was forced to calm herself. "As well, if anyone else in your department, or mine, or any other police officer handled the reports, their prints would probably be on them."

The woman behind her finally spoke. "We'd also need to identify the chain of people fingering the reports from the time of discovery until now, Captain."

Bohumil reluctantly nodded.

Jana turned in her chair to face the woman. "Thank you, Officer. Perhaps you have a nose for this work." She turned back to Bohumil. "There'll soon be a vacancy in my unit. Can you guess who it will be?"

The captain took a deep breath.

"It wasn't Seges who informed on you."

Each tried to outstare the other. Jana broke contact first, realizing how juvenile she was being. Another issue was also probably disturbing Bohumil. Jana had to deal with it.

"I didn't have anything to do with the death of Ludovit in Switzerland, Captain. The Swiss police will tell you I couldn't possibly have fired the shots that killed him. There was no reason for me to participate in a plot against him. I think Ludovit saw someone in the crowd, and they recognized each other. The person in the crowd was quicker to shoot. I think that person may have been after me, and Ludovit may have tried to stop him."

Bohumil had a quizzical expression on his face. "You think he tried to save you?"

"I think he may have." She waited for the information to sink in. "If that's the case, if Ludovit tried to stop someone from killing me, we have to ask ourselves why the killer was after me. Then, perhaps, you may explain the presence of the reports in my house."

"Are you saying that the shooter may have been after you because, in some peripheral way, you have something to do with this investigation?"

"Possible." She thought through the events. "You searched my house to find an item you thought was there. Were you searching to find these reports, or was it some other piece of evidence you hoped to find, an object that you'd been told would be there?"

The captain fiddled with his pencil, not replying.

"A suggestion: you have insufficient evidence to take me into custody. There are leads that you have to pursue, and leads that I have to pursue. We each have to go ahead."

The door to the office opened. Jana shifted to see who had come in.

It was Peter. He and Jana exchanged glances. Jana felt the earth giving way.

They said nothing to each other.

"I think we are finished for the moment, Commander." Peter gestured toward the door. "You're free to go now."

Jana quickly looked around the room before she left. It was not apparent, but it had to be there. There was a microphone in the room, and Peter had listened to the conversation between Jana and Bohumil. That way, both men could hear exactly how she responded and would later compare their observations.

Jana did not look at Peter as she left the room. She took the stairs so she wouldn't have to see the people who were still waiting in the entry hall. Jana wasn't up to facing anyone. It was all she could do to walk down the steps without breaking into tears.

Chapter 30

Trokan was right: her house was a mess. She worked on it all morning and into the early part of the afternoon, and had almost finished when there was a knock on her door. Giles, his jeweled glasses prominently perched on his nose, stood outside, smiling up at her. It made Jana very uneasy. Giles knew the rules: he couldn't come to her house under any circumstances. And the rules of the police department were every bit as explicit: police officers couldn't privately associate or socialize with informants or known criminals. Even worse, Jana was expecting them to set up a police observation of her, and her home, because of the ongoing investigation. An officer on surveillance would have unquestionably seen Giles come up to the house. Jana opened the door, but rather than letting Giles come in, she prodded him further out.

"Walk back to the sidewalk, Giles." She took his elbow, edging him down the walk, Giles protesting her lack of hospitality at every step.

"You know the game, Giles," she continued. "You never come to my house. You stay away from my life." She looked around for Spis, his bodyguard. He was sitting in a car, his face and head bandaged. The flesh outside the swathe of the bandages was bruised red, black, and purple. He appeared to be in pain. Nonetheless, Jana kept her eye on him while she talked to Giles.

"Spis looks like he was beaten. Generally, he's the one who does the beating."

"That's why I came: to tell you." He shook himself free of her hand. "To advise you of what happened. We just got back from the hospital." He brushed himself off, adjusting his glasses. "I sent Spis on an errand. The older Guzak brother, Kristoe, was waiting for him with a club and before Spis knew it, he had been beaten into this condition." Giles gestured at the car. "You should have seen him. Bloody all over, cuts, huge gashes in his head, teeth knocked out, four broken ribs, and bruises everywhere. He was a mess. The only reason he's not dead is because of his impossibly thick skull." Giles smirked at his joke. "People tried to stop it, so Guzak ran before he finished the job. He would've killed Spis if it had gone on any longer."

"To get back at you," Jana offered.

"Naturally. It was the first step to get to me. With Spis out of the way, there is an open road to killing Giles." Giles grimaced at the thought. "That's not joyous for me to contemplate. It hurts my stomach. I couldn't eat breakfast this morning." His voice took on a whine. "You owe me favors. Time to pay me."

"I've given you all the favors you're due."

"I provided you with information just a few days ago," Giles protested. "Are you going to let him kill me? Look what he did to poor Spis. Think of what he will do to me. I'm the one he's really after."

"I asked you if you wanted your favor then or in the future. You chose to take it then."

"This is part of that favor. You told me about Guzak. Take the next step. Do something about him. Will you let him kill me? What kind of a policeman are you?" Giles's voice was rising into a wail. "I am lost. Giles is a lost soul." He covered his face in his hands, first making sure that his glasses were pushed up to his forehead and out of harm's way. "Giles has just been thrown away, garbage to be disposed of without hesitation because he's of no further use."

Jana ignored Giles's histrionics for a moment, looking for the officer who had been assigned to watch the house. She was across the street and down the block. It was the same detective who'd intervened between Jana and Sabina. Jana raised her hand in the woman's direction to show her that she knew she was there; the woman raised her hand in return. She would report Giles's presence and that Jana had refused to admit him.

"Who are you waving at?" Giles was wary, apprehensive about the woman. "She's not a neighbor."

"Not a neighbor," Jana agreed. "A police officer."

"Why is she there?" His attitude abruptly changed. "I know why. Last night, you were taken to police headquarters and questioned. She's part of that."

Jana put her arm on the little man's shoulder. It was not to comfort him. "Giles had better tell me how Giles knows this fact, or Giles will find himself behind bars again." Jana's voice was cold and threatening. "I asked a question of Giles. How does he know?"

"You don't have to accuse me, Commander," Giles pouted. Then his pout turned into a sly, knowing look. "All right," he acknowledged. "By a strange coincidence I learned about this. People who ordinarily would never talk to me 'revealed' you'd been brought to the main police station. They told me about the other people as well. It's all over Bratislava. Pick up the newspaper. Your name's not mentioned, but others are. It doesn't take much to extrapolate from the facts set forth."

He removed her hand from his shoulder, letting it down gently. "I'm not spying on you like your own people are. Don't even think that, dear Commander." He brushed off his shoulder where her hand had just rested. "Lint gathers on the oil left by a human touch."

Sometimes Giles drove her crazy with his idiosyncrasies. She had to fight the urge to throttle him. It was worse today, when she had very little patience to wait the little man out.

"Giles, you're smug. Self-satisfied. And irritating. Those aren't great traits for a man in your business. Then again, you're always like this when you have information to sell. You need to realize that I've no credit or money to buy with unless you have the goods that I want. I told you before: one hand washes the other. What kind of merchandise do you have for me today?"

He put on a woebegone expression. "Ah, you want more, always more, in return for helping poor Giles."

"You need protection. Is that behind your visit to me?"

"I don't want protection. People like me can't walk around with police officers as bodyguards. It's bad for business. I just want Guzak out of the way. Deal with him. Arrest him for what he did to Spis."

"We can put more men on it."

"Good. More men. That's a start. What else can you do to get him?" He snapped his fingers. "I know, post a reward. Put out a full-scale alert for the pig. Can you do that?"

"I can," Jana acknowledged.

"Decided, then."

Giles stuck his hand out, hoping to seal the contract with a handclasp. Jana ignored it.

"What is it?" Giles asked, appearing bewildered.

"Your information, Giles."

"Yes, that." A look of disdain appeared on his face. "Always tit for tat with you. Why isn't friendship more meaningful for police officers?"

"Giles, I told you before, we're not friends."

"I refuse to believe that, not after all we've been through together."

"We haven't been through anything together. If you remember, I was the one who put you in prison."

Giles ignored her statement, played at pondering what he should tell her, seemed to decide that he couldn't get any more favors from her, and came out with what he had.

"A person working in parliament is involved. This person is helping to ship goods in and out of Slovakia. Exchanges are being made, which that individual is facilitating."

"Drugs?"

"I tried to find out, but this is a very closed circle. I can't get to anyone inside."

Jana lost patience, her voice becoming abrupt.

"Giles, there must be hints. Anything would be helpful."

"Commander, if I knew what they were bringing in or what they were taking out, or who was doing it, I might have asked to participate." He was whining again. "Not that I would involve myself in anything illegal. Just, perhaps, to facilitate things. You know?"

"I know."

"I've been trying to identify this person of influence. No one knows who it is, or they don't want to tell me. The street says that this person has influential friends as well. Be wary, Commander."

"It's very comforting to know that you care about my welfare, Giles." Her tone was acerbic. "And you, you watch out for Guzak."

"Don't forget our agreement." He backed off a few steps, then went to his car. He had a brief conversation with Spis, then they drove off. Jana waited until they were out of sight, then walked over to the detective assigned to the surveillance on her.

"Hello, again."

"Hello to you as well."

Jana noted with approval that she was not at all abashed at Jana's coming over to speak to her.

"I didn't get your name last night."

"Marta Hrdlicka."

"Marta, I came over to make sure that you would not do me any favor by failing to report that I received a visitor."

"I intend to report it, Commander."

"Good. I'll be filing a report on my own."

"I thought you might, Commander."

"Marta, tell your boss, the captain, that he could be right. At least one of the people he interrogated last night may be criminally involved. It may be a member of parliament; it may be an *apparatchik* who works there."

"I'll tell him, Commander."

"I'll be looking into it. If I obtain any information of use, he'll be informed. I don't trust a lot of the people who are working with him. If he has any messages for me, tell him I want you to deliver them. Understood?"

"Yes, Commander." Marta smiled. She had just been brought further into the game by Jana. It would enhance her career. It might even lead to promotion.

Jana walked back to her house, prepared to go back to work at headquarters, wondering, when she got back to her office, how the men under her command would respond to a boss currently under suspicion of being a criminal.

Chapter 31

Everyone assiduously avoided mentioning Jana's involvement as a possible suspect. They went about their business and, when they had contact with Jana, avoided any topic other than the one at hand. Things were stiff and overly polite, but it could have been much worse. Seges tried to avoid Jana, confining himself to his office, making rare forays for coffee. Jana welcomed his absence, and used the time to go over her notes. The call from Nepal was first on her list. She dialed the Nepal number that had been logged by the phone tap in Ukraine. The operator of the Yak N' Yeti Hotel in Kathmandu answered in English. Jana asked for the desk manager. After they spoke for a minute or two, he transferred her to the business office.

Jana gave them Solti's name. There was a long silence. Then the person in the office said Jana should talk to the hotel director. When the director finally came on the line, he was suspicious; *too* suspicious for a simple call of this nature. Jana had to assure him over and over again that she was a police officer and that she was calling on official business. One oddity that Jana picked up immediately was that the director of the hotel knew Solti's name as soon as she mentioned it, not even requiring her to spell it.

"Mr. Solti was a guest," he finally acknowledged, adding that the guest's first name was Josef.

"Do you have a home address for Josef Solti?"

After a pause, the director gave her an address in Hungary. Jana asked if Solti's bill had listed any outgoing phone charges, and, if so, the phone numbers. There were noises and a pause as the man searched through his records. He told her the charges, then rattled off several telephone numbers that had been called. One was in Hungary, which Jana recognized immediately as the phone number for the house where the man had been reported dismembered. Another was in Vienna. There were two other calls to a number that had been the subject of the tap in Ukraine. The last was to a number in Bratislava. She would have to look that one up.

Jana thanked him and was about to hang up when she realized that he had not responded to her expression of gratitude. All hotel employees, particularly at the top levels, were unfailingly polite. There was something more, an unusual event. Perhaps Solti had not paid his bill; perhaps he had had an altercation with the staff, which the director was reluctant to volunteer. Jana probed for it.

"Was the bill paid?"

"We had an imprint from his credit card. It was taken at the time of registration. The bill was run through it."

Jana almost kicked herself for not asking about the card first. They could run its number, get an account of his travels, and profile Solti on his spending habits. The director recited the credit card number.

It still did not feel right to Jana. They generally took an imprint of the card again at checkout, ripping up the first imprint since it was required merely as a security measure.

"Solti wasn't there to pay the bill himself. Why?"

"Are you sure you're with the police?"

Jana intuited what had happened to Solti.

"Was he killed in the hotel?"

There was silence on the other end. The director finally coughed.

"He was killed while on a hike. We did not sponsor the hike, so we have no legal responsibility for his death. That has to be understood. An assistant manager merely suggested to Mr. Solti that he might enjoy participating in a hike that took place every Saturday. We have discussed the matter with the assistant manager and are convinced that Mr. Solti went on the hike solely because it was called to his attention."

When the director had finished his disclaimer, Jana reassured him that she believed the hotel was not responsible. There was an audible sigh of relief over the phone.

"I think the way they killed him was horrible. I was asked to identify his body, and it was almost impossible. They shot him in the head. Awful." He was now twittering, ridding himself of anxiety surrounding the death of his guest. "Why they would do that to anyone is beyond me."

"Who did it?"

"The government people think it may have been Maoists. They acted like typical Maoists; a gang of them confronted the hikers."

"Was anyone else killed or injured? Anyone threatened or robbed?"

"The bandits let everyone go after they killed Mr. Solti. He was trying to get away, and the Maoists wouldn't permit it. I personally think they were shocked themselves at what they had done, and so left without doing anything to the other hikers."

Jana knew better. The killers weren't shocked. They'd accomplished what they'd set out to do, then vanished into the hills. Jana asked the director what had become of Solti's personal belongings. The director twittered again. The hotel had shipped them, at the hotel's cost, the director stressed, to the home address Solti had given when he'd checked in.

Jana thanked the man, hung up, then went to the next number on the phone tap list, the Bratislava number that seemed so familiar. As soon as she began dialing, she recognized the telephone number of the Slovak parliament, the same Bratislava number that the dead Guzak brother had had.

The voice that answered was unmistakable. The loud, gravelly tones of Sila Covic grated through the phone. Jana stifled her surprise. At Jana's insistence, Covic agreed to a meeting if Jana could make it within the next hour. Jana hung up, then realized that in the present circumstances, she had better have a witness present. She needed backup.

Jana didn't want Seges along. Who else could she use? She needed a police officer who would not be worried about the damage to his career that association with her might generate. She called Jarov, the cop who she had forced Seges to relieve from sentry duty. He owed Jana a favor, and would make a good observer. They arranged to meet at parliament.

The encounter with Covic got off to a strange start. There was no secretary in the anteroom to Covic's office, so Jana knocked lightly on the inner office door. When there was no response, she and Jarov walked in. Covic was sitting on her built-up chair behind her desk, her eyes closed, her hands in a praying position, meditating.

Jana waited a full minute; then she and Jarov pulled chairs up to the desk and sat. After a brief interval, Covic lowered her hands, opened her eyes, and regarded both police officers with wide eyes as if she could not understand who they were or what they were doing in her office. Jana felt compelled to reintroduce herself.

"Police Commander Jana Matinova. This is Officer Jarov."

Covic began the conversation without any pretense of courtesy. "Why are you here?"

"I called for the appointment," Jana reminded her. "I have to ask you a few questions about a murder investigation we're conducting."

Covic stared at Jana as if she was insane. "I thought you were here for the other thing." She meant the corruption investigation. "What could I have to do with murder? Who was murdered?"

"Two killings took place in Bratislava this past week."

Covic shifted her body to a more comfortable position, looking incongruously childlike in the full-sized chair.

"I read about it. Who were they, and why do you imagine that I had anything to do with them?"

"Do you know a man named Josef Solti? Or a man named Veza?"

Covic looked blank.

"No." She stopped herself. "Maybe. I don't recognize the names. I've a great memory for names, but I meet a hundred new people a day on this job, so it's possible I may have met them, yet not remembered them."

Jana read Covic the telephone number that had both been called by Solti and found in Guzak the Younger's pocket.

"My office telephone number," acknowledged Covic.

"If you don't know them, why would they call here, Madame Covic?"

Covic laughed, not a pleasant sound.

"Because of my public image, I get calls in this office for many of the members of parliament. If my secretary is here, she takes them and forwards them. If I'm here alone, I tell the caller at the other end to dial directly, and give them the number. But, if I think the caller is crazy or has an ax to grind, I hang up. Most of the time, during the day my phone is so busy they won't get through. Which is why I meditate. Otherwise I'd smash the phone to pieces."

Jana's hopes fell. There would be no way to connect Covic directly with any of the calls to the office. There was no use leveling an accusation.

On the off chance that she might know him, Jana mentioned the name Vlad Markus, the man who had been murdered and cut up in Hungary. For a split second, Jana thought she saw a sign of recognition. But if Covic knew the name, she recovered so quickly that Jana could not be sure.

There was a knock at the office door. Ivan Boryda stepped inside. He was surprised at seeing Jana and Jarov. Jana felt some of the same surprise at seeing him. Boryda was no longer a simple member of parliament: he was a deputy prime minister in the new government.

"Good afternoon, Ivan," said Covic, her voice softening. Covic knew who she had to be nice to. Now that he was a deputy prime minister, Boryda was one of them.

Boryda didn't bother to return Covic's greeting, focusing instead on Jana.

"How are you, Commander? I saw you at that debacle last night. Ugly, wasn't it? Nothing will come of it. That captain's looking to make headlines, like so many of them." Without waiting for an answer, he turned to Covic. "Any calls for me?"

"Nothing for you."

"Thank you." He nodded at Jana, then walked out.

"You see," Covic made a point. "They all come in here for their messages."

"He's a deputy minister, not a member of parliament. Why do you take his calls?"

"He *was* a member, so calls still come for him here."

Jarov finally jumped in. "He must have a cell phone. Every politician has a cell phone, at public expense."

Covic shrugged. "They don't give out their cell phone numbers except to people they're close to." She looked at Jana. "We are through, I hope. I've things to do."

Jana and Jarov left Covic still sitting at her desk, calling people on her desk phone.

Jarov snickered. "Now I know why gnomes are the bad people in fairy tales."

Jana didn't like the comment.

On the other hand, she acknowledged to herself, there was some truth in applying it in Covic's case. The woman would have fit into one of the Grimms' fairy tales very easily.

Chapter 32

Jana called Grosse at Europol, gave him the information about Solti's credit card, and asked him to run it through the banks. It was always quicker if the request came from Europol, and Jana asked for priority on it. Grosse was pessimistic, but he promised to do his best. Two hours later, Jana was pleasantly astonished to find the computer printouts sitting on her desk.

The records went back for fourteen months, with a computerized note attached indicating that this was a new account and number, replacing one that had been stolen. They offered to forward the records of the prior account upon request. As she scanned the data that had been sent to her, Jana made a mental note to ask for the other records. The address listed for the account was the one given to her by the hotel in Kathmandu. That made sense. Solti would know that his credit references would be checked. What surprised her was the breadth of Solti's travels during the period the card had been used.

Jana counted the countries and cities that Solti had visited. There were twenty-six countries and forty-one cities. He had made multiple visits to a number of the cities, dispersed over four continents. The most frequent sites were in Europe and Asia, with the most numerous visits to Kathmandu, Myanmar, and Hong Kong in Asia, Moscow, Bratislava, and Kiev in eastern Europe, London, Strasbourg, and Amsterdam in western Europe, Havana, Cali, and Asunción in South America, and Montréal and New York in North America. If Jana hadn't known that he was an associate of criminals, she might have guessed that he was a salesman, going from place to place to sell his company's wares.

There were a few things that Solti could have been involved in. Smuggling was the first she considered. Perhaps he had been a mule, transporting contraband from city to city? Jana dismissed the notion. Mules were not used over and over, particularly not on the same route. They became too obvious. Their essence was anonymity.

Jana forced herself to think of an operation with this breadth as an international corporation. If this were a corporation, Solti could be likened to one of its executives, going from place to place, making sure that the supply lines were correctly set up, checking on personnel, making sure deliveries arrived on time.

Jana liked this theory. If there were an international network, they would need a mid-level person who made sure all the cogs and wheels were working smoothly. Contraband, whatever it is, is invariably very costly. It must be delivered on time and to the right people. Otherwise, there would not only be a loss of valuable merchandise, but anger and distrust would develop between the intended recipients and the shipper. And with gangsters, that generally meant war. Deaths were the byproduct of war. The more Jana thought about this possibility, the more verification she saw on the pages of the credit card report. She needed to chart it out.

She called Seges, telling him to get her an easel with a large pad of paper. Seges, with his usual reluctance, first had his coffee before placing the materials on her desk.

Jana wrote the names of the cities down according to continent, then country. She listed the dates visits were made to particular cities in chronological order, correlating dates with visits to other cities. The major routes he had followed leaped from the paper.

The start and finish appeared to be Nepal. From Kathmandu, the most-used routes were through Hong Kong, then to either Montréal or New York. The alternate route again started in Nepal, then went through to Moscow, from there to Budapest, Kiev, or Bratislava, then on to one of the three cities listed in western Europe, from there to Asunción or Cali in South America, and finally on to either Montréal or New York. Those cities were likely to be the hubs for further regional distribution of whatever was being smuggled. The trips back to Nepal sometimes included those same locations. Solti was either checking on the sub-routes or collecting a different type of contraband that went the other direction. Or perhaps he was collecting payments, Jana reflected. It was still all very conjectural.

Jana told Seges to replicate the chart and copy the records that Grosse had sent her. Then she telephoned Officer Marta Hrdlicka, asking her to come to her office. Marta arrived just as Seges finished his copying and set the records on Jana's desk. She asked him to leave, closing the door behind him. She wanted no one to know what had been discovered and the conclusions she had drawn, except Marta, who would convey them to the captain. As for Seges, he was glad to leave. This was all over his head.

Marta was her usual alert self, listening and taking notes. Jana gave her the copies of the records and the charts. She advised Marta to tell the captain everything she had been briefed on, but to do it privately. Marta began to thank Jana for the confidence she was showing in her.

Jana held up a hand to stop the young woman. There was no need for that. She watched Marta walk out, pleased with her selection of a liaison. Marta's eagerness reminded Jana of herself when she had been new on the force, willing to do anything to become a respected police officer. Marta would make a good one.

Jana checked the telephone numbers she had retrieved from the younger Guzak's body. One was for a Vienna location. Guzak had come from Kiev, but both cities had been major destinations for Solti. Jana dialed the number. The operator came on the line and announced that it was the United Nations in Vienna. Jana hung up without replying.

The significance of this new information required her to phone Bohumil directly. He was out for the day but would be checking in within the next few hours. She left a message for him to call her. She almost asked for Marta, but decided against it because she wanted to discuss the significance of the Vienna telephone number directly with the captain. That a thug like Guzak was ready to phone the United Nations was shocking; it indicated that someone in the Euro-complex the UN had in Vienna was involved in the ring.

Jana went over the other names that had emerged in her investigation. The next one on her list was Midi, the man who had been the main conspirator in the Hungarian-based ring. Midi was the Slovak and "the bankroll." Jana called Seges, telling him to check for Midi in the telephone directories, in the property registry, and with the police registration lists in all the stations in Slovakia; and not to forget the lists of cell phone subscribers. There was a barely audible groan on the other end of the phone. Seges mumbled about trying to get off early because of the overtime he had put in lately.

Jana knew how to overcome that hurdle. She told him it was for Captain Bohumil, which brightened him up, which in turn reassured Jana that Seges would do the work in a thorough way. He still wanted to get into Bohumil's unit.

Jana decided that it was time to deal with two other issues. First and foremost, she had to speak to Peter and get their relationship resolved. She had to know why he had taken on an investigation that had her as one of the possible targets at the same time he was romantically involved with her. She also had to speak to Sofia. The meeting that Jana had stumbled on between Sofia and Kamin still rankled. She had pushed it to the back of her mind, overwhelmed by the pressure of her investigation. But she had to find out the real reason for the meeting. Then there was the diamond necklace. Why had it been placed in her apartment? To give Bohumil's unit proof that Jana had been involved in corruption? Possibly. But maybe not. Maybe there was another reason.

Jana had to delay contacting Peter. All the telephone calls that ran through the police anti-corruption investigation division were periodically voice-monitored. The same system also automatically recorded all incoming and outgoing numbers. Peter was on the staff of the attorney general, but, because he was assigned to the special investigation division, she thought his calls might be monitored as well. Jana was upset and angry with him, but didn't want her call to create further difficulties for him.

So discussing Kamin with Sofia came next. Their connection was bizarre, and it had to be wounding for Sofia. The man was repulsive. Sofia would find him disgusting and would do anything to avoid close contact with him. She certainly would not wish to be alone with the man in her office. Whatever had forced Sofia into that meeting had to be brought out and aired.

Jana called Sofia. She was not in her home office, nor at her home phone number. Her cell phone was not answering. Jana tried the parliament building. The call was forwarded to Sila Covic's receptionist. The receptionist indicated that

Sofia was not expected in parliament today: she was flying to Vienna and was probably already at the airport.

Jana was dismayed. Vienna again. And now with reference to Sofia.

Jana went to the parking area and located Trokan's car, opened the door on the passenger side, and reached below the seat, fingering the upholstery under the cushion. She suffered a momentary scare when she could not locate the diamond; then she peered under the seat and saw a piece of the necklace chain peeping out. She extracted it, relieved that it was still there.

She held it up. The gem glittered as brightly as ever. It was so beautiful and seductive, shimmering magically in the light. Jana almost hated to put it away. She forced herself to rewrap it and placed it back inside her bra.

Chapter 33

Jana went home that evening planning on loafing, clearing her mind by doing absolutely nothing. The neighbor across the street, bulky in a heavy jacket worn against the cold, stared hard at Jana as she stood before her door. There was nothing new to the woman's dislike of Jana, but the look seemed even more hostile than usual. Jana nodded at her. The woman turned away, so Jana walked into her house. A nervous-looking Sofia was sitting on the couch, waiting for Jana, her bag packed for Vienna next to her on the floor.

Jana paused, nodding to Sofia, not very surprised to see her there. In the past, Sofia used to come over at all hours of the day and night. She knew that she was always welcome and the door was never locked. Jana took off her coat, hung it up, then walked over to her overstuffed chair next to the couch.

"I understand you are going to Austria?" Jana asked.

"For a few days." Sofia's voice had a tentative quality. "Inter-government stuff."

"No private business?"

Sofia seemed to think, then tried to make a joke. "Maybe some Viennese pastries." She forced a smile. "How have you been, Jana?"

"I'm tired." Jana relaxed and sat back in her chair. "You're lucky you caught me here. I'm generally not home until much later."

Sofia nodded.

"More problems?" Jana finally asked Sofia.

Sofia stiffened. Jana could generally read her friend's face. She was thinking about what to say. Whatever Sofia had come here to speak about, she still cared that it might be received with rejection or anger.

"Better to tell me now rather than later, Sofia. Things have a way of building up when you wait."

Sofia got the needed courage to speak. "I did something I felt I needed to do, but I am not proud of the way I did it."

There was another uneasy silence. Jana went over their last meeting. They had been very, very uncomfortable. Finding Kamin in the same office with Sofia, talking together as if nothing had happened years before, had felt wrong then; it felt wrong now.

"The meeting with Kamin?"

"In part."

"Only in part?"

"Yes." She sighed, then forced herself to go forward. "I was afraid of the Party. I was afraid of him. I was afraid of making waves, of not complying with the rules of the political game that every politician has to play if they want to succeed. There was a fear of making enemies, fear that I might be rejected by the public. So, I met with him."

"What could be so important?"

"He wanted me to vote on a bill in parliament granting him, and others in the old administration, immunity from criminal prosecution for their past official acts. They'd bent the rules, and the laws. Now they claim all kinds of reasons they should be given immunity: the need to maintain public confidence, to stabilize the economy, to calm multi-national companies that may fear prosecution because of their possible illegal interaction with the prior government. A number of legislators are afraid for their own skins, so almost everyone is getting behind the bill. They want my support as well."

Jana immediately understood why. "Your support would give them legitimacy, true?"

Sofia mocked herself with an ugly sound from deep in her throat. It was filled with self-loathing.

"If the woman who fought corruption supports the legislation, it must be good, right?" Jana asked.

"That would be their reasoning, I suppose."

"So, why not simply say 'no'?"

"Because of something else." There was a look of despair on Sofia's face. "I was overconfident, and a little stupid. No," she corrected herself. "I was very stupid."

Jana had seen Sofia's expression on many other faces. It was always there when a victim felt he had stepped over some line and might himself be embarrassed or incriminated.

"Is he holding something over your head? The affair with Boryda?"

"In part," she reluctantly agreed.

Sofia went silent again, struggling to articulate the problem. It was the same internal battle she had gone through at the Café Gremium.

"You can't go on like this forever, Sofia. Time to spit it out. It's the only way I can help you."

"I don't know if you'll help me after you find out what I did."

"Try me."

Sofia reached into her handbag and pulled out an envelope, handed it to Jana, then closed her eyes as if she did not want to see Jana's reaction. Jana removed the folded page of a newspaper, opened it, and scanned an article that had been circled in marking pen. The story was about some charity social function. The photograph that accompanied it caught Jana's eye. At first glance it was innocuous enough. Sofia was merely standing next to the hostess of the party.

Jana took a closer look at the photograph. Her friend was dressed in a gown made of velvet. Very pretty, but the dress was unimportant compared to something else in the photo. It was what was around her neck: a diamond necklace. Jana recognized the necklace. She looked at Sofia. Her friend still sat with her eyes closed.

Jana pulled the necklace out, comparing it with the photo. No doubt, they were one and the same. She checked the date on the page. It was the week before Jana had found the diamond in her home, hanging from a ceiling beam.

"Sofia!"

Sofia's eyes snapped open.

"Why did you leave me the diamond without any explanation?"

Sofia tried to find the answer.

"Dread and panic. Terror. The article was mailed to me. I didn't know what to do. It was meant to scare me. I tried to tell you at the restaurant. Impossible. I was too afraid. My throat closed up. The words could not get past the constriction. So, I gave up trying to tell you. Except, as soon as I left the coffee shop, I knew I was lost if I didn't. I needed help. I came over here to wait for you. And I panicked again. I wanted to throw up, to beat myself, to die. I had to get rid of the necklace, to get it out of my life. So, I hung it where you found it, and fled."

"What was I supposed to do with the necklace, Sofia?"

"You're a police officer, Jana, as well as my friend. I thought you might find out where it came from. You would have to investigate. What else could you do?"

Jana sat in silence, trying to understand Sofia's logic.

"You put me in jeopardy, Sofia."

Sofia sat back on the couch, closing her eyes again, her voice very low. "I was not thinking clearly. I didn't mean to do *that*."

Jana watched the gem sway as she held it suspended from its chain. A huge stone, exquisite, radiating a cold fire.

"You could not have afforded a gem like this, Sofia. Did you get it from your deputy prime minister?" Jana answered her own question. "No. He could not have afforded it either, not on his salary."

Sofia moved her head as if in pain. "I *thought* it was from him. I hoped it was, when it was delivered to me by a messenger. There was no card. I was so excited, thinking he still loved me. I called him, even though I was not supposed to. He could not get me off the phone quickly enough, but. . . ." Her voice took on a wry note. "He managed to assure me that he had *not* sent me the diamond before he hung up." She opened her eyes, her face taking on a grim look. "No words of love. He was just dealing with a pest. Bang! End of call!

"He was at the party the night I wore the necklace. I wore it, still believing he had sent it to me. That he really wanted me to acknowledge his gift. But he avoided me all evening."

"When was it sent to you, Sofia?"

"Just after the news media found out about the affair Boryda and I were having."

"Did you ever get any glimmering of an idea of who had sent you this precious bauble?"

"Not even the whisper of a suggestion." Sofia's voice took on an added sense of anxiety. "When Kamin called for the appointment with me, to ask me to vote for the bill, I thought it was him. He phoned the day after I received the newspaper article. It's his way of operating."

"Did Kamin mention the diamond to you? The article that was sent?"

"Not a word."

"Why him, then?"

"Who else? He corrupts people. I thought he was trying to bribe me. That's the reason I originally came to you. Everyone would think I had sold out on some bill or other in order to get that kind of jewel. They'd believe I was taking graft."

Sofia sat on the edge of the couch, beginning to rock back and forth, trying to contain her internal tension. "I'm being assaulted on all sides, Jana. I am being driven crazy. Everything is disintegrating. My life is collapsing." She looked at Jana directly for the first time. "Jana, help me like you have always helped me. You're the detective. Find out why this came to me. Please, please, please help me!"

Jana mulled over her friend's distress.

"You're telling me the truth, Sofia? You have no idea who sent you the diamond? Or why it was sent to you? No inkling at all?"

"I swear, Jana. There's no one else who would have a reason to give me this." Her voice went up another notch. "I have no idea at all. And that's why it frightens me so much." Her eyes moved to the diamond, fixing on it for a moment, then moved back up to Jana's face. "I never expected this, never."

Jana looked at her friend. Sofia looked back, her eyes pleading for help.

Sofia had acted badly, putting Jana in jeopardy.

She had not considered Jana's needs.

No matter.

Sofia was her childhood companion.

Sofia was her friend.

They were bound together.

They both started when there was a loud knock at the door.

It was Mrs. Milanova, the woman from across the street, her arms folded over her chest, panting out chilly breaths in frosty puffs, looking both angry and self-righteous.

"Why aren't you *there?* You can't just ignore things so you can come home early."

Jana had no idea what the woman was talking about. The woman fumed on. Jana let her run her course.

"You think you can rest while all these murders are taking place in Bratislava. That's not what you're paid to do. You should be out there catching whoever did them."

Jana wondered what had brought on this outburst.

"We're trying, Mrs. Milanova."

The woman's voice went up a notch.

"You call this trying, having a chat with a friend while people are being killed? Two this past week; two more today? You are not doing your job."

Two today? What was the woman talking about? "You've heard about two murders today? On the TV?"

A flush of triumph rose like a tide over the woman's face.

"I knew it! You people don't know what you're doing. How can you claim to be protecting people? Are you even sure your shoes are on? Look at the TV, great detective that you are." She scurried away, now shouting so other neighbors would hear her. "The police force is corrupt. They beat up a woman's husband, they put him in the hospital, but they can't find criminals." She got to her front door, turning to shout a last imprecation at Jana. "You should be put in prison. All you do is hurt the innocent!" She went inside, slamming the door behind her.

Jana ignored Sofia, switching on her television, at the same time using her cell phone to call her office. The TV popped on just as the phone was answered by one of her detectives.

"Matinova here. Has there been another murder?"

She saw it unfolding on TV. There was a crime scene just two blocks from parliament. Two people had been killed, both women. They had already been identified. One was Sila Covic, the Red Devil. The other was officer Marta Hrdlicka.

Jana began yelling at the detective for not immediately informing her. When Jana finally ran down, she was even more surprised at the reason she had not been called. Trokan had given her men explicit instructions that she not be informed. He had taken personal charge of the investigation.

They had not wanted her at the scene.

Chapter 34

J ana was confused. Why had Trokan stepped in? What could have caused these two women to be murdered? Why Marta Hrdlicka? She considered every piece of evidence, every report, every small bit of data she had on the case. She tried to put these new deaths together with the others to make a cohesive whole. The solution did not appear. She had to know more.

Two hours later, a call finally came from Trokan. Jana drove directly to police headquarters, reporting as requested to Captain Bohumil's office. The two men were waiting for her. And Peter. Recording equipment had already been set up, which meant she was a suspect in the new murders.

There was a grim feeling in the room. All homicides create a harsh atmosphere, but the investigators go forward in a businesslike way, their jobs leavened with office gossip, dirty jokes, shop talk, and a gallows humor that diffuses the dismal events. It was different now in Bohumil's office. There was an overlay of gloom and depression as if they had been personally injured by the recent events. Even Trokan, who was normally able to weather the worst circumstances with a modicum of good spirits, looked bleak. Jana knew the cause: one of their own was dead. And, from the way Jana had been initially shunted aside, they thought the deaths were attributable to the ongoing investigation that she had already been questioned about.

"Marta Hrdlicka, the officer who was acting as the liaison between you and Captain Bohumil, was killed."

"I saw the report on television," Jana acknowledged.

She sat down in the only unoccupied chair, trying to come to terms with the grisly events. Marta had helped Jana; Jana had tried to help her. Now she was gone, and Jana was mourning her with a grief that was already turning to fury.

"How was she killed?"

Trokan answered. "They were both shot. The Covic woman was shot through the head. A contact wound. Marta was shot twice in the body, with a final shot to the head at close range."

"Like the Guzak killing. Body shots, then the shot to the head to make sure." Jana forced herself to concentrate on the essentials of the case. "We have to compare the ballistics in both cases. Why were the two victims together?"

Bohumil stirred uneasily. He wanted to go in another direction. "There are questions that we need you to respond to before we get into the specifics of this case."

"All of these cases are tied together. They have to be discussed and investigated as a whole."

"After you answer our questions," Bohumil insisted.

Trokan shot Jana a warning look, telling her to follow Bohumil's direction. He threw in a question just to give her a moment to reflect, and to calm her down. "You know why we didn't call you to the scene?"

"I'd like to know your reasoning."

"How would it look later? You are a possible suspect in an ongoing investigation; you are a possible suspect now."

Jana nodded. The decision not to summon her to the murder scene was also protection for her. No one could now be accused of ignoring a possible conflict of interest, nor of a cover-up. In a country like Slovakia, with so much distrust of officials, there was a need to be cautious.

"Ask me what you need to know."

"You saw Marta Hrdlicka today," Bohumil began. "Tell us everything that was said or done during your meeting."

For the first time, Jana realized that the papers on Bohumil's desk were the materials she had given Marta for him. Their asking her to relate what she and Marta had talked about meant that Marta had left the office before Bohumil's return. Marta had not had the opportunity to explain the import of the documents.

Jana related the substance of the meeting; Bohumil and Peter examined the contents of the papers as she spoke. There were a few questions. When they had been answered, Trokan nodded approvingly at her.

"Very nice. You pulled things together for both investigations." There was satisfaction in his voice.

"The commander called me *after* she had given the papers to Marta," Bohumil reminded him. "She should have given them to me directly."

"A small point, Captain," Trokan reminded him. "Commander Matinova has handed you a significant piece of evidence that advances your investigation." He waited, expecting Bohumil to thank Jana. He did not. Trokan's voice become harsher. "You can voice appropriate gratitude when you're ready."

A captain always listens to a colonel.

"You have done well, Commander," Bohumil finally said.

"Thank you." She smiled inwardly. Trokan was still her friend.

Jana thought about the phone call she had made to the captain, instinct telling her to hold off giving the real reason for the call. "I was calling to ask you if you wanted a personal briefing by me, rather than by Marta. You were out, and I thought Marta or you would call me if you had any questions, so I didn't pursue it."

Bohumil resumed his questioning. "Do you know why Officer Hrdlicka left the unit to meet with the Red Devil? She left word that she was meeting her, but told no one why. When I came back to the office, she had already left."

"You checked the phone log?"

He nodded. "She received a call just before she went. She was described as 'excited' after she got the call."

"The conversation was recorded?"

"It came in on her cell phone. So, no record."

Trokan followed up. "We checked with Covic's receptionist. She said that Covic rushed out, telling her that she was leaving for a meeting. It was an appointment that had not been entered on Covic's calendar; therefore, we conclude it had been made on the spur of the moment. They met a short time after that, and both were killed almost immediately."

"Witnesses?"

"One. She saw a fleeing man from the rear. She described him as very tall, in fact so tall that he would be considered a giant. Not a particularly reliable witness." A smile finally appeared on his face. "All shooters look bigger to witnesses. I've never met an eyewitness who didn't have problems with their memory of events."

Jana tried to settle any lingering doubts Bohumil might have about her being the murderer in this case.

"What time were they shot?"

Peter gave the times of death.

Jana turned back to Bohumil.

"I was in my office then. Check with our people."

Trokan nodded. "We did. They confirmed it."

Bohumil finally managed to articulate his last lingering doubt about Jana. "You could have had an accomplice. The Guzak killings were carried out by two people."

"If I were going to kill, I'd never use an accomplice, Captain. They're always around later to testify against you." She got up. "Unless you have further questions, I have work. May I go?"

Bohumil nodded. "One more thing: when you have the police reports, I'd appreciate your sharing them with me."

She walked out.

Jana didn't return to her office. She couldn't have worked there even if her career had depended upon it. Instead, she drove to the location where these latest deaths had occurred.

When she arrived, media representatives were still prowling about, taking photographs, stopping everyone who passed by, trying to get quotable comments. The wind was whipping up, the clouds deepening, a harbinger of the next storm moving in. Cold enough for snow tonight, Jana estimated. But if it held off until the morning, it would be too warm for snow. Just more sleet or freezing rain.

There were still two police officers at the spot where the shootings had occurred; a small area where the bodies had been found was still taped off. Jana walked over to the tape. One of the officers recognized her and saluted. As soon as the press people saw the salute, they began trotting over, hoping to get an additional angle for a story, a statement from Jana, anything that would spice up their reportage.

Jana slipped under the tape, using her pen flashlight to look at the bloodstains. She ignored the reporters, who continued to hurl questions at her. She stood looking down at the chalk outlines. It was easy to identify where each had fallen. The Red Devil's outline was much smaller than

Marta's. Jana felt like she should be in church praying for both of them, though she was not religious. She wondered if either of the two dead women had been. It would not have helped them.

One of the television crews turned its lights on Jana, catching a picture of her with her head bent over the blood stains. Jana shaded her eyes from the lights, then walked back to the tape, ducked under it, and left the death circle. The television crew kept filming, the reporter thrusting his microphone under her nose.

"Were they friends?" He pushed the microphone even closer. Jana pushed it away; the reporter thrust it back again. "We don't want to lose your comments."

She pushed the microphone away again and walked back to her car. The television team finally dropped away.

Jana felt a sense of loss.

It would have been nice to have had Marta as a friend.

Chapter 35

Jana drove home, wanting to sort out her emotions, only to find a man sitting in the dark on her front step. In the dim light, she could not see his face or recognize him from his body configuration. She decided that precautions were called for and eased her gun from its holster before she left the car.

He had been resting his head on his knees. When he heard her approach, he stood, giving her a wide smile. Jana felt relief course through her. It was Vilem, Peter's cousin, the man from the spa whom they had laughingly renamed Groucho. In fact, the only name that Jana remembered at that moment was Groucho. She put her gun away.

"It's so good to see you, even though you nearly shot me," Groucho said.

"I couldn't make you out. You might have been the tax man, or a dark mountain spirit."

They hugged each other, and Jana invited him into the house. She bustled around making coffee for both of them, apologizing for not having anything to eat with it, at the same time wishing he would get on with the reason that he had come to her house. Groucho had to be a messenger from Peter.

Jana eventually asked why he had come to see her.

For the moment, Groucho lost his smile. He held up a finger across his lips for silence.

"I have to speak very softly," he whispered, moving even closer so he could talk directly in her ear. "Peter called me. He had to use a public phone. He thinks they may be listening on his line."

"Who is listening?" she muttered back, wondering why they were whispering in her living room.

"He said it wasn't the government. He would know if it were the police or his office, or someone else in the bureaus. He found out by accident. There was a buzz on his land line, and the company sent a man to fix it. The technician found the illegal connection. Then Peter brought people from his department to go over his house, and they found listening devices. He wanted you to know so you could check here."

"In my house?" Jana whispered back.

Jana couldn't quite believe that anyone would eavesdrop on her phone calls or install listening devices in her home. She couldn't help looking around her walls, wondering what was behind the pictures now, or in the cupboards, under the chairs, or in the lighting fixtures. Abruptly, Jana was uncomfortable in her own home. She didn't like the feeling.

"Did he tell you who's behind it?"

"They haven't found out who's responsible. They left the listening devices alone. They're hoping they can track the transmissions. If so, it'll take another day or two. They're not sure if that will work. That's why he called me for help. He said you would trust 'Groucho.'" He looked discomfited by his sudden thrust into significance. "He also gave me another message for you." Groucho gave her a sly, knowing look.

Jana felt her hopes rise and her breathing quicken. Suddenly, she was self-conscious about this response.

"About Peter and me?"

"He said to tell you that he loved you." Groucho paused, thinking. "He told me to get this exactly right. He said,

'Without you he's lost; with you he's been found. He wants to stay found.'"

Jana felt elation build inside her. He still cared for her, cared for her enough to send this elaborate message through his cousin. The nonspoken message was also evident. He couldn't personally contact her; he couldn't tell her more. But he wanted their relationship to continue. Jana couldn't contain herself. She grabbed Groucho, pulling him close in a hug, kissing his cheeks over and over again in thanks. When she finally let him go, Groucho was abashed, but glowing with pleasure.

"Thank you, Groucho." She kissed him once more, this time a quick peck. "You're a man who's brought lovely news back into my life: he still cares for me."

"Any message for me to take to him?" There was an eager stutter to his question. "He would like that."

She thought about what she should say. It had to be short, it had to be intense. "Tell him I understand." She shook her head. "No; it's simpler this way. Just tell him I love him." Jana felt relieved she could get the words out. They were too important to hesitate over. "Yes, just that: I love him, I love him, I love him."

"Three times?"

"Ten times."

"Ten times it is." He stood. "I have to go. There's a drive ahead of me." Jana followed Groucho to the door.

"Come back to Piešt'any," he urged. "The spa is waiting. We always like lovers."

Groucho walked out. Jana closed the door behind him, then leaned against it.

The relationship she needed was restored.

Almost.

Despite the incredibly good news that Peter still loved

her, there was also the information about the electronic eavesdropping. It was hard to comprehend, particularly in relation to her house, her private sanctuary, her refuge from the rest of the world. Jana could not accept the idea of her private life being laid out for strangers to paw over. If the listening devices were embedded in her walls, they were embedded in her life. That meant that her conversation with Sofia had been heard and might be used against both of them. Jana would have to guard herself more closely, guard her guests and everyone else who passed through her front door. As long as she was being scrutinized this way, the house would not be hers. Speaking in whispers was not compatible with the comfort and joy of living in your home.

Jana went to the radio and turned on a music station. A piece by Mozart was being played. She listened for a moment, then felt her gorge rising. She could not even enjoy music alone. There was a presence in the house, an alien presence, an extraterrestrial that had come from some ugly universe and invaded her soul.

Jana had to know if they were there or not.

She turned the radio's volume up to cover any noise she might make and began to search the living room, methodically, starting with her couch, then each piece in the room, thoroughly examining every one. She found nothing. She then went back and scrutinized the lamps and their sockets, then the telephone. An hour later, after examining and reexamining, she had found nothing. If anyone were going to "bug" her house, they would have planted one in the room where everyone sat, relaxed, and talked freely.

Jana told herself she should feel better. She went into the bedroom and changed clothes, putting on a comfortable old pair of jeans, then tried to straighten up the house, thinking about what had happened to Marta and the Red Devil, wishing she already had the scene investigation reports.

Jana's train of thoughts kept being interrupted. She could not rid herself of the creepy feeling that there were listening devices that she had not found. Giving in to her impulse, she went back into the living room to view the room from a different angle. She needed a different perspective. She stood on a chair, looking down from the top of the room to the floor. Jana saw it right away, the only object she had not checked.

The rug.

A wool area rug lay below the small coffee table in front of the couch. Jana stepped off the chair, removed the coffee table, then turned the rug over. There were no visible devices. She felt along the border where the fringe protruded from the body of the rug. She had it!

A hard wire ran through the border, the wire connecting to both sides of the rug. At the tip of the wire, again on both sides, there were small flat pieces where the wire was inserted, pieces the size of a very small fingernail. They were embedded in the rug itself, impossible to see and almost impossible to find. Tucked under the coffee table, no one would ever suspect that every word they spoke was being listened to and recorded.

Jana put the rug back in place, taking her cue from what Groucho had told her: Peter and his people had left their bugs alone. Jana had found out what she needed to know. There would be listening devices in the other rooms. The telephone must also be tapped. Jana's guess was that it was being intercepted from outside the house, probably where the main line connected to her home. She couldn't go out and check. If the people who had installed the tap were watching, they'd know that she'd found out about their invasion of her home.

The system they had in place, whoever *they* were, was a sophisticated one. There were two feeds, plus the wire attachment acting as an antenna, which would pick up everything said in the room. There was one drawback to this type of listening device: the limited distance from which the signal could be picked up. That meant their receiving equipment had to be close by. It could be in a parked vehicle, perhaps in a house on the block. She decided to walk through the neighborhood to see if she could spot anything out of the ordinary. She put on a jacket, then stepped outside, ready to begin her walk, when she saw Mrs. Milanova standing just outside her door. As soon as the woman saw Jana, she darted back into her house.

There was no need now for Jana to go on a tour of the neighborhood. She knew where the recordings of her conversations were being made. The woman had suddenly become aggressive, no longer afraid of Jana, not trying to hide any of her anger. Why? She thought Jana was going to be brought down. They had persuaded the woman to shelter the receiving equipment in her house, and she was now relishing the prospect of avenging herself on Jana.

None of Jana's neighbors, people she had known since she was a child, would allow anyone to harm her. Except Mrs. Milanova.

Jana now had a possible course of action.

The people who were recording her life would have to come back to get the recordings. If someone was here, in Jana's house, waiting, he could follow them and identify them and their boss. But, with all the convoluted twists this investigation had taken, with the killings that had occurred today, and with the information that had just come from Peter, who could Jana trust to keep watch?

She had to make a careful choice. She had seen the place

where Marta had died today. Jana felt at least partially responsible for the death of one officer. She didn't want to be responsible for another.

Chapter 36

Trokan gave Jana permission to speak to Sila Covic's receptionist. They had completed their murder scene investigation and interviewed her already, so there was no reason to refuse Jana. However, he did add one onerous proviso: he told her to take Seges along. Captain Bohumil would appreciate their allowing his "spy" to accompany her. There was no point in arguing, so Jana brought an uncharacteristically agreeable Seges along to parliament.

They met Zuzana Vachanova in the lobby. The legislators and their aides all nodded to Vachanova as they passed, some offering condolences on the death of her boss. All of them, except for the briefest of token glances, avoided looking at either Jana or Seges, aware that they were police investigating Sila Covic's death.

"She was well liked," Vachanova explained. "There has been an outpouring of grief at her passing."

Jana knew better. Covic had been very competent at what she did, but her acerbic nature was one that would never engender sorrow at her passing. Seges made noises of commiseration, which Zuzana seemed to appreciate. Jana inwardly thanked the powers-that-be that Seges had said the right thing for once.

Covic's inner office was being reorganized. A mass of papers and boxes, legislative pamphlets, old bills, stacks of letters, and huge amounts of miscellaneous papers was being catalogued by two assistants, readying the place for whoever took over the murder victim's job. Vachanova shooed the assistants out, then closed the inner office door behind them.

"You know," Vachanova finally confessed, "she was often hard to work with. She yelled a lot." Vachanova quickly amended what she'd said. "Although, it should be noted, she had a heart of gold. She gave all of herself and her time to her job. She worked very, very long hours." She thought about her own long work hours. "Naturally, I had to work those long days with her to keep this job. My family life suffered."

Seges made positive noises. Zuzana, wearing her best martyred look, basked in his appreciation. "Can I offer you tea, perhaps? Coffee?"

Jana refused. So did Seges, again a surprise for Jana: Seges never refused anything that was offered free. Zuzana gave them both a sweet smile, primarily favoring Seges, then looked at them expectantly, waiting for their questions.

"You indicated that Ms. Covic—" Jana began. She was quickly interrupted.

"She always liked to be called by her first name, 'Sila.' She felt it relaxed people. I know it relaxed her."

"Sila, then," Jana amended. Zuzana Vachanova was meticulous. Probably her painstaking attention to detail created difficulty in her life, but it was helpful in a case like this. She would remember particulars. Jana focused on her more closely. "I wanted to take you back to just before Sila left for her meeting."

"The last time I saw her," Vachanova confirmed.

"The last time," Seges affirmed, eliciting a smile from Zuzana.

"Did you know she had an appointment?"

"As I indicated to the other police officers, I didn't. This wasn't unusual. She often had to attend impromptu meetings.

When she went off this time, she yelled her destination at me and ran off."

"Her exact words, please."

Vachanova thought for a moment, wanting to be precise.

"'I have a quick meeting. Jholki has come home to roost.'"

"Who is Jholki?"

"I've never heard the name before."

"You're sure of the name?"

"I'm not totally sure," Vachanova apologized, suddenly tense, afraid of being criticized. "She ran out, and with that voice of hers, you know, it was often hard to pick up each word." Seges nodded at her sympathetically, and Vachanova relaxed again. "We get hundreds of calls. It didn't seem like she was concerned about informing me of the name. I could always reach her on her cell phone if she was needed."

Jana followed Seges's lead, being very solicitous. "It had to be difficult trying to keep track of everything that went through this office."

"I've had to work hard at it." There was now a self-righteous note to Vachanova's voice. Her work was her religion.

The door to the outer office opened and one of the assistants poked her head in with a question.

"Out! Out!" Vachanova barked. "The door is closed. That means we're not to be disturbed. Out!"

The assistant ducked out. Vachanova resumed her virtuous expression.

"They're very inexperienced," she explained. "They've been poorly trained. It's apparent I'll have to do a lot myself." There was now a put-upon, "poor-me" slump to her shoulders. Seges placed a sympathetic hand on her shoulder. Vachanova immediately straightened up, patting him on the hand in gratitude

Jana figured she was seeing the beginning of a new romance. She repressed a smile, then asked, "Is there any way we could find out who called just before she left?"

"Nobody called her. If they had, it would have gone through me."

"And you would have logged it in?"

"No, the only calls that are logged in are those where a message is left."

"Someone could have called her on her cell phone."

"Or she might have called *them* on her cell phone."

Jana made a mental note to find out if either woman had had a cell phone when her effects were catalogued.

"Do you keep the notes you make when you take the caller's name and number?"

"Only temporarily. We give the note to whoever it's meant for, and then we forget about it. We've done our job." Her voice had that note of piety in it again.

"Yes," said Seges, as if he were saying "Amen."

Zuzana Vachanova gave him a beatific smile. At the moment, they were each recognizing a kindred spirit. Jana wondered how long they would be able to tolerate each other if they were truly required to spend time together.

She thought back to the last time she had seen Covic in this same office, and reviewed the conversation they'd had. She remembered the throwaway question she had posed and the brief response that had materialized on Covic's face. Covic had denied that she recognized the name, but Jana decided to ask Vachanova in case she remembered.

"Please think back again to when Sila left the office. You said she hurried out the door, saying 'Jholki has come home to roost'?"

"Exactly."

"Could the name have been Solti?"

Vachanova pondered, her face finally brightening. "It could have been."

Seges nodded sagely.

"Did you ever hear that name from anyone else? Perhaps in a phone message left for Sila or one of the legislators?"

Vachanova's eyes gave the impression that she was far away, searching inside the files of her memory. She finally came out of her reverie.

"I have. Yes, I have. A man by that name called here. For one of the members of parliament. It was a long-distance call, as I remember, and the man was very urgent, very demanding. That could have been the name the Red Devil shouted to me when she left."

Both Jana and Seges were surprised at the use of the nickname. It had emerged as an epithet. Vachanova put her hand to her mouth, surprised at her own words.

"I don't know why I said that." She looked mortified. "I apologize."

"No offense taken," said Seges.

Vachanova looked at him with doe eyes, grateful.

"She was a hard person to work with," Vachanova offered. "A very hard person."

"So I've heard," Seges reassured her.

"What was the name of the legislator Solti called?"

"He was a member of parliament at the time. Now he's a deputy minister. It was Ivan Boryda."

This was a surprise. Jana had not expected Boryda to be the answer to her question. She mulled the information over. Solti had probably called from Nepal. Why would Boryda get a call from a smuggler, unless he himself was involved in smuggling? She reviewed what she knew about the man. He'd been a lawyer before going into politics. Then he'd begun his climb from local politics to parliament, and from there to deputy prime minister. There was nothing on the surface of his career that Jana could see to tie him to Solti.

Jana gave Vachanova her card, asking her to call them if she recalled any further information. Zuzana focused her farewell on Seges, who lingered a few seconds longer than appropriate. Jana and Seges finally left the office, Jana wondering how long it would take after they reached their office for Seges to call Zuzana for a date.

As soon as they got back to the police building, Jana telephoned Boryda's office and asked for an opportunity to see the deputy prime minister. The functionary at the other end of the line apologized, informing her that the deputy prime minister was out of the country on official business. He was in Vienna, attending an important committee session of the IACA.

Boryda in Vienna, as well as Sofia. Not a coincidence. Perhaps the relationship between them had rekindled. Remembering Solti's call to Boryda, there was also the possibility that Sofia and Boryda were there not for love, but on business.

Jana hoped it was not business involving the murders in Bratislava.

Chapter 37

The next morning, Seges was his old self again: complaining, postponing work. His good spirits of the day before had vanished. Later, Seges and another officer came to Jana's office to talk about an old man who had gone crazy and killed a neighbor's teenage son, who had been tormenting him. All during the discussion, Seges daydreamed, unable to focus. When the other officer noticed Seges's inattention, he teased him for wool-gathering. Seges stalked out of the room.

Jana called Seges back in when she had finished with the officer's case and chided him for rudeness to a junior officer. Seges mumbled a few words about stomach problems and seeing a doctor later if he still felt sick. When he started easing toward the door, Jana asked him how his date with Zuzana Vachanova the night before had gone.

Seges glared at Jana, before realizing who he was glowering at, startled that she knew, not realizing that he had given his intentions away when they were in Vachanova's office. He choked out a few words about meeting Vachanova for coffee, avoiding Jana's eyes.

Jana pushed the matter out of her mind, telling Seges to see if the cell phones of the two dead women had been found on their bodies. He was then to bring the phones to her without using them. Jana's instructions were emphatic. She wanted the last numbers called, as well as any other information that they could cull from the phones.

When he finally left, Jana turned to the files on the older Guzak brother. She had to make good on her promise to Giles to intensify the hunt for Kristoe Guzak, so she checked on the measures they had already taken, wondering, after she reviewed them, what else could be done. The net for the man had been spread throughout Slovakia; bulletins had been sent to all the neighboring countries; so what else was left? Jana tried to put herself into the fugitive's mind.

If he had attacked Giles's bodyguard, then he was still in Bratislava. But why? The knowledge that his brother and mother had been killed, and that whoever had killed them was probably looking for him, should have increased the pressure on him to leave. Guzak would know that the police were on the hunt for him and that Bratislava was where he stood the greatest chance of being caught. Yet he stayed, when he could have fled back to Ukraine, or gone to Hungary or any other place in the European Union.

Why was he so intent on Spis and Giles? Did that mean he thought Giles and Spis had killed his brother and mother? Was the revenge motive so great that it kept him in Slovakia? Guzak probably also knew that other people in the smuggling ring had been killed. That would place added pressure on him to run. What, then, impelled him to stay in Bratislava?

Jana massaged her temples with her fingers, trying to ease her stress. Everything in the case seemed to point to more imminent violence. She had to stop it from happening.

Guzak would provide the answers she needed, so she had to find him. Where could he be hiding? Perhaps in the underbelly of Bratislava, with the pornographers, the few organized gang members, the general thieves that every city had. He might have sought sanctuary with one of them. But most of them were known and were under constant scrutiny. Surely he would be wary enough to avoid them.

Jana put herself in Guzak's shoes. If she were him, she would only emerge from her hiding place during the day, when she could mix with the crowds of strollers, just another face, a constant blur that remained out of focus to everyone else walking past. The night was something else. Night, in a small city like this, when the inhabitants of the daytime streets went home, would strip away his camouflage. It would then become imperative for him to find a secure hideaway. But who would welcome a Guzak into their home?

Jana slapped the files closed, angry at herself for not being perceptive enough to figure out where the man might have gone to earth. She forcibly composed herself. There were still official chores that needed to be taken care of.

Because of the press of events, the corruption investigation launched by Bohumil's group and the murders of Sila Covic and Marta, Jana had not adequately briefed Trokan on what she had learned from Veza on her trip to Ukraine and, even more important, what she had learned from Sila Covic's aide. As she was buzzing the colonel to find out if he was free, he walked through her door.

Trokan eased himself into a seat, stretching his legs out in front of himself, and reclined. "I came to ask for help in the investigation of the deaths of the Red Devil and Marta."

"I'm helping."

"I know. I need more."

"I'm not much of a savior."

"Try."

"I was just coming to brief you."

"I know."

"How could you know?"

"I'm a colonel, remember? We see all and know all." He grinned at her. "All right, so I didn't know. Tell me."

Jana related the information that Solti had called the deputy prime minister from Nepal.

"Ivan Boryda?" His voice was incredulous. "I don't believe it."

"Why not?"

"I suppose it's because I don't like the idea of investigating a deputy prime minister." He made a sour face. "It makes me nervous."

"He's like every politician, always screaming 'I want more.' Some of them are just more patient about it than he seems to be. I believe he is into some kind of criminal activity."

"You're sure?"

"Nothing's sure until you go to trial and the defendant is convicted. Besides, the investigation isn't over. Maybe he's not guilty of anything. Maybe the witness is wrong."

"The man is a deputy prime minister," Trokan reminded her. "We have to be positive or we're in deep shit. Remember the rule: never charge a celebrity or a politician unless you are prepared to go to the wall. They have too many friends or admirers."

"Are you telling me to not investigate him, Colonel?"

"Don't play at being stupid. Of course not; go ahead. Just do it with care, thinking all the while of your poor colonel who will have to defend you if you screw up."

She gave him a thumbs-up.

"What else do we have?"

Jana filled him in on what she had learned in Ukraine from Veza, putting it together with the information she had acquired about Solti. Trokan's eyes got wider.

"How big is this thing?"

"Big. Every time I look at it, it gets bigger."

Trokan began reviewing the facts, making sure he understood. "We have criminals, experts at getting in and out of countries, participating in what appears to be a well thought-out operation all around the world. It would appear to be well financed, otherwise they couldn't travel the way they do. Unfortunately for them, there are fractures appearing in the organization, people are being murdered, their structure is going through an upheaval."

Trokan glanced at Jana for confirmation. She nodded.

He continued: "Except we don't know what they are doing or why it is fracturing."

"Veza surmised that a shipment hadn't gone through. There was chaos; that's all he was aware of. He knew he might be next, so he fled."

Trokan slouched in the chair even further, his chin on his chest. "What are they smuggling? Narcotics, women, government secrets?"

"They all had sidelines, looking to make an extra euro, pound, peso, or dollar. The side businesses include all of the above, but none of them were the main business of the group."

Trokan eyed her expectantly.

"So?"

"The Ukrainian didn't know."

Trokan sat upright, skepticism on his face.

"How can a smuggler not know what he is smuggling?"

"Sealed packages. All of the parcels were wrapped in heavy paper which was tied and sealed. They all weighed very little; easy to transport. They were paid wads of cash to deliver the item intact. They were ordered never to open it. If the package they delivered had been opened in any way, it was reported. Veza knew of one instance where a man opened a package before delivery. He was killed a few days later. So they were all very careful as to how they handled those packages."

"Who would they report to?"

"Solti. He was the one killed in Nepal."

Trokan grimaced. "The people doing the killing have long arms."

"Very long."

"We need to know the rest of the ingredients if we're going to make a stew."

"I'm thinking."

"They've killed one of our own people. So think faster."

"Pressing me for a solution won't help."

"I know. You're absolutely right, as usual." He heaved a large, dramatic sigh. "I'm just a wretch, trying to shift my anxiety to you. Please know this: if it weren't for the fact that we both appear to be standing at the edge of a cliff, I would keep silent. However, since we are on the edge of that long drop, I will continue to be a wretch and keep pushing."

"The stew isn't ready to eat yet."

"Increase the temperature of the oven."

Trokan got to his feet.

"There's one more thing," Jana told him. "I want you to do something when I leave for Vienna."

When Jana laid out the details of what she wanted him to do, Trokan nodded with increasing enthusiasm. His face took on the appearance of a satisfied man.

"Consider it done." He moved to the door. "I just came in for a taste of the stew." He pretended to taste something, smacking his lips. "Yup, more time needed, but a good recipe. Keep it simmering."

Trokan stretched, rolling his shoulders, trying to ease the tension in his back. "I also have another objective. Just a small reminder. Your friend Sofia gave you a diamond. You have two days left of the time we agreed on. After that, we open a case and go upstairs with it."

Jana winced.

As Trokan walked through the door, he turned back, giving Jana a teaspoon of sugar to sweeten the medicine. "I'm negotiating with Captain Bohumil to take Seges off our hands. He's thinking about it." He walked out, still rolling his shoulders.

Jana called Sofia in Vienna to find out when they could talk. Jana might find out something of value about Boryda if she could persuade Sofia to talk about him. There was also the continuing matter of Kamin. Jana was not satisfied with Sofia's explanation of her association with him. Yes, she had a lot to discuss with Sofia.

On the phone, Sofia flatly refused to return to Bratislava. Too busy right now. There were many things happening; she had to stay in Vienna.

No matter how hard Jana pushed, Sofia was adamant.

Jana hung up. She had to go to Vienna.

Which left one more thing: Jana had to find a police officer to watch her neighbor's house to see who came by to pick up the tapes they were recording. She called Jarov, hoping he was free. He was. He was not the most experienced cop in the world, but he would do.

She asked him to come up so she could brief him.

After the briefing, she checked the train schedules. Tomorrow she would talk to Sofia.

Chapter 38

Jana, not yet packed, was having dinner as she waited for Jarov so she could point out the house he was to watch, when the phone rang. It was Karina, the Ukrainian girl who waited tables at the Gremium. Jana decided not to talk to her on the tapped phone, unwilling to risk Karina's life to obtain a bit of information. She arranged to meet Karina at the Partisan statue just off Postová.

When Jana got there, Karina was leaning against the figure of the heroic Slovak partisan carrying his wounded World War II comrade. Standing near Karina was a woman who Jana didn't recognize at first, she was so bundled up against the cold. It was one of the women from Andreea's apartment, the one with the sweater who had urged Veza's girlfriend to give Jana information about him.

To get out of the cold, they walked over to the Church of the Brothers of Mercy, which Jana had sometimes attended as a child, taking seats in a chilly side-chapel pew. There were only a few parishioners sitting in the rear, all well out of hearing. In the darkly lit church, the three women were indistinguishable shadows.

"If the weather doesn't warm up, I'm almost ready to go back to Ukraine," the woman with the sweater vowed, shivering.

"We agreed that you came from Slovakia," Jana reminded her.

"I'm a Slovak through and through," the woman corrected

herself, smiling slightly. "My name is Olena, and, although it is a Ukrainian name, I was obviously born in Bratislava."

Karina nodded. "I can vouch for that."

"Naturally, you were present at her birth," Jana joked.

"Of course. I'm older than she is," Karina said, although she was plainly the younger.

Jana glanced at Karina. "You called for a reason."

"My friend"—she pointed at Olena—"has been evicted from Andreea's apartment."

"All the other girls had to leave too," Olena added. "It's impossible to live there any longer."

"Olena is staying with me for a few days." Karina related her own tale of woe. "The apartment belongs to my boyfriend from the Gremium. He says if Olena stays much longer, we'll both have to leave." She looked hopefully at Jana. "You told me I could call you if there was any difficulty."

"I can't help you find an apartment," Jana responded. "That's not the type of help I meant."

"I know," Karina affirmed. "But if Guzak leaves, the girls can return."

Guzak's name took Jana by surprise.

"He comes in every night, decides which girl he wants, then takes her to bed with him. None of us can stand him, so we left. We want him out so we can go back."

Both women looked expectantly at Jana.

"You're saying that the elder Guzak brother is now staying at Andreea's apartment?"

"Every night," Olena affirmed. "We're all afraid to say anything, even Andreea."

"And the police are after him," Karina reminded her.

"I know," Jana reminded her. "I'm the police."

Both women relaxed, satisfied that they had made their case.

"Arrest him," Karina suggested.

"Tonight would be satisfactory," Olena added. "I could move back in tomorrow if he were arrested tonight."

"That would do it," Karina agreed. "My boyfriend would be happy."

The two women waited for Jana to tell them what to do, expecting her to swing into action.

Guzak was a very dangerous man, not someone to go after alone. Sending a few inexperienced beat officers to capture him wouldn't do. It would probably get them killed. Unfortunately, trying to form a large-scale arrest crew at this late hour would take time, and a man like Guzak could leave the apartment at any moment and vanish before they could seize him. Jana had to act at once. She knew only two police officers who would respond fast enough to be her backup: Seges and Jarov. She decided against Seges. He was not a man she wanted to have to rely on in a situation like this. As for Jarov, his duties at her house didn't start until tomorrow.

Thirty minutes later, she was sitting in her car with Jarov near Andreea's apartment, with Olena in the back seat. Two beat officers who had been on patrol had been commandeered by Jana to watch the back of the building, in case Guzak tried to escape through the rear. Jarov had stopped to get protective vests for both Jana and himself, and they were finishing adjusting them as they planned their next moves. The primary difficulty, aside from Guzak himself, was Andreea. They had to remove her from the danger zone, which was why they had brought Olena along.

Two patrol officers drove by. Jana flagged down their car and placed them halfway down the block, out of sight. In case Guzak got past Jana and Jarov, they would be the last barrier to his escape.

The plan was for Olena to go to the door, knock, and call to Andreea that she was back. When Andreea opened the door, they would grab her, pull her out, and then go in after Guzak.

It went off exactly as they'd hoped.

Olena knocked. Andreea came to the door. Olena responded to Andreea's query, "Just me, coming for a visit." Andreea opened the door. Jarov grabbed her as soon as the opening was wide enough, clapped a hand over her mouth, and pulled her out of the apartment. Jana went in.

Guzak was sleeping on the couch, his pistol resting on his chest, ready for action.

Jana tiptoed over to him, gently lifted the pistol off his chest, and put the muzzle of her own gun to his forehead. She pulled the hammer back so he could hear the loud click. Guzak opened his eyes.

"Welcome back to Slovakia," Jana greeted him.

They took him to jail immediately. Jana decided to talk to him in the morning, and rescheduled her trip to Vienna for later in the day. She went home to sleep, happier now. Things just might be working out.

Unfortunately, Jana was greeted rudely when she awakened. A special edition of the Slovak newspapers had been printed to disseminate a piece of breaking news. Guzak had escaped. The details were still not clear, but it was known that he'd produced a gun and forced his way out of jail during the early morning hours.

Jana had taken his gun away right before she woke and arrested him. She had supervised a complete search of the man. Guzak had had no other weapons on his person. There was no way he could have brandished a gun unless it had been smuggled to him while he was in custody.

Captain Bohumil was right to suspect someone in the department of leaking information about his investigations.

Only it was not Jana.
Somebody else had turned bad.
Very bad.

Chapter 39

There was no use in staying in Bratislava. The manhunt was on, and it would continue without Jana's supervision. It seemed like everyone in the government was investigating Guzak's escape. Every bureaucrat in the administration put his nose into the affair, trying to discover how Guzak had obtained a gun and waltzed out of his cell to freedom.

Jana took the train to Vienna's Sudbahnhof station, then a taxi to an Ibis Hotel in the central city area, one of a chain of hotels with Spartan but cheap rooms. Trokan would not quibble over having the government pay for it. The desk clerk carefully checked through Jana's passport with the usual patented Viennese scorn. Jana was back in the AEIOU, the old Latin motto which translated as "The Entire World Is Austria's Empire." Jana gritted her teeth, registered and carried her bag up to her room. She called Sofia at the Vienna International Center. When Sofia was finally summoned to the phone, she was not very happy to hear that Jana was only a short cab drive away

"Jana, I told you I was busy."

"Too busy to see your childhood friend?"

There was a pause.

"I'm here on business, Jana."

"So am I."

There was another pause.

"We're engrossed in a round of negotiations."

"Sofia, you're still a Slovak citizen. A member of parliament. It's not so good to say 'no' to a police officer. What if the voters heard about it; the people in your neighborhood? And, besides, what if they sent another police officer to talk to you who is not your friend? It's much better to see me."

The pause was longer this time.

"This evening is the best time. At 1800 hours. It will have to be brief."

"I would like to see Boryda as well."

"Impossible. He needs to work. Utterly impossible."

"Under the circumstances, it *has* to be possible."

"He can't see you." There was tension in her voice that increased with each word. "He absolutely cannot come."

It was Jana's turn to pause. She was not in Slovakia. She had no authority here. She could try calling on the Austrian police, but that option did not really appear to be feasible. Boryda probably had diplomatic immunity. The Austrian police would avoid an international incident at all costs. Jana had to settle for talking to Sofia.

Sofia gave Jana directions. They would meet in the small conference room, which was actually named the Slovakia Room. They could celebrate as if they were having dinner at home, just the two of them. Perhaps it would be better, Jana thought, to talk to Sofia without Boryda. Sofia might talk more freely without her former lover there. Perhaps.

Jana went to the ultra-modern building complex and was directed to the correct structure. She reached the Slovakia Room a good half hour before the appointed time. Under circumstances like these, Jana made a habit of trying to feel comfortable in what she perceived might be an arena. Better to get to know the terrain before the actual battle began.

The Slovakia Room, an insignificant meeting room as

international conference rooms went, was nevertheless comfortably furnished, the conference table small enough to permit real conversation. Jana felt a small buzz of national pride, then settled into an overstuffed chair, setting her watch to ring in a half hour and closing her eyes. The watch went off on time, but Sofia had not arrived. She finally appeared a half hour late, just as a food cart was wheeled in behind her.

The cart was wheeled out, two dinners carefully placed on the conference table, provided for the women courtesy of the center's cafeteria service. The two friends had not exchanged a word, not even said hello. Both were on their guard, recognizing that Jana's trip was official and that their interview would go into a file to be reviewed by others.

Jana hadn't eaten since breakfast, and even then she'd had just a small snack, so she started right in on the veal dish that had been set out for them. After the first bite, Jana waved her fork in the air, announcing that the Slovaks knew how to cook pork better, but the Viennese certainly knew how to prepare veal. Then she took a second forkful. She chewed, watching Sofia, who picked at her food. There was no harm in making Sofia simmer. It was part of the stew she and Trokan had talked about.

"I'm very impressed by this building complex. I get the feeling, from its appearance, that the world's problems are settled here."

Sofia kept picking at her food without responding.

"The UN, those other organizations, so many countries represented here; international issues brought to the table and settled peaceably. Great things are accomplished here."

Showing more irritation than hunger, Sofia dropped her fork on her tray.

"Jana, I'm glad you think that the world's business is being attended to properly. But to remind you, it's necessary that

I pay attention to a number of those issues. That means we have to finish our talk in the next few minutes, or you and I have to go our separate ways without discussing whatever you've come to browbeat me about."

"Why would I take the train all the way to Vienna to browbeat you?" Jana continued to eat. She could see that Sofia was reaching the end of her patience. A good sign. The moment for Jana to utilize Sofia's impulsiveness and impatience was coming. Jana took another forkful. "I really like the way they made this. It's always surprising when a cafeteria takes care in preparing food. Maybe they could open an annex in Bratislava?"

Sofia shoved her tray across the table, making her point very loudly as it just missed Jana. There was a clatter of cutlery and a crash of broken dishes bouncing off a seat and dropping to the floor.

Unperturbed, Jana finished her last bite and set her tray to one side.

"Finished," she announced cheerfully, as if the incident with the dishes had never occurred, and carefully wiped her hands on a napkin. "Time for us to talk. It's always easier when the belly is full, don't you think so? People are calmer." Jana focused on Sofia, preparing to drop her bomb.

"How is your relationship with Ivan coming along? Has it reverted to what it was?"

"You asked me here to talk about Ivan?"

"Ivan as he relates to your situation with the police. Ivan has an emerging problem, and I feared that your close association with him might bring you down as well, particularly considering that the newspapers have linked the two of you. Not one person who has read the articles will believe that you had nothing to do with Ivan's business."

Sofia stared at Jana, unblinking. "I told you that Ivan and I have stayed apart since the situation became public."

"You're both here in Vienna."

"By political necessity. I'm on a parliamentary committee; he's the government person taking the point on this issue. We're here for an International Atomic Energy Agency meeting on research reactor utilization and advanced reactor design. We've been fighting for years with the Austrians to win approval to build an advanced reactor in Slovakia, and for years the Austrians have opposed it. They're downwind, and if anything went wrong they'd be endangered. For the first time, the IAEA is on our side with this issue."

Sofia's voice took on a messianic fervor that had been absent from it lately. "Ivan is leading the conciliation and compromise meetings with the Austrians. That's where I'm supposed to be right now. We do nothing but attend sessions during the day, and then have clandestine meetings with the Austrians at night. You should hear Ivan talk to these people, bargain with them, always maneuvering them toward our position. He's been absolutely brilliant.

"When Slovakia gets her reactor as a result of these meetings, then Ivan will get the credit he deserves. He'll bring our country into the forefront of nuclear research; we'll be independent of oil for industry. We'll be the leader in eastern and central Europe. We'll be able to export energy. And it'll all be because of Ivan."

Sofia's face had become more flushed with each sentence, more adulatory, her voice hoarsening with infatuation with Ivan and zeal for the program. "Only Ivan can do this. And when it's accomplished, he will use it as a springboard, perhaps to become prime minister, maybe to attain a position at an international level. Ivan Boryda is a great and wonderful man, Jana. A man of destiny!"

Sofia had the look of the true believer, but more a true believer in a man than a cause. They might not currently be carrying on their affair, but Sofia was still in love with Ivan Boryda.

Jana sat, waiting for Sofia to come down from her emotional high. It was almost time for Jana to bring her even further down to earth. She regretted it, but events had shown she had to go forward.

"You sound like you would do anything for him, Sofia."

"Anything, Jana," she acknowledged. "You would have to know him, and me, to understand this."

"And are you both equally committed?"

"We've stayed at a distance from each other. We had to stay apart, except for dealing with government affairs. But, when the scandal sheets have had their day, we'll be together again. Meanwhile, we work."

Jana dropped the bomb.

"Sofia, we have evidence that Ivan Boryda is involved in criminal activities. The evidence indicates that he's implicated in a number of murders. Are you involved with him in these crimes?"

Sofia stared at Jana as if she didn't comprehend Jana's words.

Jana repeated herself, waiting for understanding to dawn. When it finally came, Sofia's face showed a flux of conflicting emotions. Jana had raised ominous and terrible possibilities, with a crash that was much, much louder than that of the tray of dishes. Sofia tried to speak; her lips moved, but no words came out.

Jana persevered.

"Sofia, I have to know where you stand in this partnership the two of you have. Are you aware of any of the circumstances surrounding these crimes?"

Sofia's face finally resumed a hue near to its natural tone. "I think our conversation is over."

"Sofia, if you are innocent, I'm trying, for the sake of our friendship, to prevent your falling with him."

Sofia grimaced at the thought of Boryda falling. "I've understood what you said and will talk about it with Ivan."

Sofia looked at Jana, expecting that she would object to her informing Boryda of what they had just discussed. Jana said nothing.

"Well, I have to go to my meeting," Sofia announced, trying to sound as if nothing of moment had occurred.

Jana stood first. Sofia rose slowly, still absorbing what she had been told.

"He's a great man, Jana. Nothing will stop the world from acknowledging that."

"You may think so, but thinking it doesn't make it true. That's a judgment for history to make." Before Sofia walked out, Jana dropped her last bombshell. "We are looking for Kamin. Do you know where he is?"

Sofia hesitated.

"Are you interested in what I've found out about the diamond, Sofia?"

Sofia left the room without answering.

Jana watched her go, then quickly made a phone call to the Austrian police officers she knew from the regional crime committee, asking for a quick favor. She didn't even have to get off the phone: they gave her the information she was seeking in a few minutes. Jana thanked them, then took a cab back to the hotel. Immediately upon arrival, she called Trokan at his home and told him what had transpired with Sofia . . . and what she now wanted done based on what she'd learned.

Sometime this evening, or at the latest tomorrow, there was going to be a defining event in the case.

It would be interesting to see what the coming hours would bring.

Chapter 40

Jana lay on her hotel bed, fretting over the things she hadn't done and wondering why she had done other things so poorly. There were other players in the game, and she hadn't dealt with them as she could have. A long, hot bath was in order, but the Spartan accommodations at the hotel only provided a shower; so Jana turned the spray on as hot as she could stand it, letting the water cascade for a long time over the back of her neck, hoping that the muscles would relax enough to allow her to either think more clearly or simply enjoy a long, deep sleep.

She toweled herself off, slipped on a T-shirt top and briefs, blow-dried her hair, then turned the covers down and switched off the light. Virtually at the same moment, there was a knock at the door. Jana quickly turned the light back on.

"Yes, who is it?" she asked. She made sure to step out of the doorway so she was not in the line of fire if someone tried to shoot through the door. It was the wrong moment to be careless. Jana swept her automatic from the dresser, jacking a shell into the firing chamber.

A muffled male voice came through the door, as if the speaker was trying to talk quietly so the other hotel guests would not become aware of his presence. Jana stepped closer to the door.

"It's too late. Call me on the hotel telephone if you need to talk to me."

The man's voice was louder this time.

"Jana, it's Peter. I've broken every rule to see you. Have pity and open the door."

Jana opened the door. Peter focused on the gun she had pointing at him.

"Sorry." She lowered the gun, looked both ways, then tugged him inside the room, locking the door behind him. "Why are you here?"

Peter looked Jana up and down, admiring her abbreviated outfit. "I'm here because I knew you'd greet me dressed just like this. I needed the inspiration of seeing a beautiful woman again."

Jana, realizing how little she was wearing, pulled the coverlet from the bed and draped it over herself like a gown. Peter smiled while she struggled with it.

"You have an idiotic grin on your face," Jana told him. "Leering at nearly naked women is not what people expect from a prosecutor."

"Only when they don't have a relationship with the woman."

"Who said we have a relationship?"

"My cousin Groucho."

Jana fought hard to suppress a smile when she heard Groucho's name. "He must have misinterpreted."

"You were very clear, and he remembered very well." He stared at her gun. "Don't you think it would be nicer if you put your gun away?"

Jana padded over to the dresser, put the gun in its holster, and laid it down.

"In the drawer, please," Peter requested.

Jana put it in the drawer.

"Feel safer now?" she asked.

"Much safer."

He put his arms around her and kissed her. She didn't respond. He looked at her, shaking his head.

"You are out of practice."

He kissed her again. Jana responded. Then she finally broke away.

"Time for explanations." She sat on the edge of the bed. "You've left me operating in the dark. I love you. But all this craziness with you and Bohumil and the investigation that tried to implicate me, has me confused and angry."

He sat next to her.

"I had no choice. When you became a suspect, particularly after the killing in Geneva, I couldn't see you. It would have been impossible for both of us. Then, after the phone taps, it became even worse. To make it better, I *had* to make it worse.

"I knew you weren't involved. I love you, so how could I not know it? However, to demonstrate to them that you were innocent of any wrongdoing, I had to let *you* show them." He leaned closer to her. "I knew you would, and would do it easily. And you have."

His face fell. "I also knew that my part in the investigation would cause hurt. For which I apologize. But for us, in the long run, it was for the best." He sighed, looking at her, hoping she would forgive him. "When I could, I sent Groucho to you."

They both smiled.

"Dear Groucho! He liked being the go-between for lovers." Jana remembered the man's delight when he heard that she still loved Peter. "He is a nice man, nearly as nice as his cousin Peter."

"Nicer," said Peter. "Remember, I'm a public procurator."

"And I'm a police officer."

"Does that mean that the only ones who can tolerate us are each other?"

"It must."

They kissed. Jana reached over to turn out the light and slipped off her remaining clothes. They made love very tenderly.

The next morning, while they slept in, the phone rang. It was Trokan.

"Get the sleep out of your eyes," he ordered. "Is he there?"

Jana looked over at Peter, still trying to wake up. "Yes, he's here. How did you know?"

"I told you before, I'm a colonel. Besides, I called his office first. They told me he'd gone to Vienna. Where else would he be going but to see you, right?"

"Thankfully, true."

"As you predicted, it happened."

"Who was it?"

"Sabina."

"I thought it might be."

"We set up the camera. She went through the files in Bohumil's office, then went to your office and pulled the files there as well."

"You arrested her?"

"She's in a cell in the Darensky substation."

"They'll try to get to Sabina before I'm ready to see her. Keep her protected."

"There are two officers right outside her cell at all times. When do you come back?"

"One more task here, then back to Bratislava. I'll interview her as soon as I get in."

Jana hung up and lay staring at the ceiling.

"Your colonel?" Peter asked.

"Yes."

"Good news or bad news?"

"Both."

"How so?"

"We've found out who's been leaking information to the probable killers."

"Who is it?"

"One of Bohumil's police officers. The partner of the man who was killed in Geneva. Sabina Postova."

"How do you know she's the one?"

"She ransacked our police files last night. I was responsible for triggering the trap. It snapped on her."

Peter got up on an elbow to look down at her. "I could swear you were with me last night. Besides, with what we were doing, you didn't have the time."

"I told a friend of mine something yesterday. Sabina found out about it. To find out about what I told my friend, my friend had to either tell her, or tell someone else close to her. We laid a snare for Sabina if she acted on the information. She did. But now my friend may be implicated."

He lay back down. "What pointed you to Sabina?"

"Guzak's escape. Inside information was leaking out. Then there was the killing in Switzerland. How did the killer know I was going to be there, in this small town on Lake Léman? Someone had to have told him."

"The killer may have been following you."

"Not me; *them!* He followed the police officers who were following me. How did he know they were going to follow me? She told him.

"He was supposed to execute me. But Sabina's partner recognized whoever it was, and tried to stop it, which got him killed. It had to be clear to her just from the crime scene alone that I had nothing to do with the killing of her partner. Yet she accused me."

"Who's the friend?"

Jana found it hard to say Sofia's name. Peter saved her the trouble.

"Your friend Sofia."

Jana stayed silent.

"You're going back to Bratislava?"

"This evening."

"Why not now?"

"I have to talk to Deputy Prime Minister Ivan Boryda's wife. I've always wondered what kind of woman marries a man like that. This is the most opportune time to find out."

"But first. . . ."

She turned to look at Peter.

"A little bit of love."

He pulled her over to him.

Chapter 41

The lady was traveling with her husband. Knowing that, it was easy to find out where they were staying. Hotel guests in Europe are required to provide their passports to hotels when they register; the names are routinely furnished to the police. The Austrian police, always models of efficiency, checked the hotel lists and referred Jana to the hotel where Klaudia and Ivan Boryda were. Everything is near the Ring, the center of the city of Vienna, and the Im Palais Schwarzenberg Hotel was within walking distance of Jana's room.

When she got there, the hotel stunned her with its opulence. Im Palais Schwarzenberg was in the middle of a Viennese park, redolent of the days when Johann Strauss, father and son, were composing waltzes for Emperor Franz Joseph. When she first walked into the lobby, Jana would not have been surprised if some majordomo of the old imperial court had come to scold her for not using the servant's entrance. Fortunately, the people at the desk could not have been more extravagantly polite.

They swiftly located Klaudia Boryda in the conservatory-style dining area and escorted Jana to a tranquil area of tables bearing linen tablecloths, crystal glasses, and expensive china, where the guests were silently served by impeccably dressed waiters. The maitre d' took over from her escort at the entry to the dining area and led Jana to the table at which Klaudia Boryda was seated.

The woman, in her fifties, dressed in a well-cut, expensive suit, stood and extended her hand to Jana.

"Commander Matinova, a pleasure to meet you." She gestured for Jana to sit, picked up a crystal water glass, and took a sip. "I wondered what you would look like. There are not many women in the Slovak police with the rank of commander."

Jana was as surprised by the woman's poise as she was by her use of Jana's name and her apparent familiarity with her career. The waiter approached, and Jana felt compelled to ask for a coffee. While she was ordering, Boryda's wife studied her, making no effort to hide her scrutiny.

"You are younger looking than I thought you'd be."

"Thank you," Jana politely replied, making her own assessment of Klaudia Boryda. The word "impressive" sprang to mind. Intelligent, a planner, with a touch of ruthlessness. Jana decided she would be the perfect wife for a politician.

"My husband told me that you might be looking me up. Wasn't that perceptive of Ivan?"

Too much praise for Ivan Boryda, thought Jana. The woman was praising herself indirectly.

"If I may make a supposition, the deputy prime minister told you that I was in town and you deduced I might look you up."

"Why would I think that?"

"You're totally unflustered, which means expectation and preparation on your part. Ivan told you that I had met with his mistress, which means he was sufficiently worried about me to tell you about it. He didn't know how to handle it and wanted your advice. You're long-term allies. You'd have prepared him, and prepared yourself at the same time."

Jana was impressed by the woman's control. She hadn't even blinked when Jana mentioned her husband's mistress.

"The woman is not currently his mistress." Klaudia

Boryda tore a small piece off a breakfast roll, put a dab of jam on it, then nibbled at the piece. "It's a dead issue."

"She still has hopes."

"I can't blame her. My husband is very attractive."

"Why do you think it's a dead issue?"

"I know my husband. He won't give up what he has. And he would have to if he took up with her again. Ivan uses people. He still has some use for her. However, it's progressively becoming smaller."

"Why is that?"

A smile flickered across her face. "I told him it was over. And, like all good husbands, he is attentive to his wife's wishes."

Jana listened carefully to her tone. There was too much assurance in her voice. She described her advice as if it had been given by a master to her slave.

"He's a reasonable man," his wife added.

"Does the fact that Sofia was important to him bother you?"

"Men have a gland that women don't. They persist, from time to time, in exercising it. I will not allow myself to get upset over the exercise of a tiny gland."

Jana realized that the waiter was unobtrusively pouring a cup of coffee for her. He set the pot down next to the cup, then disappeared as quietly as he had appeared.

"A very comfortable hotel," Jana remarked. "Service without a fuss, a beautiful setting, gorgeous grounds. Very old money, I would think, comes here."

"Yes," Klaudia Boryda acknowledged. "Old money."

"Are you saying that you come from old money?"

"Old enough. We recovered well from the communist era."

"That must be good for you, and better for Ivan. Where did it all come from?"

"You're implying that I have another source of money other than my family?"

"A politician always needs money. Moreover, the higher his aspirations, the more money he needs. Your husband, for example."

"I would agree."

"Have you both undertaken the task of getting more money to feed his aspirations?"

"People are very generous to Ivan."

"He has no side business?"

Klaudia Boryda's face became absolutely devoid of expression. She didn't realize that eradicating all emotion was, in itself, a statement.

Jana had been thinking about the diamond that Sofia had received in the mail. Sofia had immediately associated the diamond with Ivan Boryda. He was her lover, which made it natural for her to assume that he had sent it. He had denied it, but had immediately broken off their affair. Jana had assumed that he had become concerned about bad publicity in the media, which could mean the death of his political life. But maybe there was another reason.

"You and Ivan Boryda have been political partners for years. I would assume that means you are also the keeper of his political and business secrets?"

The woman's face remained a mask.

"I will take your silence as a positive response."

"Take it any way you wish."

"Do you like diamonds?"

Nothing about Klaudia Boryda gave anything away, except her failure to answer.

"All women like diamonds," Jana answered for her. "So that means we both like diamonds."

Jana felt for the two top buttons on her blouse and opened

them, pulling Sofia's diamond out far enough that it could be seen.

"Isn't this a beautiful jewel? A perfect, unflawed diamond, rare for its size. Would you like me to take it off so you can examine it more closely?"

Klaudia Boryda finally betrayed an emotion by the curl of her lips, the flair of her nostrils: triumph.

"A beautiful stone, indeed. I think I've seen it before. I wonder where?" She pretended to be thinking, putting on a performance. "Ah yes, it comes to me. I have a marvelous memory on occasion, particularly when an event strikes me. When I first saw that diamond, I remember the woman who was wearing it for the entire world to see. Your friend Sofia. I'm sure other people at the party saw her wearing it. If you wish, I can give you some of their names. Do you want them now?"

Now Jana knew how the diamond had gotten to Sofia. Klaudia Boryda had sent it. It had been a snare for Sofia. And she had walked into it blindly. There is an old saying, "Give people what they've always desired and it will kill them." People had seen Sofia wearing the diamond. The diamond just might destroy her.

"I'll ask you to provide me with the list when we both get back to Slovakia," Jana said reluctantly.

But Klaudia Boryda was still smug, believing that her trap had worked. She couldn't resist rubbing it in. "I would think, Commander Matinova, that it would be impossible for a mere legislator to have acquired a gem of that quality, they earn so little. Where do you think she obtained the money to purchase a diamond? Oh, goodness!" she feigned shock and disbelief. "You don't think she's corrupt, do you? Perhaps she took bribes? It would be horrible if she did. And even if she didn't, the press will convict her without giving her a chance to explain." A cold, pitiless note entered her voice. "Of course, I'm sure she has a logical explanation, aren't you?

"Do you have any other questions to ask me?" she continued. "If not, perhaps you will leave. I'd like to sit here alone, enjoying a quiet cigarette. Everybody makes such a fuss these days about smoking that I feel uncomfortable smoking with anyone nearby. You understand, I trust?"

Jana decided to stay for another moment. "You laid it all out, a road map for her to follow. You knew Sofia would wear the diamond. People would talk. You hoped the police would question her, they would find the diamond, and her career in parliament, and her affair with your husband, would be over. Your husband knew what had happened as soon as Sofia called him about the diamond. And he had to stop seeing her."

"Ah, you're trying to get your friend Sofia out of this by blaming me. It's wrong of you to do that." She took out a cigarette and lit it. "If I don't hear from you in the next few days, I'll call your supervisor, perhaps even the minister, and tell him about the diamond that you have in your possession. I don't think you'll chance that. Take my advice: turn it in. Start the investigation. Or else they'll be investigating you."

Jana rose and carefully tucked her chair in. In a dining room like this, it would be uncivilized to leave anything out of place. Jana took a step backward, almost bumping into the hovering waiter. She gestured at Klaudia. "The lady will pay for my coffee." She walked away.

Jana now knew where to focus the rest of her investigation.

How had the Borydas come into possession of such a diamond? It would be interesting to find out.

Chapter 42

They met at their usual spot, the Gremium Café in Bratislava. This time it was not hard to get Sofia to show up. Jana had simply told her that if she didn't, her next stop would be jail. They converged on the café from Vienna: Jana traveled by train, and Sofia was driven by a reasonably priced limousine service. Jana toyed with the idea of accompanying Sofia, but decided that she didn't want to spend that much time alone with her in the back seat of a car.

Jana arrived first and nodded to the manager of the Gremium. He looked worried when he saw her. Jana got a wave and a big smile from Karina, who bustled over, quickly cleaning the table and bringing Jana an espresso on the house. Her voice dropped to a whisper as she leaned over with the coffee. "The girls are still worried about Guzak. When are you going to catch him?"

Jana shrugged. "They're scrubbing all the corners, hoping the cockroach will crawl out. So, soon, I would think. It would help matters if you would get word out on the street that I would like to talk to him."

"Guzak?"

"Guzak," Jana confirmed. "I will help him if he helps me. I have a task for him."

Karina was lost. "He doesn't like to work, except as a 'you know what.'"

"Just get the word out."

"Okay."

The manager scowled his disapproval at Karina, then dropped his gaze, turning away, when he saw Jana watching him. Police officers are never loved, Jana reminded herself, except by the very young and the innocent. Minutes later, Sofia arrived.

"Nervous" was the word to describe Sofia. She moved constantly, licking her lips, smoothing imaginary wisps of vagrant hair, her words coming out in short, faltering bursts. She knew that Jana had discovered something, and the discovery did not bode well for her.

"Let's get on with it!" Sofia demanded, glancing around the restaurant in an effort not to meet Jana's eyes. "As you know, I have to get back to my work."

"Sofia, I talked to Ivan Boryda's wife."

Sofia was jolted.

"And how is the bitch?" she finally got out.

"She sends back her hate."

"Let her rot in hell." She finally looked at Jana. "Okay, you saw her. She hates me; I'm going to get her man. What else did she have to say?"

"That you're going to go to prison for corrupt practices and taking graft. She seemed particularly happy about how you are going to lose your seat in parliament and be drummed out of the party. Or even happier, as you've already lost Ivan Boryda because you never really had him. I ended the meeting having learned that you have been set up by a very manipulative lady."

"Ivan hates her. He's told me that over and over again."

"Some successful marriages are made in hell."

"You said I've been set up. How could that be?"

"The diamond."

Sofia had not expected that.

Jana went on. She had to air it all out. "*She* sent you the diamond, Sofia, not Ivan. She wanted you to wear it at the party
for all the world to see. She wanted Ivan to see it. She wanted
the other guests to notice. Accordingly, when the rumors of
your being corrupt came out, and she made sure they did,
everyone would point to the diamond as proof. *Voila*, Sofia is
no longer a rival for her husband. Poor Sofia is in jail."

Sofia visibly wilted.

"If you had told me about the diamond when we met at
this café earlier, we might have arrived at this point sooner."
Jana drank her coffee, signaling Karina to bring her another
one. "When Ivan saw the diamond, he knew. He wouldn't
talk to you at the party, isn't that right? And after that, but
before the scandal of the love affair between the two of you
was all over the media, he'd broken off your liaison, telling
you not to call. Correct?"

A very weak "yes" fluttered across the table.

"Wearing the diamond frightened him," Jana mused
aloud, not really sure if Sofia could answer. "Why would he
respond so immediately, and so forcefully?"

"I don't know," Sofia painfully admitted. She had an unexpected thought. "Maybe the diamond belonged to his wife?"
Her eyes pleaded with Jana to say she was wrong.

Jana concluded, "No, not her diamond. But not his either.
Otherwise he wouldn't have responded as he did. Something
else forced him to distance himself from you after he saw you
wearing it."

"Why? I would never have harmed him."

"I don't know the 'why' yet." Jana looked intently at Sofia.
"I need you to be truthful, Sofia. Did you tell Ivan that you
had turned the diamond over to me? Did you tell him that
you did it so your good friend Jana Matinova would find out
where it came from?"

There was no more avoidance and denial from Sofia. Her emotions were chaotic, showing on her face. She tried desperately not to cry.

"I . . . thought he . . . should know."

Jana waited a moment, before continuing, to allow Sofia to control herself.

"When you told him, he got frightened, and he told his wife, as he always does when he's worried. After that, the anti-corruption group in our office began to investigate me for corruption. The captain in charge said a reliable informant had told him that I was involved in criminal activities. They searched my house; they searched me.

"I believe they were looking for the diamond. I suspect that this 'reliable' informant was Klaudia Boryda. There's no better way to shift blame than by pointing the finger at someone else."

Jana decided to give Sofia a bit of comfort. "You tell Boryda everything. That's nothing to be ashamed of. All women tell their lovers things." Jana paused, gauging Sofia. "Did you also tell him about the conversation we had the other day, when I informed you that we had evidence implicating him in a smuggling ring and several murders?"

Sofia folded her hands on her lap, as if waiting for her teacher to tell her what to do.

"I don't know why I did, Jana. We . . . were working . . . and he asked me what was bothering me. He knew I was upset. And I . . ." She hesitated as if trying to decide what had motivated her. "I . . . just . . . it just came out."

"Things often just *come out*, Sofia."

"The diamond. Everything began to go wrong when I got the diamond."

"Even without the diamond, these things fall apart sooner than later."

Sofia sat, looking within herself, making an effort to control her emotions. "I don't know where to turn, Jana. Maybe you should give the diamond back to me. I can flush it down a drain. Get rid of it."

"Sofia, we have two days. Then I have to turn the diamond over to my supervisors. By doing this, we'll show that we haven't tried to hide anything. Both of us will have that going for us."

"The newspapers . . . the TV. . . ." Sofia's voice trailed off.

"Yes." Jana nodded at the rest of the unvoiced thought. "They'll come after you, and me. More pain. Sofia, I have to find out how the diamond originally got into Klaudia's hands."

"I don't know!" Sofia's voice was strong again. "I swear, Jana, I don't know."

"I have one more question, which you have to answer and answer truthfully. Otherwise, you lose me as a friend, and both of us may lose this battle. You understand?"

The little-girl quality had left Sofia; her posture was erect again. Her voice, when she spoke, was direct, her eyes focused.

"Ask me what you have to."

"Good. Why did you see Kamin?"

Sofia closed her eyes and sat unmoving.

"Sofia, you have to tell me why you and Kamin met in your office. Was it because of Boryda?"

Sofia's eyes opened again. "The Party needed money. We couldn't win without it. We couldn't keep the coalition together. Kamin had money. I met him at a party. He came over to me. He knew me, Jana. He remembered me, somehow. He apologized and said he had been drinking when the assault happened. He offered to make amends.

"I was shocked that he recognized me, shocked that he had

remembered. We talked. He said he had heard of the Party's need. He wanted to donate money, through me." She looked at Jana, beseeching her friend to understand. "The Party, the people, we could accomplish so much more with the money. I accepted his offer."

Jana tried to understand her friend. It was not up to Jana to judge her. She was the one who had been injured, and she was the only one who could decide whether to have dealings with Kamin. Sofia had made her decision. It was not the one Jana would have made, but it was Sofia's choice.

He had known what to say. The physical force he had used on Sofia so many years ago had transmuted into another type of force, manipulation. How had he known what avenue to take to persuade Sofia? Where had Kamin found the words to compel Sofia to do what he wanted?

"Was Boryda at the party where Kamin approached you, Sofia?"

Sofia nodded.

"Had you told Boryda what Kamin had done to you when you were a child?"

Sofia rocked forward, then back, before she could force her words out.

"I told him."

"I thought you might have." Jana considered the new information. It led to another conclusion.

"That means that Klaudia Boryda knew as well."

Sofia's hands went to her face, then covered her ears. She couldn't stand to hear any more.

Jana got up. It was best to leave Sofia alone for a while to absorb the appalling information she had just been given.

"The coffees are paid for. Leave a tip for the waitress. She's a friend of mine."

Jana left, glad for once to be walking into the cold air.

Chapter 43

The small Petržalka substation was a place to keep drunks and petty criminals until they could be moved to the main jail, across the Danube in the central city. Most of the time, the transfers took place within hours. The substation was a cold, unfeeling place with exposed plumbing, dirty walls, and a toilet that didn't flush properly and ran all the time.

Jana hadn't visited it in years. When she walked in, she made a mental note to scream at the budget people either to close the place or totally rebuild it. It was not fit for human habitation.

Sabina sat inside one of the cells, wrapped in a blanket. She did not acknowledge Jana's presence.

Jana, who had not yet had time to go home, was still lugging her Vienna overnight bag. She put it down on the least dirty part of the floor, then walked over to Sabina's cell, signaling one of the guards to let her in. Sabina continued to ignore her.

"Sabina, we are not friends. However, we both have duties as police officers, and I've been designated to talk to you before the department takes action to terminate you. Let me warn you, as the regulations require, that you are subject to disciplinary action as well as criminal prosecution. Do you understand?"

There was no acknowledgement from Sabina.

"I must also tell you that if you refuse to speak to the officer delegated to question you—in this case, me—about an official investigation, the department has the right to dismiss you immediately, with loss of all salary and benefits. You would still be subject to prosecution by the attorney general for your criminal acts."

Sabina began to pay attention.

"On the other hand, if you talk to me, the department will wait until the end of the prosecution, if there is a prosecution, and will take no action until then. In other words, if there is no prosecution, then you will not be fired. Understood?"

Sabina glanced at her.

Jana continued as if Sabina had replied in the affirmative, pulling out her small notebook, referring to her notes.

"Last night you went into my office and searched my files. They caught you on camera; did you know that?"

There was a blink of interest, accompanied by a shrug. Sabina let her blanket slip off her shoulders.

"You might have convinced the world that you were there for another reason if not for the film. I understand you made notes on the Guzak case, notes on the trip I took to Ukraine, and particularly careful notes with respect to the smugglers I've been investigating." Jana checked to make sure Sabina was listening. "We have the notes you took. They were in your apartment. Of course they're in your handwriting, so they're very incriminating."

Jana closed her notebook. "I'm sorry your career has to end this way."

Sabina remained silent.

"I am not going to ask you how or why you got into this, nor how much money you were paid, or why you betrayed your comrade Ludovit so he was killed."

Ludovit's name produced an immediate response. Sabina reacted as if she had herself been assaulted. She physically attacked Jana. There was a brief struggle. The guards entered the cell and pulled Sabina away from Jana, knocking her to the ground. Sabina continued to struggle until she realized it was hopeless.

Jana waited a few moments to make sure Sabina was going to remain composed, then told the guards to put her back on her bunk. The guards hauled her up; one of them sat next to her and the other remained by the door. Jana sat next to her on her other side.

"Sabina, let's be frank with each other."

The woman snickered.

"You and I both know that anything you say, I'll report, just as you would. However, I'll give you a guarantee. If you answer one question, just one, I'll report that you were completely cooperative, and that the department should wait until the attorney general has taken action before they take any further action against you."

Jana waited while Sabina digested the offer.

She finally looked at Jana. "I did not have any part in killing Ludovit. He was my partner. I didn't know he would be shot. I thought *you* had set him up to be killed."

"Why would I kill him?"

"I don't know. All I knew was that there were shots, and you were there. I figured you had to be responsible one way or the other."

Jana opened her notebook to make another short entry. Sabina had not seen the shooter.

"Under the circumstances, not a sound conclusion."

"You felt nothing over Ludovit's death," Sabina accused.

"I keep my feelings to myself during an investigation."

"I don't like you, Matinova, not even a little bit. I never have."

"You've made that absolutely clear."

"You have a question for me? Just one question, and one

answer, and the department will take no action until after the attorney general decides what to do. I keep my salary; I keep my benefits? Is all that correct?"

"Pending the action of the procurator's office."

Sabina mulled the answer over. "Okay, what's your question?"

"Who told you to search my office last night, and what to search for?"

"That's two questions."

"There may be two questions but there's only one answer to them."

"The agreement will be honored?"

"I've already said it would."

"Klaudia Boryda."

Jana was shocked.

Sabina saw her response. "Surprised, aren't we?" Sabina gloated.

Jana could see that Sabina was telling the truth.

"Did you tell her that I was going to Switzerland before I left?"

"That's another question. Our agreement means I don't have to answer it. So, piss on you."

Jana agreed. She had contracted for only one question. "I might be able to get you more from the department if you continue to answer my questions."

"It's over. Get away from me."

The set of Sabina's face told Jana that she was finished cooperating.

Jana put her notebook away, thinking of Klaudia Boryda. Despite what Jana knew about her, she'd had no idea she was involved this deeply. This meant that Klaudia was involved in the Guzak killings, the smuggling ring, and Guzak's escape. It also had to mean that both the deputy minister and Kamin were involved.

There was one consolation.

It probably ruled out Sofia.

Jana left the cell, picking up her suitcase. The two officers locked the cell behind her. Sabina came to the bars.

"They know about you."

"Who?"

"Important people."

"I expect so."

"It's larger than you think."

"That may be."

"They're going to kill you."

"I hope not."

"Right this minute, they're coming for you. Be sure you glance around when you step outside." There was pleasure in Sabina's voice. "Be afraid."

Jana walked out.

The jail looked even worse on the outside: cracked masonry, peeling paint, rusty metal. If jails were places that should advertise "Stay out of here if you know what's good for you," it communicated that warning very well.

But it was not alone in its ugliness.

Jana was on the outskirts of the old, neglected, and decrepit housing development called Petržalka. The high-rise buildings were an enclave of low-income families, a jungle of structures that trapped every one of the households that lived inside it.

Jana began walking toward the Carrefour supermarket area, where the taxis stopped. She had not gone twenty feet before she realized she was being stalked. The absence of noise made it clear. Like the creatures in the African jungle, the resident animals living in this jungle knew when the predators were on the hunt, and went silent.

Jana set her suitcase down, opened it, and rummaged

through her clothes, pulling out her gun, making sure that whoever was watching her knew she was armed. They would hesitate, perhaps think twice about coming after her. Jana checked the gun, made sure a shell was in its chamber, and slipped it back inside its holster in the small of her back. She began walking again, setting a steady pace, staying away from the buildings, then taking to the streets, using the parked cars as partial cover.

Jana was nearly at the market when she saw the woman. She stood at the other side of the huge market's entrance, out of the way of the large crowds of people coming in and out. The woman casually read her paper, a cart full of groceries in front of her so that she blended in with the other shoppers. If Jana had not recognized her, she would have passed close enough for the woman to have shot her at point blank. She was the woman Jana had seen in Vienna, in the café with Kamin. Jana had watched them brutally kill a man on the street. She was part of a team of human hunters. That meant her partner was nearby, perhaps behind Jana, ready to attack if the woman distracted Jana enough so that he could succeed. Jana hazarded a quick glance to her rear as she snapped the safety of her gun off. She estimated the time it would take her to get to the entrance of the market, assuming that before she could go inside, the woman's partner would appear. The man must be in the lot, among the cars, and he would fall in behind Jana at the last minute. There was no doubt in Jana's mind that they would use the same method that she had witnessed in Vienna.

Jana had to surprise the two killers before they could act. She took a few more steps; then, when she saw the woman put her paper down and begin walking toward her, Jana dropped her overnight bag to the ground and broke into a run, heading for the market's massive entrance. To her left, Jana saw rapid movement in the parking lot. She had to deal with the woman first. Jana paused, took quick aim, then snapped off a shot at the woman, who stopped and crouched behind a line of shopping carts. Jana had gained a few seconds. Her partner would be unable to catch up with Jana before she got into the market. She took off at a dead run again.

Carrefour was a massive complex of goods. The French company that owned the mega-market undertook to supply all of life's material comforts except cars—which they stocked parts for—and funerals. Televisions, clothing, groceries, building supplies, the store was chock-full of goods, a one-stop-shopping experience. It was a cavernous structure. And it was filled to overflowing with people.

As soon as Jana entered, she realized she had a problem. She could not shoot in a crowded area like this, but those chasing her would. The shot that Jana had already fired was having its effect. People were milling about like a herd of cattle frightened by lightning and thunder. When they saw Jana with a gun in her hand, they began to flee in all directions.

Jana ran down the center aisle. People paid less attention to her as she moved deeper into the store. They were too intent on filling up bags, baskets, and shopping carts. A child stared at Jana as she went past, noticed the automatic in her hand, and tried to call it to the attention of his otherwise preoccupied mother, who was more interested in the variety of hair rinses on the shelves.

Jana reached the back of the market and went through a door to the storage area. Goods were piled on shelves all the way to the ceiling, busy employees running around, forklifts cruising, everyone hustling.

There had to be a loading platform in back, where trucks

pulled up and workers offloaded merchandise. She saw natural light at the back of the storage area, an opening to the outside world, and ran for it.

As soon as she emerged, the first shot was fired at her. Her life was saved by the unexpected intervention of a large forklift. The bullet ricocheted off its metal sides. Jana spun and darted down the delivery dock. She had underestimated the gunmen. The two in front were the stalkers; the hunters in the rear were there to shoot her.

Jana dodged in and around the litter of crates. Workers scattered or simply stared at her open-mouthed. She was weaving around a particularly cluttered area when she ran into one of the people stalking her.

He had climbed onto the platform to try to locate her. He was as startled as Jana when they suddenly confronted each other. The man snapped a shot at her at the same time that she fired. His shot went wide. Jana thought she had hit him, but didn't wait to see. The others behind her were gaining ground. Their aim would be better.

Jana took the only way out. A large open-backed truck was moving away from the platform, its merchandise offloaded. Jana leaped the gap between the dock and the truck and dived behind the few boxes that remained on the truck floor.

Prone, Jana looked around the edge of a box and saw one of the gunmen frantically searching the platform, joined quickly by the two who had followed her from the front of the store. Relief flooded her. They had not realized that she was in the truck.

Jana stayed behind the cartons until the truck rolled across the Nový Most bridge, over the Danube and into town. She jumped off the back of the truck when it stopped for a light in the area near the Carlton in the southern part of the Old Town.

Sabina was right. They were coming after her.

Thirty minutes later, as Jana was walking into police head-quarters, she remembered her overnight bag, abandoned in front of the mega-market. She called the Carrefour's man-ager on her cell phone. He was courteous, but sorry to report that no one had turned in the bag. There had been a problem at the market, so things were a bit disorganized. A terrible shooting had occurred, and the police were looking for wit-nesses. If onlookers had information, the manager told her, the police were asking for them to call. He proceeded to give her the number for the police that he had been given. It was Trokan's cell number.

She called it. Trokan was still at the scene. Yes, he told her, he had her bag. It had been picked up in front of the Carrefour. It seemed there had been a shooting in back of the market. Could Jana, by any chance, have shot anyone today?

She told him she had.

It might have saved him some time and trouble, he sug-gested, if she'd telephoned him about it earlier. He was angry. To prove how angry he was, he hung up on her. Jana called him back. This time he listened very politely, then told her to wait at the station for him.

Before Trokan returned, Jana wrote up her reports on the Carrefour event, as well as on what she had learned from her Vienna trip and her conversation with Postova.

The man Jana had shot, who was likely to die, had been identified by his passport. He was an American. This did not make the colonel feel any better. American diplomats were notorious for demanding quick explanations, and Trokan was in no mood to deal with their complaints. On the other hand, the incredibly vast computerized records the Americans kept should yield quick information as to his identity.

After reading a summary Jana had prepared, Trokan suggested that they provide a bodyguard for her. Jana turned the suggestion down. He next urged her to take a vacation out of the country. She had too much work, she explained; besides, the case was now coming together. And they had the injured man in the hospital to interview. That would mean more information. Ten minutes later, Trokan received a call from the police officer stationed at the ICU. The American had died.

Trokan mumbled a few incoherent syllables under his breath, then told Jana to go home until he informed her that she could come back to work. Trokan had some explaining to do to the minister, and it would be better if she was beyond reach.

She walked back to her office, passing Seges, who looked altogether too smug. The word must have swept through the office that she had been involved in a shooting, and he seemed to think Jana was in trouble. Jana imagined unpleasant things happening to him, then grabbed her bag and drove home.

Chapter 44

Jarov was sitting on the front steps of her house, ostensibly unconcerned as to whether the neighbor across the street noticed that he was watching her. Jana was too tired to reprimand him. She carried her bag inside the house, dumped it on her bed, then went into the kitchen to make herself a cup of coffee. Jarov followed her.

"I needed some sun, so I thought a little tanning session on the front porch would be nice." His expression told Jana he was putting her on. "Don't you think I look better when I'm not so pale?"

This was not the rough-edged Jarov that Jana knew. She put the coffeepot down and stared at him. No question, the man was teasing her.

"Okay, game over," she said. The Cheshire-cat look on his face confirmed her perceptions. He had new information. "I suppose I get Twenty Questions. If the listening devices are still in this house, you're not worried about them. Which gives me the answer to the question I haven't asked: the miscreants who bugged my home came by last night and took their equipment out of the house across the street."

Jana went on without waiting for a response from Jarov. "You followed them when they left. You know where they stored everything. Which means you have information as to their vehicle, the place where they stored the materials, and maybe, if you followed them farther, as to where they're staying. Otherwise, you wouldn't have been sitting on the steps."

Jana was enjoying herself for the first time today. "I guess I've already won our game. Do you want coffee?"

Jarov's jaw fell somewhere around his ankles.

Jana made enough coffee for both of them.

"They must also have removed the listening devices from this house. I was out of town, so they felt they could come and go freely." She finished preparing the coffee and then took two cups from the cupboard. "Which finally brings me to a question you should be able to answer: Where did you hide when they came into the house?"

"The closet in the bedroom." He reddened slightly, the recollection of hiding in a woman's bedroom closet discomfiting him. "I had no alternative," he tried to explain. "Otherwise I might have given everything away."

"Everything," she agreed, smiling at his embarrassment. "And where did they go?"

"To a business on Obchodná."

"Were there two men in the car?"

"Yes."

"Did one of them have his face or head bandaged?"

Jarov realized that Jana was emphasizing that he had long ago lost their Twenty Questions game.

"Yes."

Jana knew the name of the business.

"The store has a sign in front that advertises 'Antiques from the Golden Ages,' correct?"

Jarov couldn't keep his admiration from showing.

"Were you following me while I was following them?" he asked.

"I was in Vienna. You know that." Jana had to fight the temptation to continue the game, then decided to take pity on him. "A man involved in the case is named Giles. Another suspect is Spis, his bodyguard. Giles owns Golden Antiques."

Jana poured coffee for both of them, trying to sort out the confusing details. There had to be two groups. One had tried to kill her that morning. The other belonged to Giles. Otherwise, why would he have bugged her house? Then there were the killings of the smugglers. No question, the key to the entire mess was the nature of the items being smuggled.

Ivan Boryda was working on the Slovak fission program with the IAEA. Could they be into smuggling parts of atomic weapons, shopping them to various countries? It would be an incredibly lucrative business. Every nation in the world that did not have atomic weapons wanted them. But these packages that were being smuggled were not heavy, nor extraordinarily big. Jana shook her head, trying to clear the fantasies out. This one was too complex and too farfetched. She dismissed the notion.

"Can I go?" Jarov inquired. "I've been up all night."

"Have you talked to the woman across the street?"

"Not yet. No time."

"Go home and sleep for a few hours. Then get a statement from her. She will lie at first. If you push her, she will break. Watch out for her husband; he likes to fight. My guess is that they paid her money, which she has kept in the house so the tax man won't get a chunk. Confiscate it. And find a photograph of Giles and Spis at the station and have her identify them."

Jarov left just as the phone rang. Jana answered it, thankful that the listening devices had been removed. It was Daniela.

"Hello, Grandma Jana."

After the tension Jana had been subjected to, the day was swiftly redeemed by a simple telephone call.

"Daniela, it's lovely to hear from you. Are you in Switzerland?"

"Yes. We're still in Geneva."

"Has Grandma Mimi let you call me?"

"Oh, no. She's still mad at you. I just decided to call."

Jana felt some of her joy drain away. If and when Mimi found out about the call she would blame Jana, further straining their relationship. Since there was nothing Jana could do about it, she decided to continue her conversation with Daniela and enjoy the moment.

"I'm sorry she's still angry. I'm not angry at Grandma Mimi."

"I know, Grandma Jana. I just wanted to tell you how much I liked going to see where Charlie lived."

"Even if the statue was not like him?"

"It was like him enough."

"I'm glad. I hoped you were not too frightened by what happened."

"I felt sorry for the man who was hurt."

"So did I."

"I called for another reason, Grandma."

"What's the other reason, Daniela?"

"I think we're leaving here."

Were they going back to the United States already? It felt wrong. The family had not been in Geneva as long as Jana understood they'd planned to stay. Daniela's grandfather could not have completed his work. Daniela was also in school there. Why would they take her away from her studies at this time?

"I had hoped to see you before you went, Daniela. I'm disappointed."

"I wanted to see you also, Grandma Jana."

If she could talk to Mimi again, maybe Jana could persuade her to let her see her grandchild before they actually left.

"Maybe I will be able to see you before you go."

"We're leaving today. We're in a big rush."

A rush suggested a crisis.

"Is everyone okay? Was anyone in the family hurt? Was there an accident?"

"I think it had to do with what happened the day before yesterday, at school."

"What happened at school, Daniela?"

"A man and a woman came to pick me up. They said they were from Grandma Mimi, and that Grandma had been hurt, so they had been sent to get me. But the school wouldn't let me go. The school told Grandma Mimi, and she was upset."

A chill went through Jana. *They* had gone after her granddaughter. There was no doubt as to why they had tried to take Daniela. It was to get at Jana, a way to stop her from going forward. Maybe their failure to get Daniela had impelled them to try to kill her today.

"Is Grandma Mimi there with you?"

"In my bedroom, packing for me."

"Daniela, I want you to bring Grandma Mimi to the phone so I can talk to her."

"She'll be mad that I called you."

"She'll be mad at me, not you. It's important, Daniela. Tell her I told you that it's absolutely imperative that I talk to her."

"What does imperative mean?"

"It means she has to come at once."

"Okay, Grandma Jana."

There was a thump as the phone was laid on a table. A minute later, the receiver was picked up.

"You were not to call here! Why are you calling?" was Mimi's opening salvo. "I don't want you to talk to or see

Daniela. Do you hear me?" There was a note of hysteria in Mimi's voice.

"I heard about the attempt to take Daniela from school. It may happen again. Leaving Geneva may not stop attempts to take her. You have to guard her very closely, at least until you hear from me. Do you understand what I just said?"

There was a frightened silence on the other end of the phone. Then a faint "yes" came through the receiver. "It's connected to what happened to that man in Vevey, isn't it?"

"Yes, more of the same," Jana confirmed.

"Who are they?"

"Criminals."

Again there was silence that lasted so long, Jana thought Mimi had walked away. Then there was a sigh on the other end of the line.

"We're going back to America."

Jana's voice took on additional urgency. "That may not be enough, Mimi. You have to place a guard on her; the administrators at her school in the States must be made aware of the problem. We can only relax when these people are stopped. And, they can only be stopped here, by me. Do you understand, Mimi?"

There was no audible response, just faint breathing.

"It'll be over soon, if that's any help," Jana assured her. "But you can't ease up on your precautions until I call and tell you. So please say you understand. She's my grandchild as well as yours."

This silence was even longer. Then Mimi pulled herself together. "I understand!"

"I'll call!" Jana emphasized. "Please tell Daniela that I love her. And I'm as sorry as I can be that this happened. I never conceived of the possibility that anyone would go so far as to try to harm my grandchild. Thank you, Mimi."

Jana hung up.

Nothing was as it should be.

Things had taken a turn for the worse.

Chapter 45

Jana was in a deep sleep, dreaming that a group of ferocious bears with huge claws and giant teeth were chasing her across an ice-covered lake where there was no place to hide, when the persistent banging on her bedroom window woke her up. She slipped her gun from under her pillow, went to the window, and tried to awaken fully before she slid the drape aside. When she did, Trokan's face popped into view. Jana opened the window.

"You sleep like a dead woman," he said. "I've been trying to rouse you for five minutes."

Snow fell around Trokan. His cap was already covered, and the wind kicked up flurries. Although he was in full winter uniform, he had to slap himself to keep warm.

"What are you doing out there?"

"Attempting to get a Slovak commander of police to do her job. So if the sleeping princess would get dressed and meet me outside, ready for duty, I would appreciate it. Wear your uniform."

He stepped away from the window and out of Jana's vision. She brushed her teeth, tried in vain to fix her hair, hurriedly dressed in the warmest clothes she could fit under her uniform, and was out the door and inside Trokan's car within minutes. The driving snowflakes obscured the windshield even though the wipers were going at top speed.

"Asking me to come out on a night like this is beyond the call of duty. Why didn't you just telephone?"

"The last I heard, your phones were being tapped. I have to be sure that our activities aren't monitored."

"They took out the bugs while I was in Vienna."

"Good for them. Please tell me, then, why is the bug in my office still active?"

"I would say that there are a lot of people who want to know what we're doing."

"Which is why I came to your house rather than telephoning you. Who knows where the listening devices are?" He rapped the steering wheel with the palm of his hand in anger. "How do you figure out who is on which side these days? The police are the ones who are supposed to be doing the eavesdropping. They're not meant to be the objects of surveillance. This is crazy-making."

"Even crazier when my colonel comes to pick me up in the middle of the night in a snowstorm, then doesn't tell me why or where we're going."

"We're going to the hospital to interview the American you shot."

Jana eyed Trokan cautiously. "Colonel Trokan, I was in your office when you learned that the American had *died*."

Trokan broke into a sly smile. "I set up that call. Whoever's listening thinks the thug is dead. If he's dead, he can't talk. Therefore, they have no reason to kill him. Hence, Trokan and Matinova will have some quiet time with the gentleman who tried to end your career. If they are bold enough to infiltrate our office, get into our jail and help a prisoner escape, and also to try to kill a commander of police in broad daylight, then they would think nothing of eliminating this man." He kissed the back of his hand in mock appreciation of himself. "Oh, Trokan, you sly devil. When you're gone, will there ever be anyone else like you?"

He reached into the back seat, grabbed a folder, and dropped it in Jana's lap.

"Courtesy of the USA's marvelous system of record-keeping."

Jana began going through the papers in the file as Trokan chattered on.

"They identified him through their tattoo database. Can you believe they have voluminous records of people's tattoos? He turns out to be a longtime criminal. The usual: a swamp creature, predisposed to violence, involved in organized crime. His only conviction was for passing counterfeit money which had been printed in Korea. The Korean counterfeits show that he has some international connection."

"If the money was printed in Korea, they would need a means to smuggle the money into other countries."

"You think this ring is smuggling counterfeit money into countries around the world?"

"Maybe. The packages were described as of various sizes, which might mean differing amounts in each shipment, or else different goods. I think we must ask the patient what's inside those packages. You asked me to wear my uniform. Do you have a strategy in mind?"

"It's a biological necessity for every officer who has reached my exalted position in the police to be sneaky, underhanded, cunning, and devious. I've been thinking about this all day, which means it will be extremely underhanded. The man you shot never went past elementary school. All he knows is what he's learned on television in the United States. This means, to him, it will be credible that in places like Slovakia we routinely execute people."

"He thinks we may kill him, so we play on his survival instinct?"

"Correct."

"Am I the good police officer or the bad one? It's always a challenge to be the good one."

"I don't speak English well enough to be the good police officer. There's another factor: when a woman is sympathetic, they think it's sincere. No one ever trusts men."

"I wonder why."

Jana reviewed the folder, which contained the man's history. He had spent his entire life preying on the weak and innocent. If there was a heaven and a hell, when he died he would go directly to hell. There'd be no mourning; there'd be no tears. Everyone would breathe easier. He was the type of man who would be sent to kidnap her granddaughter. And if they didn't like Jana's reaction to the kidnapping, he would be one of those delegated to kill the little girl, and he'd do it without hesitation.

Jana's anger at the man grew as they got closer. He was an abomination on the earth. If they tried to play good cop/bad cop, he would see right through their ploy. Any threat to him had to be real. Jana had to convey that she was prepared to act. And then she had to act.

It took nearly the rest of the journey to the hospital for Jana to convince Trokan that his plan wouldn't work. When she had finally convinced him, she called ahead, giving one of the officers stationed at the hospital detailed instructions. As they walked toward the hospital room, the two waiting uniformed officers saluted. There was an empty wheelchair next to them.

"You're sure this is what you want to do?" Trokan asked.

"I'm sure. It will be the only thing he'll respond to."

"It can go very wrong. Be careful, Janka."

"Sometimes more than care is needed."

Jana entered the room by herself. Trokan stayed outside to instruct the officers on exactly what was expected of them.

The man lay in bed, shackled to the metal frame. He eyed Jana as she checked his chart. Her shot had caught him in the collarbone, breaking it; ricocheted down, miraculously missing the lung; and broken a rib. Fortunately for him, the bullet had remained intact. It had been easily extracted.

The man's eyes followed her. The anesthetic from the operation had worn off. He was aware of where he was and certainly aware that Jana was a police officer.

She sat in a chair near the head of the bed.

"You're very lucky," she told the man in English. "The bullet should have killed you." Jana had brought a folder with her. She consulted it, then asked, "Your name is Adonis?"

"Whatever you want to call me."

"And you have nothing to say?"

"Not a thing."

"You're sure?"

He didn't answer.

"If you have nothing to say to me, then there's no reason to keep you alive."

Jana looked the man over. "Adonis, I need to get some information from you so we know what to do . . . after this is over. Your next of kin? We generally cremate." She pulled out her notebook. "I don't need much. We know almost everything else about you."

"Whoever shot me got the wrong man."

"Then why did you have a gun? And why did you fire?"

"Who said I fired a gun?"

"I did. I was a witness."

Adonis looked at her more closely but still did not recognize her.

"You're a bad shot," Jana said. "You failed. There is no room for failure in your job. All sides want to kill you now."

"I don't know anything about 'sides.'"

"There's only a short time before you're executed. We would like to know where we should send the remains. Of course, I'd also like to know details surrounding the attempt to kill me."

He laughed. "Next you tell me I'm going to be taken down to the cellar, tied to a chair, and shot once in the back of the head. Piss off."

Jana smiled without humor.

"In this country, when a police officer is shot at, there is always retribution."

The man stared at her, not quite comprehending.

"I've been delegated to kill you. You're looking in the face of death. My face. I assure you, you'll soon be dead."

The man stared at her, unblinking, expressionless.

"My name is Jana Matinova. You tried to murder me."

Jana could see his reaction. Adonis's expression changed: he realized he was alone in a room with the woman he'd tried to kill.

"I talked to my granddaughter yesterday. You, or your people, tried to abduct her. I cannot ever allow that to happen again. A message has to be sent. Payment has to be exacted."

The man pressed himself back against his pillow, trying to get away from her.

"I sentenced you to death as soon as I heard you had survived."

"I'm gonna just lie here," Adonis said. "I'm not gonna say a word."

Jana sat and watched him.

"There's no reason for you to stay," he muttered. "Get

the fuck away from me. I'm not looking at you any longer, bitch." He turned his face away. As soon as he did so, Jana knocked on the door to the room. The door opened, and the two police officers rolled the wheelchair in. They walked over to Adonis and one of them pulled the I.V. line from his arm. Adonis let out a yelp of surprise and pain.

"What the hell are you guys doing? Get the fuck away from me!"

They unfastened the shackles, dragged the man from the bed, and dropped him into the wheelchair.

His cast impeded his movements as Adonis struggled. One of the officers held him down while the other took a roll of heavy duct tape and wrapped it around him, strapping his arms and legs to the chair while he cursed them, trying to break away.

When the officers were through, they looked at Jana. She took the roll of tape from them and faced the man in the wheelchair.

"I'm a patient in a hospital," he said, as if that would dissuade her.

"And I'm an executioner. This is your last chance to tell me what I need to know."

"Fuck you," Adonis said, and Jana taped his mouth shut. She nodded to the two officers, who wheeled Adonis, still struggling, out of the room. Jana followed them. Outside, Trokan looked worried.

"You still want to carry on, Jana?"

"No question, Colonel."

Trokan waited as she and her men took the prisoner to the elevator and descended to the basement, then walked to the end of a long, water-stained cement corridor, stopping when they reached a large rusted metal door. One of them unlocked the door; the other wheeled Adonis into the room.

Jana took a last glance down the corridor to make sure no one was following, then stepped into the huge, empty, darkened room. The police officers walked out, closing the iron door behind them with a loud *clang*.

The man in the wheelchair was beginning to sweat. It was time to ratchet up the pressure even more. Jana ripped the tape from Adonis's mouth.

He tried to spit at her.

Jana smiled, took a step back, and pulled out her gun.

He began screaming. She waited for a few moments, until he had worn down.

"No one can hear you," she informed him. "They had orders to go back up to the hospital area. They were only too glad to obey. They know what is going to happen. No one wants to witness an execution." Jana snapped the safety off, then levered a shell into the chamber of her gun, cocking it.

Adonis stared at the gun.

"This is not right," he got out.

"Why is it not 'right'?"

"I haven't had a trial."

"Of course you did. I was the judge; you were found guilty. Now I'm going to kill you." He began to shake. "You can still stop me. All you have to do is answer my questions." She paused. "However, I would urge you to keep silent."

He gaped at her, not quite understanding.

"I *want* to kill you. If you don't talk, I'm empowered to put a bullet in you. I would like nothing better. So, what do you want me to do, kill you or not?"

He continued to stare at her.

"Not convinced?"

She walked around behind him.

"What . . . the fuck . . . are you doing?" he stammered out.

"Taking aim. I'm not going to put a bullet in your head

with the first shot. For what you people almost did to my granddaughter, you've earned a slow death." She hesitated, then considered the words she'd just spoken. It was for the sake of her grandchild's future. She fired. The bullet struck the muscle near the juncture of his neck and shoulder.

He screamed. "I'm shot! Jesus, you shot me!"

"Of course I shot you. I told you I would." Jana stepped closer to view the wound.

"Bullets do terrible damage. If I were to remove the tape now, you wouldn't be able to use your right arm." She prodded his shoulder with the gun barrel. He groaned. "Ah, it hurts. Good. Pain teaches us. The next one will be on your other side. Then, a bullet to the head."

"For god's sake, don't kill me. Please don't kill me."

She took a few steps back and recocked the gun. The *click* of the hammer sounded very loud.

"Prepare yourself, Adonis."

The man pleaded with her. He would talk, he blurted out. Anything, if she did not shoot.

Jana let him go on for a moment. Then she uncocked her gun and walked around to confront him.

"A good decision, Adonis." She looked down at him. They both knew her threat had been genuine.

"You will be arrested for shooting me." His eyes showed the depth of his malice.

Jana shook her head. "I think not. I shot you, from behind, when you tried to escape from custody. That's always a good story, isn't it? My boss will accept that. So will yours . . . maybe."

Jana put her gun back in its holster. She wouldn't need it any more.

She felt a tinge of regret for what she'd done. Then she pictured her grandchild, having fun, no fear in her mind, no terror in her heart. That regret was short-lived.

Chapter 46

Eva and Soros were watching Kamin's house when they saw Jana drive up. It was hard to miss her, still in full uniform, as she walked to the gate with assurance.

Eva was disappointed. "There have been murders in her city, she's been the target of an assassination attempt, and she still walks around as if she's the lord of all she surveys."

Soros disagreed, but only slightly. "She's required to look confident. She's a commanding officer. They're never supposed to show fear. It would send a bad message to the troops."

"It'll destroy her one day. Maybe today."

"Maybe today," Soros agreed. "If she gives us the opportunity."

They watched Jana pick the lock on the gate. It came off within seconds.

"She's very good at that."

"Professional," Soros commented.

"She's going to go inside the house."

"No question."

The man they were waiting to "see" was inside the house.

"She doesn't know he's inside."

They looked toward the house. The shutters on the lower windows were all closed. The lawn and bushes were still in reasonable trim, although the yard was unkempt, a few stray pieces of paper lying on it, some leaves blown under a hedge.

Jana had entered the yard and was now circling the house. She was on the alert, ready for a surprise if it came.

This time Eva's comment carried a tone of approval. "She knows the untended appearance of the yard may not be real."

"We know that she's resourceful after what happened yesterday at the market."

"They're right to want her dead."

"Soon," he assured her.

"What will happen inside?"

"It depends on him."

"You can't rely on him to do it."

"Look at her. She's not sure if the house is occupied. That's bad. It may give him an edge."

"It may make her more alert."

"He'll know she's coming in."

"Yes."

"It depends on who takes the first shot."

"It should never depend on that, which is a good reason not to get into these situations: too many imponderables."

Jana returned to the front door. They watched her attempt to make a cell phone call. Her disappointment was apparent. She put the phone away and stared once more at the house.

"She was calling for officers to back her up," Eva ventured. "She wasn't able to reach who she wanted."

Jana walked to the front door, tried it, then resorted to picking this lock as well.

"She should have waited for the other cops."

"Yes, but she's courageous. I admire courage."

"Courage kills people."

"Much of the time."

"Whichever one comes out of the house will then become our business."

"Everyone may be happy after our day's work."

"*I'll* be happy."

They watched Jana go inside and settled down to wait for whoever was left alive to emerge.

Chapter 47

Jana put her lockpicks away, pulled out her gun, and shut the door behind her. The house was fully furnished, though there was a light film of dust on the furniture. It confirmed the impression: Kamin had probably left a few days ago. She listened.

Quiet.

She relaxed slightly.

Adonis's information pointed at Kamin, but according to him there had been a lot of people giving orders; too many of them conflicting. This buttressed her hypothesis that there were two groups. But she could not tell who was on which side. One thing was sure: she had enough now to justify picking up Kamin, an event she had been looking forward to for a long time. So she had come straight from the hospital to the house where she had followed Kamin once before.

Jarov had not answered his cell phone; Seges was out of the question. But she had been too eager to confront Kamin to wait. It was an emotion that every young police officer has to get over in order to survive, she warned herself.

She began to prowl the first floor of the two-story house. She saw nothing unusual until she got to the kitchen. There was a smell of garbage. Jana examined the kitchen garbage pail, pulling out two cans of half-eaten food. She then checked the counters in the kitchen. The one near the garbage didn't have the same coat of dust on its surface. Somebody was using the house.

Jana went to the door, then used her cell phone again. Jarov answered at last. Jana gave him the house's address, telling him to pick up another man, even Seges, and come there as quickly as he could: she needed assistance in making an arrest.

She hung up and tried to decide whether to wait. Again, her eagerness to arrest Kamin propelled her out of the kitchen and brought her to the stairway that led to the second floor. The nap on the stairway runner did not show any footprints until she was halfway to the landing. A very large impression of a sole and heel marked the rug. A man was upstairs. Jana cautioned herself once more: he might have heard her prowling around the lower floor.

Jana had a choice: she could back down the stairs with her gun at the ready, or she could continue up to confront whoever she might find. She was already halfway up. Having come this far, she decided to go all the way.

The carpeting helped, but she could not stop the stairs from squeaking. She had almost reached the landing when an arm snaked over the top of the stairs, a gun pointed at her. Guzak's head appeared. She froze. The man had lain prone at the top of the stairs in wait for someone. He looked surprised to see that it was her.

"No, I'm not Kamin," Jana said.

His surprise began to fade.

"From the greeting you gave me, I suppose you were going to shoot him. You should be having second thoughts by now. I don't think you want to kill a police officer, Mr. Guzak."

The gun continued to point at Jana's head. She was developing a cramp from standing still, her weight on one foot.

But if she moved, Guzak might misconstrue her intention and shoot her. Sweat was beginning to drip down her back.

"I came to arrest Kamin. Perhaps you and I are on the same side."

The gun did not waver.

"I talked to a prisoner in the hospital. He said Kamin had arranged to kill your brother and your mother. I think he was also responsible for your uncle's death in Hungary. I'm after them, Mr. Guzak. We can help each other."

The barrel of the gun wavered for a moment, then steadied, centered on her forehead.

"I tried to get word out on the street that I wanted to talk to you. It would be mutually beneficial. I hope you heard it."

He nodded slightly.

The cramp in Jana's leg was becoming unbearable. She willed herself not to move.

"Think about it, Mr. Guzak. I arrested you; you escaped. You didn't harm anyone during your escape. Not a huge crime." The pain had become excruciating. "Think about it: you shoot me, the neighbors hear it, they call the police. The police come, that ends your hunt for Kamin." She did not tell him that Jarov would arrive soon.

"I can offer you a fresh chance to get Kamin. I propose a partnership with the police. If the police are on your side, and you're on theirs, there's no way for him to evade us. We'll have him in a box. The man who murdered your mother and brother will be taken down."

The pain had become unbearable. She had to change position.

"I'm going to sit on the steps while we talk, Mr. Guzak. My back will be to you. You'll still be able to shoot me if you wish. However, before you do, I'd like to tell you about my plans, so please listen." She slowly began to shift position. The relief was enormous. She kneaded her calves and thighs.

"I'll describe the evidence I already have, and how you fit into it. If I am wrong, I want you to correct me. At the end of our conversation, I'll tell you how you can help. Is that understood, and acceptable to you?"

She waited a few seconds to let him digest the proposal.

"If my mother and brother had been murdered, I'd do anything to avenge myself on the people who killed them. Think. You'll never have a chance like this again. You and I can do it."

Guzak grunted. Jana took it for a "yes."

Twenty minutes later, Jana walked out of the house with Guzak, just as Jarov and Seges drove up. They put Guzak in their car, Jana got into hers, and they drove away.

There had been too many police officers at the scene for Soros and Eva to go after their prey. They could only watch them drive off, untouched.

They were not happy.

Chapter 48

Jana called Andras in Hungary and gave him the address for Solti she'd obtained from the hotel in Kathmandu. She asked Andras to check it out. If Solti had any personal belongings there, she asked Andras to forward them to her as quickly as possible.

The connection between Kamin and the two Borydas was tenuous at best. Their link had to be money, dirty money. The rule in all corruption cases is to follow the money. Sofia had told Jana that the Party needed financing, and that Kamin was going to provide it. Jana needed to talk to Sofia again, to persuade Sofia to tell her where the linkages were between Kamin and the Borydas.

Sofia's love affair had gone bad, had clouded her judgment and her honesty. But if anyone could sway Sofia, Jana could. She drove to Sofia's house, then walked around to the side where Sofia's office was, once again climbing the stairs, hoping that this time she would be more successful.

She knocked on the door to the office, then walked in without waiting for a reply. Sofia was at her desk, working on papers, tears silently streaming down her face. Something had happened.

Sofia looked up and put the papers aside, waiting for Jana.

"As one of your constituents, I've decided to come to you as a legislator, a reputable member of parliament, and state my grievance."

Sofia's tears continued to flow. Jana went on.

"I've knocked on doors all over the city, and nobody wants to talk to a woman whose best friend refuses to talk to her."

Sofia almost smiled.

"It's lonely not having a best friend any more."

"Aren't we best friends any more, Jana?" There was regret in Sofia's voice.

"Best friends can argue, can give and take, without being apprehensive. I'm talking to a woman who I used to call my closest friend. Do you think, if we try again, that it's possible we can regain what we once had?"

Sofia thought, then shook her head. "I no longer have any friends. Politicians, I've found out, don't have them."

"Real people have them. A *few* politicians are real people."

"I haven't met them."

"I have. I think you're one of them."

Sofia proffered a tremulous smile.

"Can you take off your politician's hat? We have to think together. We have to have an honest give-and-take."

There was a wistful note in Sofia's voice. "There's good in politics; you just have to find it."

"Sofia, when politicians do the things that they feel are necessary to be *successful*, nothing is beyond them. They become bottom-feeders, or worse."

The tears began to slow down. "Are you being honest, Jana?"

"I'm trying to be."

"You're not."

"How so?"

"If you were being honest, you'd acknowledge that you've come here only to get information about Ivan Boryda. You're here as a policeman, not as a friend."

"I'm here, at this moment, as a friend so I don't have to come back later as a police officer."

"You haven't come to get information from me that would help in a police investigation?"

"I'm here to get information on people who have taken money they shouldn't have, and, in turn, have dragged down a friend of mine. But she may no longer be the reformer, the woman who wants to help the people of this country. She may no longer be the people's servant. She may have joined the predators."

"I hope not." Sofia's voice became stronger. "I don't want to be."

"Are you the same woman who ran Transparency? 'A person's ideals are the person,' you used to say. Do you still believe that?"

" . . . Yes."

"Are you still serving the people, or yourself? Or the Borydas? Or Kamin? What ideals can anyone have who serves *them?*"

The tears had stopped. Sofia's face had taken on a faraway look, as if she were remembering herself at another time.

"Ivan Boryda is gone, Sofia. He won't come back. He can't leave Klaudia. She won't leave him, not voluntarily. And both are tied up with Kamin."

Jana pulled out the diamond, letting it hang from the chain. Their eyes followed the sway of the diamond.

"This is one of the keys."

Sofia's eyes focused even more closely on the diamond.

"Explain."

"Kamin has been financing Boryda for a long time. Long before you arrived on the political and personal scene. Long before I saw him in your office."

"He said Kamin would make him prime minister."

"Boryda needed money; the money had to be funneled from Kamin to Boryda. You became the go-between. Boryda remained untouched. You took the risk."

Jana studied Sofia, trying to read her. It was very important not to make a mistake now. "You arrived late in the
game. There was another person who had received the
money before you. It was Klaudia Boryda, wasn't it?"

Sofia nodded.

"Was there a lot of money involved, Sofia?"

Sofia hesitated. "Hundreds of thousands."

"A huge amount."

"Enormous."

Jana thought about the sums of money that had been
flowing into Boryda's hands. "It comes down to a question
of control. The more money involved, the more people want
to manage it, to possess it. You were sucked in because Ivan
Boryda wanted to escape Klaudia's domination. You were the
tool he needed to transport the money from Kamin. Klaudia
knew that if she lost control of the money, she would be
unnecessary. She had to get rid of you."

The beginning of comprehension dawned on Sofia's face.

Jana twirled the diamond around on the chain. "We
know that Klaudia sent you the diamond and you walked
right into that trap. There's still the question of where
Kamin got the money to finance Boryda. There's also
another question, perhaps even larger: *Why* did he want to
finance Boryda? What could Boryda do for him? And why
all the killings?"

"I don't know, Jana."

Sofia's face was open. She was telling the truth.

"Boryda and his wife are no longer in Vienna. They're not
in Bratislava. Do you know where they are?"

"At the schloss."

"They have a castle?"

"In Austria, near our border. I tried to call him." She
shook her head. "One last attempt to get him back. He told

me we were through. Then he called me Kamin's whore, and hung up. That's why I'm crying, Jana."

"He wanted to hurt you, Sofia."

"He succeeded."

Jana had one more account to settle with these people.

Chapter 49

The schloss was located in Austria near the small town of Rohrau, close to both the Slovak and Hungarian borders. It had taken a full day of persuasion by Jana and her associates in Hungary and Austria to prod the Austrian police into action. The Austrians never did anything that was not according to the letter of the law, and for an operation of this type they needed permissions and approvals from Vienna and, it seemed to Jana, everyone else in the Austrian government. However, when the last of the permissions came, the operation was carried out without a flaw.

The police officers were spaced out around the castle's outer wall, the largest group focused on the rear, backed by woods. They had brought scaling ladders so they could mount the wall. Jana and most of the police were at the front. Jarov and Seges were delegated to watch over Guzak until the operation began. The Austrians had even brought a tank-like vehicle that could punch a hole through the wall and provide cover for them if they needed to assault the main building.

When the deployment was complete, Jana signaled Jarov and Seges. The four of them, along with Jana's Austrian counterpart, a man named Linden, walked to the large entry gate. Linden's men had the gate off its hinges and on the ground within minutes.

They followed the long, curving path through immaculately tended lawns toward the twin-turreted eighteenth-century building known as Schloss Bruckner. The police in the rear scaled the walls and advanced toward the rear of the huge mansion, ready to break in when the signal came. Jana picked up the pace, hoping to get inside before any violent confrontation could happen.

As they progressed, Jana took in the grounds and the schloss itself. The building was stately, beautiful, ivy-covered. There were plantings everywhere which would, in the summer, make this a green paradise. The perfect condition of the estate testified to the care that had been taken. It was an Eden for the wealthy, and the Borydas were now wealthy.

Before they had come to the schloss, Jana had asked that the Austrian police go through the land records for the last century. The locals confirmed that the building and grounds had been in terrible condition for decades, until it had been purchased three years earlier. The new owners had spent enormous amounts of money to re-landscape, restore, and redecorate the castle, inside and out.

The new owner was a woman who claimed an aristocratic lineage that nobody believed. However, as long as she paid her bills, the locals were only too happy to feed her fantasy.

Jana, too, had done her research. Klaudia was using her maiden name, to keep Boryda off the land records.

They walked up to the huge front door. Jana rang the anachronistic contemporary doorbell. A few moments later, a nondescript man dressed in a suit and tie opened the door, gazed at the police officers with some surprise, pointed them in the general direction of the interior of the building, and informed them that the Borydas were in conference.

Jana had a vague impression of familiarity, but she went with the group, through the massively chandeliered reception area, into a large hall at the end of which were the carved doors the butler had pointed to. As Jana grasped one of the ornate metal door handles, Linden held a hand up for her to stop.

"They'll be out in a moment."

Jana wondered if it was Austrian courtesy, or the respect for authority the massive schloss engendered, that made Linden ask that they wait. Jana's patience lasted for all of thirty seconds. She pulled the doors open and stalked inside. The others quickly followed her.

They plunged into a chamber that could have served as a ballroom. Klaudia and Ivan Boryda were seated as far away from each other as they could get. Klaudia Boryda appeared stiff and uncomfortable, because she was quite dead. She had been shot twice in the chest. Ivan Boryda looked stiff and uncomfortable, but he had only been shot in the shoulder.

As soon as Jana saw Klaudia Boryda's body, she remembered the identity of the man who had greeted them at the front door. Jana had only glimpsed him previously when he had been part of a murder team, beating a man to death on a sunny day in Vienna. Jana whirled, yelling for Jarov to follow her, then ran through the outer room to the front door.

"Stop the man who let us in!" she commanded.

Jana raced for the front gate. She saw a car appear around the corner of the house and accelerate toward the front entrance. Jana shouted to the police at the front gate. No one seemed to pay any attention. The grounds were so extensive, they were so far away, that they could not hear her.

She took an extreme measure to get their attention: she pulled out her pistol and fired several shots in the air. The men at the gate took notice and tried to block the car. At the last moment several of them were forced to leap out of the way as the car rammed through. A fusillade of shots by the police ensued.

As soon as the car was out of Jana's sight, she heard the

thump of metal against stone. Jana sprinted, arriving at the gate to see a cluster of police, their guns drawn, surrounding the car, which had slammed into the schloss's outer wall. The man who had killed Klaudia Boryda was dead.

They got Ivan Boryda to a clinic in Hainburg, a small town close to the Danube. The clinic was surprisingly large and well equipped. The medical personnel wheeled Boryda into surgery, and within forty-five minutes they wheeled him out again and put him into a room, which the police secured. The wound was superficial, the doctors told them, so Jana could interview him.

Jana walked in, accompanied by Officer Jarov and Guzak. Boryda visibly winced when he saw Guzak.

"You know Mr. Guzak, I see."

"I've never seen him before," Boryda mumbled, very deliberately keeping his eyes averted.

"Mr. Guzak says he has seen you on several prior occasions."

"That would not be unusual, considering that I've made so many public appearances."

Jana turned to Guzak. "Where did you meet Mr. Boryda?"

"At his home in Bratislava."

"Many times?"

"Lots of times."

Jana turned back to Boryda, inquisitively.

"He's lying." Boryda's tone was not convincing. He was trying to look wan and in pain, but could not quite pull off the role of the invalid.

"Your wife is dead."

"The doctors told me. I'm devastated," Boryda claimed. His tone was not convincing. "She was a great human being." He went into a rote summary of all the wonderful characteristics his wife had had, what a personal bereavement her death was and what a great loss to the Slovak people. "She will be missed," he concluded his speech, giving them a preview of what he would say to the media.

He disgusted Jana. She leaned close to him. "You killed her," she declared. Boryda stared back at her, suddenly wary.

"Why?" Jana demanded. "Did you hate her so much?"

Boryda practiced looking shocked. "How could you say that? I *loved* my wife."

Jana was even more disgusted.

"No one will buy that lie. You were having an affair with a legislator." Jana deliberately didn't mention Sofia's name. "It's been all over the Slovak news for months."

Boryda was not contrite. "That has nothing to do with my wife's death."

"It certainly doesn't look good." She indicated Guzak. "What Mr. Guzak tells me is also rather disquieting. He says that you and your wife have been involved in smuggling activities, in money-laundering activities, bribery, election fraud, and in taking money from government contractors." She stopped herself. "You know all about it, so I don't have to spell it out." She turned back to Guzak. "You told me that there was a missing shipment in your smuggling venture. Is that correct?"

"We delivered it. I think *he* took it. They thought *I* was the one. They blamed everybody except him. People are getting killed because of it."

Jan turned to Boryda. "You've been spending huge amounts of money on the schloss, huge amounts of money on your campaigns. Where has this money come from, Mr. Deputy Prime Minister?"

"My wife had money."

"No. She *wanted* money. There's a difference. That's true,

isn't it, Mr. Deputy Prime Minister who is now never going to be Prime Minister?"

Boryda didn't answer.

"You were shot in the arm, Boryda; the fleshy part of the arm. No real damage. Your wife was murdered, shot at close range, while you were in the same room. Explain that."

"The man came in and shot her. We wrestled for the gun. He was enormously strong, and he threw me across the room. Then he shot me." The words came out as if memorized, a bad actor mouthing a bad script.

"Not good, Boryda. You wanted her dead. She was interfering with the life you wanted. So 'out with the old, in with the new,' right?"

He sat up in bed, the invalid's role forgotten.

"I didn't kill her."

"Let me tell you about the man who fired the shots, including that stupid flesh wound in your arm. He worked with a woman; they were a team. He wouldn't have come alone to kill someone . . . unless it was a setup, an easy murder. When we arrived unexpectedly, we spoiled your play."

"You're not a police officer in Austria. You have no right to arrest me here."

"The Austrians are ready to talk to you when I'm finished. I assure you, they'll arrest you no matter what you say. Furthermore, you had to know that Mr. Guzak's brother and mother were going to be murdered."

His normally ruddy complexion had paled. "His mother was not supposed to be there."

"Things never quite go right when murder is planned." Jana watched Boryda collapse. If Jana hadn't known how slight his wound was, she would have sworn he was dying. "The records we'll find at the schloss, all the money you've spent, the money in your bank accounts, all of this will bring you down."

She turned as if to go, stopped and turned back.

"There is one other thing: Kamin! Things might go easier for you if you help us get him. He's the spider at the center of the smuggling web. I want to kill the spider.

"How do I do it, Mr. Boryda?"

Chapter 50

Jana didn't need Boryda's information on Kamin after all.

The two-day-old aroma of a dead body had forced the neighbors upstairs and downstairs to call the police. The police went to a small apartment at the city's north edge overlooking Staromestská Drive, found a body, and called Jana's people, who in turn called her.

Jana, who was forewarned about the condition of the body, limited her capacity to smell by a liberal application of camphor salve inside her nostrils. When she walked into the room, Jana immediately realized who was sitting propped up in the bed, a book neatly placed on his lap. Kamin looked as if he had fallen asleep while reading. But he had closely patterned bullet wounds in his body, and one, at very close range, to his head. A large powder burn on his forehead indicated just how close the shooter had been.

He give the impression of being surprised, almost shocked, his lips drawn back in a rictus as if he was ready to argue with the person who had startled him. The room was clean, his bag packed. Jana checked the book on his lap. It was a religious tract about a sect headquartered in India.

The name Solti suddenly came to Jana's mind. Nepal, the country where Solti had been killed, was next door to India. Jana checked the back of the book. It gave her the sect's contact information in a number of cities around the world. She made a mental note to call one of them when she got back to the station. Maybe they would know something about Solti or Kamin.

The bullets that had killed Kamin were of a small caliber, like the bullets that had killed the younger Guzak. Jana told the coroner's assistants to inform the coroner that she wanted an immediate autopsy. She then instructed her people to take the slugs from the body to ballistics as soon as the coroner released them. She wanted to compare them with those from the Guzaks' bodies.

Everything in the room, except Kamin, was neat and tidy. There was nothing of any personal value, except Kamin's unopened bag. A search of the bag merely produced clothes and a Dopp kit containing the usual shaving and bath articles. Jana tore the lining out of the piece of luggage, without results.

The people in the neighboring apartments had no information. All they knew was that the man had moved into the furnished flat, and that was the last they ever saw or heard of him until the aroma of death began leaking out of the apartment. The landlord was even less helpful: he had never even seen Kamin. The rent arrived in the mail; the landlord had left the key in the unlocked mailbox for Kamin to pick up when he'd moved in.

Jana went back to the office, slightly depressed. The long-sought-after confrontation with Kamin would never take place. She wanted personally to excoriate him, to skin him alive, to watch Kamin being drawn and quartered. Jana had worked so hard to get him, putting together a case against him piece by piece, hoping to make him squirm as a result of her skill. Now that satisfaction had been denied her. His death alone was not enough.

She called Sofia, even though the ballistics comparison had not yet been made. Jana was sure that Kamin had been shot with the same gun that had killed the younger Guzak and his mother.

When Jana told Sofia about finding Kamin's body, Sofia expressed no feelings. There was no affect from Sofia, no anger, no rage, no horror, no satisfaction of revenge, no satisfaction of any sort. Most of all, there had been no relief, no sense that a weight had been taken off her shoulders with the knowledge that Kamin was dead.

Jana had dealt with rape victims before. They had different responses. Jana checked her memory bank. In another case she had handled some years back, the victim had bottled up her anger, suppressed all her fear, until one day she ran into the man at a market where she was working. She'd killed him with a screw driver. She had stabbed him twenty-nine times, her bottled rage suddenly surfacing. Jana had a gut reaction: one day all those feelings would boil out of Sofia. Jana prayed Sofia's would not be as violent a catharsis.

Jana telephoned Karina, the waitress at Gremium, asking her for another favor. Then she began putting the pieces of her case together, charting the information, setting the witnesses in their proper places. Jana stepped back, looked at the picture she had developed, then realized she hadn't yet gotten in touch with the religious sect. Jana phoned the London branch and reached a pleasant lady who spoke heavily accented English and tried to question Jana about her religious beliefs.

The woman did not know Solti and had never heard of Kamin, but she was interested in the fact that Jana was with the police. Was Jana, by any chance, investigating the murder of the Master and the explosion during services in Mumbai, India this past year? No one had ever been caught. Wasn't it time the police did something?

Jana extracted the details from her. The information was followed by more proselytizing. Jana managed to terminate the conversation with some difficulty, although managing to remain polite.

One more factor to be considered.

Jana registered the date of the event, then made an appointment with Colonel Trokan, asking him to have Captain Bohumil at the meeting. As she was preparing to go to the conference room, a large package arrived from Hungary. It was the luggage containing Solti's belongings.

Jana went through the tightly packed clothes, all still neatly in place. Then she cut the lining out of the suitcase. When she had finished, she left the clothes on the floor of her office, closed the suitcase, and carried it to the conference room.

Everything had come together.

The colonel and Captain Bohumil arrived on time. Seges, his usual obsequious self when either of them was around, brought in a coffeepot and cups. They exchanged some general pleasantries. Trokan told a small joke, which received an even smaller response. As soon as Seges left, Jana started the briefing.

She began with the dates of the murders, including the ones in India. These came as a surprise to both Trokan and Bohumil. She then related everything she knew about the smuggling ring, the murders in Hungary, the killing of the Guzaks, both mother and son, the death of Klaudia Boryda and, finally, that of Kamin, which had only been discovered that morning.

"The killings were not only ruthless, but methodical, and pursuant to a plan to eliminate a group of people."

"What group?" Bohumil asked.

"A cadre: worker ants in an organization, people who had become liabilities. There was a line of communication, a network from India through Europe, then into North and South America. Then there was a breakdown, a large one, when a shipment that the network specialized in went missing."

"Kamin was one of these people?" Trokan asked.

"Yes. I think Solti, the man killed in Nepal, was the general manager of the network. The Indian sect, with temples in a number of major cities around the world, was probably an alternative route for the organization. It had a superb capability for a criminal group: followers who would deliver items without any questions. Then there were the smugglers, professionals who knew what the safe routes were. Most of them had family ties to one another, or long-term relationships."

"Smuggling what?"

"An organization's lifeblood."

"What does that mean?" Bohumil grumbled.

"What makes any company successful?" She looked at both men, not really expecting an answer. "Money, of course. In the criminal world, particularly the organized criminal world, how do you pay for what you buy? How do you pay for shipments of stolen goods? For example, how do you pay for shiploads of narcotics? How does the buyer pay the seller? How does the seller pay his people overseas?"

"Gray money. You launder transactions. You do it through bank transfers," Bohumil ventured, still unsure of where Jana was going. "What does that have to do with these deaths?"

Trokan was beginning to understand. "Money transfers. But international money transfers are now scrutinized. Banks check deposits more closely. Illegal transfers of large amounts are picked up. Anti-money-laundering laws are in place. Computers locate illegal deposits. And every country in the world is checking everyone else's faxes, e-mails, and telephone calls. It's hard to transfer illegal cash now."

"They had to find a new way to do it, an alternate route," Jana added. "They set up a reliable method, one the banks and their monitoring efforts did not reach."

"They smuggled cash?" Bohumil asked, his voice and manner disbelieving. "Have you ever seen how much space a million dollars or a million euros take up? The package would be enormous. Multiple packages would have to be sent on a continuing basis, which would make it even more impractical."

"Worse," said Jana, wearing her best cat-ate-the-canary look. "They would still have to keep the money in a safe repository when it reached its destination. Where would they store it? Banks are the only safe place. But they couldn't go to a bank and deposit this money, as we know." She looked to Bohumil, then to Trokan, waiting for them to answer.

As before, Trokan made the leap. "The diamond that your friend Sofia was sent."

Jana nodded, appreciating Trokan's effort. Bohumil was now even more bewildered than before.

Jana was still wearing it. She took it from her neck for the last time, letting it dangle on its chain to be admired. Then she placed it in the center of the table.

"Were they trading diamonds?" Bohumil asked.

"Not trading. Paying with diamonds."

"How does this diamond tell you that?"

"Not just this diamond. These. . . ."

Jana opened Solti's suitcase, pouring the contents into the middle of the table, a rain of diamonds. They sparkled, one on top of the other, piling up into a small tower of brilliance that seemed to fill the space on the table, and more.

"How much is it worth?" Bohumil finally gulped out.

"I don't know," Jana admitted. "Millions," she hazarded.

"Millions," echoed Trokan.

"How do we know these aren't just simply stolen gems?"

"A theft with a description of diamonds like these, of this

size, would have been news all over the world. Nothing like this has been reported, nothing even remotely close."

Bohumil reached out and gingerly took one of the stones and stared at it. "Very beautiful," he crooned, entranced.

Trokan finally nudged him. "Put it back."

Bohumil was discomfited. "I was just looking at it." He put it back on the pile.

"Inventory the diamonds after the meeting," Trokan ordered Jana. "Where did we find them?"

"In the lining of Solti's suitcase. My guess is, he became greedy. He took the contents of a package. When the empty package came to the end of its route, the question for the intended recipients was a tough one: who in the chain had taken the contents? They didn't know."

"So they decided to roll up the entire network?"

"Kill everyone," Jana confirmed. "An object lesson for anyone else who might think of doing the same thing."

"The smuggler in Hungary," Trokan suggested.

"And all the others," Jana added.

"Why Klaudia Boryda and not Ivan?" Bohumil asked, his eyes still on the heap of diamonds on the table.

"She took a diamond. Just one. From a package. She thought she could take only one and get away with it, even if it was a big one. My guess is, she also raided other packages. Who would know, she must have thought. But the bosses who ran the network could tell, by the weight of the package."

"Why would they have spared her for this long?"

"Because of her husband, the deputy prime minister. It puzzled me for a while." She made an apologetic gesture. "I should have seen it right away: He had diplomatic immunity. He walked through customs without any examination. What a lovely prospect for them: he was the perfect smuggler.

Then Ivan Boryda revealed that he would happily continue working with them as a transporter of diamonds even if they killed his wife."

They sat in silence, focused on the pile of diamonds.

Trokan finally broke the spell. "Enough!" he demanded, standing.

Bohumil followed the colonel's example, standing, but still staring at the gems, having a hard time breaking away from them.

"Don't forget to inventory them, Commander," he reminded Jana. "And write up your reports," he ordered. "I want them quickly as you can. I need to inform the powers that be."

"I will, Colonel."

"I appreciate your hard work, Commander," Bohumil said.

"I want to talk to Commander Matinova for a minute," Trokan said. The captain nodded to Jana, then walked out. Trokan waited until he was sure that Bohumil was out of earshot.

"What about the person who killed Kamin? And the one involved in the Guzak killings?"

"I'm working on it."

"And the killing of the Swiss police officer?"

"Soon."

"Good."

"I want some leeway in handling one of the suspects. The woman."

He stared at Jana. "As long as it does not come back to our doorstep."

"I understand."

He pointed at the diamonds, a grin on his face. "Too bad you can't keep any of these."

He left just as Jana's cell phone rang.

Karina had come through again. Her network of street friends was proving quite valuable. Jana thanked her, promising to stop by soon.

Events had worked themselves out.

Jana now had the information that she needed about the woman.

Chapter 51

The team went to Giles's Golden Ages Antiques on Obchodná and served the search warrant on the employees in the showroom. They arrested Spis in the back for being in possession of an unlicensed firearm and confiscated his Webley. Without his weapon, Spis physically deflated in front of Jana's eyes.

They had to cut their way through the locking devices in the gate that barred their way to Giles's quarters. Giles would not come down to open it, refusing to believe they were police at first, then simply refusing. When they finally cut through, they ascended cautiously and found Giles seated at his desk, wearing his trademark jeweled eyeglasses, burning papers in a large metal trash basket.

They doused the fire. The group of officers accompanying Jana then began a meticulous search of the upstairs area, comparing the description of the objects stored in the loft apartment with the "stolen goods" lists they had brought along.

"I hope you will not be angry at me for making you wait," Giles entreated Jana. "You know I value our friendship highly."

"You value whatever you can use," Jana replied. "Have you had enough time to burn your records?"

Jana knew that he had. The gate was built not only to keep people out but to allow Giles time to dispose of anything he had that might incriminate him.

"I would think so." Giles poured himself a cup of tea from an ornate china teapot. "Delicious tea. A new one I'm trying. It's called 'Rouge Metis.' I ordered it from Mariage Frères in Paris. Let me pour you a cup."

"Thank you, no." She gestured at one of her men, handing the teapot to him. "Check this. Its design is unique. Identification should be easy." Her officer took the pot away to check against his lists.

"What are they doing?"

"Searching for stolen goods."

Giles sniffed the bouquet of the tea in his cup, displaying a lack of concern; then he took a sip of tea, his expression beatific. "Ah, wonderful. You are missing a truly sublime flavor. I suggest you call your man back so I can pour you a cup."

"He'll bring it back after he's confirmed that it's stolen."

"No!" said Giles, an expression of simulated shock materializing on his face. "I can't believe that. The seller assured me that it had been in his family for more than a hundred years." He took another sip. "Awful, how people lie to you. You expect them to be honest, and then they cheat and defraud you."

"Giles, we've compiled a list of every piece of antique furniture, silverware, china and bric-a-brac that has been stolen in Slovakia and every surrounding country, including Germany, for the last several years. We're prepared to compare these lists with your inventory over the next few days until we've gone through every item."

"A terribly hard task."

"Very hard."

"I wish I could help. Unfortunately, I'm an honest trader, so I couldn't possibly be of assistance."

The officer who had taken the teapot away came over, still carrying it, pointing to an item on one of his lists. Jana thanked him.

"You will never guess what my officer discovered. It's Limoges, nineteenth century, stolen a year ago, along with other objects, from a Czech banker."

One of the officers mishandled a piece of crystal. The glass shattered when it was tipped over.

"For goodness' sake!" Giles was distressed. "Please tell your men to handle these items with care. These are precious objects. Precious. And they must be treated with reverence."

"Are you a reverent man, Giles?"

He took on a self-important look. "Of course, Commander."

The same officer came over a moment later, holding a large silver-and-gold chalice. He showed Jana another entry on the lists. Jana read it aloud to Giles.

"Gold and silver, inlaid with enamel. From the Franziskanerkirche in Salzburg. Stolen just six months ago from the Franciscans. A church. I thought you were a reverent man, Giles."

"When it comes to beautiful things, I am a reverent man, Commander."

"You're going back to prison, Giles."

"All antique dealers, at one time or another, mistakenly buy goods that have been stolen. That's not enough reason to put them in prison."

"Giles, we'll find more. And after that, even more of them. You won't be able to explain them all away, Giles, particularly since you've burned your records, which we'll also mention to the procurator. Add in your prior conviction, and you'll be away from these lovely objects that you worship for a long time."

Giles put his tea cup down, pursing his lips. "You're always willing to trade for information, Commander. We should really talk about that possibility."

Jarov was one of the officers conducting the search. He

placed an open box of shells on the table in front of her. Jana checked the contents. "A number of shells are gone." She read the label on the side of the box. ".32 caliber. Not many of these made any more." Jana thought of the old Webley that had been taken from Spis. Not a match for the shells. "If the shells are here, the right gun will be here. I want that weapon."

Jarov went back to his search.

Jana fingered one of the shells.

"You killed a Slovak police officer, Giles."

Giles looked at her through wide, innocent eyes, removing his glasses intensifying the effect.

"What Slovak officer?"

"In Geneva."

"I've never been to Geneva."

"A lie."

"Never."

"I thought we were friends, Giles. You always tell me how much you value my friendship."

"You've always refused my offers of friendship, Commander." His voice had a note of indignation. "Are you saying, at long last, that you want it?"

"It was always too late for that, Giles."

"Then why bring it up?"

"Because you tried to kill me, and trying to kill a person you ask to be your friend is deceitful. Then again, being a criminal is deceitful itself, isn't it? Giles, why did you fly down to Geneva to kill me?"

For the first time he looked dismayed. "How could you think I would do such a thing? You're completely wrong." He paused for effect. "This is a conversation I no longer want to be engaged in."

"The police officer who was shot knew his killer. How did

a Slovak officer in Switzerland recognize the man who killed him? The obvious answer is that the killer was a Slovak. The dead man's partner was working with the killer. She refuses to name him. Even more proof that he was a Slovak.

"Whoever the killer was also had to know what I looked like. He was after me. The murderer could have been given a photograph, although photographs are not ideal for an assassin who is identifying his victim quickly. No, the killer knew me."

Giles indignity turned to outrage.

"I cannot believe you are saying this. A man you knew tried to kill you. Therefore, because I know you, the killer has to be me? You have gone crazy. This is ridiculous. . . ." He sputtered to a stop. "No friend would ever say such things. We are no longer friends."

"Giles, we've already agreed that we're not friends."

"I couldn't concur more," he huffed.

Jana decided to lay it all out for him.

"How does an organization become an organization? It has to be put together by a person with a certain expertise. How does one put together a smuggling organization? You get a man who knows about smuggling goods. They came to you and said put together our organization of smugglers. Working with international criminal groups is very lucrative. You accepted their offer. Except, soon afterward you went to prison on another charge. When you came out, they didn't need you any more. Other people had taken your place."

"You put me in prison." Anger suffused Giles's face. "How dared you put me in that terrible place?"

"You came out. You went back to business on your own. Then things happened to the criminal association you had set up. Merchandise was lost or stolen. The chiefs of the organization, who had previously paid you so much money, came back to you to try to find out why. You had very few answers. That was when the killing began in Europe."

"I would never kill my people."

"You didn't have to. They did it all."

"So, you see." He brightened up. "I was not involved."

"I showed you the diamond. You told them about my visit. They knew it was missing. You signed and sealed Klaudia Boryda's death warrant. Then they told you to kill me. It was an opportunity to get back into their good graces. My trip to Switzerland was your perfect opportunity. Except that one of the cops following me saw you, and you had to shoot him."

"I would never have done that. Shoot a police officer? I am a coward."

"Cowards kill from ambush. The cover of the crowd was ideal. It was a perfect moment for you. At least it was, until the police officer you killed recognized you."

"Garbage, all garbage."

Jarov returned. He had a small automatic in his hand. Jana glanced at it. She didn't need to examine the weapon.

"The bullets we found will match the bullets in this gun, which will match the bullet used to kill our policeman. I knew you would still have it, Giles. It's the nature of your business; it's your nature. You're a collector, Giles. You can't throw anything away. It will be the death of you."

Giles struck a confidential pose. "Let us examine reality a little closer, Commander. We still can do things for each other. I have information about this group of criminals. Not that I am admitting the killing, but I do have information. We can work things out so that there is a plus for you and a plus for me. Win-win, as they say." His voice got quieter so he would not be heard by the other officers. "Simply lose the gun."

"We'll find the flight that you took to Geneva, Giles.

We'll talk to the airlines. There were only a few flights to Switzerland at the right time."

He leaned back, away from her. "So, we don't do business." He shrugged. "The French will, the English will, the Americans will do business. I have things they'll want. They'll pressure the Swiss. I know the Swiss. They're business people. They'll understand the need to put business first. They'll be forced to deal with me. I'll walk away."

"Perhaps. There is always a 'perhaps' in a criminal case." She watched as Giles's eyes searched her face. He was not at all confident. Jana felt better. "You killed someone in Switzerland, a bad place to kill anyone. To the Swiss, neatness comes first. Order is all-important. You disturbed their orderly existence, a horrible thing for them. They need to keep their lives tidy; they're outraged by murder. You committed a cardinal sin in that little country. I think they won't deal, Giles."

He folded his arms across his chest.

"We'll see."

Jana contemplated the court processes and the needs of government agencies, which she knew so well. They all made compromises. She considered the compromise she was going to have to make later that afternoon.

"We'll both see, Giles."

There was no further need for Jana to be there. Her men would do their job.

She left without saying good-bye.

Chapter 52

Jana arranged to meet Seges and Guzak at Stefanik Airport, just to the side of the small terminal. Jana's instructions to Seges had included explicit directions on cleaning up and dressing the man. The change in Guzak was extraordinary. His long, unkempt hair had been cut and styled, and his perpetual need for a shave had been reduced to a narrow moustache that added a touch of sensitivity to his perpetually sneering upper lip. When glasses had been added, along with the presentable white shirt, tie, and suit, which covered up his tattoos, and polished shoes, the man almost looked like your everyday businessman.

"Almost" was the key word.

If you looked through Guzak's eyeglasses and into his eyes, you could see the intensity of the permanent rage barely contained by heavy lids. It was not important, Jana thought. His disguise was good enough to fool the casual observer, particularly one who had never before seen the man in the flesh. It would be good enough to deceive the woman. She wouldn't be looking for him when they passed each other.

What a shame, Jana thought, that the greater good had to be served by letting this man go free. Jana could not trust the courts on this one. She tried to comfort herself with the ultimate purpose it would serve. Yes, the world would be a better place without her.

They could see the front entrance from where they sat. Fifteen minutes later, she arrived. She was let out of a car driven by Andreea, the woman who had given shelter to Guzak. Guzak emitted a grunt of anger. Jana touched his shoulder to remind him what he was there for.

There was no question who the woman moving into the terminal was: the woman from Vienna, the one who had held a gun on Jana while her partner beat a man to death. It was the same woman who had participated in the killing of both mother Guzak and the younger son. It was the same woman who had been involved in the killings in Hungary, the surviving assassin of the team responsible for deaths around the world. The woman thought she was leaving Slovakia without a care; that no one was even aware that she existed.

She had made an appalling error for a professional in her line of work.

The three waited until shortly before the plane was due to depart. Seges then went to the airline counter to verify that the woman had boarded the plane and that it would take off very soon. They walked to the boarding area.

"No question that you will be able to identify her?" Jana asked Guzak.

He nodded, impatient to get on with his task. "You're sure she's the one?" Guzak had to force the words out, barely controlling the violence inside himself. "She killed my mother?"

"And your brother."

Guzak started for the boarding area gate. Jana blocked his way. For a moment, Jana thought he was going to attack her.

Jana faced him down. "Remember, not on the plane. You are to do nothing on the plane. Do you understand that?"

Guzak reluctantly nodded.

She handed him a slip of paper, the order from the court that Seges had obtained.

"The court has ordered you to leave Slovakia. If you come back, you'll be coming back to prison. Do you understand that as well?"

"I understand."

Seges handed the man his ticket.

"You're free to go."

The man immediately went to the boarding area, gave the purser his ticket, and boarded the plane. When it took off, Jana turned away. She hoped that Guzak would wait until the plane landed. It would be best for the other passengers.

Some things in life are necessary.